P9-CEM-114

The Fourth Crow

THE FOURTH CROW

D. W. Smith

St. Martin's Press
New York

Library of Congress Cataloging-in-Publication Data
Smith, Dan.
    The fourth crow / by D. W. Smith.
        p.   cm.
    ISBN 0-312-05091-7
    PR6069.M444F68   1990   90-37180
    823'.914—dc20   CIP

First published in Great Britain by Macmillan London Limited

First U.S. Edition: December 1990
10 9 8 7 6 5 4 3 2 1

PART I

St Basil's

Chapter 1

Detective Sergeant Peters was cold, irritated and tired, thirsty, out of cigarettes and in need of a pee. He shrugged the collar of his fur-lined leather jacket higher round his ears and turned into the November wind.

The street was in a prosperous part of north-west London. That didn't make the night any less abominable. It didn't make 2.30 a.m. any earlier, or six and a half hours of surveillance – with only the odd break for coffee in a hamburger bar long since closed – any easier to handle. He sniffed, wiped a cold, gloved hand across his nose, then on his trousers, and wondered if he was starting a cold.

'Pete, make the back door,' a voice crackled at him. It was Austin, Detective Chief Inspector, in charge of this miserable outing. 'Quick shufty, then call in. Acknowledge.'

About bloody time too, Peters thought. He reached into his jacket pocket for his short-wave radio. 'I'll be quiet as a mouse, guv,' he said. Without increasing his pace, he made for the target of their activity, a first-floor flat in a large apartment block. He was going to go in down the alley at the back, through the gate, across the garden, up the fire escape and in through the back door. As he walked, he beat his hands together to get some feeling going. On each step, he put his feet down with extra firmness, rolling exaggeratedly from heel to toe, to restore some circulation there too. He heard Austin tell Royce and Cowie to cover him, and Truscott and Feather to take up position at the front entrance.

He turned into the alleyway. It was unlit. A few vehicles were parked along it – one of them was a Mobile Surveillance Unit – and there were several garages. Between two of them was a double gate. It was padlocked on the inside, but cut into it was a door secured only by a Yale lock. Peters stopped there and saw a shape coming at him through the dark. He eased back into deeper shadow until he was sure it was Royce. Then he took his woollen gloves off and started in on the lock, Royce holding the torch, trying to keep it steady despite his shivering. It should have been easy, but Peters

7

fumbled and had to try three times, blowing on his fingertips to warm them, before it gave way. As he opened the door Cowie appeared. He was to wait there while Royce and Peters went in.

They nipped through the door. Behind it was an area of tarmac where delivery vans could pull up. Then there was a path made of loose stones leading to the flats. Peters hopped over the flower-bed and on to the grass. It was white and crisp with frost, but even so their feet would make less noise on it than they would on the path. Royce crossed the flower-bed too, but went half through a rose bush which brought muttered curses from him and an angrily hissed 'Shut it' from Peters.

As they faced the block from the back, there were two fire escapes. The one they wanted was on the left. One flight up, the flat they wanted was on the left again. There was no light coming from its windows, nor from any of the other flats. The only lights were on each landing of the two fire escapes.

They ran quietly over the grass and paused at the foot of the iron staircase. Peters half unzipped his jacket, experimentally loosened his gun in its shoulder holster and led the way up, testing each step carefully before putting his full weight on it.

The door to the flat was simplicity itself. A good lock, but Peters was equipped with the right keys to open it and had the benefit of a little light on the outside landing. There was no bolt on the door. That surprised him. He'd more than half expected he'd have to climb in through a window. He noticed that, if he had needed to do that, he wouldn't have had to break any glass. One of the panes in the window by the door was already missing. He opened the door carefully – thankfully, it didn't squeak – and eased his way in. Something rustled under his foot – some rolled-up newspaper. As he took his foot off that, it brushed against something which rolled across the floor – a small empty can of some kind. Peters pulled his gun out. Behind him Royce held the door open with one hand, gun also at the ready.

They were on the threshold of a large modern kitchen. Diagonally to their right was the door which gave on to the hallway. It was open. There was an odd smell, a mixture of odours Peters couldn't quite identify – fustiness, certainly, perhaps some old cooking smells, maybe a hint of beer. He looked round the kitchen. There was some more paper on the floor, a few cans and a couple of empty bottles. That probably explained some of the smells. He paid them no more attention than was necessary to be sure he didn't step on them or kick anything else and crossed the floor on tiptoe.

8

He stood in the doorway. Immediately to his left was the door to the sitting-room – open again. His heart was pounding and the combination of adrenalin and cold made him shake uncontrollably for a few seconds as his eyes adjusted to the greater darkness of the hall.

Then he heard a noise; like a soft footstep, faint but distinct under the whistling of the wind through the broken window. It seemed to come from the sitting-room. He stood absolutely still for a moment, heard the noise again. Definitely a footstep. Definitely the sitting-room.

He tightened his grip on the gun and held it raised by his shoulder, barrel pointing up to the ceiling. With his left forefinger he made a stabbing gesture at the wall which divided kitchen from sitting-room. He took a quick look over his right shoulder, saw Royce raise a thumb and step out of the kitchen on to the landing. He'd have his WT in his hand already, thumb depressing the transmit button, muttering 'Contact, contact' into it.

In the car in which he'd sat for so long, Austin got Royce's report and jerked upright. He turned to the man sitting beside him. 'They *are* there,' he said. 'Truss,' he said into his mike, 'make the front. Dutch, cover at the back. Cowie, in.' He turned to his companion again as he started the engine: 'Surprise, surprise.' Naseby said nothing. He was wondering how and when the targets had got past Austin's team without being spotted. He was also wishing he'd responded to Austin's urgings two hours ago and called in for permission to enter the flat. They drove slowly and quietly to the building's front entrance and parked there.

Peters stayed where he was. He tried to relax his breathing, turning his head from side to side to get the stiffness out of his neck and shoulder muscles. Mentally he shook himself like a dog to try and forget the cold. The sound came from the sitting-room again – such a small noise, barely audible, so soft – but nothing else, no whispering. He took quick glances at Royce who was in the landing doorway again. He saw Cowie arrive and Royce step back outside to use the WT.

A second after Royce told him Cowie had arrived, Austin heard from Dutch that he too was in position. A minute later, Detective Inspector Truscott said he and Feather were covering the landing outside the flat's front door. 'Royce, tell him to do it,' Austin said.

Royce acknowledged, moved back to where Peters could see him, waited till the Sergeant glanced his way, pointed dramatically at the sitting-room and mouthed the words, 'Go, go.'

9

Briefing them earlier that evening, Naseby had said he had no information about whether the targets would be armed. Peters was taking no chances. He crouched, moved so he could see round the wall into the sitting-room, using the door jamb to hide most of his body, slipped the safety catch off, knelt in the classic position with the weapon held outstretched in both hands, finger not on but by the trigger. He felt rather than heard Cowie tiptoeing across the kitchen to the hall doorway.

The sitting-room was a bit lighter than the hallway, still quite dark – and he didn't dare use his torch and make himself a perfect target – but enough to see by. There was a sofa and two chairs, and what looked like a coffee table. Nobody was visible, but he heard another small movement. Then Cowie slid quickly past him into the hall, taking up position so he too could cover the sitting-room, though he couldn't see into it as well as Peters.

'I am an armed police officer,' Peters said. 'Stand up and raise your hands.'

There was no answer, no sound of movement.

'I say again, I am an armed police officer. You are to stand up and raise your hands above your head.'

This time there was a sound, a quick movement. It came from behind the armchair in the far corner. That was where the bastard was hiding – or perhaps bastards. He wriggled his shoulders to loosen them before he reissued his warning. 'I repeat, I am armed. My weapon is loaded. You are to surrender yourself now.'

Another quick sound and this time Peters saw something. It moved very fast. Before the image had taken shape in his brain, almost before he knew it, he fired. There was an inhuman screech of pain which got caught in the echoes of the shot, the crack as the front door splintered under Truscott's weight, the shouting of Royce into his WT.

Austin didn't need Royce to tell him. Out front the noise wasn't very loud, but he recognised it immediately as a shot. Once Royce stopped screaming at him and cluttering up the airwaves, he ordered everybody in and leaped from the car himself. The front door had been damaged as Truscott and Feather made their unsubtle way in; it was too secure to get past silently – that was why Peters had gone in round the back. Apart from anything else, it had an alarm connected to the caretaker's flat and the local police station. They were probably already on their way and the large man wearing a dressing-gown, blocking Austin's way and loudly demanding what the hell was going on, was probably the caretaker.

Austin ducked his shoulder, rammed the man in the chest and sprinted up the stairs. By the time he got into the flat his detectives were crowding into the hall, lighting up the place with their torches – none of the lights appeared to have a bulb in it. He pushed his way through and found Peters in the sitting-room, leaning against the window sill. Even in that dim light, Austin thought he looked sick. Peters waved his gun towards the far corner behind the armchair. Austin took a torch from Truscott and went to have a look. Peters's shot had hit the tail of a mother cat trying to defend her brood of kittens.

There were a lot of things Austin could have said about that. To his credit as a senior officer, he kept them to himself. Peters shook his head sadly, left the window, handed his gun to Austin, walked into the hallway where the other detectives also kept whatever they were thinking to themselves, pulled his torch out and switched it on, opened the bathroom door, went in and used the lavatory.

That, at least, was some relief.

Chapter 2

The background to the cat's injury began nearly three years earlier when Jerzy Pretkiewicz arrived in London as the Deputy Press Attaché at the Polish Embassy. He was forty-three years old and had just finished a posting in Prague. Before that he had been, among other places, in Bonn. There in 1981 he had been approached by West German counter-intelligence. They were interested by his incompletely masked support for Solidarnosc. But the sympathy with the independent trade-union movement which brought him to their eyes was also the reason why he turned the approach down. The wind of reform in Poland warmed his commitment to his country; it was no time to be thinking of defection.

Disappointed, the West Germans kept him on their books, and when he went to London the file was passed as a matter of routine courtesy to the British Security Service, MI5. There it went to Department K8, responsible for monitoring non-Soviet diplomats. By March, K8 had tagged him as one of those Eastern bloc diplomats who did not mind, in private and off the record, being moderately frank; it was clear he believed Poland was in a poor state. Solidarnosc and the hopes it had generated had long since been snuffed out. Reform at that time seemed to be in Poland's past, not its future. The head of K8 passed the expanded file to his colleague who ran K5 – recruitment – who had a long think about it.

He was reluctant to authorise an attempt on Pretkiewicz. It was too likely to produce nothing or worse. If he had reported the first approach, he would have been primed by Polish intelligence to expect a second one, and perhaps to accept it so he could be used to feed disinformation. But the head of K5 was equally reluctant to reject the opportunity out of hand. The Director of K Branch, Neil Deakin, had been in post for one year. He was pushing everybody hard. He wanted agents, he wanted results and he wanted them tomorrow. When the problem was referred to him, he decided the risk was worth taking. Many things had changed in Poland. Perhaps Pretkiewicz had changed too; in one respect he certainly had: the file from the West Germans reported that he'd had his wife with him in Bonn but not in Prague; no more did he in London. Divorce presumably. If he turned them down, nothing would be lost. In case he turned out to be a fake defector, they would cover themselves by treating his early product with caution.

Pretkiewicz was given a code-name. For Eastern bloc defectors except from the USSR, K5 used girls' names. They had started with 'Abigail' and gone steadily through the alphabet. By the time they got to Pretkiewicz they had just done Louise, so his file was entitled 'Lucy'. The recruiters cast their line out in April. Pretkiewicz looked interested and had a quick sniff of the bait. Then he ducked back under water and K5 stalked him upstream for a while. In June they got a definite tug on the line. They played him for three months before they finally hooked him. At a discreet meeting, terms were agreed and procedures for passing on information established. At it, he was asked about the West German approach. 'I rejected it, but I kept it to myself,' he said.

'Why didn't you report it?' he was asked.

'I didn't want to be seen as the sort of person who might be approached by Western intelligence,' he replied. That got satisfied nods. It had the ring of authenticity.

But there was still some doubt about him, so Deakin took personal control of the file. He established a mini-section, answering directly to him, with a translator and two desk officers: Kelvin Hay fixed the drops, pick-ups and payments; Gerald Thomas digested the Lucy material and farmed it out to the rest of K. Some of it was not useful for counter-intelligence; that went straight to Deakin who kept it in his purse, extra coinage when it was necessary to buy favours from MI6.

As press attaché, Pretkiewicz had no access to real secrets unless he went out of his way to get them. Deakin decreed he should not take that risk nor receive any of the spy's tools of the trade – micro-camera, one-time pad, microdot equipment and so on. That was not only out of concern for his safety. If Pretkiewicz was a plant, Deakin did not want to hand any gifts to the opposition.

His early product was gossip, stray remarks he overhead, sum-maries of confidential documents which passed across his desk in the ordinary course of things. He had a feel for the significant and a talent for explaining its background. He provided general intelligence about the Eastern bloc embassies in London, their staffs and concerns, together with analyses of the thinking back home in official Warsaw.

Each month he deposited an envelope in a pre-arranged place. It contained a report hand-written on ordinary notepaper. From a different place a few days later he collected another envelope; in it was the counterfoil of a bank paying-in slip so he knew his retirement fund was building nicely, together with a list of any subjects he was particularly asked to look out for and instructions for the next drop and pick-up.

After Lucy had been operating for a year, Thomas wrote a report and pronounced him genuine. Half his material was banal, but the rest was new. Significantly, it tended to fit the pattern of what K Branch already knew but expanded it. Even more significantly, when it contradicted K's existing information, further research normally proved Lucy was right and K was wrong. In the exceptional cases, his inaccuracy could be put down to error, misunderstanding or incomplete knowledge. Twice Lucy himself later corrected his mistakes. Thomas got a pat on the back and was assigned as a desk officer in K2 – counter-espionage against the KGB. Hay, still answering directly to Deakin, ran Lucy and parcelled out the product.

At the end of November, Lucy's monthly report mentioned an English journalist called Brown. At a press conference, he had overhead a *sotto voce* conversation in which his Soviet counterpart described Brown to a colleague as 'most valuable, extremely influential', adding that Brown had good sources and reliable information which he collated and analysed efficiently. What made this interesting was that the Deputy Soviet Press Attaché, Scherchinskiy, was in the Register of Foreign Hostiles as a major or colonel in the KGB and an agent-runner. The man he'd been talking to, a Tass reporter, was also KGB-listed.

Brown, too, was on file. He had been the object of surveillance since 1982. Timothy McKellen, the head of K2, remembered him from those days. McKellen had spent most of his career in F Branch, which watched over domestic subversion, alternating between monitoring the IRA and the British left, and had switched to K only three years before as part of an effort to bring new blood into counter-espionage.

To brief the K-men, Brian Jensen was called in from F7, the section that monitored the smaller left-wing organisations and the unorganised left. Wesley Brown was thirty-nine, divorced with two children whom he saw each week, living by himself in Blackheath, editor of a monthly magazine, *World*, which had a circulation of 35,000, almost all by subscription.

'He's an interesting case,' Jensen said, 'though not untypical. Very left at university. Sit-ins, London demos, all that sort of thing. Called himself a revolutionary, mixed in that crowd. Stayed that way for a few years after graduating. Then he seemed to calm down a bit. Got his Ph.D. done – economics, specialising in Third World development – and in seventy-eight he did a year at Unesco in Paris. When he came back he did a spot of lecturing, a consultancy or two for Unesco and the World Bank, began to write journalism as well as academic articles, got his book published. Around that time it became clear he'd changed his spots a fair bit. Still supported all the appropriate causes, of course, and was secretary of his local peace group when it started up. But he joined Labour and became what you'd have to class as a bit of a moderate. Sort of person who was pleased as Punch when Kinnochio became leader. And adept at riding several horses at once. Has friends among the Liberals, even the Soc Dems. No official position in the peace movement any more, but he knows all the right people there. In fact, he's got contacts all over the place. He became editor of *World* in, oh, late eighty-one. His writing covers much more now than just economics. Does a lot of stuff these days on defence, arms control, the EEC, US and Soviet foreign policy – you name it really. Doesn't just write for his own rag either. Gets published all over the place.'

'Any sensitive material in those articles?' Deakin asked.

'Any?' Jensen snorted. 'The latest count is sixteen which reveal classified UK information. And in ten of those, plus eight others, there's sensitive stuff on other Nato governments. To be fair, about half of our secrets he picks up in the US where, of course, they're still a lot freer with that sort of thing than we are. And some of the foreign gen had been published abroad before, but never here. Still, when you subtract those instances, he's still a pretty strong dealer in secrets on his own account. And the rate at which he does it has increased over the years.'

Deakin asked if that was why surveillance had been authorised.

Jensen shook his head. 'Frankly, try keeping a close watch on every hack who's up to that lark and you'd need an army. Anyway, we started it in eighty-two and he wasn't so deeply into the classified game then.'

So Deakin asked what the reason was.

Jensen exchanged a smile with McKellen and blandly asked, 'The reason it was authorised, or why it was requested, sir?'

Deakin smiled in turn. He knew well the tactical difference between the two. 'The real reason,' he said.

15

'His contacts,' Jensen said. 'Quite inordinate range of them, including people either not on our lists, or not prominently there. Putting him under the 'scope has given us a much better picture of the whole radical-stroke-peace field in this country – and several others too, which is good when we need to trade with friends. It shows us the ebbs and flows of participation, seniority, influence, that sort of thing. Availability of resources being what it is, we can't watch everyone so closely. Brown was a strategic choice.'

Deakin nodded. 'Just out of interest,' he said, 'how did you justify it?'

'The Short Reason was contact with Argentina during the Falklands war,' Jensen said, referring to the three or four sentences which the Home Secretary had to see before approving surveillance. 'Turned out to be pretty innocent stuff, actually – a minuscule anti-war group there. But handy.'

'And since then, naturally, you've not raised the matter again at that level and, as long as nobody remembers, you can keep your eyes and ears in place,' Deakin added approvingly.

'Any hint of anything that would interest K?' McKellen said to Jensen.

'Not till now. Unless there was another push to plug press leaks. He sees Sovbloc dips, of course, but so do lots of people, journalists included.'

'There may be nothing in it,' Deakin said after Jensen had left, 'nothing more than the irritation factor anyway, but I think he's worth a closer look, a bit of research. Gerald, you'll do that, will you please?'

By Christmas, rooting around in Registry and press files, Thomas had expanded the picture considerably. He'd made a list of Brown's articles on Soviet arms control policy over the years, showing how at every turn Brown had argued for new Soviet initiatives *before* they were announced in Moscow. That was not the sort of cross-checking which would occur to F Branch, but its significance was obvious in K.

'Preparing the ground like that,' Deakin said as he filled his pipe, 'is definitely the pattern of not just a *bien pensant*, but a knowing agent of influence. And he deals in classified material too. Interesting mixture.'

Thomas had also found three mentions of Brown in various reports over the past seven years. They all came via the Secret Intelligence Service, MI6, but at such a high level of classification that when they reached MI5 they had gone nowhere, which was why

F7 hadn't known about them. Armed with Deakin's authorisation, Thomas had dug them out.

One originated with the CIA: Brown had frequent contact with three people in Washington listed as Cuban agents of influence. One came from a source in the Moscow office of Tass, well known to K Branch as a cover for KGB operatives, and why not since British journalists on foreign assignment were traditionally regarded as likely agents for MI6? It was a report about the London Tass correspondent: Brown was mentioned in passing as someone he saw frequently. It was not the same reporter Scherchinskiy had praised Brown to, but Thomas checked and found him listed under Foreign Hostiles. The third came from French intelligence who'd six times in three months seen Brown meeting with a man they were then investigating, who had later been tried and convicted, and who was now in prison waiting for his appeal to be heard.

'Suggestive,' Deakin said through his pipe-smoke. 'Highly suggestive.'

'We've been as good as asked three times to take a look at him,' said McKellen, 'even if we happened not to hear till now.'

'Yes, I think we should steal him away from your old chums in F,' Deakin said. 'You'll take the file on, Gerald. I'll set up the hand-over.'

It was quickly done in the dead period between Christmas and New Year. Soviet agents were given bird names. 'Cormorant' was the last one they'd used, so Brown was 'Crow'. 'Suitably enough,' McKellen said.

'How so?' Deakin asked. 'This is not an ill omen I hope.'

'No, I was referring to the crows of St Basil's. There's some folk-tale about them, similar to our one about ravens at the Tower.'

'St Basil's?'

'The church in Red Square.'

'Ah yes, Tim, quite so, most appropriate. As long as the KGB has agents, the Soviet threat will never evaporate.'

Chapter 3

The first step was to raise the level of the telephone taps on Brown. Of four degrees of tapping, Brown had been on the third; all his incoming calls were recorded, plus any outgoing call to a number on a list held by A2, the technical support section. His coverage was upgraded to the second degree; now all his calls to any number would be recorded. Conversations were transcribed if they contained key words which alerted the monitoring system. Thomas wanted to take Brown right up to the top level, with all calls not only recorded but listened to as they happened, but McKellen ruled against even asking A2 to go that far.

He did, however, agree when Thomas made the case for comprehensive personal surveillance. Authorisation came in late January. From then on, not only was Brown's mail read and his every phone conversation recorded, but he was followed wherever he went by the Watchers from A4. The telephone taps also picked up sounds in each room where there was an extension. Thomas wanted to go for a full-blown search combined with emplacing proper bugs. 'Too risky,' McKellen said. 'Anything he's got – if he's got it – will be well hidden. I'll bet he has thousands of books and tons of paper and periodicals. It'd take hours just to check through those. And you may be surprised how hard it is to pull out of those left-wing pigsties without leaving traces.'

'But the information value of in-place listening—' Thomas started.

McKellen cut him off. 'If the bastard's KGB, he might even have the equipment for a rudimentary sweep. It's too early. Watch and wait.'

He even refused permission to get hold of Brown's address book. 'He'd publish the fact immediately,' he said. 'Counterproductive, and in any case unnecessary. Eyes and ears only.' But he compensated Thomas twice over. He allowed him to approach Deakin and ask if a request for information on Brown could be inserted in the next set of instructions to Lucy. And he authorised

18

routine anything-further-known requests to be sent to MI6, the CIA and the SDECE – French intelligence.

Brown received a voluminous mail, appeared to be in regular correspondence with people from over a dozen different countries, and seemed to spend at least half of each day talking on the phone. His energy was fantastic, his social life complicated, his political, academic and journalistic contacts unending. The Crow file expanded rapidly. About once a fortnight, he met with Eastern bloc diplomats, normally from the Soviet Embassy, usually for lunch. Among these meetings, several were with Scherchinskiy. When Thomas got advance warning from the telephone taps, he arranged discreet bugging operations. Most of the conversations were simply a matter of Brown asking questions, offering analyses and seeing how the diplomats responded. He pressed them especially for their views on Gorbachev's reform programme and the new Soviet foreign policy.

In May, he had lunch with Jerzy Pretkiewicz. Till then, Lucy hadn't learned anything with which to respond to the request for information on Brown. He reported it when the lunch date was made, of course, and his next envelope after it contained some interesting material.

Before the lunch, Pretkiewicz was called in by his superior who said, 'I am informed it is essential not to discuss sensitive matters with Mr Brown.'

'Informed by whom,' Pretkiewicz asked, 'and what sensitive matters should be avoided?'

His boss did not answer, saying instead, 'You are to understand the need not to cause embarrassment.'

The lunch, Pretkiewicz reported ruefully, was in fact very boring, because he had to steer the discussion away from all the interesting issues Brown raised. A couple of days later he met Scherchinskiy at an embassy reception and mentioned his lunch with Brown. He praised him and asked for the Russian's opinion. Scherchinskiy was non-committal, changed the subject and soon drifted away. The following afternoon Pretkiewicz was called in by one of his own embassy's security officers and warned against loose talk. He asked what was the occasion for this reproof. He was told it was merely a helpful suggestion to ensure he did not give a bad impression to anybody, especially representatives of Poland's allies. Informal warnings tended to follow immediately on an infringement of propriety. He assumed it was a result of his query to Scherchinskiy. He replied that he was always interested in expanding his contacts in British journalism but would accept the advice in the spirit it was given. This seemed to satisfy the security man.

'Warned off,' Thomas said.

'But warned off what?' Deakin asked rhetorically.

The next item in the jigsaw came in July. With no prior sign that he had spotted the Watchers, Brown disappeared on the Underground. One minute it was a routine job of surveillance, next he was lost.

Thomas interviewed one of the unfortunate pair of Watchers, to supplement their dry report. 'Brilliant, it was,' the man said. 'Near the end of rush hour, still crowded. Brown got on the Northern Line at Camden, going south. George followed him in. I got into the next carriage and stood by the window. At Euston chummy got a seat. At Leicester Square he didn't move, then suddenly he got up and nipped through the doors as they were closing. I got off – had to fight the doors – but George didn't. I couldn't see Brown. Then I heard a northbound train come in on the other platform. Had to tread on umpteen pairs of feet to get through and made it just in time to see the doors close neatly behind our man and he's away. I tell you one thing: I've never seen the two-train trick pulled on the tube. That was special.'

Three issues arose out of the incident. The first was whether to call the Watchers off. Deakin decided not to. 'The very fact that he dropped his tail so neatly is revealing,' he said. 'If he does it again it may give us a pattern.' The second was why he'd done it: 'Where was Scherchinskiy?'

'Apparently at home,' Thomas replied.

'Interesting,' McKellen said. 'I wonder who he was off to see. Time will tell.'

'If it doesn't,' Thomas suggested, 'perhaps you'll reconsider a search.'

'Perhaps,' McKellen conceded. Then he raised the third issue. 'And where do you suppose he got such training? Dig back, Gerald, dig back.'

At the beginning of September an article by Brown appeared in *World*. It questioned whether government research on defences against chemical warfare at Porton Down was as innocent as was claimed. There was evidence, it stated, that the scientists were developing a new generation of weaponry. It was designed only to be severely disabling, Brown wrote, but it was potentially lethal. This was happening despite the government's ostensible support for a treaty banning chemical weapons at the Geneva disarmament conference. The article gave no hint of its sources.

Thomas arranged for an assessment. 'It's mostly on track,' said the man from the Ministry of Defence. 'He's clearly not got a lot of the information – missing about a third of it, I'd say, as far as the actual facts are concerned, if you want a quantification. He's exaggerated how far the research has gone, which is typical, and he's stressed the lethal side, which is misleading, again typically. He's also wrong, of course, about the point of the research. Otherwise, he's pretty much on the mark.'

Deakin tapped the stem of his pipe lightly on his nose. 'There's a possibility here,' he said. 'The question is, where's the other third of the information? Well, perhaps he just didn't get it. But if he got that much, why not the rest?'

'You mean the rest went to Scherchinskiy?' Thomas asked.

'Possibly. By publishing what he has, he suggests to us that he's not got the real goodies. He leads us astray. Look, he's saying, all I do is a bit of investigative journalism, maybe dipping my toe into illegality, but nothing *really* naughty. It would be a very neat exercise. Espionage at the core of it, combined with mischief-making and camouflage.'

'But it draws our attention to him,' Thomas objected.

'It was already drawn thither, Gerald, and he knows that.'

'If we suppose he gave the rest to Scherchinskiy,' McKellen said, 'does it fit his pattern of movement?'

'He had lunch with him two days after he two-trained the Watchers,' Thomas replied. 'Arranged at short notice – one day's in fact. So we didn't have time to sort out a bugging. Not that it would have helped us much.'

'No,' said Deakin. 'I doubt they discussed it over the *coq au vin*. But we did have eyes on him?'

'Yes. He hadn't dropped them that day. And they had a clear view too. Also had Scherchinskiy's own tail there, of course. But, well, you know.' Thomas finished weakly, but the other two did know. Trained operatives, even under trained eyes, could easily effect an invisible hand-over. It was impossible to see literally everything they did.

There were two investigations at Porton Down: one run by the establishment's management – and the real one. The first turned up nothing. The ferrets from K1 – responsible for counter-espionage in government departments and establishments – found five people they wanted to have a closer look at. Thomas gave K1 the list of people Brown had seen over the months of surveillance, but none of the five figured on it – not surprisingly in view of Brown's disappearance on the tube – so the task became to discover if any of them had any mutual acquaintances with Brown. They were all put under surveillance, but it would be a slow job weeding through them to find the culprit.

Thomas again wanted a proper search of Brown's home and offices. McKellen demurred. 'Too late,' he said.

Thomas objected because it was the opposite reason to the one given before and asked leave to appeal to Deakin. 'The point is,' he said, 'that we don't see everything he does and everybody he meets, or hear everything they discuss. He goes to see people in their homes; we can't be sure we know who else is there. There's private meetings he goes to in organisations we haven't got fully covered inside. He could be given documents then and we'd be none the wiser. He can make calls from public phones like anybody else. Our information is really very incomplete.'

McKellen let him appeal, but the decision went against a search on the grounds of risk.

Two weeks later Thomas told McKellen, 'He's done it again. Off the train to York on Saturday. Slipped the leash at Peterborough. His ticket was for the whole way to York, but he was long gone by then.'

Scherchinskiy was accounted for that weekend. It was the middle of October before a possible explanation emerged. This time, it came not from *World* but from MI6. A source – in the usual fashion, there was no statement of who, when, where or how – reported that information from the Bath naval design centre had turned up in Moscow. Did MI5 have any comment to make on how this might have happened? Indeed, MI5 did have a comment: there had been a break-in on 15 September. Was MI6 not aware of that? It had been included in a routine inter-service report.

It turned out that no great problem was caused by the material which had found its way to Moscow. It was the outline of designs which had been rejected for the next generation of destroyers. That was why the designer in question had them in a desk-drawer in his office instead of a high security safe. They were yesterday's secrets.

But they were secrets. Deakin gave the MI6 report to McKellen who let all his desk officers see it. Thomas spotted the coincidence of dates. 'On Thursday the fifteenth, the plans disappear,' he said, 'and on the seventeenth, Brown drops out of sight. A month later, they're in Moscow. What do you think?' But there was only coincidence to go on. They allotted it a 50 per cent probability.

By then they were already in the throes of dealing with another new addition to the Crow file. The October *World* carried an article by Brown which detailed discussions the British Defence Ministry was having with the French and, separately, the Americans about developing a new air-launched nuclear missile. 'It's not just he's got the issues straight,' said the man from Defence. 'He's got every bloody detail off pat too – when the meetings were, who was there, who said what, the lot.'

Everybody was furious – the French, the Americans, Downing Street, the Ministry of Defence, the Foreign Office. The K1 ferrets got to work. Thomas updated them on who Brown had been seeing and talking to. They looked at all the people involved in or with knowledge of the talks. Most were very senior; K1 put them under the microscope even so. But once again none of them could be shown to have had any contact with Brown and the hunt was on for mutual acquaintances.

'Of course,' McKellen said at a meeting, 'there is a different possibility: the leaks could be on the other side of the Channel and the Atlantic.' The man from the Foreign Office perked up at that and proposed making inquiries of US and French counter-intelligence.

'We can remind them we've already asked about Brown,' McKellen added, 'and heard nothing back apart from an acknowledgement.'

Afterwards Thomas commented to McKellen that the proposition didn't stand up: Brown hadn't travelled abroad in the last four months.

'I know that,' McKellen said loftily. 'Just trying to take the heat off us and put it on somebody else.'

Even as those inquiries continued, Brown did another vanishing trick. It was at the end of October and was the best one of all. He arrived home very late one Friday night; next morning he wasn't there. The Watchers camped out at the end of his street in a draughty flat saw him returning on the Sunday afternoon.

'How did they miss him this time?' Deakin asked.

'A chap in Brown's street drives a huge artic,' Thomas explained. 'It was parked outside his house on Friday. The Watchers reckon he left through his side entrance, which they can't see from where they are, made a quick dash to behind the lorry, then simply walked in a crouch behind the parked cars the sixty or so yards to the corner.'

'But they could have seen him when he got to the main road.'

'If they were looking, sir, but they'd already seen him get home so that's where they were looking, if you catch my drift.'

'Scherchinskiy?'

'Was under our eyes the whole time – again.'

'Well, I wonder what horror he's got in store for us this time. This is getting too much. It has to stop.'

Chapter 4

Even as they considered how to stop Brown, the CIA answered the query arising from the leak about the air-launched missile talks. The first half of the reply was unpromising. No relevant US official could be shown to have had contact with Brown, or with any of his long list of Washington acquaintances. Inquiries were continuing. The second half was dynamite.

It was a transcript of part of a debriefing session with a Soviet defector who'd come over four years earlier. With MI5's two information requests in mind, they put Brown's name to him. Though he knew little about him, for he had never served in London, he was definite that Brown was an agent of influence whose investigative journalism was a cover for digging out information to embarrass the West and pass to the USSR.

'In principle,' Deakin said, 'there's two ways of stopping him. We can pull him in for a little chat, warn him off and hope that will do the trick.' He lit his pipe. 'Or we can step up our watch on him and see if we can't catch him in the act – receiving or delivering information, meeting clandestinely with the wrong sort of person. Whatever. The disadvantage is we don't know when we'll get the chance.'

'There is a third way,' sir,' said Thomas. 'The search.'

'No,' McKellen said. 'We're unlikely to find anything damaging, and he's almost certain to know we've been there. He is ultra-professional. His streetcraft is evidence enough of that. We still don't know how he got the information on either Porton or the missile. The ferrets have made no progress on either front. That again indicates his proficiency. And it all stands as a warning against going off half-cock.'

'And calling him in, Tim?' Deakin said. 'Your feeling on that?'

'It would make a good article. He'd probably get an advance for his next book on the strength of it. Might keep his head down for a bit, but it could strengthen his hand in the long run. If we ever moved against him, he'd simply cry vendetta. Another case of half-cock.'

'So you opt for catching him in the act?'

'Only option,' McKellen said conclusively.

'I agree,' Deakin said. 'Sort out a summary, Gerald, for me to take to the old man. What's the headline?'

'Agent of influence and information,' Thomas replied, 'with an exceptionally high degree of training. We haven't pinned down when he got that, but my money's on the year he was in Paris with Unesco. It was after that his colours seemed to change.'

'Perhaps. Probably. Reasons for closing him down?'

'One,' said Thomas, 'to deny his talents to the opposition, both as agent of influence and as spy.'

'That's two reasons,' McKellen said. 'Three, it would force the KGB to rejig their order of battle in London, and that itself would be revealing.'

'Four,' said Thomas, 'it would discredit the anti-nuclear agitators and other groups he's associated with, including in the Labour Party.'

'And five,' Deakin concluded, 'it would awaken a broad swathe of opinion – centre and a bit to the left – to the realities of life and break them from their Gorby-mania.'

'Reasons four and five,' McKellen pointed out, 'presuppose we do it with maximum publicity.'

'Quite so,' said Deakin. 'Let's not hide our fire on this one, eh?'

They discussed operational requirements. 'Urgent level on intercepts,' McKellen said. 'Gerald will need immediate reporting from real-time monitoring of Brown's phone and same-day transcripts. Also stronger coverage from the Watchers.'

Deakin agreed, instructed Thomas to write it up and arranged to see the Director-General the next day. But before that he went to a routine liaison meeting with MI6. 'The Sixers,' he told McKellen when he got back, 'have got wind of an unusual amount of opposition activity. They seem to be giving their top influentials warning of the next propaganda wave. Usual sort of thing. Get the proposals aired in the West this month and they'll be taken up by the flexible Freddies in the Kremlin next.'

'Arms control, is this?' McKellen asked.

'Mainly. In more general terms it's their reaction to the US elections. Six has a source – or they've received news from somebody else's source, more likely – which they call Gerhardt – so it's definitely not a German. He's in some embassy. He picked it up from a message in the KGB station officer's in-tray.'

'When?'

'Over the past two weeks is all they'd say.'

'So Brown may have been getting his orders during last weekend's Indian rope trick.'

Later that day, Deakin told McKellen that the Director-General had authorised Brown's arrest on the basis they'd agreed. The media follow-up and intensified surveillance were also approved. Deakin instructed Hay to put into Sunday's instructions to Lucy a request for information about Brown or Scherchinskiy, especially the latter's forward plans, and to use the emergency procedure to provide it immediately if it became available.

The first news, however, came from MI6's Gerhardt in the middle of the following week. A message to the senior KGB officer at whichever embassy Gerhardt worked in listed London among those cities of Western Europe where a special effort would be made in the following two weeks to promote the USSR's new disarmament proposals. Maximum personal contact was ordered. 'Good,' McKellen said. 'Brown hasn't yet had his marching orders. The issue now is how he'll get them.'

On Sunday, Thomas was called in to see the transcript of a telephone conversation. It was Brown, saying to a friend whom he'd evidently planned to see on Tuesday, 'Sorry I can't make it, mate. I've got a late date in Hampstead, don't you know, ten o'clock. Can't afford to miss it, I'm afraid. Just come up.'

'Hampstead?' said Deakin on Monday morning. 'Do we have anything there? Or, rather, do they?'

Thomas had already checked. 'A flat in a place called Windsor Court, not far from the Heath. Rented but not occupied. I've sent a Watcher up to check that's still the case. The rent's paid regularly, and the lease is in the name of a Liechtenstein-based holding company which appears to be untraceable. It's been on our lists since early summer, but we've not spotted any activity there so far, though hostiles have been seen there twice in that period.'

When the Watcher returned, he reported the flat was still empty, though semi-furnished, and that one of the neighbours had seen somebody there already that day. 'A foreign looking gentleman,' she said.'

'We may be on,' Deakin said. 'That could well have been the sweeper to be sure it was clean.'

By evening, the last piece of the jigsaw was in place. At lunchtime Lucy signalled he would make a drop at 6.30. When he finished work he called in at a pub on his way home, something he often did – it was more or less his local. Hay was there too. After a drink, Lucy went to the lavatory and left an envelope tucked behind the toilet-paper holder. Hay made sure he was the next one in and retrieved it. Lucy left immediately, but Hay waited another twenty minutes. At 7.10 he was back at Curzon Street, by 7.30 Lucy's message was translated, and five minutes later Deakin conferred with Thomas and McKellen.

'Scherchinskiy has an appointment in Hampstead tomorrow evening,' he said. 'Lucy's exact words are: "At the inter-embassy meeting this morning, I managed to sit near S. We discussed treatment of the SU's next arms initiative. It will be made at the UN next month. No details were made available but general preparatory groundwork was discussed, and a reception at GDR tomorrow was mentioned. Speaking privately, S's senior asked him if he could be there. Also quietly, S said yes, but he would have to leave early as he had to be at Hampstead Heath by ten. Is this of any help?"'

'That's it,' said Thomas. 'Do we do it?'

'Yes,' said Deakin. 'The old man gave me authority to pick the moment. This is it. See Naseby tomorrow morning, and get him to line up Austin. His team's the best for this, don't you think?'

'Yes, he's a good man,' McKellen agreed. 'Served us well several times.'

On Tuesday morning Thomas briefed Naseby who handled liaison with Special Branch and who in turn briefed Austin. While those preparations were made, the Watchers kept their eyes on Brown. In the early evening they reported he'd done another disappearing act. 'Good,' said McKellen when Thomas told him. 'How'd he do it this time?'

'The bus routine,' Thomas said. 'There were two pairs on him – one front and one back – with a third waiting at his next port of call.'

'What was that?'

'Pub by Blackfriars. He'd arranged to have a drink there with another journo at six thirty. Anyway, he hopped on a number eleven at the lights by the National Gallery. That dropped the front tail and half his back pair. One of them managed to get on the bus with him. Says he smiled at her.'

'Cocky bastard.'

'At the Aldwych he jumped off in the middle of the traffic and zipped off into the LSE. She ran after him but lost him in the crowd at the entrance. Called in extra help, of course, but it was too late. The place is an absolute warren. By the time they had all the exits covered he was probably long gone. I've had them wait there though.'

'Of course. What about the pub?'

'I've let them off. The chap he was seeing there turned up, had a drink, then he got a phone call and left.'

'Fine. He's going to some trouble over this, not surprisingly. What about our KGB chum?'

'Still at the embassy.'

'At this time? When's that East German reception Lucy mentioned?'

'Already started.'

And Scherchinkskiy was not spotted leaving the embassy and certainly not at the GDR's reception. Thomas and McKellen waited together for ten o'clock to come by. At midnight McKellen left saying, 'One of us had better get some sleep.' Thomas nodded gloomily.

The first question he asked himself, after Naseby had called him and he'd told him to tell the Special Branch to take a quick look at the flat, was, 'Where did I go wrong?'

By the time McKellen arrived at eight on Wednesday morning, took one look at his unshaven, crumpled and dispirited desk officer and said, 'Oh shit,' Thomas had heard all about the cat and stopped asking himself that question. Now he wanted to know, 'Who's going to make them pay?'

Chapter 5

'Well, let's be thankful for small mercies,' Sir Nigel Laker said. 'At least the cat didn't make the evening papers. What happened to it by the way?'

'I am assured it's all under control,' Hanson replied. He had an Edinburgh accent, softened by a lifetime in London. 'Its tail has been amputated and I'm told the desk sergeant at the local police station has offered to adopt it and see the kittens into good homes.'

'So the cat dropped its tail too,' Sir Nigel said. His voice was low, cultured, authoritative and, from time to time, mildly amused. 'How the hell did it get there?'

'As far as they can make out, somebody – some tramp – has been using the place to drink and sleep it off. The cat would appear to have got in by the broken window through which this tramp effected his own entrance into the flat. However, Nigel, touched as I am by your concern – and I'll make sure the Feline Defence League or whatever it's called gets to hear of it and taps you for a donation this Christmas – I assume there is another purpose behind your invitation?'

'Yes, Jock,' Sir Nigel said, 'I'm only delaying the inevitable. These occasions are detestable. I feel we shall only survive if we have the rudiments of civilised existence. I propose to decamp to the corner and lubricate the faculties. You'll join me? Scotch?' He pushed the box of cigars across the desk as he rose. 'Help yourself. The darker leaf is an acceptable Havana imitation, the lighter a rather pleasant Dominican.'

The room was large, high-ceilinged, furnished in a style which reflected centuries of the assumption of power. It was lit by a single, classical, green-shaded lamp on the expansive mahogany desk. When Sir Nigel had poured two generous measures of whisky and selected his own cigar, he crossed to the far corner and switched on the standard lamp. He sat in a wing-chair and gestured Hanson to the sofa.

'I invited you round both because you have an interest,' he

said as they lit up, 'and to run through some options with you.'

'Ah,' Hanson said. Despite his effort to mask it, relief was evident enough in his voice for a practised ear.

'You thought you were here to receive the ticking parcel,' Sir Nigel accused gently.

Hanson shrugged. 'That shot,' he said. 'Of course, not just the cat but also the Branch has been kept out of the newspapers. However, they are intrigued, the neighbours worried, the caretaker and owners furious, and the local division quite beside itself. The Minister expects questions in the House any moment and wants to know what answers he shouldn't give. After a day like that, nothing bad is unexpected. So what's *your* problem?'

Sir Nigel covered a pause for thought by attending to his whisky and cigar. There was a great deal of delicacy in what he was about to do. Formally he and Hanson had the same Civil Service rank: Deputy Secretary. The Scot was head of the Police Department at the Home Office. As much as it could be said of any one person, and that was not much, he ran the country's fifty-five police forces. Sir Nigel, however, was effectively the senior of the two. He was the Chief Intelligence Co-ordinator, Chairman of the Joint Intelligence Committee, situated in the Cabinet Office, responsible for well over a billion pounds of secret expenditure each year. The cause of his seniority was simple: where Hanson had access to a Minister of State and on occasion the Home Secretary, Sir Nigel could, when occasion demanded, have access to the Prime Minister.

The delicacy lay in the fact that he was about to seek Hanson's assistance. It hurt to do that – both to rely on a man who was effectively junior and to go outside the intelligence world for help. There was the further problem that by doing this he was going behind the back of another Home Office Deputy Secretary who was supposed to be responsible for the Security Service.

'I am not convinced,' he began, 'that we can automatically lay the blame for Operation Crow's failure at the door of Special Branch. It may be. It needs assessing. But there are, I'm afraid, other possibilities.'

'In the Security Service?'

'Quite.'

'Where, as in the Branch come to that, I suppose we are confronted with the usual pair of possible explanations: either a fool or a rogue.'

'Quite,' Sir Nigel said again, and then lapsed into silence. He was a tall, lean man, his thin face normally an expressionless mask. But tonight the worry lines were more visible than usual, the skin on his prominent cheekbones looked tauter, his eyes were shadowed with fatigue.

'How do you gauge the procedure?' Hanson asked.

'To begin with, the Red Book, I'm afraid.'

Hanson frowned. That was the weekly digest of top secret material provided to Cabinet ministers on a strictly confidential basis. 'Is it wise to let the whole world know?' he asked.

'The times have taught us not to spring security surprises on the Prime Minister,' the Co-ordinator remarked blandly. He did not bother to explain why. It was no secret. There had been too many such surprises in recent years, too much expenditure of political capital dealing with the Security Service's old and dirty linen. 'An accounting will be demanded, of course. Some form of inquiry.'

'At what level?'

'There are various possibilities. The Service, naturally enough, wants to run it. I am inclined to resist that. I think they've already made up their minds. I would value your thoughts.'

'Not the Security Commission,' Hanson suggested. 'Neither necessary nor desirable.'

'Nor, on this issue, particularly useful.'

'It hardly needs saying it must be not only confidential but also small scale.'

'Though that should not be taken to mean half-hearted,' Sir Nigel said.

'If Five Hundred can't do it on grounds of bias, nor can Special Branch. And neither would accept the Sixers rummaging around in its affairs.'

'Out of the question. Infringement of territorial rights.'

'So perhaps *noblesse* obliges?'

'An eminent outsider? Difficult. Anybody with security experience is caught on the bias objection. And I doubt any of the usual tribe could fit the bill without staff. He might deliberate on material unearthed by someone else but would hardly know how to grub around in the dirt himself. Which still leaves the task of finding a candidate to conduct the investigation, and makes one wonder why bother with an eminence at all.'

'Are you telling me,' Hanson said, 'not least by my presence here, that your thinking has embraced the possibility of seconding a police officer?'

Sir Nigel did not at first respond directly. 'What I need,' he said, 'is an outsider who knows his way around. Not *of* the security world, but with a feel for it. A competent, experienced investigator, able to work alone and sustain the effort in the face of whatever comes his way. It may be that a police officer would fit the bill. It is a suggestion I am open to, if you have a nomination.'

'And what might there be,' Hanson asked, 'coming his way?'

'Contradictory, confusing and unclear evidence. Some unwillingness to co-operate – the usual response to an outsider. Beyond that – who knows? If we are dealing with a penetration, then perhaps deliberate obstruction and even interference.'

'You ask a lot,' Hanson said. 'An experienced investigating officer, of whom there are many. He needs to be tough: no problem. As well as great competence and integrity, you want proven qualities not only of perseverance – which is common – but also of independence, so he can work without his usual back-up, which is rarer. And he must have some experience or feel for the world you move in. Quite a shopping list.'

'Do you have such a man?'

'I know one. But I must tell you, he is independent, he does persevere.'

'You mean?'

'That on the last occasion I called on him for a special task, he caused some difficulty precisely because of those qualities. Let me put it like this: if he's set a task, you can rely on him to do it.'

'But if he's called off before he thinks he's finished— '

'There are some detectives,' Hanson interrupted, 'who are like hounds on a fox. If you change your mind about blood-sports after you've unleashed them, it may be too late.'

'Indeed?' Sir Nigel said lightly. 'It would surely depend on how serious you were about your change of heart.'

Hanson resisted the temptation to consider the implications of that casual remark. 'I don't think you've answered me yet,' he said.

Silence hung between them for several minutes. Sir Nigel finished his Scotch. 'I think a two-stage operation may be advisable,' he said finally. 'A preliminary sweep and initial report. Then time to catch our breath and consider.' He glanced at Hanson. 'In the preliminary stage, and in the follow-up if we get there, the task will not be redefined.'

Silently he added to himself, 'Except in extreme circumstances.'

Hanson nodded. 'I shall need a memorandum to define his task, and I presume you will want to check his credentials. Will you require more than his file?'

'Yes, but you don't have to provide it. What is his name?'

PART II
Parliament of Crows

Chapter 6

While the two civil servants were picking delicate paths through their tangle of predicaments, the man Hanson had in mind to cut their way out of it was in a police cell trying to cut a deal.

His intended bargain was with a hard case who, according to repute, had gone soft. That turned out to be ill repute for him, when a pair he'd once chased out of London decided to take their chance to settle old scores, and worse repute for them, when he pulled out a flick-knife and sliced them up with all his old skill.

If the pair who jumped Billy Hughes had been smarter, they might have run from the smile which greeted them when they confronted him in the alleyway. If they were smarter, they might have read something in his eyes, even in that poor light. They weren't, they didn't, and the price they paid amounted to ninety-five stitches between them.

It seemed ill luck that night was not confined to them. There was a pair of witnesses who recalled seeing a police car just round the corner and ran to do their civic duty. At Tottenham Court Road police station, Detective Inspector Herd had Hughes charged and put in a cell to think things over. Then he called Detective Chief Inspector Harry Fathers. Hughes was a barracuda in a sea where Fathers and his section of the Serious Crimes Squad at Scotland Yard were hunting two big sharks.

Fathers arrived half an hour later, offered a quick 'hello' and thanks for calling him, and asked, 'Queen and Yarrow here yet?'

'Queenie's in the bar,' Herd said.

'I think I disturbed Yarrow on the job,' Fathers said. 'Probably take him a while to get out and over here.' A flickering movement of the small scar at the corner of his mouth suggested he found his interruption of Yarrow's love life amusing.

He probably does, thought Herd. He looked at Fathers. Even at this hour, the DCI was impeccably turned out. It was said that in his own office, at the right time, he'd loosen his tie, put his feet on the table and swig some whisky with the best of them, but this was not one of those times. The white shirt didn't look like it had been worn all through a long day. The well-tailored, double-breasted suit he wore under his Burberry didn't look in the slightest bit rumpled. His dark hair was as neatly brushed as usual. He was six foot two, weighed around thirteen stone and, turning forty, didn't seem to have developed a paunch yet. His record as a detective won him a lot of professional respect, but few of his colleagues got close enough to know if they really did dislike him or just found him stand-offish. A lot of them had difficulties with the way he looked, as if it expressed permanent disapproval of their own appearance and dress-sense. Next to him, most people looked a bit slovenly. The few who did get close enough either liked him a great deal or couldn't stand his clever guts.

Fathers was shown to Hughes's cell where he opened negotiations. The trade he was offering was a lighter charge in return for information – the usual thing.

Hughes was a medium-level operator on the fringes of Soho. He owned or controlled a handful of restaurants and clubs, had his fingers into local prostitution and got a percentage of the pimps' take, ran a tidy protection business and didn't trouble anybody very much as long as things stayed quiet. His kind tended to hurt only those who were partly or wholly on the wrong side of the law – except the punters they rooked, but that was the way of things – and under normal circumstances the police would leave them to their own devices.

But the last few months hadn't been normal. Along with several other similar figures, Billy Hughes was under pressure from a new pair of players in the London game. A long-time small-timer from Hackney – a man called Garston – had teamed up with an American arrival – Connors, from Boston it seemed. The American appeared to have brought a lot of money which, together with Garston's numerous contacts, made it possible to recruit freely. They had become a formidable pair.

Garston's base of operation in east London was obviously not enough for them. They had started to go for bigger prizes, muscling their way into the West End. Their methods were direct. Restaurants and clubs were broken up. Protection dues collectors were intercepted, beaten up, their takings taken. Three pimps had been badly cut around the face when they refused to hand over a percentage to the new force. There was growing talk of some of the little people running for cover, leaving the old firms' protection and joining the new. Rumours spread that Billy Hughes had gone soft. People he'd

38

elbowed aside the hard way in previous years were lining up to take him on. But Hughes's problem was simply that he faced superior force; in himself he was unchanged.

Well, thought Fathers, he proved himself tonight. When the hard men lost their edge, previously beaten rivals often wanted a go at them. The resulting fights had been known to end in a killing as the intended victim's taste for violence came back in a frenzy. But Hughes had punished his attackers with controlled viciousness. The street talk had been well wide of the mark.

But now it was possible he could help Fathers. Facing what could be several years inside, and at the very least a few months on remand in custody, perhaps Hughes would be fearful that his little empire would slip out of his grasp and therefore be willing to provide some information – which he doubtless had – in an attempt to get the new predators off his back.

As soon as he offered the bargain, Fathers knew it was futile. Hughes was not the toughest looking person you would encounter in London, but he had a permanent air of authority which came from knowing he'd never had to back down or take a beating in a straight fight. He was no more prepared to trade than he had been to stand there and be taken when two wallies from out of town tried to jump him. He was also shrewd.

'Look, Dad,' he said reasonably, 'what you're offering me now is no better than my brief'll get me anyway in a few months. These gits went for me and I defended myself. You can have me on the dangerous weapon, possession of – I'll put my hand up for that – but on an assault charge, the jury'll see mitigating circumstances and sling it out.'

'You know so much,' said Fathers. 'Just think about it. I'll have the pair you shivved plus the beak on my side when we go into court, and two witnesses to tell about the brutality of your attack. If you want to chance it, go ahead. Your choice, your funeral – or your sentence. And while you're waiting trial, you know things aren't going to stand still on the streets. So think about it. Remember, I'm not asking you to grass in open court. Just some hard squeaking so we can line up Connors and Garston.'

'Who're they?'

Fathers left Hughes in his cell and went to the bar. Sitting at a table he found Detective Inspector Laurence Queen and Detective Sergeant Elliot Yarrow. They were sitting in silence, as they usually did when they were in each other's company with nothing relevant to say about the immediate inquiry, though they were both gregarious enough in general. The reason for this was very simple: they didn't like each other.

The year before, a small-time thief who was an informant of Yarrow's had got to hear that Queen was taking bribes. In fact, Queen had been posing as corruptible to tempt a villain into offering a bribe. The scheme had worked, but Yarrow's informant got in the way. So Queen hit him several times with a piece of wood and the informant ended up in hospital. Yarrow had yet to forgive Queen, who in turn distrusted the Detective Sergeant for his upright moralising and sentimentality.

Fathers bought a round of drinks and sat down. He recounted the negotiation. 'Not so soft as they make out,' Queen remarked through a cloud of cigarette-smoke. He was a few years older than Fathers, shorter, heavier, wore suits which shone at the elbows, knees and seat and usually clashed with his shoes, tie and just about everything else he was wearing. 'Hasn't lost a bit of it. Didn't think he had.'

Queen was the expert on the underworld. More than a few people thought it had been easy for him to pose as corruptible because he was. Perhaps – but he'd never been caught. Fathers had several times tried to have him transferred, but never had any success, and over the years had come to a sort of working relationship. On the other hand, he regularly blocked Queen's promotion, not out of personal animosity but because he didn't think Queen was the right material for DCI. Queen more or less knew this and resented it. Equally, he resented the obvious fact that Fathers thought Yarrow had the qualities to go a long way in the force – past Queen eventually. It didn't make for an easy partnership.

Now Yarrow wanted to know how the out-of-town pair had got to Hughes. Fathers asked what difference it made. Yarrow shrugged. 'Coulda been a set-up,' he said.

Queen pursed his lips and shook his head. 'You saying they got to someone?' he said, disbelief curdling his voice. 'Or p'raps these two gits from Glasgow are on Garston's pay-roll. Or maybe even Guy White.'

White was Hughes's top muscle.

'Could be,' Yarrow persisted. He turned to Fathers. 'Or p'raps those two heard the jocks were going after Hughes and decided to lend a helping hand. I dunno. But I'd like to know where White was.'

Queen mumbled and shrugged, lit another cigarette and allowed the smoke to filter out of his mouth, up through his straggly moustache and back into his system via his nostrils.

'Then find out,' said Fathers.

Yarrow nodded. As they rose from the table, he muttered to Fathers, 'Like a word, guv.'

Queen cast a look at Yarrow. 'D'you want me back 'ere in the morning?' he asked Fathers.

'Don't think so. I'll talk to him myself and see if he's prepared to deal. If not, we've got time before it comes to trial.' Queen nodded and went to the bar for another drink. 'What's the score?' Fathers asked.

'I just saw one o' my snouts in the book when you were downstairs. Bit of luck really.'

'And you want the charge pulled. What is it?'

'Wheels for a B 'n' E.'

'I'll have a word and see if they can lose it.'

'Actually, guv, I've a different thought.'

'Yeah?'

'Keep the charge, but get a low bail.'

'So when he's out he can get to work earning his dear old liberty,' said Fathers, nodding with satisfaction. 'Yarrer, I've hopes we'll make a rozzer of you yet.'

Next morning Fathers called in at Tottenham Court Road and offered the deal to Hughes again, but with no more success. After a brief chat with Herd he went to the Yard. 'Seen Yarrer?' he asked Queen.

The DI sniffed. 'Ain't you just been to Tottenham Court? Thought you might've seen him there. Didn't he go back to see about his snout?'

'You don't miss a lot, do you, Queenie?'

'Not when a skipper takes you aside to say what by rights he could say in front of me, specially when I can put an eye across the Occurrence Book.'

'Well, if you want him to tell you about his snouts you shouldn't duff them up. Anyway, talking of keeping quiet about snouts, get the one you've lined up in Hackney and haven't told me about to tell you what those bastards are really up to.'

'Talking of not missing much,' mumbled Queen.

At eleven, a summons came from Chief Superintendent Bastin. There would not be many more of them, Fathers reflected with a sort of nostalgia. Bastin had only a month left in charge of the Serious Crimes Squad – he was going the week before Christmas. His last year before retirement would be spent at Bramshill Police College. It was a final, gentle departure from the force for a man who'd been steadily easing off during the past several years.

Fathers had had his moments with Bastin, as he always did with his immediate superiors, but as the Chief Superintendent had relaxed his pace much of the tension between them had disappeared. Fathers was dimly aware that Bastin had, if not exactly a paternal attitude to him, at least an avuncular one, prepared to tolerate his misbehaviour and defend him to higher authority on the grounds of his clear-up rate which, at about one-third of all the cases he handled, was nearly twice the Metropolitan CID's average.

Fathers assumed Bastin wanted to know about the Connors and Garston investigation, but the Chief Superintendent cut him off and handed him a letter. 'Take a deep breath and read that,' he said.

Fathers read. The letter was from Hanson. In a way which was not to be refused, it asked that Fathers be seconded to him for two weeks, possibly longer. 'Before you start up,' Bastin said, 'the AC's OK'd it.'

The Assistant Commissioner's say-so didn't mean much to Fathers. 'Does he know what I've got on at the moment?' he demanded. 'No, he doesn't. Because I haven't even told you yet. Billy Hughes got picked up on a knifing last night. That leaves the way open for Connors and Garston. Could be their big chance.'

'I doubt that would've changed his mind,' Bastin said. 'He's not going to turn down Hanson on this. I told him about your work-load, and he waved it aside – said you'll have to ride both horses at once.'

'Both?' Fathers exploded. 'If only there were just the two of them. But in any case, why me? Has Hanson forgotten?'

'I doubt it,' Bastin said gently. He certainly wouldn't forget how Hanson had sent Fathers to New York, then wanted him reprimanded for reporting that, in all probability, the US government had had a British researcher killed for stumbling across embarrassing secrets and not keeping his mouth shut. He had kept Hanson away from Fathers' throat, and the fuss had died down. But it was a surprise that the Home Office wanted Fathers' help again.

'But I can't bloody do it,' Fathers said. 'No way. What's the AC up to with his ride both sodding horses? Apart from Connors and Garston and their nasty ways I've got— '

'I know,' Bastin said with quiet firmness, 'but it's not me you should be telling it to, nor the AC. I can't do anything about it and he won't. Talk to Hanson.'

'I bloody will,' Fathers said getting up.

'Yes, well, I sort of meant you should persuade him but you'll probably try to do it your way. By the way, the new man's just been named.'

'Your replacement?' Fathers said distractedly.

'Yes. Chap called Myers. Frank Myers.'

Fathers stood stock-still. Bastin looked at him. 'You know him?'

'I know him,' Fathers said. They had been Detective Sergeants together fifteen years ago, before he came to the Yard. 'I do know him.'

'And don't like him,' Bastin sighed. 'Well, I suggest you try forgetting that. You'll need to get off to a good start with him. From what I hear, he's a real hot shot.'

'You could say that,' Fathers said, the tightness of his jaw belying the casualness of the words. 'When's he start?'

'Formally, on the fifteenth of next month. He'll be here for a week or so before that.'

Myers, Fathers thought as he stormed back to his office and got his coat, bloody Myers – why him? And bloody Hanson. Why me?

Chapter 7

Fathers saw no change in Hanson in the four years since they had last met. The Scot was average height, balding and stocky, just as he had been before. He had added no weight, lost no more hair and still wore the sort of dark suit and quietly distinguished tie favoured in Whitehall – a Home Office mandarin to the last detail, unchanging, preserved in formaldehyde.

Equally, Hanson saw no change in Fathers, neither his appearance nor his manner. Tea had barely been provided before he started to be offensive. After complimenting Fathers on some of his recent successes, Hanson began to explain why he had called him over. 'We have a problem, a Five Hundred problem,' he said.

'You mean MI5,' Fathers interrupted.

'Indeed,' said Hanson. 'The Security Service.'

'Then would you mind saying so?'

Hanson took a breath and reminded himself of what he knew about this man, both from his file and from personal experience.

'It's always easier when you people speak English,' Fathers added. This might have been an anti-Scottish insult; Hanson was not sure but thought it wasn't beyond Fathers. 'It's tough enough keeping up with our own slang without you making it worse. And there's no reason for it. Except to seem clever.'

Hanson took another breath. He assumed Fathers was trying to provoke a row so the assignment would be given to somebody else. Well, he would not give him that pleasure. He smiled, sipped his tea, and began again: 'Two nights ago, a security operation fell apart on the point of producing a major *coup*. We want to know why.'

'Tuesday night?' Fathers grinned. 'This isn't the cat-killing episode, is it?'

'Er, that is to say, the cat was winged rather than killed,' Hanson said. He, too, couldn't resist a brief flickering smile. 'Or, perhaps I should say, tailed. I'm surprised you know about it.'

'Oh, it's all over the place. Won't be long now before it seeps into the papers. Probably be up to a pack of dogs by then. Anyway,

I'm afraid I can't help you. Got too much on my plate right now.'

Hanson ignored the last remark, steepled his fingers, took on the air of an Oxbridge don and outlined Operation Crow and its breakdown. 'Your task,' he concluded, 'is to find out what happened, what went wrong – whether the problem is a leak or simple incompetence – and to do so with your usual speed and ingenuity.'

Fathers disregarded the flannel and poured himself a second cup of tea. He took a sip and looked at the polished bureaucrat. 'You really do dislike me, don't you, Mister Hanson?'

Before Fathers' arrival, Hanson had readied himself for a discourse entirely unlike the ordinary run of things between civil servants. Even so, this took him aback. 'Why do you say that?' he asked. He could think of nothing else to say.

'Why else do you always give me the shit end of the stick?'

This was the Fathers Hanson had expected. But again it caught him off guard. He cleared his throat noisily. His first reaction was to want to point out that 'always' was an exaggeration – this was only the second occasion. But it was hardly the appropriate response.

'My wife,' Fathers added conversationally, 'often asks me if I'm the only policeman in London.'

'I take the point, but it may be that you *are* the only one who can handle this problem, certainly the only one I could identify at short notice.'

'Well, try again,' Fathers responded, 'because I can't do it for you.'

'Mr Fathers,' Hanson said firmly, 'I think we've been here before. Four years ago. Let me make it clear that you have been seconded and will do the job. There is no alternative.'

Fathers launched into an explanation of why there had to be an alternative. He listed his section's current cases, explained the particular importance of keeping track of what Connors and Garston were up to and added a dozen other considerations, considerably salted with exaggeration.

Hanson let the torrent of words exhaust itself. Then he said, 'This is a two-stage process. Your first task is to go through everything in the operation and see if an explanation for its failure emerges. If so, your task ends there. If not, identify the most promising lines for further investigation, which you may or may not be called upon to undertake. You have *carte blanche* to interview everybody involved in the operation, whatever their seniority in Special Branch or the Security Service. They have been instructed to answer all your questions fully. If they are less than properly co-operative, I will

45

see they're put straight. This inquiry is top priority and one hundred per cent confidential. I have assigned you an office here from which you will work. For security reasons you will have no investigative or secretarial assistance. You will have your own outside line which does not go through the Home Office switchboard, but of course conduct the minimum of business by phone.' He indicated a stack of folders on his desk. 'Here you have details of the operation, the target, and what happened on Tuesday. Also the names of all those involved at any level and how to contact them plus their full service records. Through me, you can have access to any further files you judge relevant.' He rose and picked the folders up. 'Do you have any questions?'

Hanson walked round his desk, ready to hand Fathers the folders, implying there would be no questions. Fathers remained in his chair. 'No,' he said, 'but something to say all the same. I'll conduct the interviews in the office you've set up for me if you like, but I'm not working there otherwise.'

'Mr Fathers— '

'There are several reasons, but only one that will appeal to you. If you want what I'm doing kept secret, the worst way is to withdraw me from my office at the Yard just now. The underworld in London is about to be shaken up in a very big way. If you want to set tongues wagging at the Yard, there's no better way than pulling me off the case exactly when the explosion's about to come. If you think a couple of lads wouldn't try to figure out what I'm doing just for the fun of it, you don't know them, and if you think they wouldn't succeed, you don't know anything.'

'There is no higher classification, Mr Fathers, than the one given to this inquiry. Whatever the gossip at the Yard or the modified version provided to the press, the fact is that the whole operation is still surrounded by total confidentiality, a security net which your colleagues, however able— '

'Do you know what a security net is?' demanded Fathers. Hanson was caught off guard again. 'It's a lot of holes tied together with bits of string. About as much use as a security blanket, but it doesn't give such a strong illusion of safety.'

Hanson made no response, reflecting on this further proof that Fathers had not changed in four years – unless it was change for somebody to take all his worst characteristics and emphasise them. Fathers calmed down a bit and continued, 'Now look. You obviously have a problem, because you can't trust either MI5 or Special Branch to investigate themselves or each other.'

Hanson nodded, comforted by the thought that if Fathers had not lost his proclivity for wild insults, he had not lost his sharpness either.

'So you've picked me to bail you out. But if you want the job done properly you've got to let me do it my way. Or pick somebody else.'

Despite the truculence, Hanson relaxed as he listened. Fathers was quibbling over details but had effectively accepted the job. In fact, he sensed a quickening of interest in the detective.

'And that means I can't drop this case. It's not just that to do so would be wrong in terms of the case itself. It's also the business of security.'

Hanson reflected for a moment. If he insisted that Fathers drop his main current inquiry, the man would probably keep going on it anyway, not only because he was cussed, but because he knew he was right. He shrugged inwardly and surrenderd. 'Time is of the essence. I've given you two weeks, but I want that to be the outside limit. Can you manage it as well as this other thing?'

Fathers had no idea if he could. For a start he didn't know how many people were mentioned in the awesome stack of paperwork Hanson was holding. But having gained as much as he had, he decided to see what happened and make it up as he went along. Bastin, he thought, would have been proud of him. All he said was 'I never run one case at a time.'

'And you will work alone,' Hanson insisted.

'There's one other thing,' Fathers said. Hanson readied himself for another rude volley. 'What I know about MI5 wouldn't fill the back of a postage stamp. I'll need an organisation chart for it, together with a description of its routine security procedures.'

Hanson relaxed and smiled. 'That will be no problem,' he said. 'You'll have them both in the morning.'

Over lunch, he provided an abridged version of the conversation to Sir Nigel Laker, who listened carefully and at the end said, 'He sounds quite an impressive chap.'

'He is, and he obviously has a point on the security angle. Best to let it seem like a lower-level task rather than set the Yard gossips going – and they are incurable, you know. Bunch of old women.'

'Just like Five and Six.'

'On the other hand, setting this laddie loose gives me the feeling of launching an unguided missile.'

'You don't mean unguided, Jock. You mean self-guided.'

'Maybe. What I mean is neither you nor I can guide him.'

Sir Nigel raised his eyebrows as he speared a piece of steak. 'Too often,' he said, 'that's the way of the world.'

Hanson looked at him in puzzlement. He supposed the Coordinator was talking about a different world. He enjoyed a contemplative sip of claret and the talk turned to other matters.

Chapter 8

The office Hanson had provided was little bigger than a cubby-hole. It was decorated, if that was the word, in a dull green. Somebody had put an unimaginative landscape picture on the wall, presumably to harass any occupant with the knowledge that there was a larger world outside – precious little of it was evident from the window. The furniture was a desk, two chairs, a filing cabinet, a coat-stand and a safe on which stood an electric typewriter. The only distinguished thing about it was the two phones on the desk – one of which, so the secretary who showed Fathers there said, was the outside line especially hooked up for him. She was obviously impressed by that; the way she made it sound, it might have been directly connected to Downing Street. While Hanson and the Chief Intelligence Co-ordinator dined on steak *au poivre* at the latter's club, Fathers munched a cheese sandwich and took a first glance at the files.

Even before he sat down he'd decided to start with the Special Branch. Including Austin there were unlucky thirteen of them. To Fathers, as to most other policemen, they were the spooks, or the funnies. They weren't quite proper policemen, but almost. And the degree of fellow feeling he could acknowledge with them, though limited, made them as good a place as any to start. It would at least reduce their anxious time spent waiting for his summons. He read Austin's report on what had happened and decided to bring in Naseby, the MI5 liaison officer, as well in the early stages, to get a different overview on it all. Then he read Peters' report and sympathised. Only those who had been on outings like the one on Tuesday could really know what they were like.

After that he read an outline description of Operation Crow – there was a lot more detail he would have to sift through, but fortunately there was also a handy summary – and decided that in MI5 he'd start with the three officials who had run the show. That would give him the shape of Crow and perhaps point the way ahead.

For Fathers understood one thing all too clearly. He had no sense of strategy for this inquiry. He hoped it would develop as things went along. And if it didn't? He brushed the thought aside.

He'd come into contact with MI5 once or twice in the past, enough to include anybody he'd met from it in the general category of spooks and funnies, and enough to know that he and they operated in very different worlds by very different criteria. They worked constantly in the dark, trying to light it here and there so it at least approached gloom. They worked on hints and nods and probabilities. Well, some of the time so did he. They worked in a world of secrecy and deception where surface appearances were always designed to mislead. Again, so did he sometimes. But there was something different about their world. Was it that the stakes were higher? Or their sense of fundamental conflict with an enemy clearer? Or their belief in their mission and duty deeper? He'd had only enough contact with them to know there was a difference – not enough to define it.

He decided to start that afternoon. Austin and Naseby were as good a place to begin as any. He'd nip back to the Yard, tell his section he'd be gone for the afternoon, collect a recorder and a bunch of cassettes, and start the first interview at three. The next day he could intersperse the Special Branch detectives with the three key men from MI5, carry on with the former across the weekend and then explore further into the deeper recesses of MI5 the following week.

He worked out a rough timetable, got on the phone and started to make appointments. When he spoke to the Special Branch officers he began each time, 'Hello, this is DCI Fathers. In connection with last Tuesday night, I'd like you to present yourself at the Police Department in Queen Anne's Gate at . . . ' The only exception was with Austin, when Fathers began, 'Hello, Tracy, Fathers here. In connection with . . . ' Phoning the MI5 men he began, 'Hello, this is DCI Fathers. In connection with Operation Crow, I'd like . . . '

Nobody objected to the time and day he set, nor would he have allowed them to. He had his orders and they, evidently, had theirs.

At eight o'clock that evening, Deakin called McKellen and Thomas into his office in Curzon House in the West End. It was a good deal handsomer than Fathers' temporary accommodation, though as yet they hadn't had the chance to compare. It was large, quietly decorated, distinguished by three handsome oil paintings, marred by the high-security safe in the corner.

'Tell me about this Fathers person,' said Deakin through his pipe-smoke. 'I don't know him, but I'm told he's sharp, that he smells skeletons in cupboards but has none of his own.'

'You know more than we do then,' said McKellen.

'I got a call from Austin to tell me all about it. They're his words. He's already been done – two hours going through Tuesday's procedural details.'

'Naseby's been in too. Likewise a couple of hours' worth. So we know he's nothing if not thorough, but also a fast mover.'

'And what else do we know about him? Gerald, did you manage to see his file?'

'A good record,' Thomas said, 'outstanding even, and a clean rating, though it seems he's managed to ruffle more than a few feathers in his time. Doesn't look like much of a team player. But there's an oddity.'

'How so?'

'There's a reference to an assignment he undertook four years ago. It says it was for the Home Office, Foreign and Defence. And that's all.'

'And the further file reference?'

'Isn't there,' Thomas said. 'In fact, I hunted around through that year's files and there's nothing. No mention of Fathers, and none of a joint op between the three ministries. The slate's been wiped.'

'An oddity indeed,' Deakin said. 'Any thoughts, Tim?'

'Obviously something that's classified above the level of his file. Classified to a very high degree, in fact, if it's been effectively withdrawn. I suspect it means he's been around our world a bit, which may mean he's not such a bad choice for the job.'

'Hmm,' said Deakin. That was not the conclusion he drew from Thomas's news. 'Any outsider is a bad choice. The old man told me he was set to handle this internally, but the Co-ordinator overruled him. I'm hoping that's because he thinks it would be unwise to have the Service haul the Branch over the coals. Which it would be. However, I'm not confident about that. The DG's shut us down on Crow and that usually means only one thing – that the evil eye is being turned our way.'

'The Service has crossed Fathers' path before,' Thomas said. 'I think the episode may be rather revealing – worrying even, in view of what you've just said. It's an operation back in eighty-one. He was co-ordinating a straightforward police operation in the Christmas period, putting teams of detectives into all the big shops and on the streets, with the aim of catching pickpockets. Since the word was that the INLA was going to do a spot of Christmas bombing, somebody got the notion that, whatever else Special Branch and the Anti-Terrorism Squad could be asked to do, F5 could take a free ride and use Fathers' detectives for short-range preventive security.'

'Did it work?' Deakin asked.

'Yes and no.'

'Oh? Why the no? The man was uncooperative?'

'Er, no and yes, actually.'

'All right, Gerald,' Deakin said with a smile, 'unpick the paradoxes for us, please.'

'Obviously, there was a briefing followed by written authorisation. And there's a reply from him, saying that if one of his chaps trips over a bomb while he's lurking in the ladies' lingerie, he'll be sure to let us know.'

'A joker. But did he actually do what he was asked to? Don't say yes and no again, please.'

'It seems he did, in that there's a copy of an instruction to his chaps, saying there may be an INLA bombing campaign, so keep your eyes skinned and report anything suspicious immediately. But he seems not to have changed his arrangements in any way.'

'And did anything happen?' McKellen asked. 'Bombs? Arrests?'

'Neither – except of pickpockets – but that was probably because the police told the press how they were protecting all the Christmas shoppers. There's an exchange of memos on that, with F5 complaining about the publicity, and Fathers replying that if it scares the INLA off, it'll have achieved its purpose.'

'Well,' said McKellen, 'by his lights, you can hardly fault that, can you?'

'By his lights,' said Gerald. 'But surely that's the point. First, his lights and ours are different. Second, he didn't actually co-operate to any degree, beyond telling his men to keep their eyes open, which was what they were there for anyway.'

'But since there were no Christmas bombs,' McKellen said with some exasperation, 'how could you complain? He was asked for preventive security and he provided. I doubt if he was even involved in the publicity side of it.'

'I think,' Deakin said with a glance at McKellen, 'that Gerald is bothered by the attitude, especially as revealed, perhaps, in the lingerie memo.'

'Attitude is rather crucial at this juncture, I'd have thought,' Thomas agreed gratefully.

Deakin examined his pipe which had gone out. 'It's the element of the outsider again,' he said. 'Now, I expect this Fathers will want to know all about Crow. Most of it's not relevant to his inquiry and you are therefore to ignore that part of your instructions which emphasises answering all questions fully. Let me make myself clear: keep it tight on Crow and especially do not reveal anything about the sources, particularly Lucy. Hay has not been mentioned in any of the written reports and there's no reason why he should be interviewed. That's a formal, even if oral, instruction and supersedes previous ones. I – well, I regret having to issue it, because I realise it simply makes your interviews harder, but I take the view that security requires it.'

Thomas nodded enthusiastically, but McKellen looked sceptical. 'We know,' Deakin continued, 'why Crow failed. But we cannot necessarily expect a police officer to come to that same conclusion when he is investigating his colleagues. The risk is that he will go haring off on endless false trails, most of them through our carefully constructed operation which, I may add, I am determined will be up and running again as soon as all this has blown over. We are not going to let Brown slip. And above all Lucy is not to be compromised.'

McKellen nodded at that. 'Damage limitation,' he said.

Despite that, Deakin was not happy with McKellen's attitude. Clearly the Assistant Branch Director had not grasped the risks of Fathers' investigation. But Deakin had and, though it was possible his caution would prove unnecessary, he decided to prepare some defences just in case.

The first thing in preparing for any campaign is to know the enemy. When he left Curzon House he stopped off at a wine bar he knew had a phone in a cubicle. He called a friend at home. It would not have been politic to phone him at work, because he worked for the Chief Intelligence Co-ordinator. At home, however, his friend could talk freely. 'Tell me about this Fathers,' Deakin said. 'I want to know what we're up against.'

'In what sense, up against, Neil?'

'In the sense that I do not welcome outsiders being asked to rummage around in our affairs.'

'Well, sorry, but I couldn't get to the Chief on this one. Dealt with it entirely on his own. The only reason I know about it is because I went through the Red Book material as usual.'

'When is he to report?'

'Two weeks.'

'And what is it about this Fathers that recommends him so strongly?

'Can't help you, I'm afraid. It was a Home Office nomination. All I gather is that he's apparently handled a similar matter before.'

'That would be the operation four years ago, would it?'

'Well, if you've seen the file . . . '

'No, I've not seen the file. I've seen *his* file, but that isn't in it. Merely a reference. It's been withdrawn.'

'Oh, well in that case— '

'But I assume the Co-ordinator has seen it.'

There was a long silence at the other end of the line. After waiting a time, Deakin said, 'And if he can see it, so can you.'

'Neil,' his friend appealed.

'Christopher,' Deakin replied with ironical, icy weight.

Fathers at that point was breaking all the rules by reading the Crow file at home. He was sitting at his dining-room table, making notes on a large pad of paper.

He totted up what he'd learned so far. Apart from the broad outline, that consisted of his interviews with Naseby and Austin. The former had only been brought into the picture on Tuesday morning. The background was not explained to him. He had the names of Brown and Scherchinskiy but they meant nothing to him. No more did they to Austin who had been given the bare bones later that morning – including a street plan of the relevant area of Hampstead, with all the names deleted. He'd been told a flat was to be watched and two people arrested – no names, no time. He'd learned the actual address about half an hour before going to Hampstead – he'd needed that to get the search warrant approved by a magistrate – and the names only minutes before leaving. That was when the rest of his team had been briefed. There was no doubting that the information flow had been tightly controlled.

So where, Fathers wondered, does that leave me? The basic goal was obvious: identify the source of the incompetence or leak which had scuppered Operation Crow. If the problem was incompetence, it was most likely the fault of Special Branch. But Brown had dropped his MI5 tail on the afternoon of last Tuesday. It might be because he'd spotted his trackers, then, that he hadn't shown up for the evening meeting with Scherchinskiy. Then again, he'd spotted and dropped them before. What to make of that?

If it was a leak, it could as easily be from K Branch as from the Special Branch. Naseby was obviously a possibility. So too the magistrate who signed the warrant. That was already a fair number of suspects. But lurking in the shadows there were yet more. The people who'd been tracking and bugging Brown, for example. In addition, the files revealed that before K Branch took over F Branch had been watching Brown. So there were people who knew he had been under a fairly light surveillance at one time, and that something had then happened. A double agent in F Branch could have passed that information on and its significance have become clear to somebody – in London or Moscow – who knew Brown's real role. On the other hand, a spy in F Branch would not have known about the operation on Tuesday night, nor much about Crow as it developed across the year, unless the leak could be traced back to a tongue wagging out of turn.

And that, of course, was another problem. Nobody was very likely to admit that they had spoken to people they shouldn't, either inside or outside MI5 – or Special Branch as the case might be. If the problem was a loose tongue, it was most unlikely he would either identify whose it was, or to whom the tongue in question had been wrongly loosened.

Fathers looked at the pad of paper and watched his list of potential suspects grow. As he tried to make sense of it and spot the best avenues to investigate, he found it hard to follow his convoluted thinking through a series of unfounded suppositions. The problem was he had nothing firm to go on in this alien world. Every time he tried to transfer an idea from his mind to the paper in front of him, something got lost in the process.

His concentration wavered. He fiddled with a loose screw in his reading glasses and wondered where Sarah was. She was out two or three times a week these days – usually, so she said, seeing films or concerts with a friend, occasionally for meetings of a local history circle she had joined. This evening, typically, it had been the baby-sitter who greeted him when he got home. She told him Sarah had gone to a film. Gary and Samantha were upstairs, long asleep. He'd paid the sitter, helped himself to some leftover salad – even in winter Sarah tried to keep the uncooked content of their diet high as part of the programme she'd adopted nearly two years ago for a fit and healthy transition into middle age. At least she'd stopped foisting it so aggressively on him. Then he'd settled down to work with a whisky and the cigar he permitted himself at the end of the day – and increasingly, despite his best efforts, at plenty of other times in the day as well.

Sarah, he thought. A different kind of problem. She seemed

to have stopped even putting up a show of being the faithful wife waiting for him at home. And he couldn't bring himself to blame her. In her shoes, he'd be pissed off with him too and not slow to find other things to fill his time.

And then there was the day's other development. The real shocker. His new boss. Of all the people to get the nod for Bastin's job, why did it have to be somebody he'd worked with and finally fought with fifteen years ago? The CID was a small world, but did it have to be that small? He doubted Myers would have forgotten him, but perhaps time would have eased his resentment. And then again, Fathers thought gloomily, perhaps it wouldn't.

He went to bed at midnight and drifted off to sleep, wondering if he really would be able to keep up to the mark on Connors and Garston at the same time as solve Hanson's Five Hundred problem. He woke up when Sarah got into bed beside him. His eyes automatically took in the red figures on the radio-clock. It was after one. 'You're late,' he murmured. 'Good film?'

'What?' she said. 'Oh yes, great. Tell you about it in the morning.' She lay down on her side with her back towards him and quickly fell asleep.

Problems, he muttered to himself, trying to find a comfortable position. Hundreds of them. Five Hundred. At least.

Chapter 9

On Friday morning Fathers called in briefly at the Yard, announced to general puzzlement that he'd be away for the day and got to his new office at the Police Department before nine. He checked on the internal phone that the reception desk was discreetly aware he'd be having a stream of visitors all through the day and then started reading the personal files on the people he was to see. After about half an hour he became aware of an unmet need and, phoning first to be sure Hanson was in, went along to see him. It seemed a strange thing to bother him with, but the mandarin was disposed to be sympathetic.

'Indeed,' he said, 'it's an indispensable prerequisite of my own working method too. You'll want to be independent of the normal system, will you not? Convenience if not security considerations would suggest you should be personally equipped. I'll see to it right now.'

He picked up a phone and dialled. 'Our guest has brought a matter up. I believe we have somewhere a spare one of those electric filter things that makes reasonably tolerable coffee. D'you know where it is and whether it's in working order? . . . Ah, excellent, I'm sure it will more than suffice . . . You will? That's most kind. Thank you so much.'

He hung up and turned to Fathers with a smile. 'She knows where it is, she'll dust it down, try it out and, if all is well, give it to you in twenty minutes, together with fresh ground coffee, milk and a stock of sugar.'

'Thanks very much, but no need for milk or sugar.'

'You will, however, need this,' Hanson said. It was the MI5 organisation chart.

Once properly equipped for human life – better equipped than normal, in fact, because the machine worked well and the coffee was excellent quality, a world away from the nauseous concoction dispensed in quick-melting plastic cups by the machine outside his office at the Yard – Fathers spent a concentrated hour and a half getting to know MI5's structure and reading the necessary files and dossiers.

The first interview was with Gerald Thomas. He was thirty-seven and looked to Fathers more like a youngish merchant banker than a counter-espionage official. He had the sort of thin aristocratic face which always looks intelligent and competent. On entering the unpleasant little office, he cast an eye over the pallid decor and pursed his lips momentarily as if deprecating the necessity of meeting in such down-market surroundings. But he asked how he could help and announced he was entirely at Fathers's disposal. This seemed unlikely. The narrow nose, tight mouth and strong chin reflected a habit of command, not service. Fathers could not believe Thomas would ever willingly put himself entirely at anyone's disposal.

He began by asking how many people in MI5 knew about the Tuesday night operation.

'Knew in full?' Thomas said. Fathers nodded. 'In that case, myself, my section head and our Branch Director – McKellen and Deakin respectively.'

'Not the Director-General?'

'I understand not. Authorisation for an arrest had already been given.'

'Naseby,' Fathers said. 'You forgot to mention him.'

'You asked about those who knew in full. Naseby did not. On Tuesday morning I told him what had to be done, where and when, but not why. He was not indoctrinated into the background. It's the need-to-know principle: he was told only what he needed to know in order to get the job done.'

Fathers grunted. That was what Naseby had told him. 'How about your secretary when you asked for the files before briefing Naseby?'

'I already had the files,' Thomas said. 'Except for the flat, which I checked out myself.'

'What does that mean, checking it out? From the Registry?'

'No. It's on computer. I simply called it up on my terminal and printed it straight out.'

'Would there be a record of that?'

'Yes. All computer transactions are automatically logged in the Joint Computer Bureau with the file number and user code. I think the head of JCB checks all daily use at the end of the day, or maybe the next morning.'

Fathers made a note on his pad. He hadn't thought yet about the question of computer security. It would be worth going into.

He wondered if it was really true that every one of the probably countless computer transactions logged up in MI5 in an ordinary day would or even could be checked so quickly.

He pressed Thomas further on the question of who knew – fishing for a hint that maybe somebody from F7 had known. Or the A4 Watchers, or A2's Tappers. Thomas quashed each possibility in turn. Need-to-know, he said, dictated that they would not know. When Fathers asked if he was absolutely sure, he tilted his chin and said, 'Absolutely? An absolute is a very big thing. But to use a formula you're doubtless familiar with, I am sure beyond reasonable doubt. There was no need to inform them, no point to it. I certainly didn't, and I can't imagine that either of my two seniors would have, nor—' He checked himself. He'd been about to say, 'Nor Hay.' He'd remembered Deakin's instruction just in time.

'Nor who?' Fathers asked.

'Er, nor would I think it right if they had,' Thomas said.

He did tell somebody, Fathers thought. Who and when? He decided not to press directly on the issue and switched to constructing a picture of what Thomas had done on Tuesday after he'd briefed Naseby. By his account, Thomas's day was a model of non-communication. From the point of view of security, it sounded suspiciously perfect.

Fathers decided to be even more indirect and asked Thomas how he had learned about the meeting between Brown and Scherchinskiy. It was all in the report which had been written on Wednesday – primarily by Thomas with some amendments from Deakin and McKellen – but he wanted to check out how uncommunicative Thomas had been on the Monday and Sunday. However, Thomas was most unwilling to explain how he'd learned about the meeting. They began well enough when Fathers took a page from one of his files and said, 'Towrope.'

'Telephone tap,' replied Thomas. 'It's the generic code-name.'

'Ah. What we call Tinkerbell.'

'Do you? Bit of a giveaway.'

Fathers ignored the dig. 'That was on Sunday.'

'Yes, Brown saying he'd be in Hampstead at ten on Tuesday.'

Fathers nodded. 'Lucy,' he said.

'A source,' Thomas replied. And that was all he would say. Fathers tried several times before he finally sighed, took off his glasses and said, 'May I ask what your orders are about this inquiry?'

Thomas frowned and looked unhappy.

'Because my understanding is that you have been instructed to answer all my questions in full.'

'Indeed,' Thomas said, 'but I am not wholly sure— '

'About what?' Fathers snapped.

'About the relevance of— '

'Have you been instructed to judge the relevance of questions before answering?' Fathers demanded. 'No you have not. You have been instructed to answer.'

Thomas erased the frown from his features and assumed a mask of bland impassivity. He said nothing.

'I think, Mr Thomas, you are heading for some trouble. It appears to me that you are wilfully ignoring your instructions.'

'I feel sure,' Thomas said, 'that you will have in those files all you need to know. All that has been judged necessary. However, I don't know what's there. If I answer you on sources, I may inadvertently tell you more than need-to-know requires. That would be bad procedure.'

Fathers decided to turn the screw. 'You can guess what inferences I might draw from silence, bad memory, half-truths and so on. You may have the best of motives, but you are making a serious misjudgement and I will not be able to ignore it.'

Thomas shrugged. 'If it's a misjudgement, so be it,' he said. 'I'll take responsibility for following what I consider proper procedure— '

'At the expense of your orders,' Fathers cut in.

'Just as you can take responsibility for pressing me for access to sensitive information.'

Oh-ho, thought Fathers, one threat in return for another. 'Gerhardt,' he said.

'A source,' Thomas said. 'It belongs to our friends south of the river.'

Fathers was puzzled for a moment, then he remembered where MI6's Century House HQ was. 'Yes,' he said, 'that's what it says here.'

'Well then, you know what you need to.'

If he mentions the words 'need' and 'know' in the same sentence one more time, Fathers thought . . .

He tapped his pencil on his notepad. It was no longer worth asking Thomas who he'd talked to on the Sunday or Monday when the information about the meeting was coming in. Except for that one slip – the loose 'nor' – he was too smart to be tricked into saying anything he didn't want to, and too resilient to be blustered out of the strength of silence. In fact, nothing was worth anything very much any more with this interview.

'That's all,' Fathers said abruptly.

Thomas looked at him, rose and left. When he got back to Curzon House, he had a quiet word with Deakin. 'Worst fears confirmed,' he said. Deakin nodded and thanked him, wondering if his friend Christopher had been able to lay hands and eyes on that withdrawn file. It looked as if Fathers was going to be an enemy, and the state of knowledge about him was still deplorably low.

Fathers, meanwhile, asked Hanson to provide him with a K2 staff list. He was going to talk to them all, find out who Thomas had chatted with on Monday and Tuesday, and press them for a detailed account.

Chapter 10

'DC Lloyd? Sit down. You know the rules. You're not to talk about this interview to anybody – not that it happened, nor who interviewed you and, for your life, not what I ask or you reply. Got it?'

'Yes, sir.'

'That includes your mates, superior officers, typists, your wife, everybody. Clear?'

'Yes, sir.'

'Oh, and it includes your girlfriend.'

Lloyd flushed and bit off a protest. He supposed that, working for Special Branch, he should know that few things about anyone's private life could escape the state's prying eyes.

'Eighteen months ago your promotion was denied. Do you know why?'

'Yes, sir.'

'Inadequate attention to procedural detail. Let's see how you've come on since then. We're going to go through everything you did and said on Tuesday, both in the van and before it.'

'Do you mind if I smoke, sir?'

'Yes.'

Lloyd pulled out a packet of cigarettes.

'I said yes. That means I do mind. That means don't smoke.'

Lloyd shoved the packet back into his pocket and stared at the desk. He took a deep breath, willing the colour in his cheeks to subside, hating the man opposite him. The anxiety he shared with everybody else involved in Tuesday's operation – during which he'd been in one of the Mobile Surveillance Units – had been multiplied by the peremptory telephone instruction he had received to present himself at the Police Department for interview. That it was DCI Fathers who was to examine him only made it worse. He was known to be sharp – in both senses. Everybody respected him, but there were few who liked him, and Lloyd now understood why. Three blows below the belt already – deftly aimed as well, at sex, seniority and smoking – and he hadn't got properly started yet.

In fact, once Fathers got going it wasn't too bad. Lloyd actually had nothing to fear, since he hadn't spoken out of turn about Tuesday's outing, nor heard anybody else doing so. When they had covered the time between DCI Austin telling him he'd be needed that night and the moment when they left the Yard, Fathers turned to the dreary hours spent in the van watching the flat and listening. He pressed for any hint that they might have missed something, but since, as Lloyd pointed out, the reason for having two men in the van was so they could take turn about at twenty-minute intervals watching the scanner screen, and since they'd followed that routine precisely, there was nothing even Fathers could find fault with.

'Equipment.'

'No problems with it, sir. Always had good resolution on the screen and picked up the smallest sounds. We clocked DS Peters going in and heard him make the lock, heard Royce talking on the WT, and of course we heard the shot. There's no chance we missed a thing.'

'Fair enough, Lloyd. That's it. I hope I'll not need to bother you again. If it makes you feel better, everybody has to go through it. The stakes here are pretty big. You'll want to know how you stand, and the answer is that if everything was by the book, you're OK. Remember, not a word.'

'Thank you, sir,' said Lloyd, relieved it was over but not quite believing the assurances from the stern figure opposite him.

After Lloyd had let himself out, Fathers ran his hands through his hair. Despite the tailpiece to the interview, he felt like a rat. He picked up the internal phone and dialled. 'Next one.'

He carried on being nasty to Special Branch detectives in quick succession, taking only a fifteen-minute break for some fresh air in St James's Park, eating a sandwich as he walked. But however much he discomfited them at the start of each session, what he got was exactly the same as he had from DC Lloyd: nothing. Each account gelled with the others, with what he'd learned from Austin and Naseby and with their written reports. Despite the anxiety he instilled in each one, he found no discrepancies, and from none of them did he pick up the whiff of a lie or a half-truth.

As an interlude from cudgelling his quasi-colleagues, Fathers had Timothy McKellen to fence with. He was a few years older than Thomas and he looked worried. Too intelligent, thought Fathers, to coat himself in that veneer of confident helpfulness

Thomas started with. He knows what kind of mess he's sitting right in the middle of. But when, having received another picture of a day spent assiduously following routine security procedure, Fathers asked about the sources, McKellen was no more forthcoming than Thomas had been.

'I think it's not a necessary part of your remit to have access to the Lucy file,' he said. 'In any case I have no authority to release it to you. The nature of Lucy's information was a meeting between Scherchinskiy and Brown. I think you already have that. Similarly, the fact that it was confirmed by Gerhardt and by a telephone intercept. And that is all, I think, that you need to know.'

Fathers pressed again, making veiled and not so veiled threats as he had with Thomas. Finally McKellen said, 'I would like to be in a position to answer your questions fully,' he said, 'but I am not.'

'Do you mean you have received an instruction not to answer on the sources?' Fathers said.

'I mean that I am not in a position to answer fully.'

'I'm afraid I shall have to pursue this.'

'I expect so,' McKellen agreed dolefully.

Fathers shrugged and took McKellen back through Operation Crow as it had developed. McKellen's tension seemed to ease as he talked about Brown and give way to a different emotion – distaste, overlaying a suppressed but profound anger.

'He really is wickedly clever, you know,' he concluded. 'Slippery. Meeting his KGB control openly, publishing some but not all of the information from Porton – that sort of thing. It makes it all the harder to pin anything on him. I mean, by themselves those are not the basis for publicly accusing him of being an agent. Indeed, we'd be accused ourselves of going over the top. That was why we had to catch him in the act. And it's what makes Tuesday so desperately frustrating.'

Fathers finished by asking McKellen when he first thought Operation Crow might not succeed.

'When Thomas and I waited way past the appointed time on Tuesday.'

'Not before that? The way he'd dropped your tracker dogs whenever he wanted to, for example. That didn't bother you?'

'It told me we were on to a big fish. That he was a skilled opponent. But not that we were going to fall flat on our faces.'

'When that happened, wouldn't it have been better to remove the tail?'

'You have to remember,' McKellen replied, 'what our original

purpose was in having A4 on him. The point of the whole operation, in fact. We had strong indications about Brown. Watching him was designed to back them up. And the fact that he could so easily drop his tail, and by very high-quality manoeuvres, and that each time something damaging happened – it was extremely informative. Take the last time he did it – on Tuesday itself. It confirmed that later on he wanted to be out of our sight.'

Fathers scratched his hair. 'I've got a report about how Brown dropped his tail,' he said, 'but how do you think Scherchinskiy gave you the slip?'

'The most likely explanation is that he hid in somebody else's car as it left the embassy area, then got out at a convenient point – just outside a tube station, for example, and in heavy traffic. From there he would take a circuitous route to his eventual destination to ensure he had no tail. Of course, that's only supposition.'

'OK, and then at the end of it all, as you say, you fell flat on your faces. Why do you think you did?'

McKellen examined his hands for a minute before replying. 'You're asking my opinion,' he said and shrugged. 'In that case it's because the Branch screwed up. But it's only an opinion. I doubt you'd expect a different one from me.'

'I doubt I would,' Fathers agreed. He thanked and dismissed the head of K2. What McKellen had said, implying he'd been ordered not to tell Fathers everything – or anything, in fact – about Lucy and Gerhardt, was something to put to his boss when his turn came round later on. First, though, Fathers had a couple more Special Branch detectives to bully.

By six o'clock, he was feeling like limp lettuce which, he reflected glumly, was entirely appropriate, because he'd just phoned Sarah to say when he would be home and discovered she was off out for the evening again, leaving some leftovers in the fridge for him – and, though she didn't specify, he was prepared to bet that old salad was exactly what he would be eating for dinner. Again. Apt as it might be, however, it was not the right state of mind for taking on the man responsible for all counter-espionage conducted inside the United Kingdom.

When Deakin sat down, he immediately commented that he'd been waiting for—

'Yes, well, I've got a job to do,' Fathers cut in, feeling a spark of life at this sign of hostility, 'I can't skate over detail with one person for fear of keeping another waiting.'

Deakin was in his late fifties, turned out like a senior civil servant,

tallish, slim and dapper. Much to his displeasure, he was asked to confirm that on Monday evening he, McKellen and Thomas had decided to arrest Brown and Scherchinskiy and deny that he had talked casually with anybody about it at any time thereafter.

'Absolutely not. I told nobody. I resent the insinuation.'

'Resent away,' Fathers suggested, and took Deakin through the details of how he'd spent Tuesday. Deakin remarked that if this was how Fathers was pursuing his inquiry it was no wonder he kept people waiting.

Fathers looked over his glasses and asked, 'And where did you have lunch?'

When they'd made it through Tuesday, Fathers said, 'What orders have you received about this interview?'

'To present myself when required, to answer all questions fully and to maintain total secrecy thereafter. Which I have done and will do.'

'And what instructions to the contrary did you give McKellen and Thomas?'

Deakin looked at him blandly. 'None,' he said, with just the right inflection to tell even such a practised ear as Fathers's that he meant it.

Fathers sniffed. 'Then why haven't they answered my questions fully?'

'I don't know. What questions have they not satisfied you about?'

Fathers was not about to mention his conviction that Thomas had talked loosely about the Tuesday operation. 'The sources,' he said.

'Ah,' said Deakin. 'Now that I can understand.' He pulled his pipe from a pocket. 'Do you mind?'

'I do actually,' Fathers said. 'It's such a small room, you see.'

'Yes, so it is,' Deakin responded evenly. He looked slowly round the room and tapped the bowl of his pipe on his knee. 'Well now, I presume you're referring to the sources code-named Lucy and Gerhardt. The latter is not ours but an asset of our sister service. Presumably in a foreign country, unless they've broken the agreement again and gone fishing here at home. But that's fanciful, I think. I hope. In any case, they haven't told us who or what or indeed where Gerhardt actually is. Nor would we expect them to.'

'And the nature of Gerhardt's information?'

'I really feel I cannot specify. Gerhardt belongs to Box Six, and I think that is where you should direct any queries.'

Fathers thought about that. It sounded convincing; it had the

authentic ring of territorial disputes between two large bureaucracies. 'But Lucy's yours,' he said.

'Yes.'

'Tell me about her.'

Deakin fiddled with his pipe for a while. 'An embassy source,' he said finally. 'Extremely sensitive. Which explains why neither McKellen nor Thomas would tell you anything. I should add that neither of them runs Lucy. They may also have had some regard for demarcation.'

And once again Fathers had reached a dead end. Deakin would not tell him anything more about the source, nor about Lucy's information. It seemed like a conversation with Hanson might be necessary. 'Have you had contact with Lucy since Tuesday?' he asked.

Deakin unscrewed the bowl of his pipe, examined it and put it back together. He shook his head.

'Perhaps you should. Lucy may have some information on any reverberations in her embassy in the wake of Tuesday.'

Deakin put his pipe in his mouth, sucked on it, then regretfully tucked it back in his pocket. 'I did think your remit was to inquire into the reason for Crow's breakdown, not give the Security Service operational directives.'

'Lucy was one of the sources of the information that Brown and Scherchinskiy were meeting on Tuesday night.'

'Correct.'

'In which case she may be able to help explain what happened.'

'Impeccable logic, Mr Fathers, but inadequate. It's too risky. A face-to-face with a valuable source is an infrequent event. It's something we prefer not to organise unless it's absolutely essential. Far too risky.'

'I don't see that you would have to arrange a meeting,' Fathers objected. 'How do you normally get information from Lucy?'

Deakin took a moment to formulate a non-reply: 'There's a procedure for its provision.'

Fathers resisted the temptation to respond with an ironic 'Good heavens'. Instead he asked, 'Does Lucy simply provide it to you, or do you ever ask questions?'

'There is a procedure for requesting information about a specified issue,' Deakin replied, making Fathers wish he'd succumbed to his ironic temptation, 'though the bulk of Lucy's product is not in response to our prompting. But you see, there's something you may not understand.'

He pulled out his pipe again and fiddled with it for a few moments. Then he jabbed it in Fathers' direction to emphasise his points as he offered a brief lecture on spying: 'It is a general rule of intelligence, counter or otherwise, that we put the least possible stress on our major assets. They live and operate under conditions of great strain, as you may imagine – constant anxiety, double lives, fear of discovery and its consequences, their need to gain approval by providing information, so forth. If you directly pose a question to such an agent, he – er, or she – will try to answer it. The attempt, especially if it is a very specific question, may entail taking risks which lead to discovery. Anxiety and eagerness to please, you see, are double-edged swords, for while they keep the product flow going, they can also cause carelessness. For this reason, our general— '

'I understand,' Fathers interrupted as politely as he could, 'but let me put it to you that the stakes involved in the failure of Operation Crow are such as to justify the risk of asking— '

'I think,' Deakin cut in with equal politeness, 'that in that case you do not understand the risk – Lucy's vulnerability, the consequences.'

Fathers paused. Deakin's obduracy was fluent and plausible. Arguing with him was like fighting through a pile of cotton wool. And, he reminded himself, this was not a world he was familiar with. Deakin was telling him that asking Lucy this question could pose unacceptable risks. Did he have a basis for saying Deakin was wrong? Did he have the right?

Deakin felt Fathers's hesitation and pressed home his advantage. 'The question, in any case,' he said, 'would be in my judgement irrelevant. To your inquiry, that is.'

'Oh? You know the explanation for Crow's failure, then?'

'Its breakdown,' Deakin corrected him sharply. 'Temporary. I think the explanation's obvious.'

'I thought you might,' Fathers said. 'It's probably why I'm conducting the inquiry and not you.'

Afterwards he regretted that remark. Apart from anything else, it let Deakin see how much he'd got to him. Deakin himself also thought about it when the interview was over. As Thomas had said, his worst fears were indeed confirmed. On his way home he phoned his friend Christopher again, from a privately placed public phone in a different bar.

'Yes, I've seen it,' Christopher said, 'and you're not going to like it.' He outlined the contents of the file on Fathers' visit to

New York four years before, the conclusions he'd arrived at, the rules he'd broken, the trouble he'd caused, the angry responses of three government ministries.

Deakin thanked him and hung up. Perhaps I do like it, he thought. Perhaps this is just what I needed. It defines the man.

PART III
Crow's Nest

Chapter 11

The night sky was leaking randomly. Fathers turned up his collar and hoped he'd avoid the downpour when it came as he threaded his way through the maze that lies west of Victoria Street. Since Sarah wasn't going to be in when he got home, he'd decided to call on Joseph Perry, the magistrate who had signed a search warrant for the flat in Hampstead three evenings ago. He was welcomed into a prosperous front parlour and offered a drink which he politely declined.

When the initial niceties were completed, he checked – not that he had doubted it – Austin's account of when the warrant had been signed. That done, he started in on the magistrate himself, who, of course, could not help but wonder why he was being questioned about his whereabouts and company from seven till midnight on Tuesday.

'I'm afraid I can't tell you, Mr Perry,' Fathers replied, 'but I do assure you that it's important.'

The magistrate gazed thoughtfully at his gin and tonic. 'The warrant was for Special Branch and the grounds were suspected offences under Section Two of the Secrets Act,' he commented. 'Am I to understand this is a security inquiry?'

'Some loose ends which need tying up. That's all.'

'I suppose,' the magistrate said, his colour rising, 'that the bust or whatever you call it failed and that I'm under suspicion for having tipped the wink to whichever birds flew the coop.'

'No such thing,' said Fathers quickly. 'Everybody who had any knowledge about the outing on Tuesday is being asked the same questions. It's a new aspect of post-operational assessment that we want to make routine.'

'I know how you work,' said Perry, ignoring Fathers' hastily assembled gobbledegook. 'Nobody is not under suspicion for your sort. Well, I've always been prepared to be co-operative with you, and I would've thought that should place me well above suspicion. I don't take kindly to the ferrets snooping around questioning my loyalty, thank you.'

'Now, Mr Perry, there's no question of snooping around or of you being under suspicion—'

'I understand that your function is an important one. Essential, in fact. That's why I've always been helpful at my end of things. But there is a limit. I suggest your function is better fulfilled by going after the real enemies of the state than by harassing its loyal servants.'

My Christ, thought Fathers. Now even the magistrates have picked up the language of police harassment. We must be in a bad way.

'I don't think,' continued Perry, 'that I'm prepared to answer your questions or stand by while anybody I might have spoken to or seen on Tuesday night is similarly bothered – and I'm not saying there was anybody, you understand. Your Commander will be receiving a stiff letter of complaint, I promise you. And I hope its consequences include something unpleasant for you. There are certain people, Chief Inspector, who are not to be treated in this way.'

Perry got to his feet but Fathers remained in his chair. 'If I can make one last try, sir,' he said, 'to assure you that you are in no sense under suspicion and that there is no question of harassing anybody. In fact, there's nothing for you to be under suspicion of.'

'No, I don't think you can try. Please leave.'

On the pavement after the front door had been slammed dramatically behind him, Fathers shrugged on his raincoat and considered what the episode might have meant. As he made his way towards the Yard to collect his car, he assessed the pros and cons of the three obvious possibilities.

One: Perry had nothing to hide and was sincerely outraged to be under suspicion. In which case, he was either too angry to bother with Fathers' insistence that he was not suspected of anything, or too shrewd to fall for such platitudinous nonsense.

Two: he had something to hide which was unconnected with Fathers' inquiry – an evening spent with a mistress, prostitute, male lover, for example. In which case, if he couldn't bring himself to tell the truth, he'd surely have done better to lie, to spin a story about an innocent evening spent in front of the television perhaps. Then again, he'd had no time to prepare one and most people lie better with a little preparation. Or he might have been astute enough to fear Fathers would spot a lie, even if he didn't know what the truth was. Which made bluster a better strategy. Except that, like many people who hide irrelevancies in the course of police inquiries, he was then bound to become the object of greater scrutiny. But then most people didn't realise that. Perry might be shrewd up to a point, and perhaps no further.

Three: he was a Soviet agent who, by passing on the address of a Special Branch raid had alerted its targets to their danger. In which case, he would have had reason and time to develop a lie, since he knew the operation was going to fail before anybody else did. And he would surely realise that refusing to answer innocuous questions was a good way to become the object of more attention. On the other hand, especially if he knew he was not a very convincing liar (but aren't all agents convincing liars by nature and training? No matter), his bluster could've been a double bluff, designed by its very obviousness to dissuade Fathers from thinking he was the source of the leak.

The key question was how he'd jumped so quickly and accurately to the conclusion that Tuesday's operation had failed. There were two possibilities: either he was an agent, or he was clever. Or three: Austin could have told him. Four: somebody else could have. Five.

As he crossed Victoria Street Fathers gave an impatient shake of his head. But his irritation was not directed at the convolutions into which his inquiry was taking him, nor even at the rain which was becoming heavier. He was annoyed that the magistrate had mistaken him for a Special Branch man. It was the first time that had happened. And he didn't like it. I suppose if you deal with spooks too much, he thought, you get to become a little like them.

On the other hand, he added to himself, of four people who wouldn't answer all my questions, there's two who've done it in a suspicious way.

Driving home, he managed to feel quite pleased about that and even had the traditional 'Thank God it's Friday' thought, before he remembered he'd booked interviews for the weekend. That soured his mood, and he felt even more vinegary after he paid the baby-sitter, wondered what sort of a fortune she was making these days and asked himself why it was he who paid for Sarah's gadding about. Then he reminded himself that it could as easily be expressed as paying for his own long working hours, shook his head to clear it of such thoughts and went upstairs to tuck Gary and Samantha in and give them sleep-time kisses. He looked in the kitchen. He had been right. Supper was leftover salad, which he munched morosely and washed down with beer in front of the television news. He was idling his way through the paper with some gentle jazz on the stereo when he heard the front door.

Sarah's smile was warm and gentle as she walked into the sitting-room. 'Hi,' she said and bent over to kiss him softly, stroking his cheek. Then she straightened up, an abstracted look replacing the smile, turned her caressing hand into a fist and rapped him gently on the head with her knuckle.

As she took off her coat, he saw she was wearing a smart black dress with flowing sleeves and a lowish neckline. Black was also the colour of her patterned tights and shoes, the whole offset by the brilliant silver and sparkly red earrings which dangled under her jet black hair. The effect was simple, elegant and attractive. The dress was loosely cut to hide the waistline she thought was thickening – a product, she believed, of age and insufficient commitment to exercise and healthy eating. Her husband resolutely claimed it was the product of her imagination. She was a couple of years younger than he, six or seven inches shorter and determined to age well.

'Where've you been?' he asked, following her into the kitchen.

'History circle,' she said as she opened the fridge door. 'Mm, I'm starving. Did you finish off the salad?' She closed the door, took an apple from the basket on the dresser and bit into it voluptuously.

'Interesting?' he asked.

'Yes, very.'

'What do you do in this history circle?'

'Oh, it's all about the local area. You know. I told you. It's mostly oral history at the moment. We had somebody in talking about the war round here.'

'And how was the war round here?'

'Mixture of good and bad. Just like life, I suppose, only sort of more so. Rationing, hardship, various clever cats getting more than their fair share, fear of the bombing, fellow feeling, community spirit, living for today 'cause you might be gone tomorrow.'

He put his arms round her and bent to kiss her, but she bit again into her apple, butted his shoulder with her forehead and twisted away.

'You're smartly done up for a history circle.'

'Oh, you don't know the half of it. We're all very formal.' She smiled, but it looked forced. Her eyes weren't in it.

'But your best party dress.'

'Oh, come on, Harry, this was my best party dress three years ago. How was your day?'

'Like the war, but without the fellow feeling and community spirit stuff.'

'Oh well. God, I'm tired. Glad the week's over. Bed. You coming up now or later?'

'Later.'

'Night, then.'

When she'd gone he opened another beer and speculated gloomily and fruitlessly – about a history circle you dressed up to go to, about her smile when she came in, the warmth of her first kiss and the immediate change of mood. Slowly, reluctantly, but inevitably, he went back to the sitting-room and got the local newspaper out of the pile in the corner. He checked through the events listings. There it was: regular meetings on local history, 7.30 p.m. at the library where Sarah worked. Each Wednesday.

When he got into bed she was sleeping deeply with a light smile playing round her mouth. But where were you really? he asked her silently. And who with? If it wasn't a man, who was it? And why not say? If it was a man, how long have you been seeing him? Is that who you were with last night till one in the morning? Is it serious? Are you . . .

He tried to stop his mind from working. It refused.

Chapter 12

It was lucky the interviews Fathers had set up for Saturday were all in the afternoon. He had promised earlier that week to do some Christmas shopping with Sarah in the morning. After a productive session during which he restrained himself so well he lost his temper only twice, he put her and several carrier-bags into a taxi at Oxford Circus at 1.30, then walked down most of Regent Street, cursing and sweating his way through the crowds before he found a cab for himself. The Special Branch detectives found him particularly aggressive that afternoon. They put it down to natural irascibility and instinctive nastiness, not realising that Christmas was to blame.

They fretted their ways through his insults and trick questions without producing anything of interest. They might have been consoled if they'd known they were followed by their Commander, from whom Fathers insisted on getting a detailed account of his brief acquaintance with Operation Crow and everything he had done on Tuesday. He felt guilty, however, that although he had included Commander Scott, he didn't treat him with quite the same boorishness as he had the others. After all, Scott was a senior officer and, while Fathers had a reputation among the upper ranks for a certain wildness, he was not stupid. He didn't think he'd pulled his punches enough to miss anything, and the fact was that Scott hadn't been told what Naseby wanted when the MI5 Liaison Officer phoned on the Tuesday morning to ask for automatically given permission to get Special Branch assistance. Nor had Austin passed on any details. But it felt like a betrayal of something, not to be as nasty to the Commander.

'You obviously realise,' he said when he'd finished, 'that Austin's team is the likeliest candidate to carry the can. What with the cat and everything. But it is a real possibility. How good are they?'

'You're thinking about an advance guard coming in?' Scott asked. 'Giving the place the once over and spotting our chaps.'

'Something of that sort.'

'Well, you know well enough. It's really quite straightforward to cover that. I suppose you've had Tracy's own report? Which includes the street deployment plan.'

'Yes. Looks sound. But it all depends on how good the blokes are who have to do it.'

'True enough,' Scott said. 'I'd say there's a couple of lads who've got a few more ropes to learn yet, but Austin knows that and I'm confident he wouldn't put them in situations they couldn't handle. By and large it's a good team and well led. They've handled some tricky tasks in the past and come out on top every time.'

'It would be useful to see some reports of previous ops,' Fathers said thoughtfully.

'I can send you some. Covering how long?'

'Say, the last dozen or so?'

'Certainly. Send them here?'

'Yes please – addressed to Mr Hanson. And mark the package – oh, what would look convincing? How about "Home Office Surveillance Technique Evaluation Project"?'

'Full marks,' said Scott. 'I'll send them round on Monday.'

As the Commander was putting his coat on to leave, Fathers said, 'You may be hearing from a certain Joseph Perry.'

'Oh? Who's he? Not the magistrate fellow, do you mean?'

'That's right. He said he'd be writing to you. I'd like to see it.'

'If you say so. Why will I hear from him?'

'Because I annoyed him.'

'But why complain to me? Oh, because he took you for one of mine.'

'That's right.'

Scott chuckled. 'I'll bet that pleased you.'

Fathers spent Saturday evening at home, trying to put his suspicions about Sarah out of his mind along with the circuitous second-guessing involved in hunting a traitor. She made it easier, with a degree of vivaciousness which had become unusual. When the children were in bed after a game of Monopoly, in which Samantha had shown her usual calm ruthlessness in bankrupting the rest of the family despite the way they blatantly ganged up against her, the parents sat down with a bottle of wine and spent a while teasing each other about Christmas presents. They went to bed early and made love, but perhaps because it was a few weeks since they had last done so, or because one evening of closeness could not wholly erase his doubts, or perhaps the problem was that she did not desire him so much any more, not as much as her lover if there were one – in any case, it was not satisfactory to either of them.

He tried to say something about it. Sarah cut him short. 'Never mind,' she said. 'If we worry about it, we'll only make a thing of it. It's not important. Go to sleep.'

But it is important, Fathers thought, listening to her maddeningly even breathing. He finally faded into sleep and woke sweating in the small hours from a dream that was not quite a nightmare, in which Sarah bought a restaurant from Billy Hughes and sold it to a Soviet agent who had the face of Thomas, the voice of Deakin and the clothes of Queen. When he got back to sleep, Commander Scott brushed the snow off his gloves and gave full marks to Samantha for buying up a set of Monopoly properties in Soho, while Deakin portentously announced in Hanson's voice that Sarah could come in from the cold and spend her retirement in anonymity, pseudonymity, amity or enmity.

It was a night that left him exhausted, when he was roused by Samantha and Gary insisting he join them to watch the children's programme on television. He half dozed off while watching, and somehow the fresh-faced and impossibly bouncy presenters got mixed up in the semi-waking remains of his dream, running a club where secret agents from half the countries in the world met and discussed Sarah's lover.

When she was dragged from bed by Gary to eat the breakfast Samantha had prepared, Sarah responded to her husband's drained look with anxious affection. But he would not let himself be drawn by her – could not – into saying what the problem was. 'It's not last night, is it?' she said quietly to him when the children had gone off to dress.

'No, no,' he said, 'I'm just feeling a bit tired, that's all. Nothing to worry about.'

So she assumed he was nursing some problem to do with his work. He rarely talked to her much about that sort of difficulty and she'd learned to suppress her irritation at his frequent bouts of inwardness. She shrugged now and, as the morning went on, regained her brightness of the evening before as they pottered round the house. She accepted his announcement that he had to go into the Yard in the afternoon with unconcern.

But it was not to the Yard that he went. Instead he turned up at his dingy Police Department office. There was always a skeleton staff there at the weekend, and he'd arranged one interview for the afternoon – the unfortunate Detective Sergeant Peters. With him, as with Scott but for a different reason, Fathers did not adopt the crude cruelty of his sessions with the other Special Branch detectives. He did not need to shake Peters out of his confidence, because he didn't have any. Instead he wanted to win his trust.

'I'd like to know what anybody else would've done,' Peters said at one point. 'I heard sounds, light footfalls. How was I to know it was a fucking cat? This was a target – that flat. I was checking it in case anybody'd got in without us spotting them.'

'And naturally when you heard the noises you thought they had,' Fathers said.'

'Course I bloody did. What else? You know what some bugger said? Why didn't I switch the effing lights on? As it turned out, fat lot o' good that would've done. There was no bulbs. But even if there had been— '

'You'd've been a sitting target.'

'So Naseby tells me when he gets in the flat, there was no chance the pair we was after would've shot their way out. Fine time to say so. Prat. Didn't say it at the briefing, did he? We asked if they'd be tooled up and he simply says nothing known. Which means they could be. Blokes not in the firin' line – it's easy for them to be wise afterwards. They don't have to take the risk.'

Peters pondered for a moment. 'Mind you, better it was a cat than some other innocent. Tramp, for example.'

They spent three hours together. Once Peters had got his resentment out of his system, they went in minute detail over everything that happened between eight o'clock when the team deployed and the time that Peters got the order to go in. Fathers asked about the cold. 'Yeah, it was bad,' Peters agreed, 'but, you know, it's part of the job, isn't it? And I mean, I've thought about it and – well, I reckon it's part of the story of what happened with that bleedin' animal.'

'Tensed you up, you mean?'

'Yeah, together with the adrenalin and, you know, the whole situation once I was actually in the flat. But the thing is, you're asking about the cold on the streets, and what I've thought is that it can actually help you. As long as you keep moving, which you do, you're cold but not like an ice block or something.'

'You mean that just like it tensed you up in the flat, it kept you aware on the street.'

'More or less, yeah.'

'So you don't think you could've missed somebody because of the cold.'

'No,' Peters said firmly, 'not me and not any of the other blokes either. Thing is, if it's raining, that's different. You tend to walk with your head down a bit, but with the cold you hunch down sort of, but it actually works to keep you alert. You know?'

Fathers did know. By the time they'd finished, he was convinced that the incident of the cat did not prove – did not even suggest – that Peters had made a mistake earlier. He was experienced, he knew his job on the streets, he understood the system and his comments about the effect of a cold night on awareness were soundly based.

'What're you going to do now?' Fathers asked when they'd finished.

'Wait till the fuss blows over, then maybe I'll see about a transfer,' Peters said. 'Somebody called me Moggie the other day.'

Fathers grinned. Unexpectedly, Peters did too. 'Yeah,' he said, 'but I got a feeling it's a joke that's gonna wear thin in a few years.'

Fathers gave him some advice. 'Reputations travel,' he said. 'You may not lose it by moving. Might do best to accept the tag and get on with it.'

'Does that mean you're going to clear me?'

'I couldn't answer that even if I wanted to,' Fathers said. 'You know that. But I'll tell you what I've told all your mates. If everything was done by the book, you're OK. The cat's a different problem. Firearms certificate and all that. But that's not my job. If you come out of my part of it all right, that's the next hurdle you'll have.'

Fathers felt better for not having been mean to Peters and pleased with himself for a productive change of tactic. He got home buoyantly, only to find the family's day had soured into tantrums. His hopes for a repeat of the evening before, except with better love-making, were dashed by a diatribe from Sarah about the demands his job placed on him, the way they took priority and how little he cared for her. Having snarled the children into bed well before their usual hour, she went to bed early herself, grumpy and tired and complaining of a headache. He cursed everything roundly, did the washing-up, and went to the sitting-room where he put the music on, smoked, drank whisky and read the Sunday papers. He kept his mind resolutely off MI5 but his resentment at Sarah's outburst, and his guilt in the face of it, led to more meandering thoughts about whether she was being unfaithful to him. He got into bed woozily, fearing another round of dreams, but if he had any he could not recall them when he awoke, hung over, to the beginning of another week.

Chapter 13

Monday morning Fathers had set aside as a chance to show his face at the Serious Crimes Squad and find out what his section was up to. The week was beginning traditionally. Most people looked tired and half of them seriously the worse for wear. Everybody wanted to see him and if they hadn't been feeling so ill would have been clamouring for his attention.

The inevitable exception to the general decrepitude was Yarrow, who had an irritating look of health and cheerful contentment. He had obviously spent a pleasant, restful weekend in which booze had not figured large. He was dressed smartly, as he always was these days. As a Detective Constable he'd gone in a lot for leather jackets, but with promotion he'd adopted a new style. The fact that it was closer to Fathers' had earned him a lot of teasing from his colleagues, but the main sartorial influence on him was not his boss – it was his girlfriend, Rita. They'd met a year and a half ago and were steadily working themselves towards marriage. He virtually lived with her these days. He warned her constantly about the perils of being married to a detective – long hours, fatigue, obsessions with particular cases, sporadic dangers and the anxiety they cause in lovers and spouses. She insisted she could take them, then fretted and harried him whenever they reared their heads.

Though the new Yarrow was smarter, he would never quite approach his DCI's elegance. For one thing his blond hair was stubbornly untidy. For another his eyes were irredeemably shifty. They rarely seemed to settle on anything for more than a second, especially when he was in the company of suspects and senior officers. That combined with his lack of size – he was only average height which is small for a policeman – and relative youth to disarm colleagues and adversaries. It frequently induced contempt in those he dealt with, which gave him the advantage when it came to the crunch and he could catch them off guard. Though he was never quite sure if Fathers really liked him, he was regularly chosen as skipper for big cases, so he assumed his boss respected him – and that was good enough.

In fact, Fathers did like Yarrow – but not when the younger man chose to hum not quite inaudibly and tap out a gay little rhythm on the filing cabinet. Queen clearly didn't like it either. He looked as fragile as Fathers felt and twice as broken down as usual. The worn patches on his brown suit shone with unusual clarity today, perhaps in an effort to compensate for the lustreless state of his eyes. He also didn't like the fact that he'd spent the whole weekend traipsing around learning nothing from his string of informants. And he liked it even less when it turned out Yarrow had news. He'd come in to find a phone message on his desk. When he returned the call, an informant offered a link between Connors and Garston and a weekend bank robbery in Hammersmith.

'Can the rest wait?' Fathers asked.

'Not for too long,' Queen muttered.

'This evening?'

'Fair enough.'

Fathers called the Hammersmith CID to arrange for Queen and the enthusiastic Yarrow to horn in on its investigation of the bank robbery. The younger detective walked out whistling, leaving his superiors to grimace at each other. It was the first time Fathers could remember feeling anything in common with Queen.

'Why don't you have a chat with Hughes?' he said. 'He's due in court again on Thursday. See if he's ready to trade now. Hobble over to Hammersmith with Bubbles out there, then when you've recovered leave him to it and go see Billy.'

Queen nodded, shakily lit a cigarette and walked out. Pardoner came next, the other Detective Inspector in Fathers's section. Where Queen with his unprepossessing, even seedy appearance and air was one sort of police archetype, Pardoner was another. Tall, slim, late thirties, always dressed in a combination of sports jacket and dark slacks with a white shirt and striped tie, pleasant, masking a careful, almost pedantic approach to the job of detection under a veneer of knowing flippancy.

'My nappers may soon be caught napping,' he began.

The news was so good that Fathers managed a smile. Pardoner was handling a long investigation of a gang which had turned kidnapping into a production-line industry. They were highly professional and operated on a fixed pattern. The victims were small children whose families were well off without being among the very richest. Ransom demands were in the region of ten to fifteen thousand pounds,

84

which the victims' parents could usually find without too much difficulty in the two or three days they were allowed. Every victim had ben returned physically unharmed, and the kidnappers seemed to be as gentle as possible. A bed, toilet and television were always provided in the small, evidently soundproofed rooms in which the children were kept, where they were fed on a diet made up mainly of burgers or fish-fingers, chips and beans. Naturally, no child ever saw a kidnapper's face or was able to recognise where they had been held. Inevitably, the police were rarely informed of the crime till the victim was safely home.

It was a frustrating case. Pardoner's work on it had mostly consisted of centralising information, which only added to a well-established picture of extremely professional criminals. He had twice thought himself on a verge of a breakthrough but without enough evidence on which to base a case. Now, however, he thought he was about to make real progress.

The kidnappers operated nation-wide. A slip-up had let one victim in Manchester identify the street where she'd been held. Her description of the inside of the house tallied with evidence from victims of three previous kidnappings. It was obviously regularly used. Manchester CID had pinpointed the house and put it under permanent surveillance.

'But,' Pardoner finished, 'there is a bijou problemette I'd rather like your help with.'

Fathers frowned. In Pardoner's vocabulary small difficulties were mega-problems. Insurmountable obstacles were usually bijou.

'We's in dispute,' the DI explained. 'When the house is next used, I want to go easy, watch the action, follow the bad guys, find the big wheels and roll the whole lot of them up.'

'Makes sense, but don't watch so much telly.'

'Manchester, on t'other 'and,' said Pardoner, briefly adopting what Londoners think of as a Mancunian accent, 'want to move in straight away, lift whoever's on the spot and claim a triumph.'

'Of which they've had precious few recently.'

'You said it, boss, not me. I'm dealing with a Super and I'm not allowed to think such things, let alone say 'em.'

'And you want me to pull rank and step in.'

'Sort of.'

'Hmm. Bastin's a better bet. He does that sort of thing very well and he's got more rank. I'll ask him. Any other problems?'

'Not if I can get Manchester to start behaving itself. Though some of us would like to know why you're never around.'

Fathers shrugged. 'Just getting out and about and seeing things,' he said. Pardoner's response suggested he was not convinced. Nor were any of the others who asked that morning.

After lunch he returned to Queen Anne's Gate and went to see Hanson. He explained about the falsely addressed package Commander Scott would be sending, asked for a security file – 'Perry, Joseph,' said Hanson without inflection looking at the note Fathers gave him – and described his problem with the men from K Branch: 'They're giving me the run-around over sources of information on last Tuesday's event. Can you sort it out?'

'Is it germane?'

Fathers reminded himself he was asking for help and cut the sharpness from his voice as he said, 'I wouldn't ask otherwise.' Hanson made a note, and passed over the K2 staff list Fathers had asked for on Friday.

Fathers spent the rest of the day finishing off the Special Branch detectives – still no hint of any loose tongues, departure from procedure or anything else untoward – and making appointments for the rest of the week. Then he sighed, locked the files away in the safe and went to find Queen and Yarrow to do some real police work in a pub.

As he put the drinks on the table – a beer for Yarrow, a whisky for himself and one of each for Queen – both Detective Sergeant and Detective Inspector began talking. When each found he couldn't talk the other down they stopped and Queen glared at Yarrow who would have glared back if he'd been able to keep his eyes still. Fathers jumped into the silence created by this uneasy stand-off and asked about Hammersmith.

Yarrow shrugged: 'Routine job. Saturday night and Sunday mornin'. Tunnelled in, blew the strong-room door, took the cash and most of the safety deposit boxes. Coulda been any one of half a dozen firms. I got Bunn, Hands and Petty at work finding out what the most likely villains was up to over the weekend. If I hadn't got this call this morning, there'd be no reason to think Connors and Garston was part of it.'

'What about your snout then?' Queen asked. 'Trust 'im?'

'I don't reckon he'd call up with something unless he was pretty sure of it,' Yarrow replied. 'I'm going to go have a word with him when we're through here, start putting the screws on, see if I can get some more names. I suppose it could just be pub gossip. Dunno really.'

'No,' said Queen, 'not really.'

'All right,' Fathers said before Yarrow could rise to Queen's bait, 'what about Billy? Get anything?'

'Nope,' said Queen. 'No deal. Doesn't seem to mind a spell inside. Which is odd when you think about it, specially if you know what I know.'

'What's that?' Fathers asked.

'It's the talk of the town,' Yarrow said. 'News hit the streets this afternoon.'

'It didn't all hit the streets,' Queen objected snappily. 'Half of it you know only because I told you, because I have my ears in the right fucking places and don't go running off on false trails about Guy bleedin' White.'

'That's not a false trail,' Yarrow said. 'She broke a leg.'

'Stop it,' Fathers said before Queen could come back. 'Who broke a leg?'

'You remember I was wondering how those two jocks got to Billy?' Yarrow said with a sidelong half-glance at Queen which suggested complacency. 'Well, turns out Guy White's wife is laid up with a broken leg.'

'And what do you make of it?'

Queen butted in as he rummaged in his jacket pocket for a cigarette. 'What I take our young Fabian of the Yard to be suggesting is that it's no accident. That it was done to put the frighteners on Guy White, who's known on the streets as the Gorilla, not just because of his name, but also because he looks and behaves like one, and what's more that it bleedin' worked and he left the way clear for two nobodies to get to Billy.'

Yarrow's theory dismissed, Queen fished in another pocket for a box of matches and lit up. He took a long thoughtful drag, relaxed and let the smoke trickle through his moustache.

'Gorillas are actually very gentle creatures,' Yarrow objected, accurately if irrelevantly.

'Were it not,' Queen continued with elaborate care, 'that Guy's so fucking hard, there might be something in it. And before you come up with the idea he's gone soft, just remember those three who got clobbered the week before last when they were rolling Billy's restaurant. They had Guy White written all over what was left of them.'

Fathers thought about that. 'Do we know how it happened?'

'Apparently she says she fell down the stairs,' Yarrow said.

'Any word from your snout?'

Queen sniffed irritably. 'Not on this. Honestly, guv, I reckon this is making something out of nothing. It's – it's trivial. Now the stuff I got, that really does add up to something. To a right dog's dinner, in fact.'

'Although it is trivial, it is undoubtedly queer,' said Yarrow, adding in response to Fathers's raised eyebrows, 'Lestrade in "The Adventure of the Six Napoleons".'

Fathers grinned. Yarrow was given to quoting from Sherlock Holmes stories, thus displaying his quirky sense of humour, his extraordinary memory and an odd taste in reading for a detective.

Fathers lit a cigar and pondered. For all that could be said about Queen and often was, his instincts on things like this were not usually far wrong. On the other hand, Yarrow's instincts were not to be ignored and on this occasion they chimed with his own. He had a feeling Queen was blinkered by his dislike of Yarrow. 'Well, maybe it's making something of nothing,' he said at last. 'But maybe not. I reckon it's worth looking into.'

Queen nodded reluctantly. That was a firm decision, Fathers' equivalent of a direct order. 'I s'pose Sherlock didn't actually find out where Guy was last Wednesday?'

Yarrow resisted the needle and replied straightforwardly. 'Early evening he was at the hospital according to the ward sister. One of Mr Herd's skippers saw him at the Primrose about nine.'

'Later?' asked Queen.

'No word, which, if you'll forgive my presumption, seems queer to me.'

Queen stubbed his cigarette out. 'It does pong a bit,' he conceded. 'I'll sniff around.'

'And, Yarrer, get the local manor to ask a few questions in Guy's street,' Fathers instructed. 'See if any odd bods were around when the accident happened. Now, what's the dog's dinner you were squabbling over?'

'Item number one,' Queen began.

'Have you heard this, Yarrer?' Fathers cut in.

'Yeah.'

'Then get another round in, will you?' He pulled out his wallet, but Yarrow waved it away and went to the bar.

Fathers turned to Queen. 'Leave the needle out, all right? I don't need it, nor do you and nor does this case. Go on.'

'Number one,' Queen repeated with a wriggle of his shoulders, the furthest he was every likely to go in registering a reprimand of that sort, 'the bit your sparrer says is common knowledge. Two of Billy's best overcoats are buttoning on the other side.'

'Who?'

'Tom 'n' Jerry.'

'Yates and Fenner,' said Fathers quietly. 'That is news.'

'This is not just buying in muscle,' said Queen. 'This is running down Billy's strength and his stock something considerable. Point two, an offer's been made for the Primrose and White's talking terms.'

'You mean a sale?' said Fathers.

'I mean a sale,' Queen agreed.

'The Primrose,' Fathers said. 'Billy's first place, where he started – more or less.'

'And the nicest little earner he's got, far as his legit side goes.'

'And Connors and Garston are buying?'

'Through a middle man, o' course, but that's right.'

'Who?'

'Boyars.'

'That slippery bastard's put his head up again, has he?' Fathers sipped his whisky. 'Who'd you get this from?'

'Whoah,' said Queen, glancing at Yarrow who had just returned from the bar and was engaged in trying to put four glasses on the table without spilling anything, 'I'm not sure I want to say in front of him.'

''S all right,' Yarrow replied sitting down. 'When I hit him it won't be with a piece of wood.'

Fathers ground his teeth in irritation, then blinked with surprise as Queen chuckled with apparently genuine amusement. 'My snout in Hackney and the barman at the Primrose,' the DI said.

'So it's a true bill of goods,' Fathers said quickly to remove any temptation Yarrow might have had of mimicking Queen's earlier distrust of his informant. 'But what makes it a canine supper? It happens. One lot of villains lose out, another moves in. What's the problem? I mean, I know why I don't like it, but what's complicated?'

Queen drained his whisky, swallowed half his beer and went through the business of finding and lighting another cigarette before replying. 'Doesn't feel right,' he said. 'As we know from last Wednesday's piece of work, Billy's not gone soft, whatever the talk, and nor's Guy. So what's he up to? And is he playing solo, or what?'

'What do you think?' Fathers asked Yarrow.

'Sounds like Guy's acting on his own. You can say it's not like him, but it fits in with him leaving the way open for those

two to get to Billy. Then again, I don't know Guy the way some
of us do.'

Fathers grinned wryly. The particular way in which Queen knew
White had from time to time been the subject of some speculation.
'All right,' he said, 'let's assume White's ratting on Billy – maybe he's
been bought out, maybe he's decided Billy's a loser. Then we assume
he's trying to sell up, take the money and run. So he needs Billy out of
the way. He leaves him unminded so two out-of-town thugs can have
a go at him. That doesn't work, but we're kind enough to have him
remanded in custody. Supporting evidence includes the news about
the sale and the fact that Tom and Jerry seem to have decided the
same thing as White and signed up with the oppo.'

'And Guy's old lady,' Yarrow interjected.

'Maybe,' Fathers said. 'Now what you're saying, Queenie, is
that all that may add up, but not set against what you know about
White.'

'And Billy, come to that,' said Queen.

Fathers looked at him.

'Look,' said Queen, 'start from the fact that part of Billy's clever-
ness is he knows when to be reckless. Put the pressure on him too
much and he turns wild. Doesn't give a damn. Blow everybody
up, himself included, as long as he causes grief where it counts.
Remember how it was, the time Gelchin tried to push Billy out?
Fucking near did get blown up when Billy started putting torches
to his clubs. Finally decided it wasn't worth it, arranged peace talks
and left Billy to his own patch. That's Gelchin you're talking about,
for Christ's sake. The king. You don't forget that, do you?'

'No,' said Fathers.

'Nor does anybody else. Guy remembers for a kick-off.'

'You mean he knows Billy'd go for him later.'

'And get him. Guy's not soft neither, like I said, but it's not
soft to wonder if your house'll be fire-bombed, or a roofin' con-
tractor with a high-powered rifle's gonna be given your name and
number.'

'OK. You've made your point. It's not likely Guy would sell
Hughes out.'

'It's just not on,' said Queen. 'Nor is the pair of 'em giving in to
Connors 'n' Garston. They'd not cut and run. They'd try – at least
try – to carve out a place for themselves.'

'So maybe Connors and Garston are tougher than Gelchin,'
said Yarrow.

Queen looked at him, the sneer turned on at full strength.

'Or they're ignorant,' Yarrow persisted. 'Or smart enough to realise Billy's time is up.'

'Or this,' said Queen, 'or that, or something else.'

'If the skipper's wrong,' said Fathers, 'what've you got to put up instead? If White's not selling Hughes short, or if they're not cutting their losses and going, what is happening? What's your theory?'

Queen shook his head. 'I don't work from theories,' he said shortly. 'I don't like what I see and I want to know more about it. That's how I work.'

'OK. So work like that. Get the evidence. Somebody'd better talk with the pair Billy turned into diced beetroot. Find out why they came into town just then. We're just whistling in the dark at the moment. We need facts.'

'It is of the highest importance in the art of detection,' Yarrow said thoughtfully, 'to be able to recognise out of a number of facts, which are incidental and which are vital. Otherwise your energy and attention must be diss – dispitated – or something, instead of concentrated.'

Queen turned an irritated eye on Yarrow. The younger man shrugged. ' "The Reigate Puzzle",' he said. 'Makes sense to me.'

'Dissipated,' Queen growled. Fathers looked at him with interest. The DI didn't normally admit to knowing long words.

Chapter 14

The Primrose was a private club which admitted only members and their guests. Queen was neither, but he didn't let that bother him as he went to the bar, accepted a drink without paying for it, briefly checked with the barman that there was no more news to be had, brushed a 'hostess' aside and went to a corner table where he half watched the two dancers on stage. He had no doubt his presence would be reported up the line.

After twenty minutes White made his appearance. 'Laurence, old pal,' he said, 'let's talk out of the noise, shall we?' Without waiting for a reply he led the way through velvet curtains beside the stage to an office whose nameplate declared it belonged to the manager. It was a smallish room, decorated and furnished with cheap plushness.

Queen had not exaggerated much when he said Guy White looked like a gorilla. He was in his mid-thirties, about six foot tall, heavily built, big-fisted, his neck almost invisible between his shoulders. His hair was jet black and grew in thick, tight curls. He seemed to live in permanent need of a shave. Somebody had once managed to flatten his nose with a knuckle-duster. He looked every bit like Billy Hughes's top muscle, but he was more. As shrewd as he was hard, he was Hughes's deputy, trusted keeper of most of his boss's secrets, source of valued advice on everything from business management – in which he had a first-class degree – to the critical staffing questions of who was reliable and who deserved a working over.

White closed the door, showed Queen to a chair, took off his overcoat, unbuttoned his dinner jacket and flicked his fingers across his velvet bow-tie. He paused at a side table to pick up the whisky bottle and poured two large measures, set one glass in front of Queen, sat down behind the desk, leaned back and rested his massive feet on the desk. 'Well, Laurence, to what do I owe this enormous pleasure?'

'Cut the crap. And it's Mr to you.'

'Nice whisky, don'tcha think, Mr Laurence? Pure malt, of course. How's things?'

'Shaping up, thanks. And you?'

'Keeping busy, thanks – all hands to the deck now, what with you lot fitting Mr Hughes up in that malicious way your sort have.'

'Fit up, fuck off,' said Queen unemphatically. 'Don't you mean, all hands to the pumps? Sinking ship and all.'

'Sinking ship, Laurence? You've been listening too much to those twopenny guttersnipes you keep on your books. Dunno why you bother. Told you before: if you want it straight, here's the place to come.'

'Oh yes? And how's the wife?'

White shifted slightly to look straight at Queen, and beamed. It was not a pleasant sight. Above the open mouth and flattened nose, his eyes held no warmth at all. 'Is that what you've come about then?'

Queen didn't like White smiling at him. He sniffed, swallowed some whisky and pulled out his cigarettes, but made no other reply.

'I'm touched by your concern,' said White switching his smile off. 'Silly cow. Slipped on the kitchen floor. Still, they do say the home's more dangerous than the street, don't they? Here, don't smoke those mucky things. Have one of these.' He pushed a box of cigars towards Queen. The detective took one and lit up.

'I must say,' continued White, fussily fingering the cigars until he selected one which satisfied him, 'that I'm impressed as ever by the way you sleuth-hounds get on to these things. Do it yourself, did you? Or was it one of your minions?'

'We wondered where you were last Wednesday night,' said Queen. 'Yarrow looked into it and come up with this.'

'Yarrow. Oh yes, the little bloke with the funny eyes and lightning in his fists. Karate king of the serious crime plods or some such. Black belt and then some. I hear he might even be good enough to give me trouble. Smart little bugger and all, they do say. He's on my tail then, is he, this orientally trained terror of the underworld?'

'Pongs a bit, Guy, you have to admit that.'

'Pongs? How d'you work that out?'

'How come two gits like that got close enough to have a go at Billy?'

White puffed on his cigar for a while. 'Carelessness, I suppose,' he said through a cloud of smoke.

Queen stubbed out his cigar and lit a cigarette. 'You're so full of bullshit,' he said evenly. 'Anybody ever tell you that? Connors and Garston are putting the squeeze on Billy and everyone else, the word's out he's ripe for the picking and you're trying to tell me he strolls around without someone covering his back?'

'That's a good cigar you've wasted there, Laurence.'

'So maybe your wife's leg got broke as a little warning, which you took, to leave the way clear to Billy, but the pair who tried it on weren't good enough, despite the talk.'

White started to laugh, apparently with real amusement. 'I've heard the talk,' he said. 'I'll give you that, I have heard the talk – doubt if I'll hear much more of it though.'

'Maybe you've gone soft, Guy, and maybe they've bought you out.'

This brought another burst of laughter from White. 'Yarrow's the one producing these fantasies, is he?'

'Yarrow's the skipper,' said Queen, 'but you know who's boss.'

'Daddy's fallen for this crap then, has he?'

'The day I know what he's thinking, I'll be buying the drinks.'

'Yeah, he's a deep one, your boss,' said White more seriously. 'Talking of buying though, you expecting to get a good price for this dump? They tell me it's a buyers' market at the moment. Might do better to wait a bit, p'raps until after Billy gets out.'

'Just dipping a toe in the water, Mr Laurence, testing the possibilities, weighing the options – you know how it is – or perhaps you don't, not being a man of business.'

'Dipping a toe,' Queen scoffed. He drained his whisky. 'You won't have any bleedin' toes left if Billy doesn't like what you're up to.'

White looked at him but made no comment.

'Do Tom 'n' Jerry like it? Probably do now they've jumped ship.'

'You lot always amaze me,' White said, 'with how it only takes you a week to catch up on the news. Can't say I like it much, but those two've always been a bit uppity. Not such a blow to lose them. Frees up some money in the pay-roll for a bit of new blood actually.'

'Cobblers. You're finished and you know it.'

White smiled at Queen again for a while, then got to his feet. 'Well, I see you've finished your Scotch and don't want the cigar, so let's call it a night. I've work to do. I'll tell you two things, though, both of which I hope you'll think about.'

Queen rose as well, tossing his cigarette into his empty glass. White came round the desk and laid a large hand delicately on Queen's shoulder.

'Number one, Laurence, you're paying a lot of attention to

Connors and Garston, but it's a waste of time and effort. Being a tax-payer, it hurts me to see public money misused like that. They're a pair of slags who've bought up some muscle but won't stay the course. I tell you straight, old pal, they're the wrong horses to back. About the first thing Billy taught me was that muscle's no substitute for brains. And number two, like I've told you before, when you get fed up being on the wrong side of the law, there's a place waiting for you here.'

Queen shook White's hand off.

'In the meantime,' White continued, 'you ever want to share your wild ideas with me, come right round. Always glad to see you. Going to watch the next act? Might like it. Bit more saucy than the one you just saw.'

Queen ignored the invitation and left. Yarrow's theory had sounded daft, but why wasn't White worried about Billy Hughes being tucked up in clink? Or about losing Yates and Fenner who, for all that White might say, had been major cogs in the Hughes wheel for years. The number two's confidence when his boss was hard-pressed and out of action, at least for a while, should have been hollow. But Queen knew White, and the big man didn't sound like he had any problems worth mentioning. Despite their direct ways with violence, both Hughes and White could be subtly indirect when it suited them. Was this part of some complex game-plan they'd worked out? If it was, did they think they could hold Connors and Garston off, or were they after something different?

And when Yarrow's information was that White's wife had fallen down the stairs, why had White himself said she slipped in the kitchen?

Queen was feeling extremely irritated by the time he got to his flat. He didn't like trying to think in circles.

Chapter 15

Fathers drove slowly. Though it had been a long day he had no eagerness to get home. He realised he felt more relaxed in a pub with Queen and Yarrow, finding out what they knew, testing their guesses, guiding their work, trying to suppress their bickering, than he did in his own house. It took no reflection to acknowledge that he felt a good deal more comfortable with them than he did with the poor Special Branch officers he'd been tyrannising or the MI5 officials.

But if Yarrow and Queen didn't stop fighting, there could be serious problems. Part of it was that Queen knew Fathers trusted him only so far and didn't like him, though there was no positive dislike, whereas Fathers trusted Yarrow unreservedly and liked him. He'd proven this by his response to Yarrow's promotion. The younger man had spent three years in Fathers' section before putting in for promotion to Detective Sergeant. Having passed the examination, he was hoisted out of the Squad and into uniform for a year. Fathers had pestered Bastin endlessly to pull the right strings and make sure that, at the end of twelve months, Yarrow was yanked back into his section where he wanted him and Yarrow wanted to be. He'd done the same thing when Pardoner was promoted to DI. It was common knowledge that if somebody would agree to take Queen off his hands, Fathers would be only too pleased.

Alongside his jealousy, Fathers believed that Queen's self-respect was challenged by Yarrow. Queen was given to bemoaning the rise of the new men with university degrees. He saw his own failure to proceed beyond DI despite repeated efforts as stemming from his lack of higher education and the current prejudice against men like him. He believed it came down in the end to the fact that he was working class; the university-educated Fathers, by contrast, had a middle-class background. It was his excuse, his justification for failure – and it provided an edge of resentment which motivated him to show that his rougher-hewn methods could still work. The fact that Yarrow was also working class, also with no higher education, and above all the fact that Yarrow was on the way up and was obviously favoured by at least one member of the university mafia – Fathers – it all threatened the credibility of Queen's story.

So he took it out on Yarrow. Which was all very well normally. Fathers didn't mind if the detectives in his section weren't friends as long as they carried on working reasonably smoothly and got results. And Yarrow was capable of looking after himself. But the inquiry they were running against Connors and Garston was beginning to get complicated. It was not at all clear what Hughes and White were up to and whether they were doing it together. Queen, firm in his knowledge of the mentality of Hughes and White, equally steadfast in his rejection of most of Yarrow's ideas and contemptuous of his ability as a detective, was likely to miss the subtleties which the younger man teased out. Both Queen's blunt expertise and Yarrow's ingenious guesswork were needed to unravel it all. As a theory of a partnership between two detectives, that was fine, but not if they spent all their time scoring points off each other.

Still, maybe Queen's amusement at Yarrow's remark about how he'd deal with the DI's informants betokened a new era between them. And maybe it didn't.

Fathers' mind wandered to the Crow inquiry and the three spooks he'd seen the previous Friday. McKellen had been the only one who really looked worried. It was likely that a degree of anxiety lay behind Thomas's over-acted display of helpfulness to begin with and the blind way he dug in his heels and shut up later when he made that little slip – when he let one word sneak out uncontrolled: 'nor'. Deakin, however, the big boss, had not shown any concern, except that Fathers shouldn't get to know anything about his work.

Yet surely they ought to be worried. They were all senior officers in the country's Security Service – Deakin very senior, a member of the MI5 Directorate. Here they were with a spy on their hands whom they intended to bring to book and the operation, slowly and carefully built up to this climax, had suddenly fallen apart. Their reaction shouldn't have been just worry but something much more intense – controlled panic perhaps. For if the fault did not lie with Austin and his Special Branch crew making a mistake on the night, and so far Fathers could find nothing there to put his finger on, then there had to be some sort of leak from MI5.

Perhaps that had simply not occurred to them. Perhaps they regarded the fact that Peters had shot a cat as proof that he or one of the other detectives had fouled up earlier. Incompetence by association. It was the kind of argument which sounded convincing over a drink. Not when you looked at it closely.

There again, perhaps they had had their panic in private and all he – the outsider – was allowed to see was the control.

There was, of course, another possibility which he had raised with McKellen. Had Brown been put off going through with the meeting because he'd spotted his Watchers that afternoon? But he had dropped them with his usual skill. McKellen's argument, that not being followed would have alerted Brown to danger on the day of an important and clandestine meeting, had a certain logic to it. Having lost the tail, Brown would think himself safe. It was a reasonable hypothesis. The problem was that it couldn't be checked by asking the one person who knew – Brown.

So then – combine McKellen's view on that with his own on Special Branch and that left a leak. What were the possibilities? One was that somebody very close to the operation was an agent. Another was one of them talking out of turn. The suspects in either case were obvious: the three from K Branch – mark out Thomas for a closer look on the loose tongue front; then there were Perry – worth a closer look at him too – Naseby, Austin, any one of the twelve other Special Branch men, anybody else who knew about the operation – a Watcher, an A2 eavesdropper – or somebody with computer access to the key information.

Oh Christ, Fathers thought.

From his point of view, as an investigator, there was nothing to choose between the two options. Agent or loose tongue: each would be hard to pin down. If somebody was indiscreet and word got back to the KGB at the Soviet Embassy, the question was: how did it get back? Or: via whom? Talk was only indiscreet if it was in front of the wrong person. Presumably Security Service officers didn't go round chatting about the details of their work to strangers in bars. Something as precise as 'We're picking up Brown tonight at ten' – it shouldn't be said at all; if it were, it would only be said to somebody who was trusted. A close colleague. A wife? Lover?

Like a pinball, Fathers's thought hit the buffer marked 'lover' and rebounded on to one marked 'Sarah.'

The more he thought about it, the more he was worried about Saturday night. They'd spent a cosy evening together, walked upstairs hand in hand, gone to the bathroom, undressed, got into bed knowing they were going to make love, done it, not liked it much and Sarah said, 'Never mind.'

It was like sex without love, without even attraction. She had been perfunctory and unenthusiastic when it came to it. So had he.

The amount of energy which Fathers' work drained from him, there were often long periods when bed meant only sleep, desperately trying to reduce the backlog of ingrained fatigue. They'd been married fourteen years. They both knew enough to accept that the initial intensity of passion could not be sustained over a decade and a half at the same level. That you settle for something else. But hitherto that hadn't meant – dreadful pseudo-therapist's term – unresponsiveness. It had meant, during the good times, which were many and prolonged, an even plateau of knowledge and love, of warmth and dailiness, interspersed by peaks of renewed passion, often at their sharpest exactly when they first found real time for each other after he'd been away on a case, or when – as recently – the depth of his exhaustion had ruled out sex.

Of course, there had also been bad times, a couple when it looked as if they might be about to break up. But they had always drawn back from that, and getting so close to the edge had had the effect of not just renewing the relationship but deepening it, accelerating its tempo.

Fathers didn't know what he'd do without Sarah, Samantha and Gary. They were his emotional nest, where he returned from the bitter world of policing in London. Crimes so often wrecked the victims' lives and were committed by people whose own lives were in one way or another a wreck. Not always. Some criminals seemed untouched by the nastiness they were responsible for. Some victims found astonishing depths of strength. But much of Fathers' working life was spent dealing with human wreckage. To survive you affected unconcern, grew a thicker skin, and steadily the unconcern stopped being affectation and became real. You entered businesslike into the ruins and got the victims to help you pick through the debris for items of professional interest. You learned words of comfort, formulae of assurance which reflected no real empathy, designed merely to generate enough calm for a few questions to be asked and answered.

But through it all, despite your best efforts, even after nineteen years in the force, however thick your skin and professional your attitude, you still had feelings, could still be shocked.

Fathers' pleasure at Pardoner's news about the breakthrough in the kidnapping inquiry was more than genuine. It was visceral. The abduction of children held real horrors for him. Confronted with it, the edge of his mind always touched darkness as he wondered how he would react if Samantha or Gary were stolen away from him.

He had seen the guilt and self-doubt in parents, holding themselves responsible for what had happened. He knew that if Sarah were to phone him at work one day to say that their son or daughter had disappeared, had a serious accident or worse, he would immediately regret the long years of working days which extended to midnight and later, hate himself for how much of their childhood he had missed.

But at work that intermittent sense of horror could not be allowed to express itself. It would only get in the way. The surgeon could not be afraid to cut through flesh. It could only be voiced and ameliorated at home.

However much he neglected it in favour of his job, it was only at home that he could let his emotions crawl out from the protective carapace of his properly detached approach to work. Only there that he could express weakness, vulnerability. Only there that he could ask for comfort. Only there that he could expect to get it.

And when he didn't get it he felt the walls of his life collapsing around him. Love, he thought, was basically a selfish thing. You love to be loved; committed yourself wholeheartedly to somebody in order to have their whole heart committed back to you. Behind the selflessness of commitment lay a self-centred expectation.

And there, he thought, is where I go so wrong. In what sense am I wholly committed to Sarah and the kids? It's the bit my job leaves spare which they get. Unless I'm too tired to give it them. He recalled a conversation where Sarah had described herself as a hobby he picked up in his odd free moments.

She works at a full-time paid job, runs the home, does my laundry, makes it possible for me to put so much into the job. I live off her – her work for me and the kids, the emotional strength she gives me, the place she gives me to come and rest – assuming she will always be there for me in the few minutes I have available for her. And till now, she always has been.

The change, he was sure, was in her, not him. I'm treating her as dreadfully as I always do. The difference is she's not prepared to sit and wait at my convenience any more. She's out and about. Is it any wonder – an attractive, intelligent woman – if in the course of it she meets a man and they become lovers? If that's what's happened.

He sat for a few minutes in the car after he'd switched the engine off, his depressed thoughts circling aimlessly round the question, Is that what has happened?

As he left the car he wanted Sarah to be in. Opening the front door he thought, I don't like the MI5 investigation, my junior officers are wasting their time and energy and mine by silly quarrelling, but that's all manageable. What isn't, Sarah, is that I no longer trust you. Oh, Sarah, look at me and take me in your arms because I need you.

She was in the kitchen. 'Christ, you look tired,' she said. She gave him a quick peck on the cheek.

That, he thought, is what she sees in me – not need but tiredness. Not somebody she loves, but someone with whom to go through a quick, meaningless ritual of affection. He made some small talk for a few minutes and went dispiritedly to bed. As he switched the light out another thought hit him. Stupid sod. Why didn't I take her in my arms? Tell her I need her?

Because I'm not sure of her.

PART IV

Crow's Luck

Chapter 16

Fathers had a reputation as a cerebral detective. It was one of several reasons why many of his colleagues disliked and did not quite trust him. It was equally one of the reasons why most of them had a lot of respect for him. He was well aware of his reputation, relished it and regarded it as not far off the truth. He did not think of himself as an intellectual, but there were times, he reckoned, when intellect had a part to play.

Queen qualified as a footslogger – because of the way he slogged from one bar to another buying drinks for informants and sometimes accepting them for free – which was one model for a detective. Pardoner by contrast spent a lot of time in his office, carefully and slowly compiling files. That was another model. Yarrow was a reasonable combination of – or compromise between – the two. Badly though he got on with Queen, he'd taken a leaf from the DI's book by steadily developing his own network of informants – nothing to compare with Queen's as yet, but it was early days. But unlike Queen, he did not scorn Pardoner's desk-bound method.

In days gone by, Fathers had also worked in Yarrow's style, consciously trying to meld two contrasting ways of working into one. That was one reason why he liked Yarrow: for all their differences in background, he saw some of himself in his sergeant. But now he had junior officers he could rely on for both desk and street work and, though he shunned neither when need arose, he relied more and more on a third way. Where Queen could break a case with an inside tip, or Pardoner could do it with the sheer weight of accumulated evidence, Fathers could sit and think and often beat either of them to it.

But thinking, Fathers had reflected once in a rare philosophical mood, is a strange business. So often, the conclusion came first; only later did the chain of logic fall into place. The trick was not to become so bemused by conclusions that you let the logic look after itself. That way lay arrests and charges which fell at the first hurdle, rejected by the Crown Prosecution Service or the Director of Public

Prosecutions. So when conclusions did form themselves at an early stage in any inquiry, Fathers had had to learn how to put them on hold, neither forgetting them nor forgetting everything else because of them. He had, in fact, taught himself how to do this so well that when such stray thoughts jumped into his mind he could let them ripen at the edge of his consciousness, often acting on them without quite realising what he was doing or why.

When that happened, he told himself he was acting on the instinct born of experience. And perhaps he was.

He was therefore not entirely sure why on Tuesday evening he parked his car down the road from Perry's front door. There was nothing in the magistrate's security file that would give anybody any reason for suspicion, but Fathers didn't let that stop him. It would also be a grotesque misuse of his time to sit every evening in a car watching Perry's front door, but he didn't let that bother him either – not for one night's work at least – even though there was no reason to suppose this night would be more revealing than any other.

He arrived at seven equipped with a sandwich and a polystyrene cup of black coffee and settled down to wait. Having comforted himself with the thought that Sarah wasn't at home and wouldn't be much fun even if she were, he resolutely kept his thoughts off himself. A Charlie Parker tape in the car's cassette player helped. When he'd played both sides of that, he replaced it with a recording of Stephane Grappelli.

It was eight thirty and he was wondering whether to see if there was anything worth listening to on the radio, when a car pulled up and parked a little way down the street. A young man got out, went to Perry's door and rang the bell. Fathers caught a brief glimpse of the magistrate as he let his visitor in.

Bingo, Fathers told himself. Maybe. Perhaps it's his son. No. According to the file, Perry's divorced and has two grown-up children, but they're both girls. His nephew then. Or son-in-law. Or maybe a friend. Let's wait and see.

He let a few minutes pass, checked that Perry's front curtains were drawn and strolled down the road to take the new arrival's car registration number. As he walked back, Perry's front door opened again. He carried on briskly past his car and along the street till he came to a turning, ducked round the corner and cautiously looked back. Perry was just getting into his visitor's car. Fathers let them drive off before running to his own car. Without going so fast that he'd attract attention, he managed to get on his quarries' tail before

106

they disappeared into the maze of streets which made the area a nightmare for visitors, taxi-drivers and anybody who was trying to follow somebody else.

The car in front of him headed towards the Embankment, turned west towards Chelsea and after a while cut north and ended up in South Kensington. There Perry's friend drove very slowly along one small street after another, obviously looking for a place to park. When he found one, and they got out of the car, Fathers watched them walk off, drove past them, and found a nice clear spot in a side street on a double yellow line. He didn't want to risk being seen by Perry so he followed them on a long leash – over a hundred yards – and nearly missed spotting the place they went into. It was a quiet-looking establishment which advertised itself very discreetly as a members-only club and restaurant. Fathers didn't know it, but he added the name and address to his notepad. Hoping they'd be there for a while, he headed off to find his car again, arriving just in time to rescue it from the gentle attentions of a couple of constables in a patrol car who were evidently calling for a towing vehicle to come and impound it. They saluted when he flashed his warrant card, cancelled their call to the car pound and smiled when he asked about the club.

'Kensington's best,' one of them said. 'Only three qualifications you need to join. Be male, well heeled and queer.'

'Discreet, is it?' Fathers asked.

'Very quiet. Just a place where they can hang out, relax, not be bothered. Never anything going on there oughtn't be. Not a knocking shop, pick-up joint, what have you. And not a hint of rowdiness. Oh dear me, no.'

'Fine,' said Fathers. 'Get me the gen on this, would you?' He read out the registration number of Perry's friend's car. The answer came back in a few minutes. Fathers jotted down the name – Peter Wayne – and address which was in Islington, thanked and dismissed his helpers.

How much is one instinct worth? Fathers asked himself as he got into his own car. How much time spent waiting in a car or a shop doorway?

Not that much. One good evening's work, so thank you and good-night. But as he drove home, another of those thoughts crossed his mind. Not so much a conclusion, this time, as a question. Yet not even a question, more a mental itch that, when he scratched it, resolved itself into feeling he'd lose nothing by calling in at Peter Wayne's home, especially since Wayne himself wouldn't be there.

Being young, it was very likely he lived with other young men. From whom something of interest might be learned. Or might not. Since it was not out of his way, Fathers opted to make the visit.

It was a large house in one of the more prosperous parts of south Islington, divided into two flats. Fathers rang the bell. It was quickly answered by another youngish man with a smile of welcome which vanished when Fathers produced his warrant card. 'I'm looking for Peter Wayne,' Fathers said.

'You've found him.'

'Er, you're Peter Wayne?'

'The same.'

Fathers covered confusion by fumbling as he put his warrant card back in his breast pocket. 'Would you mind telling me who's using your car tonight?'

Wayne looked at him. 'Nobody,' he said, puzzlement clearly etched on his features. 'What's the problem?'

'Could I just check with you? Is it a red BMW?'

'Yes. What's happened?'

Fathers read out the registration number.

'It's mine all right. What's wrong with it?'

'Where did you leave it?'

'Just round the corner here.'

'I don't think it's there now. Could we just go round there and check? Might be a case of false number plates. If not, it's been stolen, but don't worry – it looked OK when I saw it just now.'

'God, yes. Hold on, I'll get my shoes and a coat.'

Peter Wayne's car was not where he'd left it. As they went back to his flat, he wanted to know how Fathers had got on to it so quickly. 'Very impressive, I must say,' he added.

'It is, isn't it?' Fathers said with a complacency which was directed not at discovering a theft before the owner knew about it but at having lucky instincts. 'Can I use your phone?'

'Sure.'

Fathers called the local police station and summoned an officer to take a statement. Twenty minutes later a uniformed constable arrived. Fathers left him to take Wayne laboriously through the business of describing where he'd parked his car, saying when he'd last seen it, confirming that he'd locked it and agreeing he'd given nobody permission to use it.

The arrest was made at half-past midnight as Perry and his friend arrived back at the magistrate's house. As they got out of the car they were approached by two uniformed officers who stated

108

they had reason to believe that the BMW had been stolen and would they please come to the police station to clear the matter up. Fathers stayed out of sight.

By two in the morning Perry had been allowed to go home. He'd made a statement claiming innocence, and his friend's account supported him in that. But he would be in the embarrassing position of being a material witness. His friend's name was Gavin Stone. He was twenty-four. Since he had a good job with a travel agent, it seemed hard to understand why he had stolen a car. How he was able to do it was easier to grasp: until he lost his licence for driving under the influence of alcohol, he'd worked for a BMW dealer in the West End. When he left there he had purloined a master key. The charges against him made a nice list: theft twice – first the key, then the car – driving without a licence or insurance, as well as, following a nice evening at the club, under the influence. Fathers had him brought to an interview room.

'You've been charged,' Fathers said to him as he switched on his cassette recorder, 'had your rights explained, made a statement and you've got a nice restful night before you, then the magistrate in the morning, but not Mr Perry. How long have you known him?'

'What is this?' Stone asked tiredly.

'It's a question,' Fathers said. 'An answer means you'll get to bed sooner. No answer and you'll get there later.'

'Why do you want to know?'

'Why not? You trying to protect him? He hardly tried to protect you. Anyway, there's nothing left to protect for him now he's been forced out of the closet.'

Stone sighed deeply. 'Couple of months,' he said.

'Do you see each other often?'

'Depends what often is.'

'More than once a week,' Fathers suggested.

'Yes.'

'When did you last see him?'

'Friday.'

Which, Fathers thought, is one reason why Perry was so quick to kick me out last week. The tide of his self-congratulation flowed into a smile as he asked, 'Before that?'

'Er, Wednesday.'

'And before that?'

'Um, we spent the weekend together. More or less. Saturday afternoon till Sunday evening.'

So not on the Tuesday itself, Fathers thought. Never mind:

109

can't hit the jackpot every time. The smile stayed on his face. Stone thought it betokened sympathy. When Fathers asked him about how he and Perry spent their time together, he was ready to talk. At 2 a.m. when he'd been charged with theft, when a secret way of spicing up the evening had gone disastrously wrong, when it was obvious Joe would never want to see him again, when God knew what future awaited him – Stone needed a sympathetic ear. And here, God knew how, he'd found one.

He told Fathers about their weekend at Perry's Dorset cottage. He said that on Wednesday the previous week they'd gone to the same club they'd been to tonight. He agreed they were lovers and added that they talked long and in detail about everything. It was one of the ways he knew theirs was a very special relationship. He bemoaned his idiocy which meant all that was over now.

Fathers listened, nodding his head and smiling. Then he asked, 'Last Wednesday, for example, tell me what you talked about then.'

'Why Wednesday?' Stone asked.

Fathers shrugged. 'All right,' he said, 'Friday.'

'Wednesday if you want,' Stone said. 'I just wondered why.'

'Well,' said Fathers, 'Mr Perry is in a difficult situation. Thanks to you, I'm afraid. Unfortunately, it's my job to see just how bad a situation it is for him. And the way I go about these things when they're necessary – well, it's what I'm doing now. Developing a sense of the background.'

'Joe hasn't broken any law,' Stone said. 'Being gay's legal – or didn't you know?'

'That's not the issue, Gavin. Normally, if somebody's charged with stealing a car, any passenger who was along for the ride would be charged too. Frankly, Mr Perry being who he is, well, a different approach has been taken.'

'He didn't know I'd— '

'You've said that in your statement and that's OK as far as it goes. But you can see that, being who he is – a magistrate I mean – it can't just be left there.'

Stone absorbed this argument sadly. 'Wednesday, you said?' he asked.

'Sure,' said Fathers, 'just Wednesday. We'll leave it at that for now. Tell me all about it and I'll let you get off to bed.'

The way he said it with a smile still playing around his face, he made the uncomfortable cot in the police cell sound almost inviting. Stone proceeded to tell Fathers everything he could remember.

At the end, throwing blind, Fathers said, 'I rather thought the two of you were together the night before as well – the Tuesday.'

'No. Why'd you think that?'

Fathers said something vague and inaudible and shrugged.

'No,' said Stone, 'he was with somebody else.'

'Who?'

'I don't know. He didn't say.'

'But he said he was with someone else?'

'Well, no, he didn't, but I smelled the cigar-smoke in his sitting-room. Joe doesn't smoke.'

'How'd you know the somebody wasn't there earlier on the Wednesday?'

'Well, there was no ashtray. And I suppose the smell was too stale for earlier in the evening. And anyway I got there earlier than tonight. About seven.'

'He could've washed the ashtray.'

'No. Joe doesn't do that sort of thing for himself very much.'

Chapter 17

On Wednesday morning Hanson told Fathers that, for the moment, sources Gerhardt and Lucy were off limits to him. When Fathers demanded to know why, Hanson made pacificatory gestures. 'The feeling is that your need to know is at this point unproven,' he said.

'The feeling where?' said Fathers. 'I haven't argued my case yet.'

'The salience of the information to which you seek access is unproven.'

Fathers looked at Hanson till the civil servant began to feel uncomfortable. 'Exactly how much do you understand about police investigations?' Fathers asked. The tone was polite; the words were not. Hanson's gestures became more expansive. 'I can't tell you whether the information is relevant until I have it.'

'It is very sensitive,' Hanson pointed out.

'So is the information I already have,' Fathers countered. 'In any case, doesn't it bother you that these three officials have ignored their instructions to answer all questions fully? That refusing me access to possibly important material is explicitly against their orders.'

'That is a point,' Hanson conceded, 'but a different one. You're invited to see how far you get without that access.'

'Invited? By whom?'

Hanson gave up. 'By people who matter,' he said.

When Fathers was back in his poky room he thought of returning to Hanson and saying that, since the terms of his inquiry had been changed, he was not taking it any further. Then he shrugged inwardly; he was too deeply in to back out now.

Win some, lose some, he thought. And maybe Lucy and Gerhardt were less interesting now he had Perry in his palm. He wondered about Perry's cigar-smoking visitor. Before he saw anybody else that morning he called Austin and told him to come round.

'Sorry to drag you round here, Tracy,' Fathers said when Austin arrived, 'but my instruction is to conduct all interviews in this room.'

'Kind of thing the spooks get you doing,' Austin commented.

'Just a couple of questions. When you went to get the warrant from Perry, was anybody else there?'

'Not that I saw.'

'And did you notice anything to suggest somebody was there? Or had been? An extra coat lying around? Smell of cigar-smoke? An extra whisky glass? That sort of thing.'

Austin shook his head decisively. 'OK,' Fathers said. 'Last thing: have you seen Perry since then?'

'No,' Austin said, looking with puzzlement at Fathers when he said that was all.

So if Stone's right that Perry had company on the Tuesday, Fathers thought, it was after the warrant was signed, assuming Trace would've noticed it if somebody was there.

If and if. Assuming this and assuming that.

He carried on with his next batch of interviews – more Watchers, and more of Thomas's colleagues in K2. Perry was promising, but Fathers was not yet ready to ignore every other angle.

Early that afternoon he called in at his office at the Yard. Queen and Yarrow collared him immediately to say Connors and Garston were stepping up their activities, slowly but noticeably increasing the pressure. The absence of Hughes and the defections of Yates and Fenner were easing the invaders' path into the West End. 'This goes on for much longer,' Queen said, 'and they'll run slap into Gelchin.'

'Or worse,' Yarrow said, 'they'll hit the tongs in Chinatown.'

Fathers brushed them aside. 'Unless there's a sudden disaster,' he said, 'we'll talk Friday. And, Queenie, make sure your snouts come up with some real news about what that pair's planning.'

'Innit obvious?' Queen muttered unhappily, but Fathers took that to mean that the DI was bothered that the information was not flowing in the way he liked. He left before anybody else could bring him their problems and went to Hampstead to see where Special Branch had frozen the week before.

Windsor Court was owned by a company called Gentry Estates. MI5 had taken a look at it when the flat had been identified as a KGB safe house; nothing untoward had been revealed. The flat itself was still empty. The caretaker let Fathers in. The kitchen window had been repaired and the rubbish removed from the kitchen, though the smell of beer and cats still hung there. He asked about the man who'd come to call on the Monday, the day before the cat was shot. 'News to me,' the caretaker said. But the woman who lived across the landing was more informative. She had been going out to do some shopping when she saw a man letting himself into what Fathers privately referred to as the cat flat, the day before there'd been all that fuss. She'd assumed it was all right for him to be doing that – no reason why she shouldn't have, Fathers agreed – and hadn't taken much notice of him except that he looked foreign.

'What sort of foreign?' Fathers asked her.

'Very foreign,' she replied. 'I mean, not even European. Very black hair and sallowish sort of complexion, quite burly, and with a lot of rings on his fingers. He just sort of nodded to me – I don't think we even got as far as exchanging hello's before he closed the door behind him.'

Between being indignant about the police intrusion the previous week, the caretaker found time to add a little indignation that he hadn't been told about this man coming to visit. At Fathers' suggestion, he phoned Gentry Estates, but nobody there seemed to know anything about the visitor either and some surprise was expressed that anybody apart from the caretaker had a key.

'Well, he ain't got a key now,' the caretaker remarked. 'New lock. Needed it after your lot had their bit o' fun.'

Fathers spent an hour in the area going through Austin's notes on how he had deployed his team, comparing it with how he'd have done it himself. He found nothing to fault. Entrances, exits and all the streets around had been efficiently but not blatantly covered the whole time. The vans had been well placed in among other parked vehicles, as had Austin's car, and the men on the streets had kept on the move.

Fathers' main concern was the possibility of a third person checking the area out and seeing the Special Branch detectives. But the files on past operations sent over by Commander Scott confirmed what he had said – this was a competent team which had previously had to deal with an advance guard scouting the terrain, and done so without difficulty. As Fathers knew from his own experience, it was not that complicated to deal with. The trick was keeping your own men mobile and so arranging it that, if somebody spotted one of them, another one spotted the somebody. Of course, the later it got and the fewer people were on the streets, the more obvious the Special Branch presence would have been. But then again, the later it got the colder it was, and the quicker the detectives would move so as to keep warm, thus making themselves look more like ordinary citizens hurrying home. And the emptier the area, the easier it was to spot somebody giving it a quick once over.

Fathers got back to the Police Department convinced that, if they'd been rumbled, Austin's men would have known. He couldn't believe they'd be so appalled that they would have conspired to cover it up. Nor could he believe that if they'd covered it up, he wouldn't have got a sniff of something from at least one of them. And since he'd not found anything else to suggest any of them had talked out of turn – since it seemed, in fact, that nobody apart from Austin knew anything early enough to be able to leak it even if he'd wanted to – Special Branch could more or less be wiped off the suspects' list.

The only exception was Austin himself. Not that Fathers had any evidence against him. But Austin was the only one who knew anything about the operation more than a few minutes before it began.

Fathers filed that thought in his mental 'on hold' compartment. He had decided what to do about Perry. He had toyed with the idea of confronting the magistrate, but it could be counter-productive to squeeze too hard at this stage. His remit was to make a first sweep and identify either the explanation for Crow's failure or, if that wasn't possible, the most promising lines of further investigation. Perry was clearly one of those, but following up could not be done by a one-man team. Fathers decided he would recommend a full investigation and surveillance. For the time being, there was just one thing he could do: set in motion the process for getting a telephone tap approved.

That done, Fathers continued with his interviews. As the week went on, he came to the same view about the Watchers as about Special Branch. There was no reason he could find for suspecting any of them of anything, except of being spotted by Brown. The people who walked the streets – whether following Brown or waiting for him that one cold night – the poor bloody infantry, were not to blame.

But the way the Watchers had been used bothered him. He broached it with the head of A4 on Friday afternoon, once he'd received favourable assessments of all the twenty-two Watchers he had interviewed, plus two who'd followed Brown but whom he hadn't seen because they'd since been transferred to Belfast.

John Platt was a surprise. Fathers had expected the head Watcher to have an air of seedy nosiness, something like the least scrupulous and most cynical of the private inquiry agents he had met. A man whose career was built on prying into other people's affairs – one of the state's senior snoopers – should exude something dangerously unpleasant. But Platt's manner and bearing were closer to that of a senior partner in an amiable firm of provincial solicitors. He was dapper in dark overcoat and three-piece suit with a watch chain on his waistcoat. Tall, silver-haired, handsome, with friendly lines around his eyes and mouth, he was the sort of man whose advice anybody would seek and trust. But like a solicitor's, his advice when it came would be expressed in a way which, while courteous, elegant and grammatically precise, was occasionally next to incomprehensible.

Yet there was something which made the impression fall a fraction short. Fathers pondered it all through the interview and afterwards. He couldn't pin it down. It might have been uneasiness, or an edge of ruthlessness which came not in the words but the tone of voice, especially at the end of sentences. If it was uneasiness, it could mean nothing or everything. Fathers asked about how the Watchers had been used.

'That's a matter of policy,' said Platt. 'Is it quite within your remit?'

'Yes,' said Fathers. He had decided to out-bland them all. 'I'm frankly surprised that your people were kept on Brown's tail when he could lose them so easily and knew he was being followed.'

'We don't know he knew,' Platt said.

'Isn't it obvious?'

'It's obviously probable but not self-evidently a fact.'

'Why not?'

'When we commenced in January, the brief was to work on the basis that Brown would assume he was under our eyes. That is not to say we knew that he knew or believed he was under surveillance, but simply a statement of our working assumption. Whether he had spotted a tail and therefore knew, or had not and merely assumed, it seems there came a point when he wished to be sure he was not being followed. And whether he knew or assumed, his course of action then would be the same – a manoeuvre we couldn't counter. In the event, the first time, it was what the chaps call a two-train trick, following which he could be sure he was tailless. It proved he had at least assumed he was under surveillance. It strongly suggested but did not prove he had at some point spotted one of my people. And equally, it suggested, without proving, that he had seen the pair who were tailing him on that particular occasion.'

Platt paused. 'Do you follow?' he inquired.

'Almost.'

'But there is a difference between knowing and assuming. We operate on the assumption that the target knows or assumes. But while his actions may be no different under those two circumstances, we cannot afford to encourage him into moving from assumption to knowledge, for fear that his behaviour might then be changed in salient ways.'

'So you're saying,' Fathers said, his exasperation growing at Platt's circles of assumptions, 'that the fact that Brown dropped his trackers didn't prove he knew he was being followed?'

'Correct. Suggests, but does not prove. Precisely.'

Fathers thought about that. 'In the reports I have,' he said, 'there's no sign of him having tried and failed to drop his tail at any point.'

'I believe that is so. He appears to have a one hundred per cent record.'

'So he's extremely skilful.'

'Indeed. Evidence is not just his perfect record, but the high-quality manoeuvres utilised each time. For example, last Tuesday, the last day on which I was asked to assign coverage – or rather, the day before I was instructed to lift it – he evaded a tail, the cover and a separate back-up pair. He, however, reversed normal procedure, losing the back-up and cover first, then he lost the close-in. Usually, of course, it's done the other way round. It shows the high quality of his streetcraft that he can be thus flexible.'

'Last Tuesday was particularly important. What— '

'Was it?' Platt said. 'I was not aware.'

'You didn't know it was particularly important? Why not?'

'I assume it was decided I had no need to know.'

'That strikes me as odd.'

'You may have reasons for finding it so. We work throughout on need-to-know. We are only told what— '

'I think I understand the principle,' Fathers said, rather snappishly. 'Your people lost him four times.'

'They were lost by him,' Platt corrected, 'by an operative of extremely high standard, as we have just agreed.'

'Too good for your people.'

'Yes, but let that reflect not on their training, rather on his, and equally on the difficulty of effectuating personal surveillance against a target aware that he is or may be watched. Average powers of observation combined with, for example, an idiosyncratic itinerary, if sustained for no more than half an hour, will almost inevitably reveal the tail. The knowing target has inherent, irreducible advantages.'

Fathers was beginning to wish he hadn't raised questions of policy. On the cotton-wool scale, Platt measured at least as high as Deakin. 'What could you have done to prevent him from losing

117

'your people?' he asked, remembering the question he'd been about to put a few minutes ago.

Platt looked thoughtful for a while. 'I'm not sure there is anything,' he said finally.

'In other words, it didn't matter how many people you assigned to Brown, he could've dropped them all if he'd wanted to.'

'That's my assessment.'

'Well, if that was your view, why did you bother?'

For the first time in the interview, Platt seemed put out. He rubbed his chin, fiddled with his watch chain, ran a hand over his hair. 'I'm not sure I follow,' he said.

'The exercise seems pointless,' said Fathers. 'The evidence is that when he wanted to, he lost his Watchers. So why did you continue?'

'The information you have,' said Platt, regaining his composure, 'which leads you to that conclusion, was available to K Branch, where a different conclusion was reached.'

'Did you at any point consider the task pointless?'

'It's not my business to,' Platt replied. But that evening he did something which was not his business. He phoned Neil Deakin and recounted his interview. 'The man seems to be after a complete red herring,' he concluded.

'I'm sure you're right,' Deakin said. 'The problem, you see, is that he knows nothing of our world.' And if Watcher policy was a false trail, he reflected, it was not the only one Fathers was set on.

Austin had phoned him after his second, very brief session with Fathers. Deakin had examined Perry's file and could not for the life of him see why Fathers should apparently be pursuing an angle there. Except, he thought, because he's already exonerated his police chums and is looking for somebody else to blame. He also knew, of course, that every member of K2 was being called in. He had questioned McKellen and Thomas closely to find out why, but neither knew – though Gerald perhaps had looked a little uneasy, as if he might have said something amiss. That was borne out when he called in one of the particularly reliable K2 officers and gently tested the water to see if she'd say what Fathers had wanted. She accepted the gambit and described her fifteen-minute session with the Scotland Yard man who clearly had the idea that Thomas had talked loosely about the Tuesday night operation. Deakin had a long session with Thomas, grilling him about everything he'd done on the Monday and Tuesday, just as Fathers had done, and was eventually satisfied that somehow Fathers had got the wrong end of the stick. That did not surprise him.

Chapter 18

Fathers stumbled out of Platt's circuitous world into winter dusk. He took a stroll into St James's Park to clear his head and then walked back to the comparatively simple world of Scotland Yard where he was immediately confronted with a problem which illustrated how complex that could get too. 'Manchester won't play,' Pardoner told him.

Manchester won't play, Fathers repeated silently to himself. 'On the kidnapping,' he said aloud.

'Insisting on a quick arrest,' Pardoner said. 'And angry with it. I got a right balling-out yesterday.'

'I'll have a word with Bastin. But if he's tried already—'

'Oh, he has. That's why I got the ear-bashing. Going over the head of the Super up there.'

'Well, we'll see what we can come up with. If we can't swing it, at least you can interview the ones they pick up. They couldn't refuse that. That'll be worth something.'

'Yeah, maybe if they get some of the workers, we can prise the name of one or two members of the board out of them. Still, I'll not be the only one to be glad when you've finished this MI5 thing of yours. How long's it gonna take?'

Fathers looked at him. He tried to keep his face expressionless and to say 'What MI5 thing?' but instead he started chuckling.

Pardoner grinned. 'And that's a tenner for Cathy,' he commented.

Fathers raised his eyebrows. 'Prize?'

'Yeah. A little sweepstake between me, Cath and Yarrer – fiver each from the losers to the winner.'

'How'd she work it out?'

'Well, your absences began Thursday last week, and she asked around and found the AC had approved a secondment and . . .'

Pardoner let the sentence fade out. Fathers finished it for him: 'And then got the AC's secretary tanked up, I suppose.'

'I didn't get all the details,' Pardoner said tactfully.

'Well, knowing Cathy, I'm sure they're sordid. Don't let on, will you?'

'Course not,' said Pardoner as he left. He sounded slightly offended.

So it wasn't one of my lads who worked it out, Fathers reflected, it was Cathy. Still, I was right when I told Hanson they'd do it just for fun.

It was in many ways a relief that at least one of the secrets about his current work was out, even if only to a select few. He phoned Bastin to see what they could do about Manchester CID and the kidnapping, but the Chief Superintendent was out. He left a message, got a cup of what the automat in the corridor insisted was coffee, despite the taste, and began pushing paperwork round his desk, in the hope that if he moved it fast enough some would disappear. It didn't – except for some memoranda so old there was no point in replying to them any more, which he duly consigned to his 'file and forget' tray – but at the end of an hour he had at least turned his chaotic overload of bureaucracy into an orderly overload.

There was a discreet tap on the door. It was Yarrow, carrying a different kind of paper. The banner headline read: THE NEW TERROR ON OUR STREETS. Fathers skimmed the lurid story of nightly street-gang fights in the heart of London. 'It's not that bad, is it?'

'No. But it's not good. Here's our version of it.' Yarrow passed a folder over. 'First page has the summary. Then there's the details. The rest of it's background, specially on Connors. I've been on to the Boston police. They've sent over a thick file they had. Said they were pleased he was in London and wished us the best of luck with him.'

'Queen around?'

'Somewhere.'

'I'll read this properly, then we'll have a drink and talk. OK?'

'I'll tell him. By the way, I went to see Logan and Grey.'

It took Fathers a moment to recognise the names of the pair who'd tried to jump Billy Hughes and thus disproved the rumours of his growing softness. He winced inwardly. Not only did he not have the names at the forefront of his mind, where they should be, but he remembered now that he hadn't specified who should talk to them. It was an important point. Queen had his strengths – not least his informants, most of whom owed him more favours than they could ever pay off – but he was not too careful about detail unless he saw its immediate relevance. Yarrow, on the other hand, had his weaknesses – a little too imaginative for his own good at times – but inattention to detail was not among them. He was also, despite his shifty eyes, pleasanter than Queen – less likely to scare information out of a suspect or witness, more likely to persuade it out. If Fathers had a choice, Yarrow would have been the one to talk to Logan and Grey. But he hadn't chosen. He'd let it slip by – the sort of mistake that could beckon disaster. Yarrow had gone anyway – the sort of luck Fathers didn't deserve and would need more of so long as the better part of his mind was occupied by Operation Crow.

What Yarrow had learned from Logan and Grey was puzzling. 'He smiled at them,' he said.

'Who did?'

'Hughes.'

'Smiled at them?'

'Yeah.'

'What sort of a smile?'

'Well, Logan reckons it was a happy one, Grey says it was a smile of recognition. What d'you make of it?'

'Dunno. What's Queenie say?'

'He says Billy prob'ly snarled at them, and in the dark they mistook it for a smile. Or else they're lying.'

'Why would they do that?'

'Because they're liars.'

That was the sort of simple explanation Queen liked. As Fathers dismissed Yarrow he added, 'Not a word about your little sweepstake, eh?'

'Course not.' Yarrow too sounded mildly offended.

Fathers got stuck into reading Yarrow's file on Connors and Garston until Bastin phoned and summoned him.

Fathers explained Manchester's response to Bastin's intervention. 'We could ask them about letting Pardoner interview anybody they arrest,' Bastin said, 'but it's bad tactics to go back when first you're refused.'

'What can we do then?'

'Go higher. How're you getting on with Hanson?'

Fathers saw the line of reasoning immediately and didn't like it. Bastin saw the reluctance and persuasively went to work. 'Don't let your notorious dislike of being in people's debt get in the way of this,' he said. 'The fact is that Pardoner's right and Manchester wrong. Simple as that. The question is, what're you going to do about it? Hanson could add a bit of might to your right.'

121

Fathers sat in obstinate silence.

'Look, Harry, if what you're doing for Hanson is as important as his letter cracked it up to be, he'll want to do you a few good turns. To keep you happy and working well. Which means that for the moment you've got free run of the most powerful single source of influence in the country's entire policing structure. So what's your problem?'

Fathers stayed silent. He knew Bastin was right, but there were consequences to getting favours which he had never liked. He didn't want to end up in anybody's pocket.

Bastin poured them both a whisky and loosened his tie. 'I want to tell you a few things,' he said. 'One of them's my little secret. I'm on my way out and it's time I passed it on. I reckon you're going to need it.'

Fathers shifted uncomfortably in his chair. 'Go on,' he said.

'A lot of the time, people positively want to do favours for you. The trick is knowing who. Begrudged favours put you in somebody's debt. Freely given ones don't.'

'I can see that.'

'But the real thing is that with some people, if they do you a favour, they end up in your pocket.'

'What?'

'It's true. Look, people do favours because they want to please you. If they want to once, they may want to again – or even feel they have to. It's very simple really. Just not very obvious. The trick is to get them in the habit. If Hanson does a few things for you now, you'll have a friend in high places you can turn to whenever. And if he's a bit reluctant any time, you remind him he's done as much for you before, so why not again?'

'And what if he calls the debt in?'

'Depends. If it's no effort, do it, but with a bit of a song and dance. If it's a problem, however small, say it's impossible. Either way, immediately ask for a favour of your own, just so he knows who's calling the tune. The beauty of it is, of course, you don't have to pay the piper.'

'And what if he won't play?'

'No harm done. You'd've got your favours from him now, without ever having to pay him back. Neat trick, eh?'

Father ran a hand across his face. The subtleties of bureaucratic politics had always been beyond him. Bastin, on the other hand, was a master of them. He promised to think it over. 'Yes, have a good think,' Bastin said, 'then do it. Before you go, what's all this about Connors and Garston?'

'What's all what?'

'The paper. Is it getting out of hand?'

'Not yet. There's a lot of street-fighting, but so far they're only hurting each other. We're going to have to step in at some point. Probably next week. The trouble is, I can't figure out who's on whose side and, though Connors and Garston are obviously the bad guys, I'm not sure who're the goodies. But I know who we're against, so I suppose we're for everybody else.'

'Aren't we supposed to be for law and order, Harry?'

Fathers chuckled. Bastin's tone and timing were just perfect. As he neared his departure date, the old Chief Superintendent was becoming relaxed and expansive, often funny and even likeable.

On his way back to his office, Fathers met Detective Sergeant Gordon. 'Nice one, Cath,' he said quietly. 'Your little sweep I mean. I seem to annoy people when I say this, but I have to say it all the same: you won't let on, will you?'

'Course not,' she said, just like Pardoner and Yarrow, though unlike them she didn't sound offended. Perhaps he'd managed to say it better to her. Or perhaps she'd managed to hear it better.

As he turned away from her, a thought struck him. He went back to Bastin's office and poked his head round the door. 'I know,' he said, 'why don't you ask Hanson about Manchester, more or less on my behalf?'

Bastin looked up and beamed. 'Good, Harry,' he said, teacher to pupil. 'I can see you're really learning how to manipulate people.'

Chapter 19

'Things have quickened up this week,' Fathers commented, lighting a cigar. 'Can't doubt they're putting their stake money down, not any more.'

'Haven't been able to doubt that for some bleedin' time,' Queen remarked.

'What's your snout got to say?'

'Him? First chance, I'm going to roll him so fast he won't stop spinning till Domesday. Not a fucking word from him.'

'Why not?' asked Yarrow. 'Doesn't he know? Or is he scared? Or what?'

'The trick, Sherlock,' Queen said, 'is to make sure your snouts are more afraid of you than of anybody else. I think I'm reasonably competent on that front, you know what I mean?'

'I think I know what you mean, sir,' replied Yarrow with studied formality. 'So why's he not telling you what everybody knows?'

Queen shrugged. 'Needn't bother about it now. But I will have him. When snouts think they can pick and choose when to play, word gets round and the whole cartload turns rotten on you.'

'So what about your little whisper, Yarrer, and the bank blagging?' asked Fathers.

'I think he might be facing some grief too. He gave me the word, but not a dicky bird since, and I can't find a way to connect it with Connors and Garston.'

'Any ideas on who actually did it?'

'Nothing pinned down. It's a slow job. I'm putting the fear of Mr Queen into my man to get some actual names from him. Says he doesn't know them, 'cept he heard it was down to Connors and Garston.'

'Paid him yet?' asked Queen.

'Course I bloody haven't,' retorted Yarrow. 'Given him a score for drinks and told him there's a monkey for names.'

'Half a grand?' said Queen. 'You do look after your snouts.'

'Worth it. The bank's offered more'n that as a reward, anyway.

Worth ten times that if we can get Connors and Garston to wear it. Did you get through all that stuff about Connors, by the way?'

'I did,' said Fathers. 'You seen it, Queenie?'

'I give it a once over,' said the DI. 'Drugster, chased outa Boston when the blacks closed down on the paddies. That's the sort of thing my bastard snout hasn't told me. Whether drugs is the name of his game now too, I mean. I really am going to do him, 'less he produces pretty effing soon.'

'Any more on that front?' said Fathers. 'What about Hughes and White?'

'Still negotiating the Primrose sale,' said Queen. 'I'm told they're about twenty grand apart on the price and White's insisting on a cash deal.'

'Still dealing through Boyars?'

'Yup.'

'Has Billy given the sale his say-so?'

'Don't know.'

'What about having another word with White? Or trying Billy again?'

Queen puffed his cigarette thoughtfully for a while. 'My round, I reckon,' he said, and went off to the bar. When he came back with the drinks, he said decisively, 'I think you're scratching around a bit, guv, looking for something to do.'

'Probably am at that,' Fathers muttered. 'You don't take to it, then?'

'No, not yet. Leave it be. Didn't get anything from Billy last time. Maybe have a go after the weekend. See what happens. After all, if Billy does want out of it, not a lot you can do to stop the sale going through.'

'I don't know about that,' replied Fathers. 'I can screw up the negotiations for a bit by hauling friend Boyars in and questioning him about the Delvey fraud again.'

'But there's nothing new on that,' Yarrow objected. 'Fraud Squad gave it up eighteen months ago.'

'True, but we can occupy his time in all sorts of ways with it. I'll think about it. We might try bouncing him in and out of nick several times a week. See what gets flushed out in the process. Anything else?'

'I belled Glasgow about Logan and Grey,' Queen said. 'Only got their reply today. Somebody who fits White's description was seen drinking with them a coupla weeks back.'

'Is that reliable?'

' 'S what I asked, no thanks did I get for doubting a jock's word. 'Parently it comes from two barmen and Grey's brother.'

'So we take it on trust,' said Fathers, 'and it means Guy White tried to set Billy up.'

'How it looks,' Queen said with evident reluctance, 'but it don't make sense. Because Guy'd know Billy would take 'em out. He knew them back when Billy used to kick 'em up and down Charlotte Street every night. They're not good enough. Never have been. If he was going to try and get the job done, why not pick someone who could do it?'

'And,' said Fathers, 'there's what you've said before about Guy knowing how Billy would react.'

'I had a theory,' Yarrow said. 'I thought maybe it was slightly more complicated. That the idea wasn't to top Billy, or even close to it, but just get him tucked up inside.'

'Go on,' said Fathers. 'Bit involved, but go on.'

'So I thought maybe those two witnesses were part of it. Coincidentally there on purpose, you know?'

'And?'

'I've checked 'em out. Nothing.'

'Back to the drawing board, then.'

'But then again,' Yarrow said, 'there's the business of Logan 'n' Grey saying Billy smiled at them.' Queen sniffed dismissively. 'Yeah, all right,' Yarrow said to him, 'they could be wrong or telling pork pies, but they might be right.'

'Well, what's it mean?' said Fathers. 'If he did recognise a pair he saw off years back, he wouldn't't've been pleased to see them, would he? Unless he was looking forward to cutting them.'

'If he knew they were coming.'

Queen watched the dialogue, sniffed again and finished his drink. 'Or maybe he was feeling pissed off with life, and fancied the idea of taking it out on anybody who came along,' he said.

'If and maybe,' Fathers said with a sudden revulsion against guesswork and theory. 'It doesn't get us very bloody far. Meanwhile, Connors and Garston go on getting stronger, and some time, we'll have to do something about it.'

The weekend proved him right, as well as providing plenty of grist for numerous journalists' mills. The fights on Friday night swirled north and south of Oxford Street as Connors and Garston continued to increase the pressure. Three cars, belonging to club owners resisting their advance, were set on fire with crude petrol bombs. There were six arrests and thirteen hospital cases. Fathers

126

postponed the interviews he'd planned for Saturday morning until the afternoon and went to inspect the damage to people and property. Two things stood out: ordinary punters were getting hurt, and now that Guy White was negotiating the sale of the Primrose, none of the properties owned or protected by Billy Hughes was hit, none of his men involved.

At lunchtime he co-ordinated a case conference. It was not an easy session. Several senior officers from the Soho and Tottenham Court Road stations wanted to know why Scotland Yard had taken the Connors and Garston case over and then done nothing about it. To himself, Fathers repeatedly cursed his luck – to have had Hanson pull him into the MI5 business just at this time; then he cursed the Assistant Commissioner for suggesting he should ride both horses at once, and everybody and everything which had got in the way of him staying on top of the case. That meant he spent a lot of time cursing himself as well.

They ended with an agreement to call in as many men as they could find, cancelling weekend leave for those who hadn't gone off for a day or two, and strengthen up the police presence on the streets.

It didn't do much good. The pattern was repeated on Saturday night, and from one club the customers ran screaming as two heavies poured petrol on the stage curtains and set them alight. They exited through the back door and not one of the audience to their spectacular performance could or would offer any description, except that they were male and big.

Fathers was called out in the early hours of Sunday morning to see for himself. He avoided the club owner and the reporters, listened to the non-accounts from a few of the non-witnesses and had a greasy breakfast with Queen and Yarrow and Herd from Tottenham Court Road. They took a look at the Sunday papers and their stories and editorials on the burgeoning gang war. 'That's gonna keep your pals happy,' Herd remarked to Fathers, referring to the critics he'd had the previous day.

'Only jealous,' Queen mumbled through his bacon. 'None of 'em had a fuck's worth of ideas what to do. This ain't something comes along every week.'

Fathers was surprised at that bit of loyal support, and pleased when Herd signalled his agreement with it. 'Even so,' he said, 'they've got a point. So've these bloody editorials. We're going to have to go for something big.'

He went back to the Yard to type a memo and leave it for

Bastin to find on Monday morning. Then he sent another one to the Chief Superintendents at Soho and Tottenham Court Road, urging them to keep as many patrols on the street as possible that night and promising a master-stroke soon.

Some sodding hope, he muttered to himself as he arranged for them to be delivered. He got home in time to have a second breakfast with his family, had an hour's sleep and then joined them for a long walk in the country and pub lunch. He and Sarah talked little, but the children's energy provided a mask for the parents' distance.

Chapter 20

Fathers began Monday juggling metaphors. Was this the day he would finally get out of the foothills and pitch his base camp in preparation for the assault on the summit? Or was he nearly through a tough third round fixture with the game not over till the final whistle, Brian, and a long way yet to go to Wembley? Worth considering was the possibility that the bell was about to end round one of twelve with Mike Tyson.

Whatever – he was nearing the end of his interviews. He spent the morning polishing off the rest of K2. Good luck with Perry had been balanced by none with Thomas. Nobody in K2 had exchanged more than vague pleasantries with him in the two days leading up to the attempt to arrest Brown and Scherchinskiy. It was possible, of course, that Thomas's loose 'nor' had reflected a conversation with somebody outside K2. But Fathers felt that one word was hardly the basis on which to interview all MI5 staff working from Curzon House. In any case, he wanted to write his report the next day and be shot of it.

With K2 out of the way, there were only three interviews to do. He went back to the Yard at lunchtime to see Bastin about Connors and Garston. What he had in mind was a truly massive police presence in the West End. 'However bad this is getting—' Bastin began.

'I know,' Fathers said. 'We may not get the other divisions to cough up the necessary strength. But I want us to ask.'

'Ah,' Bastin said. 'I didn't expect that from you.'

'What?'

'A bureaucratic manoeuvre. I'll get on to it.'

Back at the Police Department, the first interview was with Peter Goreham, the Head of A2, the man who directed the phone-tappers and letter-openers. Of all the MI5 people Fathers had seen, Goreham looked the most like a spy – shabby raincoat, scruffy suit, shirt which used to be white, knitted tie badly knotted, untidy mousy brown hair, nondescript features, runny nose which he dabbed at alternately with a handkerchief he should have been ashamed of and the back of his hand. But Goreham had never done undercover work or led a double life. His thirty-year career had been desk-bound. He had graduated from listening to other people's phone conversations, through analysing the material produced by surveillance, to directing both eavesdroppers and analysts.

Knowing nothing about the failure of Operation Crow, Goreham expressed his satisfaction that an instruction earlier that month to raise Brown's telephone coverage from Comprehensive to Urgent – which meant the calls were listened to as they happened – had since been rescinded.

'Why?' Fathers asked. 'Lack of resources?'

'Partly that. Same old story. But it's also a matter of philosophy. These people – most of the time, they seem to think they can solve all their problems just by intercepting more communications. Lot of boll— bull. Excuse me. You have to work in information gathering – actually gathering it, I mean, not just using the product – before you understand how much of it is a total waste of time. Total.'

'Why's it a lot of boll-bull, Mr Goreham?' Fathers asked with a smile.

Goreham grinned a little shamefacedly and sniffed profoundly. 'Being swamped by information is as bad as being starved of it. D'you know anything about the NSA? National Security Agency. Massive American outfit. Phenomenal coverage. Listens almost everywhere to almost everything. All over the world. Transcribes the lot. Uses more paper in a day than News International in a week, I shouldn't wonder. And does it help? Of course, saturation coverage has its advantages, but at what cost – and not only financial. Loads of stuff slips through because they can't keep up with themselves. They farm out the gen at such a rate that nobody else can keep up with them either. Utterly indiscriminate. It gets to be not just a waste of time but a positive liability. Miss the important stuff because you're drowning in dross. Happens all the time.'

Goreham paused to give his nose another wipe. Fathers waited for more. He could recognise a hobby-horse when he saw one being ridden.

'And, of course, the bigger your information-gathering effort, the more staff you need. And what does that mean? Sloppy recruitment. Which not only lowers standards and produces a very long and slow learning curve, but worse too.'

'Worse?'

'Say you want to slip an agent into the US intelligence community. What's your best route? NSA every time. Ruddy open door. We nearly did the same when the computers got upgraded.'

'When was that?'

Goreham paused again, and continued after another wipe and sniff in slower and more subdued vein. 'Ah, talking a little out of turn I'm afraid.'

'Please.'

'Well, about ten years back the firm needed a lot of new computer expertise. And how do you suppose we got it? At the time, I was amazed. The jobs were advertised. Of course, you'll understand I'm not saying anything. I've no grounds to. Doubtless, all the angles were covered, as my friends in the NSA might say. In terms of security, vetting, so on. And by comparison it was on a small scale. But. Even so.'

'Risky.'

'That's how I see it. Personally I like small, tight operations. I like desk officers and section heads with a sense of priorities and discrimination. I don't like to see the consumer try to flood himself, to pretend that quantity and quality are the same. Too much of that nowadays. In all walks of life.'

Goreham paused for another sniff and wipe. 'I do apologise, Mr Fathers. Apart from that about the computer staff, I'm afraid what you've just had is a microdot version of my standard lecture to new recruits.'

'No, Mr Goreham, it's been very informative and I'm most grateful.'

It was almost regretfully that Fathers allowed the snuffly Goreham to shuffle off. It was a pleasure to find that at least one senior official of MI5 was open and communicative. Next in was George Longley, head of the Joint Computer Bureau. There was something about him which told Fathers immediately how to go about the interview: let the expert give a lecture. Get him talking and, once he was in full flow, divert him into talking about something interesting. Fathers began with a very vague inquiry about the JCB.

'If we stored data the way the Special Branch does,' Longley said, 'we'd have space for about twenty million fields.'

Fathers blinked, already struggling to keep up and unable not to resent the supercilious jargon. Longley saw the look of incomprehension and condescended to use English. 'We could hold key information on about twenty million people. As it is, we have, oh, somewhat in excess of the half million mark. More

131

detailed than Special Branch, of course, but fewer. It has around one point five mill, and rising. Their indiscriminacy let us off the hook of blanket coverage, so we were able to focus on constructing a retrieval system of speed and quality. Fundamentally, it's size which provides flexibility. And we have a capacity five times bigger than the Police National Computer. So – given software adequacy— '

'Five times bigger than the PNC,' Fathers said lamely.

'Makes you think, doesn't it?' Longley said proudly. 'Now— '

'Software,' said Fathers, recovering himself quickly. The time had come to get Longley talking about the right things. 'My interest is the security aspect, in which I gather software is a major issue. Can we just run over the major points? How about monitoring computers? I understand that's possible.'

'With great restrictions,' Longley said. 'It's essentially the same principle as television detector vans use to spot unlicensed sets. A matter of identifying the emissions and, in this case, reading them. It provides an unstable reproduction on your own VDU of what's on the terminal you're interested in. There are three reasons why it's a limited threat. Hardware can be insulated enough to make it effectively impossible. The method works only over very short ranges – maximum fifty to eighty metres. And, of course, the monitoring equipment gives off emissions, so it can be traced. At present we discount it.'

'And bugging through the phone system?'

'For communication via outside lines that is, in principle, more serious. To read the messages, the intruder must replicate our software or decode it. That's not impossible, of course, but the variation in frequencies on the wire associated with tapping means we can spot and trace it.'

Wondering if he had adequately replicated Longley's software and read the message, Fathers asked, 'Do you regularly check the frequencies to see you're not being tapped?'

'The function is inwritten to all our communication software.'

Fathers decided that probably meant 'yes' and carried on. 'How about this hacking I keep reading about? Could that be a problem?'

'If the system is undefended. Ours has very complex defences. The are two classes of problem – the innocent hacker and the real spy. The first line of defence cuts the former right out: you cannot access anything from outside the building unless the proper coded authorisation is inputted on a terminal inside it.'

'How do you get that done?'

'By using the telephone,' Longley said, raising the level from which he was condescending. 'The requirement is a combination of codes communicated by voice and computer plus a return call. But assuming the intruder crosses that barrier – which he can't without physically taking over one of our external terminal sites— '

'How many of them are there?'

'Two hundred and seventeen at the moment. Mostly in police stations for local Special Branches, some in the firm's regional offices.'

'Why can't he – the intruder – just cut into the telephone line?'

Longley's look suggested he saw Fathers as a human glitch. 'Frequency variation,' he said with forced patience. 'We'd spot him immediately. Our intruder's next problem is that he needs the appropriate personal code – one of a few authorised for that terminal. And the code changes continually. However, assuming he has achieved all that, his problems are just beginning. The next barrier arises when he attempts to access a file for which the personal code and/or terminal he's using has not been authorised. First, he can't do it. Second, an alarm registers with one of my staff. If he successfully unlocks the file, either by randomly pressing the right keys or because he knows how to circumvent the defence, there's several things we can do. First, simply abort his transaction. Second, override the system so we see in real time what questions he's asking and feed him the answers manually – the wrong ones, naturally. And in the meantime, of course, steps are taken to apprehend him, sitting in front of a VDU he's no right to.'

Fathers looked blank. Longley took pity on him again. 'It is very involved,' he said. 'Basically, nothing's perfect, but this is as foolproof as anything I've heard of.'

Fathers scratched his head. 'If I follow what you said at all,' he said, 'the conclusion is that the problem of computer insecurity you face, if any, is not the system coming under attack. It's personnel. A programmer might write a few twirly bits which somehow get round all these codes. Or someone who uses the system ordinarily might make illicit use of it if they were skilled enough. Or they might sabotage it.'

'Personnel reliability is first and foremost a question of security vetting,' replied Longley, sounding as if he were reading from a manual. 'As to programming, it's constantly checked to make sure there are no countermanding sub-programmes or hidden logic bombs. As to use, nobody has unlimited access. Your personal code gives you some things but not the lot. We operate need-to-know in the JCB as much as anywhere else. Also, our programmes are written so that use is recorded.'

'How do you check that all use is authorised?'

'We sample it at random.'

'And how long do you keep the record?'

'Permanently.'

'Really,' said Fathers.

The last interview was with Brian Jensen. In his corduroy suit, button-down shirt in schoolboy-grey and pink tie, he looked like a young 1970s revolutionary who had grown up. This was quite appropriate since in that decade he had joined several radical organisations – the Anti-Apartheid Movement, Chile Solidarity, the Anti-Nazi League, the International Marxist Group. In 1980, just when his revolutionary comrades told him to infiltrate the Labour Party, MI5 told him to stop infiltrating the revolutionaries. Several years later, there were still people who over a late night bottle of wine would wonder whatever happened to him and speculate glumly that he was probably another casualty of Thatcherite Yuppiedom. In fact, he had been promoted to be a Desk Officer in F7 – the section of MI5 responsible for monitoring the activities of unaffiliated left-wingers. Recently he had been promoted again and was the temporary head of his section.

Brown was an old case for him. It was some time since he'd been responsible for that file, but he had no difficulty remembering its broad outlines. Fathers explored the reasons for F7's initial interests in Brown, and the arguments from K Branch for transferring the file to it. Jensen explained how Brown was a strategic choice for intensive coverage.

'But none of this alerted you to his role as an agent?' Fathers said.

'No, though retrospectively one sees the pattern. Until K came up with whatever they did, I had no reason to think he was more than an irritating lefty who developed fine journalistic skills and good sources.'

'I understand. How long have you been watching Brown?'

'Me personally?'

'You F7.'

'Ah, from nineteen seventy-eight until last January.'

'You personally?'

'As Desk Officer for his file, since early eighty-two. But I'd come across him before.'

'Personally?'

'Yes. Got to know him a little. I first met him in the summer of seventy-eight. Saw him around the place over the next couple of years till I was pulled out.'

'What's he like?'

'Very smart, very personable. Sometimes rather quiet. Funny when he has a mind to be. Extremely knowledgeable. One of those people you could ask if he'd read a story in the paper that day, and he'd reply with everything worth knowing about it back to the year dot. Talks very fluently once he gets going. Reports suggest he's a pretty good public speaker too. Very clear and not over-dramatic. And, of course, he writes very well.'

'Very left-wing?'

'Not really, not by the standards of the people I mixed with. Didn't have much time for the small left groups, you know? We used to call him a right-wing social democrat, which was about the worst thing you could call anyone. He's an odd sort, very radical on some issues, less so on others. But we still liked him.'

'We?'

'Er, they.'

Chapter 21

When Fathers got home after calling back in at the Yard to read Bastin's memo requesting a major operation against the fights being caused by Connors and Garston, to hear that his boss had already learned the request would be turned down and to check on what sort of strength the police could field that night, Sarah was out again.

He sighed as he paid the baby-sitter. He had only enough money to give her half her dues. She took an IOU for the rest. He went upstairs to turn off Gary and Samantha's light, spending a few minutes with each of them, discussing school and, in Samantha's case, a boy who was being particularly mean to her.

There were no leftovers, so he scrambled some eggs. It brought back a memory of the last time he had been unfaithful to Sarah. It was in New York, working on a seemingly dead-end case concerning the disappearance of a British citizen. He had met the man's lover, there had been a spark of attraction and recognition between them, and they had made love. The first morning after, he had made breakfast – scrambled eggs – and they had joked about it, softly and affectionately, in the after-haze of a new sexual discovery. They had had two more nights together and then he'd gone to Washington, and come back the next day to learn she had been killed by a hit-and-run driver.

He'd never accepted it was an accident. A normally suppressed part of his memory of Rosemary was that he'd been indirectly responsible for her death, by spending so much time with her and using her in his inquiry. But that same day he'd been ordered back to London and had never been able to pin down who was directly responsible. Somewhere in the files of Scotland Yard and various government departments, there resided the bulky and mostly speculative report he'd written, in which he concluded that the US government was guilty of killing Rosemary, her lover and another woman – also a hit-and-run victim. The civil servants – Hanson among them – who'd received his report had been infuriated by it. Fathers himself had been sceptical of his conclusion, though confident of his reasoning.

These days, after the Iran–Contra business, it was all much easier to believe.

He sat at the kitchen table and watched his eggs congeal. He'd never told Sarah about Rosemary. There had been no point. They'd been going through a rocky patch at the time, but when he came back from America they had stitched the fabric of their relationship back together. Apart from her continual and always justified complaints about the hours he worked and the regularity with which he forgot to tell her when he would be home particularly late, they had had four pretty good years since then. But now . . .

He sat up with a start and ate his eggs. It occurred to him that Sarah was now the one who didn't bother to say when she was going to be out. She had stopped bothering about his inability to make a quick phone call to say he'd not be in till late – or at least, she had given up complaining about it. She'd also stopped trying to force on him the healthy diet she'd adopted the previous year. Initially she'd been a true evangelist about it. Each day he'd gone to work with an old ice-cream box packed with raw vegetables and salad for his lunch. That had long since stopped. He crammed the last of the cold egg into his mouth, washed the saucepan, packed the plate and cutlery into the dishwasher and switched it on, then went to get his briefcase to settle himself to work at the dining-room table. All the while he continued his lament about Sarah.

She also no longer criticised the drink he invariably poured for himself when he arrived home – which reminded him. He poured himself a whisky. And his cigars. In the last couple of weeks she'd virtually stopped complaining about them. He lit one mournfully.

That's it, you clown, he told himself. She doesn't nag me any more, therefore she doesn't love me.

But there was a logic to it, at least as convincing as Bastin's theory that someone who did you a favour could be in your debt. And she was out so much these days. He had done nothing to follow up on his suspicions. He was damned if she was going to be the object of an inquiry. But he couldn't stop himself from wondering.

He had once again broken what he supposed was a cardinal rule of security by bringing home some of the documents in the Crow case. He read through the files, making notes, beginning a rough outline of his report. His thoughts flickered intermittently back to Sarah, where she was, why, and to the distance that had been growing between them. If only I could be sure, he thought, if only I knew – but his mind balked at finding a way to confirm or disprove his suspicions.

It was after eleven when he heard the front door. Sarah walked in and waved a hand at the clouds of smoke which hung over the table.

'Hello,' she said. She sounded low. She came to the table and gestured at the ashtray. 'Do you have to? And why you try to work while you're drowning your brain in Scotch, heaven knows.'

He smiled at her, perversely welcoming her complaints as proof that his suspicions were overblown. As she moved so he could see her face properly in the light, he realised her eyes were red-rimmed. She'd been crying. He stood up. 'What's wrong?'

She came close and he wrapped his arms around her. She started to sob, fished a tissue from her pocket and dabbed uselessly at her eyes. She backed off and blew her nose.

'What's wrong?' he asked again.

She looked at him miserably and shook her head. More tears started and he put his arms round her again. She began to shake uncontrollably, threw her arms round his waist and held on fiercely.

'I'm sorry,' she said finally.

'What's wrong?' he asked for the third time.

She turned away from him as she took off her coat. 'Oh, it's . . . Well, I can't really talk about it. She asked me not to. It's so upsetting. A friend – you don't know her – she's just having such a terrible time.'

'Who?'

She shook her head. 'You don't know her. A girl I used to work with. She's been having an affair, and he's just broken it off, and her husband's found out, and she's left with almost nothing and it's really all very messy. Oh Christ.'

'Can I do anything?'

'Yes,' she said after a while. 'If you will, you can come to bed and hold me. I'm just so upset. I don't know why. It's got to me.'

He cleared his files and papers into his briefcase and they went to bed. As they lay in bed, she had another bout of sobbing and then slowly eased into sleep, comforted by the firmness of his arms around her and the shoulder on which her head rested. He was happy to comfort her – comforted himself that she had turned to him – but as they lay there, a sadly mocking part of his mind reminded him that people often referred to mythical friends to describe their own problem.

PART V
Double Backtail

Chapter 22

By the end of Tuesday Fathers had the distinct impression he was going stir-crazy. Looking back on it, he thought that might have been what alerted the hairs on the nape of his neck.

When the alarm woke them at 6.15, Sarah smiled weakly, nodded when he asked if she was all right, kissed his forehead, squeezed his hand and told him not to worry. 'What time will you be back tonight?' she asked.

'About seven, I hope,' he said. 'I'll call if I'm delayed.'

'You'll call *if* you remember *when* you're delayed,' she corrected him, but with another effort at a smile.

He got to Queen Anne's Gate before eight. There was a formidable pile of paper to go through before he could write his report: the files he'd started with, more he'd picked up along the way, notes from the interviews, supplemented by recordings of each except the one with Perry. His coffee was just made when the phone rang. He looked at it. Nobody was supposed to know the number. He lifted the receiver, clicked on his cassette record and held the microphone to the earpiece. 'Yes?'

''Allo, guv.' It was Queen.

Fathers stopped the cassette. 'How the hell'd you get this number?'

The DI chuckled throatily. 'Elementary, as whatsisname would say – Yarrow, I mean. Look, reason I called, a bloke got topped last night.'

'One of ours?' said Fathers in alarm.

'Nah, one of Hoyte's, young feller, name of Stubbs, a sticking job.'

Hoyte was another small operator under attack from Connors and Garston. 'Wasn't so bad to begin with, but he didn't find a doctor till he'd more or less bled to death.'

'And it was one of Connors and Garston's crew who did it?'

'Looks that way. They was all out 'n' about last night. I got names for about twenty of 'em. Pickin' 'em up now. Can you come in on it?'

Fathers pondered for a moment. 'No,' he said. 'Just get statements and hold the lot for further questioning.'

'They'll alibi each other.'

'I know that. They visited their aunts in pairs and later played darts together till dawn. Do it anyway. Scour the area where it happened for an eyeball. Tell me, what's those bastards' strength now? If we haul in twenty, what've they got left?'

'Almost as many again, I reckon. Maybe more if they call in a few favours – ones Garston's owed down east – and more again if they want to spend big.'

'So we can expect more trouble. Any response from King Gelchin?'

'Not that I've heard. It's early in the day yet and the news prob'ly hasn't hit the street. I'll get on it. What about your sparrer – do you want him to stay on the Hammersmith blag?'

'No. Today he can help out on this.'

'And what're you going to do about it, 'part from tell us to try and get a body to wear the charge?'

Fathers heard the note of challenge. Things were beginning to fall apart, and Queen knew it. 'I'm going to take sides,' he said and hung up.

The first person to call was Bastin. Fathers decided to wait an hour – the boss didn't get to work early these days. When he got through, Bastin had already heard the news and began by congratulating Fathers for suggesting the written request for a large operation. 'We'll get it now,' he said, 'no trouble. How do you want to handle it?'

'I'll get Herd and his Super to work out the details,' Fathers replied, 'and go over it early this evening. I want control of operational instructions. Will that be complicated?'

'No. I'll go heavy on the self-righteousness bit and they'll have no choice but to let you do what you want, how you want. By the way, Hanson said he'll help on Pardoner's Manchester problem. Don't forget to thank him, but not too fulsomely.'

Fathers promised, then called Herd. 'It's time we took the streets back,' he said. 'My boss is sorting out the authorisation. We're going to blanket the area, draft in strength from the other divisions. Can you work out deployment and requirements?'

'Happy to.'

'I'll call in to go over it early evening and give you the form. Six thirty OK?'

'Sure. Good to get some action going.'

Fathers sighed, wondering if he should take a hand in the arrests and preliminary interrogations. But if he did, he could still be busy with it tomorrow, the report wouldn't get written by itself, and Hanson would begin to get scratchy, which might get in the way of the Manchester favour.

He got on with his reading. By twelve he had worked out the basic shape of his report. He lunched on a sandwich and carried on. Although he sometimes worked alone, he usually had somebody to bounce ideas off. Normally, that role was played by his detectives. Many a time Sarah had been more or less willingly cast in the part. There had been occasions when witnesses, knowingly or not, had been his sounding-board. This time he had no such assistance, so he bounced ideas off himself, conducting internal dialogues, theorising, elaborating, disagreeing, speaking out loud as he paced his little room. He drank coffee almost continuously, broke his rule about not smoking in such a small space, tore his ideas to shreds and reconstructed them.

By two o'clock he was jumpy from the caffeine and had a headache from the smoke. He made more coffee, lit another cigar, sat down at the typewriter, put on his glasses, arranged his notes into a more or less orderly pile and drafted his report.

It took him three hours. There was no firm evidence with which to point the finger at treachery or incompetence, so most of the report was an argument about probabilities. It concluded it was unlikely that Special Branch had blown Operation Crow through carelessness. The problem was either that Brown had cancelled the meeting with Scherchinskiy when he saw he was being followed – or it was a leak, in which case the most likely suspects were Thomas and Perry. For the former he recommended another long and intensive interview. For Perry, a full investigation, mail and phone intercepts, personal surveillance. Next best bets, though only because they had the fullest information, were Deakin, McKellen, Naseby and Austin. Long shots were any one of the other Special Branch detectives. An even longer shot – but one he set more store by – was that computer security was the problem, and either somebody in the Joint Computer Bureau or anybody in MI5 with a high level of computer skills was the source of the leak.

When it was done he compared it with his original ideas. He'd promoted a few suspects, deleted others, exonerated Special Branch of incompetence and discovered computers. It didn't seem like much to show for all those interviews and files.

Tiredly he packed everything into the safe and decided on a

quick reviving drink. No, he corrected himself, a slow one. He checked his watch. Five thirty. Plenty of time before he had to meet Herd.

Fathers was not the only one to write a report that day. Neil Deakin was hard at work too. He had, in fact, been crafting a counter report on Crow's breakdown since early the previous week. He planned to send it straight to the Chief Intelligence Co-ordinator, bypassing the Director-General, as soon as he learned from his friend in the Co-ordinator's office that Fathers' own report had arrived.

Deakin's arguments were straightforward. All the officers involved in Crow were experienced, had come out clean after several security vettings and were wholly trustworthy. To point an accusing finger at them reeked of the self-destructive paranoia which had haunted the Security Service for over two decades from the early 1960s and which it should by now have put behind it. In addition, proper security procedures had been followed throughout. There was no possibility of other MI5 staff – elsewhere in K2, in the Watcher service, anywhere – knowing enough to leak. Therefore, the reason for the breakdown lay at the point of breakdown – Tuesday night in Hampstead. While a leak could not be ruled out – though Austin was as trustworthy as the K2 officials, and the rest of his team had not known anything soon enough – the most likely explanation was simple incompetence. Either Austin's mode of deploying his team or his assessment of what numbers were needed was inadequate, or one of the detectives had made an error. Probably, Deakin generously acknowledged, the extreme cold was partly to blame – blunting alertness. Likewise, that was probably why the cat got shot.

In the conclusion, Deakin inveighed strongly against the use of a biased outsider to conduct the *post mortem*. He did not make explicit use of his inside information about Fathers or about the conduct of his inquiry – the red herrings of Watcher procedure, interviewing the whole of K2, following up on Perry – for fear of weakening his position. That it had firm foundations, which would only be spoiled if he overdid the report, was shown by the way he had prevailed on the issue of keeping the key sources in the Crow file secret from Fathers.

By the end of the afternoon, Deakin was satisfied with the shape and tone of his report. He took his handwritten draft home to type up.

Going into the night, Fathers remembered his wallet was empty. He walked through to Victoria Street, setting a fast pace, trying to scatter the physical and mental after-effects of the day. As he worked out if he would be home early enough to see Samantha and Gary before they went to bed, his thoughts turned from optimistic expectation into depressed memory of the night before. His stride shortened. He shook his head vigorously. Stupid bloody self-destructive thoughts to have, he told himself irritably. The basic thing is she's extremely upset and needs my support and sympathy. That has to be there unconditionally, or what's love for? As for the rest, either she has or she hasn't. It doesn't really matter now if she has; it's bad enough that I've worked myself up into suspecting her. Why should I assume she's not telling the truth? But if she has, she'll tell me if and when she's ready. I'm not going to demean myself and her with any more stupid suspicions, far less by spying on her.

Spying, he thought. This whole sodding business has got to me. Thank Christ it's over. If we assume the assumption of presuming the knowledge, do we know the hell where we are? Life and work are two different things; especially my life, especially this bit of work.

It was as he lectured himself silently on his idiocy that the back of his neck began to communicate urgently with him.

Cutting off his homily, Fathers crossed the road against the lights. He saw a chemist's, went in and took several minutes to buy some painkillers with the last of his change. As he left the shop, he swallowed a couple of tablets, then walked on in the direction of Victoria till he reached a branch of his bank. There was a little queue at the money machine. He joined them and acted impatient, looking at his watch, shifting from foot to foot, casting quick glances up and down the street.

He saw nothing to confirm his primal danger signals, but when he had withdrawn fifty pounds he remembered what he had been told by Platt, head of the Watcher service. The knowing target has inherent, irreducible advantages. By the time a round-about ten-minute walk had brought him to the vicinity of a Scotch at his favourite pub, Fathers had no doubt. He was being followed.

Chapter 23

Fathers entered the Bunbury Arms and bought a whisky and a packet of cigars. He now needed not only to recover from his day's work but also to assess his new situation – no longer just the hunter, he'd become the quarry as well. It was, however, an open question whose quarry he was. He turned to find a table and found himself face to face with DCI Austin.

'Oh, Harry,' said Austin. 'I, er, sorry, I didn't recognise you from behind.' His voice trailed away to a mumble. He was embarrassed. Not surprisingly. He didn't know how to behave with Fathers, whether to treat him as a colleague or a threat.

'Hello,' said Fathers equably. 'Alone or with company?'

Austin slid past him to the bar and lodged his order. 'Two whiskies, two pints of IPA, please, love,' he said, giving Fathers his answer. He was there with one other detective.

'You won't hear officially for a while, and maybe never,' Fathers said quietly, 'but you can rest easy.'

Austin looked at him, but Fathers' face was turned away as if he didn't want to acknowledge he was talking with the Special Branch man. 'And the boys?'

'All of you.'

'Fair enough. Thanks for telling me. Did you know I'd be here?'

'No. Where're you sitting?'

'Over to the right.'

'See you then,' Fathers said and walked to the opposite corner.

Not if I see you first, you odd bastard, Austin thought.

Fathers sat for a while, smoking and drinking. The man who'd followed him had not come into the pub. He wondered whether it had been a fantasy produced by pressure, paranoia and poor street-lighting. It was possible. Over the past twelve days, since Hanson had called him in, he'd begun to think in strange, circuitous ways. He had convinced himself Sarah was having an affair, when the most obvious explanation for the distance which had grown between them was the amount of time he spent working and her need to fill her life with other things. He was investing no energy or time in their relationship these days. In fact, the quality and intensity of their life together had been deteriorating for several months. It was up to him to put it right, not indulge in nightmares.

Then Connors and Garston: his approach to the case was as indirect as any he had ever adopted. He had assigned Yarrow to look into a tenuously connected bank robbery where the lad was making no progress; was contemplating hoisting Boyars, who was a notoriously crooked solicitor, but for once was probably not breaking the law; demanding information from Queen's network of informants; and watching while Connors and Garston expanded their empire – instead of doing the obvious thing and clamping a strait-jacket on them.

It was all – to some degree, at least – a product of close contact with MI5. Its personnel, whatever their manifold differences with each other, exuded in common an air of conspiracy and convolution. Surface appearances were inevitably designed to deceive. Face value was a worthless currency. Look at what he'd just said to Austin. He'd deliberately told him he was in the clear, with the thought that if Austin was the source of the leak, he'd now relax. He hadn't needed to say anything. He could just have muttered something awkwardly and sidled off. It had been a free and deliberate choice to lie.

Perhaps it had all gone to his head, and produced a fantasy of being followed. Perhaps he even wanted to think he was being followed.

Yet he had been conducting a major if solo inquiry into a serious security leak. It would not be surprising if somebody who did not want it plugged – presumably its source, or somebody connected with him – had decided, at the least, to keep a close eye on him. What else might have been decided – or might yet be – was something he did not want to think about. He shivered, cast away the thought that his sanity was wearing thin, and opted for pragmatism. Safe was ever better than sorry.

He left the pub and went into the newsagents next door where he bought a phonecard and the evening paper.

The first phone call he made was to Cathy Gordon. He congratulated himself for the luck that she was at her desk. She listened to what he had to say, agreed to his request, and they hung up. The second call was to Sarah, to say he'd be home in an hour and a half. Fine, she said, sounding surprised – she'd delay their supper till then. He went back to the pub, got another whisky and killed fifteen minutes drinking it and reading the paper. It was again full of the outbreak of violence on the London streets and editorial demands that THE POLICE MUST ACT.

When the time came he walked quickly to the Yard and got his car. He drove at a normal speed, checking his mirror rather more than was strictly necessary for road safety. If he was still being followed, they were good at it. He found a spot in the police car-park at Tottenham Court Road and went in to see Herd. They sat in his office, where Herd broke out a fresh bottle of whisky and a pair of plastic cups.

'Cheers,' he said. 'Good to be making a move at last. You've seen how the papers are keeping up their this-scandal-of-violence-must-stop, make-the-streets-safe-for-decent-people campaign?'

'Yeah. I'm inclined to agree. You see, I wanted to wait until I was sure how the game's being played.'

'But your hand's been forced now.'

'That's right. Not so much by the papers, though I suppose they have a point, but in the end we can't let the streets get out of control like this. I wanted to see how the cards were falling, but now we know – or part of it, anyway. Connors and Garston are making their big push. If they win, a lot of things could change.'

Fathers paused to hold out his cup for a refill. 'Maybe Connors still has drug connections in the States. Then again, it doesn't have to be that. Or not primarily.'

'No,' said Herd, 'I was thinking about what'll happen if they just want more and more of the action. That could mean a war with the Tongs which'd make what's been going on so far look like a tea party, or they might even mean to take on Gelchin, which'd set the clock back twenty years. In the end, whatever their plans, we know we don't like 'em.'

'Yeah, and I've decided figuring it all out doesn't matter any more. It's time we let the street know where we stand. We'd rather have Billy Hughes and his like operating in a small way than see this lot in charge. We'd rather the Tongs kept Chinatown, and Gelchin the rest, than let a major gang war boil up. But we've got to show that. If the little people realise we've taken against the new force, they'll have to keep their options open. They'll have to keep paying the firms they know. Who'd want to tell Guy White to piss off, on the grounds that somebody else provides the protection these days, if they thought these days were numbered, that pretty soon Guy wouldn't have Connors and Garston on his back. So we have to hold the line for the established firms. But we can't do that just by putting the word out. We've got to show we mean it. We've got to do it.'

'Long speech, Harry. It's convinced me. D'you think the editors would like it if they knew the police response to their campaign was to side with small crime against big crime?'

'And what do they know about crime or policing?'

Herd produced the plan he and the uniformed branch had worked out for deploying vanloads of police constables throughout the areas of Connors and Garston's campaign.

'That's pretty good,' Fathers said. 'Just a couple of changes. For one thing, put plain clothes PCs into the most likely clubs.'

'Yeah, we should've thought of that. What's the other?'

'Bit tricky, this one. Deft, if I say it myself. I want one of your lads at each of the mobile group centres. So when the vans pick up the bodies and bring 'em back to the group points, somebody who knows the area's there to give 'em a quick once over *before* they're bunged down the nick.'

'Uh-huh, no problem. What're you up to?'

'Well – what've you put down for operational instructions so far?'

'Basically, keep the streets tight and snuff out any trouble as soon as it starts, and, where possible, before.'

'Right,' said Fathers. 'Here's the trick. Remember, the point is we're taking sides. A little bit of bias won't come amiss. Pick everybody up, before the fights start – thus pleasing the editors, thank you kindly – but let the locals out straight away. Don't even bring them back to the nick. Brush them down, salute, smile, sorry to have bothered you, off you go. Them foreigners get the works. Booked, held, straight into court where we try for remands in custody, the lot. And pad out the charge sheet as much as possible, without overdoing it.'

'I like it. And that's why we need my blokes on the spot, yeah, to sort out the good guys from the bad?'

'The good – well, I wouldn't go that far. They may be our villains, but they're still villains.'

'Yeah, demoralising, innit? About the best we can ever do is choose which birds rule the roost.'

'No,' said Fathers, 'it's not that bad, is it? I mean, it is in this case, but aren't there times when you get some real sod tucked up for a ten stretch, and you say, "There's a job well done, he's out of the way."'

'He's out of the way,' said Herd with determined gloom, 'and it feels good for the minute, but there's a thousand others ready to fill his shoes. It's a cesspit out there. I'm lucky really, only on the edge of it. I do not envy the blokes who're right in there, you know, just half a mile south of here. There's so much villainy and – I dunno, just plain wickedness. It's like you walk round with the permanent smell of rotting meat up your nostrils. It's just everywhere. If I worked that patch, I reckon I'd either call in the SAS, quit or get infected meself.'

'Yes, well, there's that side to it too, working the Soho manor.'

'The grease machine, you mean. I know, though I got some sympathy for the ones who do it. By being on the take they do more or less what you're planning now – pick which side they're on, which villain's not as bad as the next, which clubs're showing naughty films and which are showing the ones that are truly nasty.'

'Oh yes,' said Fathers, 'and choosing whose smack's going to fuck some poor sod's life up, and which firm's allowed to get away with having children on the game, and — '

'Yeah, all right, there're limits. I don't dispute that. I'm just saying that if you walk knee deep in shit your whole working day, it's not surprising if you start to pong a bit yourself. And that it's not always done, not at the beginning anyway, for the worst of motives.'

'Not everybody who works Soho's on the take,' Fathers objected. 'There are blokes who keep their nostrils plugged.'

'I'll tell you what, though,' Herd said, 'most of them don't get that much by way of result. They don't get close enough in to know who's who.'

'That's the problem, isn't it? Good policing means knowing the people on the manor. Knowing the community. And if it's sick, there's a risk to getting too close.'

'It's a filthy fucking world, and all the moralising and do-gooding in the universe won't change that.'

'So we just do what we can,' Fathers said, 'and not too much of what we oughtn't to. Policing's the art of the possible. Hasn't somebody said that before?'

'No, Harry, I reckon that's an original. I'll note it down for your biographer. Are you going to come along and watch the show?'

'I don't know. I'm absolutely shagged out. Bell me when the fireworks start. In the meantime I'll try to get some shut-eye.'

'OK. And tell me, will Guy thank us when he sees what we're up to?'

'If I knew what side he was playing on in what game, I might have an answer for you.'

150

Chapter 24

'It seems like when I'm out you're in, and when I'm in you're out, except for a few times when we're both in and you're not here even then,' Sarah grumbled as her husband's eyes half closed under the weight of fatigue and whisky. She was not pleased that, though home at a reasonable hour, he was not only exhausted but on call for later in the evening.

'You're out so much I hardly thought you'd notice,' said Fathers, 'or complain.' He had wanted a pleasant, quiet evening with Sarah after he had read Gary a story and talked with Samantha about how to deal with the boy who was teasing her, but as they sat down to eat it seemed he wasn't going to get it. For different reasons, neither of them was up to it.

'Of course I'm out a lot,' Sarah snapped. 'What is there to keep me in?'

Fathers knew the answer and didn't like it, so he said nothing. She grunted eloquently and started to eat. He did likewise. After a while he broke the silence. 'You'll be out tomorrow night, I expect?'

'Yes. How'd you know?'

'Because you're in tonight. And anyway, tomorrow's the history circle.'

'That's right.'

'Each Wednesday.'

She looked at him for a moment. 'That's right,' she said again.

'You going to dress up for it?'

'What?'

'Oh, nothing,' he said yawning. 'I may be in and out tomorrow evening. Can't really say for sure. How can we organise it?'

'I'll warn Susie. She doesn't mind being on call. What did you mean about dressing up for it?'

'I was just thinking about that meeting you had a couple of weeks back. You seemed rather smart for a history circle, I thought.'

'Oh, honestly, Harry, your clothes sense – for women, at least –

151

you do all right with yourself. It's just not there, is it? There's nothing special about that dress. It's smart, but nothing very special.'

'But I remember you getting that dress. It was for parties.'

'Was. Not that there've been many. Anyway, I got it when I was in my quiet phase with clothes. It felt like a party dress then. It doesn't now. I wear it out to ordinary things quite a lot.'

'It was a Friday, wasn't it?' Fathers said abstractedly. 'The meeting when you wore that dress, I mean.'

'Was it?' she said. 'Oh yes, I remember. The man who gave the talk had been going to come a while back, but he was ill. Cold or flu or something. So it was rescheduled as an extra meeting, on top of the usual ones. It was very interesting, but there weren't that many of us there, so I don't think we'll be doing that again in a hurry. Keep to the regular cycle.'

'What was it about?'

'Um, what was it?' Sarah frowned in thought. 'The war, wasn't it? Local experience of the war.'

'Oh yes, that's right. You said.'

Sarah eyed her husband suspiciously as he ate. 'What's with this sudden interest in the circle, anyway? And what I wear to it? Would you care to advise me on what would be most appropriate for tomorrow?'

'Sorry. I was only making conversation.'

'Oh, conversation. Yes, I think I remember that. It's when two people talk about things which are important to them.'

'That's right,' Fathers said emphatically, waking up under the goad of Sarah's hostility and returning her angry look defiantly.

'So tell me, for the sake of conversation, why're you on call tonight?'

'No, Sarah,' Fathers said, 'for conversation you need not only important subjects but mutual interest.'

'But I am interested.'

'Well, you don't bloody sound it.'

'You make it hard to be interested.'

'So you're not interested, then.'

'Don't you catch me out with your clever sodding little interrogation techniques. Christ, you can be so snotty.'

'You're not interested, so why ask?'

'I'd like to be interested.'

'I'd like to be Boris Becker. But I'm not.'

They glared at each other in fury – mutual, righteous and restrained. Silence hung between them again as they both pretended to concentrate on eating. Sarah was the first to soften. 'All right, I'm sorry I put it like that. Let's try again. I am interested. Really. Why are you on call tonight?'

'It's this gang warfare stuff,' Fathers said with another yawn. As Sarah's anger dissipated, so did his energy. 'Same thing as had me out over the weekend. It's getting a bit out of hand, so we've decided to step in and referee the contest, and they're going to call me when the action starts.'

'So you can be along to see the show?'

'Well, it's my show. I've got a right.'

'And a duty?'

'Same thing.'

'Huh.'

Fathers decided to doze on the sofa while he waited for the call. At eleven, Sarah covered him in a blanket and stood for a long time looking at him. Lonely thoughts chased each other through her mind and brought tears into her eyes. She half bent to kiss him gently and tuck the blanket round him, but he coughed and spluttered and turned. She shook him by the shoulder. 'Do you want to come upstairs to bed?' she asked.

He shook his head to clear it and looked at his watch. 'Shit,' he said. 'No, I won't bother.'

'Go on.'

'No, the call could come any time – in five minutes or after midnight. I'd only disturb you when I get up. Leave me be.'

'Well, at least take some of your clothes off or something,' she said, but he had already closed his eyes and gone back to sleep.

'On your head, then,' she said. 'Mine too.' And then more quietly, in case he might still be only half asleep, 'Christ, when are you going to come back to me?'

She lay awake a long time after she went to bed. 'When I'm worth coming back to,' she said to the ceiling, 'and maybe not even then.'

Chapter 25

First thing at the Yard next morning, aching and unrested, Fathers called Herd. 'Total no-show,' he was told. 'Reckon they hadn't time to line up the extra muscle, what with all the bods you had inside for questioning. But at least we'll get a good press today. Same again tonight?'

At the automat in the corridor, Fathers got a cup of what was alleged to be coffee against all the evidence of its smell and decided that, even if it seemed pretentious, he was going to start the New Year with a personal machine which made the real thing. As he walked back to his office, he signalled to Cathy Gordon. She came in behind him and closed the door.

'You were followed all right,' she said. 'Blue Montego. A driver and passenger. Neither of them looked like the one you described on the phone. They picked you up as you left here and again when you left Tottenham Court Road. I didn't follow them all the way. Cut through to Holloway and waited. When you came by, you had a different pair on your tail. A black Sierra. Then they swapped with the Montego which stayed with you till you got home. They waited about twenty minutes, then came back. I followed – lost them near Euston. But I got the numbers and called them in.'

'And?'

'False plates. No such registrations listed.'

Fathers sat in silence for a while. It was small and cold comfort to know he hadn't been paranoid.

'Do you want me to keep this up?' Cathy Gordon asked. He pondered. 'I'm happy to, you know,' she added.

'You're a love, Cathy, a true love.'

'Had we but world enough and time . . . '

'No, you've lost me there, all that culture.'

'Who is it?'

'Dunno.'

'What're you going to do about it?'

'Dunno that either.'

'Do you want me to keep on back-tailing you while you work it out?'

'Can you?'

'Sir, Mr Fathers, Guv, Detective Chief, Harry, Dad, Popsy-babe – I wouldn't offer if I couldn't.'

'You're a cheeky love, but still a love. I'm going to the Home Office in a bit. Won't be long. Can you cover me as I go, and watch me in if I call you to say when I'm coming back?'

'Nothing easier.'

'And thanks.'

'My pleasure.'

'One thing: I know I'm called Dad behind my back, but do they really call me Popsy-babe as well?'

'That's a secret,' Cathy Gordon replied and exited smartly.

'Queen, skipper,' Fathers bellowed without moving from his desk. They came in. Queen had news. 'I got a whisper who's earning his wack at last,' he rasped through his first cigarette of the day. 'You're gonna need the extra uniforms from what he says. Something special's laid on for tonight.'

'Good. What about the knifing?'

Yarrow reported. Eighteen people had been questioned, all part of the Connors and Garston set-up, all seen in the West End on Monday night, all equipped with alibis. Seven also had records for possessing or using knives and they were being re-interviewed. The knife hadn't been found and, unless one of the seven cracked, there was little to go on. Fathers thought it over, stretching to ease the pain in his back. 'Queenie, you reckon you can offer to fit them up? Each of them individually, I mean.'

'I should think I could manage that, guv,' Queen replied, lighting a new cigarette from the stub of his old one which he then tossed into his coffee cup. 'We're into finding levers, pressure for the exerting of, are we?'

'Pretty much. What's the best way? Claim you've got a witness?'

'Be better if we could fake the shiv.'

'It was a pretty distinctive one,' Yarrow put in. 'The doc says it had a serrated edge on the other side of the blade.'

'Nasty,' said Fathers.

'Right,' said Queen, 'you tell me how big it was and I'll nip out to an army surplus store and get one. I suppose,' he added to Fathers, 'you don't mind them knowing we're offering a fit-up?'

'That's the whole point,' Fathers replied. 'What we want is to break the alibis. One of them may have knifed young whatsisname.

155

Six didn't. Maybe none of them did. Could be one of the others. Or somebody else entirely. They're not going to worry about being genuinely caught for something if they didn't do it. But they'll worry about being set up by a bent screw. If any of them's a bit dumb, you may have to be explicit. But do make sure the tape's not running.'

'Stroll on, guv, when d'you think I was born? OK, Sherlock, let's go.'

'Half a mo',' Yarrow replied. 'I got something else. Always the way, isn't it? Just when you give up hope about something, it produces.'

'What've you got then?' Fathers asked.

'It's a tale of two birdies,' Yarrow said. 'I saw my snout last night, the one who told me about the Hammersmith blag, and he had a name – the wheelman.'

'Great.'

'Who turns out to be another little birdie o' mine, name of Barker, the one you got Mr Herd to agree a low bail for after I saw him in the book, that night we were round at his nick when Billy Hughes was there.'

'I remember. He was in the book for wheels then, wasn't he?'

'Yeah. And soon as he was out, he went and did some more dealing on his wheeling.'

'Naughty,' said Fathers, 'but nice.'

'You get all the bleedin' luck,' Queen complained. 'First Hammersmith just drops into your lap, and now you get a name with piss-all effort, and it even turns out to be somebody you've got an extra handle on.'

''S not fair,' Yarrow said. 'It was a real effort to be mean to my snout and make him cough up. Goes against my sunny nature.'

'So now you've given him the monkey you promised?'

'Course not. I lowered the offer each time I went to see him. He picked up fifty in the end.'

Queen tossed his head. 'You're learning,' he conceded. 'They call that psycho-loggy in smart places. You'll find him easier to deal with next time round.'

'So what're you going to do with friend Barker?' Fathers asked.

'I've sent Bunn and Petty off to find him.'

'They shouldn't lift him where anyone can see. You might want to keep him right out of it, so none of his mates knows he passed the word.'

'That's why I sent two of our lot, rather than just put out a call to the local manor. They'll pick him up when he's on his ownsome.'

'Good. Let Queen or me know if you want a hand.'

'Sure. I'll try it solo first, though.'

'Right, Fabian,' said Queen, 'gimme the gen on the knife and we'll leave Daddy to his spycho-loggy.'

'You just keep that quiet,' Fathers said.

'How'd you find out?' Yarrow asked. 'We didn't talk out of turn.'

'No,' said Queen, 'you were tight as a jock's wallet. It's all to do with who you know and whether they work in useful places. Nuff said, all right?' And with that he went, followed by Yarrow, leaving Fathers to speculate about government security and wonder about the full extent of Queen's network of informants. He went off to deliver his report on a different security failure to Hanson.

When he got back, he sat in his office and felt odd. Hanson had thanked him for his speed and reminded him that he might or might not be required for the second round of the Crow inquiry. Fathers thanked him for agreeing to try and sort out Manchester CID and Hanson explained that nothing could be guaranteed, since no CID liked to be told by the Home Office how to run a case, but that it was all a matter of knowing the right people and ensuring that the long view prevailed.

So that was that. Mostly, that was an empty feeling. The MI5 job had not been pleasant, but Fathers found himself wondering – and caring – what Hanson and whoever stood behind him would make of the report. After finishing it he had developed – in fact, he'd had forced upon him – a personal stake in the whole business by being followed, assuming that was the reason he'd grown a tail. Now he tried to pick up the threads of normality, reviewing his section's cases, deciding what should be consigned to the files and what should receive more effort.

It was not quite a return to normality, for Cathy Gordon told him he'd been followed on his way to and from the Police Department. That afternoon he was looking out of his window, thinking disconnected thoughts about MI5 and Sarah, when Queen came in without knocking. 'Counting pigeons, guv? Or is it crows?'

Fathers came out of his reverie. Was that a reference to the MI5 case? No, surely not. Just coincidence. Whatever else he knew, Queen couldn't know the name of the operation. Could he?

Queen was delighted with himself. 'Went down a treat,' he said. 'I had a shiv, told 'em about the art of faking dabs and how I was goin' to put some o' Stubbs's blood on it, and even showed 'em some of it.'

'How'd you get hold of that?' Fathers asked.

Queen grinned and put a specimen bottle on the desk. It contained a tiny amount of red liquid. 'I said we got it as it dripped from his dying body,' he said.

'What is it? Stencil-correcting fluid?'

'The oldest trick in the book, but how often it does the trick,' Queen said happily. 'Couple of 'em kept shtum, but the rest sang like little birdies. Reckon at least two of them, maybe a third, I can turn right round and put them on me snouts' list. Good day's work.'

'So what did you get?' Fathers asked.

'A name – same one, fingered by three of 'em.'

'Who?'

'Bloke called Joey Wainwright, used to be in Billy's crew. Nobody saw him do it, but three of 'em heard him talking about it beforehand.'

'Did you say Wainwright?' Yarrow asked brightly as he walked in. 'Now there's a happy coincidence.'

'Why?' asked Fathers.

'Because my man Barker says Wainwright was crow for the Hammersmith blag.'

The word 'crow' again disoriented Fathers for a moment. 'Queenie,' he said, 'did anybody put up a different name?' The DI shook his head. 'OK. Got a call out on him yet?'

'Yup. And I got a warrant to roll his drum.'

'Mugshot?'

'Yeah. He's got form, nothing much, bit of filching, couple of assaults. You want his picture?'

'A copy with every unit tonight. There's just a chance he'll be out on the streets, assuming your whisper didn't sell you shoddy goods.'

Queen snorted derisively.

'Now, what's this about Wainwright being look-out at Hammersmith?' Fathers asked Yarrow.

'That's what Barker tells me,' Yarrow said. 'He came up with all the names. But the real news is who was in charge.' He paused dramatically. 'Yates,' he said.

'Fenner there too?' Queen said. Yarrow nodded.

'Tom 'n' Jerry both,' said Fathers. 'They haven't done a bank before, have they?'

'Not that I've heard,' said Queen.

'Maybe when you sign up with Connors and Garston,' Yarrow

suggested, 'you have to do something to prove you're really one of them.'

Fathers shrugged. 'Have you put the calls out?'

'Not yet, because I was wondering what I could do to keep Barker out of it. So I thought I'd talk to you about it first.'

'You were right,' Fathers said. 'Unless we scoop them up tonight, we'll leave Yates and Fenner for later, after we've got Wainwright under wraps for the knifing. *Then* we'll bring in that pair — '

'And tell 'em Wainwright's blabbed,' Yarrow said, 'which'll leave my man out of it.'

'Yes,' said Fathers, 'that's shaping up nicely. Well done, both of you. How did Barker get to do the wheels, by the way? He doesn't know Hughes's crowd or the other lot, does he?'

'Ah,' said Yarrow. 'Thereby hangs a sorry tale. A bloke called Davy Dawes was told to find a driver, and offered it to his old mate, Cy Barker. When he told me that – Barker, I mean – he pleaded with me, really begged me, to leave his good pal Dawes out of it, and out of the kindness of my heart, I said I would.'

'What's sorry about it?'

'You never know who to trust,' Yarrow said with a sly grin. 'Dawes is my snout who put the finger on Barker in the first place.'

'Gawd, Christmas starts earlier each bleeding year,' Yarrow muttered as he put the drinks on the table. He cast a venomous look over his shoulder at the office party revellers who'd jostled him on his way from the bar, sucked the spilled beer off his hand and sat down.

'What d'you mean, starts?' Fathers scoffed. 'It's been going for a couple of months already. Almost three in fact. Christmas mail-order catalogues come at the beginning of September.'

'I wouldn't know.'

'You will when you have children. Done your shopping yet, Queenie?'

'Yeah, did it in the January sales.'

'Now that's forward planning,' Herd said. 'Myself, I say every year I'll do it in November, but it always seems to be Christmas Eve.'

It was ten o'clock. They were killing time, waiting for something to happen. Everybody was waiting. Outside a flat in Upper Holloway three CID men were waiting and watching for Wainwright. His photo had been reproduced and distributed among the uniformed officers who were waiting in cars and vans in the West End for some trouble to start. Connors and Garston's crew were waiting to start it.

They chatted desultorily. They had little in common apart from being policemen. Christmas made a good topic for them, full of tales of the common punters' seasonal stupidity. Fathers rose to get another round of drinks in. As he stood at the bar, a woman came up to him. 'Well,' she said mock coyly, 'are you going to buy me one too?'

'No,' Fathers said.

'Aw, go on, you haven't bought me one all evening. Gin and tonic.'

'I'm not with this crowd,' Fathers said. He caught the barman's eye, waved his tenner and called out his order.

'And a G and T,' the woman shouted. She looked to be in her early thirties, dressed for a party, her eyes and cheeks bright from several gins already. 'Haven't had a kiss from you either,' she added, producing a sprig of wilting mistletoe from nowhere.

'Forget the gin,' Fathers called to the barman. 'She's not with me.'

'I could be,' the woman said. She leaned against Fathers, clutching his arm against her breasts. She used the rung of a bar stool to clamber up and plant a kiss on his chin. He gave her a push, but she tried again, aiming for his mouth, slipping into his arms as he staggered backwards and held on to her. 'That's better,' she said, got his head in her hands and kissed him full on the lips. 'You're nice,' she said sliding her arm round his waist and rubbing herself against him, 'and I could be really nice to you if you like.'

Fathers put a hand on her shoulder to haul himself upright. 'Go away,' he said laughing, 'I'm not with this crowd.'

'That needn't matter,' she said, insinuating a leg round his, stroking her ankle up and down against his calf.

Despite himself, Fathers was aroused and, of course, flattered, even if she was drunk. He gave the woman another push, and managed not to put out a hand to help her as she tripped backwards. The barman arrived with the drinks, including the gin and tonic, and gave a knowing wink. 'Christmas,' he said, 'comes but once a year.'

'Thank Christ,' said Fathers, passing the money over. 'Look, dear, here's your drink. Now fuck off.'

'Not off,' she said, but she could recognise a losing cause, and knew it was wholly lost when another woman gave Fathers' arm a tug and demanded, 'What're you up to then?'

'Oops, sorry,' said the first woman. 'Just a bit of fun, love, and I started it. He's a cute one, isn't he? I envy you.' She took her drink and wandered away.

'Thanks for the rescue, Cathy,' Fathers said. 'What do you want? To drink, I mean.'

160

'I won't bother, thanks. Don't want to cramp your style. Oh, all right, if you insist, brandy.' The barman was waiting with the change, heard the new order and went to get it without being asked.

'I just came to tell you I'm clocking off,' Cathy said. 'Before we join the others, another thing. This evening, I was doubled.'

'They were back-tailing you?'

'Yes.'

The barman came back with the brandy and less change as Fathers absorbed this information. 'It's a right merry-go-round. We'll talk about it tomorrow. Let's join the others.' They picked up the drinks and started to weave their way through the throng.

'Who's your lady friend?' Cathy wanted to know.

'Dunno. Never seen her before.'

'Ah, how quickly they forget. Look, you've badly disappointed her. She's going.'

Fathers watched as his would-be seductress left the pub. She didn't appear to be with the office party crowd either. A man whose loosened tie and ruddy face proclaimed that he was one of the crowd blocked Cathy Gordon's path and announced she could only pass by giving him a kiss. Without spilling a drop, she stamped on his foot and followed up with a sharp sideways kick at his shin, leaving him furiously indignant, crudely insulting and in pain. 'That's how to deal with them,' she said.

Fathers attended to his thoughts while the others gossiped. Suddenly and apropos of nothing he said, 'It stinks.'

PART VI
Crow of Triumph

Chapter 26

In the vans parked in back streets on the edges of Soho, conversation and what passed for wit flowed excitedly. Nerves tingled in the way that says the adrenalin is ready to flow. They were too wound up to complain about the wait, the cold and the discomfort of sitting in a cramped space for so long. None of them knew how many were involved. Extra strength had been brought in from all over London. The only requirement was that they were good but reasonably cool in a fight, for trouble was expected and a lot of it. That was attraction enough for many of the ones who'd volunteered. The chance of a good fight, the ability to say in the coming days and weeks, 'I was there', if, as expected, the evening turned out to be a classic. And there were the extra rewards as well. Not a lot, but not to be sniffed at in the Christmas season with all its demands on everybody's wallet.

The police were ready.

Joey Wainwright, too, was sitting in a van, driving in from Hackney to the West End. When he spoke to the others, catching a joke and throwing it back, commenting on a girl on the pavement when they stopped at lights, his voice crackled with tension. His hand in his pocket was clamped round his knife, the one with which he'd stabbed Johnny Stubbs two nights before. He'd meant to stick it in him, but to read in the next day's evening papers that Stubbs had died had been a shock. He'd been surprised how easily the knife had slipped in. He'd heard it was hard to knife someone in the ribs, because the bones got in the way. Meaning only to scare Stubbs out of dunning him for the eight hundred pounds he owed, Joey Wainwright had deliberately chosen the ribs rather than the face. He'd thought Stubbs would bleed a bit and get stitched up by a medic. Apparently it hadn't been like that.

When the shock ebbed, he'd been scared of being caught. Before it, he'd told the others he'd been with that night, said he was going after Stubbs and would make his own way home. There'd been no witnesses, but for anybody to share his guilty knowledge was dangerous. He'd thought about going to see his family in Reading or a pal who'd moved to Bristol. But when it seemed the police were picking up everybody but him, he'd calmed down. His mates wouldn't talk. And, as the fright subsided, it had been replaced by a feeling of power. He didn't go round boasting, but he knew himself to be different. He had only just turned twenty, but in his own eyes he had grown up and from now on would hold his place with the best of them. It didn't matter if it wasn't common knowledge. The important thing was that he knew.

It had been OK working for Billy Hughes as a barman-cum-bouncer. Reasonable money, easy hours, and the feeling of being close to where things happened. But then had come the day when Tom Yates offered him the chance of earning five hundred quid, just by being look-out for a bank robbery he was organising. 'I didn't know Mr Hughes went in for that line,' he'd said. 'It's not for Billy,' Yates had replied. He'd looked at Joey Wainwright seriously for what seemed an endless time. Then he'd said, 'It's for Connors and Garston.' Joey Wainwright had nodded quickly, and that was how he came to change sides. When Johnny Stubbs heard about it, he'd immediately come asking for the money he'd lent and turned nasty when he was told it wasn't there. He'd hit Joey Wainwright before he had a chance to get out of his chair and kicked him half a dozen times. And that was how he came to get stabbed.

Joey Wainwright was pleased with himself and his life. Working for the new men – it was a good feeling, exciting, gave him a share of power.

The van came to a halt, the lights were switched off, the motor killed. They were parked in a back alley. They waited a few minutes in silent dark. Then Yates turned round from his seat in the front. 'Time, gentlemen, please,' he said. They got out, stretching stiff limbs. 'Joey, Bill, you're with me,' Yates said. 'Rest of you wait here. Five minutes. Then you know what to do. If anybody gets in your way, deal with 'em. But don't lay a finger on the girls.'

'Not a finger, Tom,' a voice confirmed to a chorus of sniggers.

'Keep your mind on the job you're paid for,' Yates snapped. He walked off briskly, the other two in his wake. They looked carefully up and down the side street as they emerged into it and then the bigger road which the club that was their target fronted on to. No sign of the police, or of any suspicious clumps of men hanging round pretending they had nothing to do.

'Stay at the door, Bill,' Yates said. 'Don't let anybody in. Scarper when the punters come out. Wait for us at the end of the alley. You and me's goin' straight through, Joey, havin' a bit of fun on the way. Move quick and don't look anybody in the eye.' He checked his watch. 'Ready? Let's do it.'

There was a man at the front entrance to the club whose job was to encourage men who stopped to look at the pictures outside to overcome their nervousness and go inside to see the real thing. Yates and Joey Wainwright paused like a couple of potential customers. The doorman eased over to them. 'Care to see it in the flesh?' he asked.

Yates nodded and hit him back-handed in the throat. Joey Wainwright followed up with a kick, whipped his knife out and ran the serrated back of the blade up the man's cheek. As he began to scream, the two of them bundled him in the door.

There was a woman in the booth where the entrance fee was paid. 'Press that alarm button,' Yates told her, 'and you'll get a faceful of acid.' She put a hand to her face and nodded palely. 'Get out of there,' he ordered. She was reluctant. 'You get out of there or I'll come in with the acid.' She came out. 'Right, downstairs with you.'

He ran her down the stairs in front of him. The bouncer was standing at the bottom. Behind him was a room with a bar where diluted drinks were sold at inflated prices, a few tables and chairs, and some rows of seats at the front. It was not very big. A full house was an audience of fifty; tonight was half full. All attention was on the low stage which was occupied by two performers, a man and woman, both naked except for the leather straps with which he had just pretended to tie her up.

Yates shoved the woman cashier into the bouncer, knocking him down, and Wainwright followed up with more knife-work. The barman emerged and Yates hit him with a chair. A few heads turned at the noise, but for the moment the act continued and the customers' expectation remained concentrated on it. They woke up to what was going on when Yates uncorked a smoke bomb and hurled it at the bottles behind the bar. As the smoke billowed, panic was immediate. Yates and Joey Wainwright barged their way through and leaped on to the small stage as the performers left it. Only one member of the audience was calm. He withdrew into a corner. He'd already used his short-wave WT radio to call for police assistance.

Backstage, all was chaos. There was not much space – a changing room for the performers, an office, a lavatory and a corridor. The men who'd come in the back had already started to break up the furniture and spill petrol round the place. The manager had come out of his office as he heard them break through the back door. He lay semi-conscious on the floor, bleeding from a head wound. 'Get the fuck out,' the women for the next act and their minder were told, and that they did. The pair who'd left the stage stood uncertain what to do, pincered between Yates and Joey Wainwright from the front and the others who'd come in the back. 'Out,' was the order and they made their naked way through the leering crowd and into the cold night. 'Get this bag of scum out too,' Yates snapped, and the manager was half carried, half dragged outside. The last to leave, Yates soaked a rag in petrol, lit it and held it till it was burning well. Then he dropped it on the sodden carpet and joined the others, leaving the door open behind him so the breeze would fan the flames.

As they got to the van they hearrd a siren. Yates yelled at them to get a move on and took the driver's wheel himself. As he turned out of the alley, headlights on full-beam blinded him momentarily. The wheel bucked in his hands, the van slewed across the street and into a parked car. He threw the door open and jumped out, knocking into a policeman who staggered but hung on to him. Yates lashed out, got free and raced down the street. 'I'm with you, Tom,' said a panting voice. He half turned as he ran. It was Wainwright. It looked like he was the only other one to get away. Behind, he could hear shouts of rage and pain.

'Down here,' said Yates. They ducked into a narrow passageway. It led into a courtyard. He looked round, decided quickly against going back to the street, picked a door and leaped at it feet first. The lock gave and they were into a poorly lit hallway, presumably the back exit of a shop. Yates cursed as he stumbled into a full rubbish bag. The next door was stronger and refused to give way to him.

'Fuck it,' he said. 'Lose the shiv.'

But Joey Wainwright was still holding the knife when three uniformed constables appeared in the doorway from the courtyard. He shaped to use it on them. 'No, you stupid bastard,' Yates screamed, and hit sideways with the edge of his clenched fist. The knife man went down clutching his head, but Yates's good sense didn't prevent him from being slammed face first into the wall.

In all there were twenty-nine arrests, no police casualties apart from the odd bruise, no members of the public hurt, though many had been badly scared. There was a considerable amount of damage to property, but no fires had spread and no tears were shed. Not by Fathers, at least.

As the small hours ground on into Thursday morning, the

phone calls of congratulation from the top brass started coming through. Serried ranks of reporters demanded press conferences, statements, interviews, background briefings. Through the day the news bulletins were full of the clash between gangland anarchy and the Metropolitan protectors of the peace. There were even questions in Parliament that afternoon and fulsome praise for the police from all sides of the House. The fact that all this was done to protect several small gangs from one big gang somehow never got mentioned.

Queen and Yarrow set to work on Joey Wainwright. He was young and inexperienced; all his previous convictions were for petty teenage thievery and a few fights. He wasn't hard or wise enough to resist the detectives' wiles as they set about disorienting him. Inside half an hour they had him believing that a full confession would give him a clean slate and the chance of a new start. In a sense it would, but only when he got out of prison. He confessed to the murder, to his part in the bank robbery – and named Yates, Fenner and two others – to armed assault with intent to commit grievous bodily harm, to possessing a dangerous weapon – which he agreed was the murder weapon – and to threatening police officers with it. Some or all of his confessions might be retracted when it came to trial, but the knife was full of evidence which could not be gainsaid. He even wanted to explain the motive for knifing Stubbs and told them about the debt he couldn't pay. That gave them a line which would be followed up later. Confirmation by friends of Stubbs that he was owed money would strengthen the evidence against Wainwright in case he decided not to make a guilty plea in court.

Yates was a different matter. Apart from demanding to make a phone call, he refused to say a word. Queen and Yarrow didn't bother with trying to bluff, bully, cajole or con him. It would have been a pointless exercise. They made a photocopy of Joey Wainwright's statement and gave it to Yates. He read it through and looked up with a sour expression. 'That's his story,' he said.

Queen admitted to being quite impressed by Yates's calm, and Fenner, who'd been picked up in the act of throwing a petrol bomb, put up just as good a show fifteen minutes later when they presented the statement to him. 'Lies,' he said, 'forgery I shouldn't wonder.'

Yarrow was satisfied, however. Nobody would look further for an informant when Yates and Fenner could see for themselves who'd talked. It was useful that Wainwright didn't remember Barker's name. To cover themselves, Queen and Yarrow showed him the mug-book, but made sure it was one which didn't have Barker's picture in it. So Wainwright couldn't identify the wheelman, whose name was thus not in the statement. Having protected Barker, Yarrow had strengthened his hold over him, to be further exploited at a later date.

Over a cup of tea, Fathers put a pin in the euphoria. 'Wainwright's up the creek,' he said, 'but Tom 'n' Jerry may yet convince a jury if they keep playing the same way. They'll say they don't know what it's all about, put up a good alibi and claim little Joey's just being malicious. Supergrasses have got a bad name these days.'

'Wainwright's not a super,' Yarrow protested.

'No, but I'm warning you to wait and see what a jury makes of it after a good defence counsel's had a go,' Fathers said. 'Still, there's no way for Tom 'n' Jerry to get out of tonight's bundle of charges.'

Chapter 27

'I said to myself at the outset,' Sir Nigel Laker mused, 'and I believe I said to you too, that he sounded an impressive chap.' He tossed the early edition of the evening paper to one side. Its front page showed a picture of a smiling 'Fathers of the Yard, mastermind of last night's Operation Clean-up'.

'In terms of publicity,' Hanson said, 'he has certainly cleaned up.'

'Impressive or no, however, he has set me a problem.'

'You find something lacking in his report?'

'No, it's a solid piece of work – or solid-looking, at least. He exonerates Special Branch as far as competence is concerned, and I would gauge that to be reasonable on his arguments, yet leaves open the possibility of a long-term penetration agent there, which is certainly wise. Similarly, he acquits the Watchers of both incompetence and leakiness, where again I find myself following and accepting his logic, yet queries the sagacity of the policy which guided their deployment. Well, there are countervailing arguments, but he has a point. It may be worth rethinking some of these operational aspects.'

'And yet,' Hanson said, 'it struck me that those were relatively minor matters.'

'Trivia,' Sir Nigel agreed, 'hors-d'oeuvre to the main fare. He gives us two main suspects – Thomas and Perry – and makes his recommendations about how to deal with them. And I follow his reasoning throughout. Perry is clearly worth a very close look, but, as Fathers says, there is no evidence against him as yet and none may emerge. In consequence he gives us further potential suspects in Deakin, McKellen, Naseby and Austin. And then, by God, he knocks us all flat on our backs and poises his sword over the entire staff of the Joint Computer Bureau.'

'Along with any other computer expert in the whole of Five Hundred,' Hanson added.

'True. A comprehensive list.'

'Yet perhaps he missed one person out.'

'Oh?'

'The Director-General.'

Sir Nigel blew out a long breath. 'God's teeth, Jock, I'm too old for that sort of joke. It's early, I know, but would you accept a pre-lunch whisky?'

'I could be persuaded.'

'Regard the arguments as made and conclusive. Take a cigar if you wish. Join me in the corner.'

Equipped for serious discussion, the head of the Police Department and the Chief Intelligence Co-ordinator seated themselves on sofa and wing-chair respectively.

'You understand, Jock,' Sir Nigel began, 'you recommended a man. I accepted the nomination. He has conducted an initial investigation and arrived at certain conclusions. On paper, as he argues them, they are logical. Phraseology leaves something to be desired by Cabinet Office standards, but the reasoning is impeccable. However, I did not conduct the inquiry. I have not seen – or heard – the evidence. If he has missed something, I cannot tell.'

'Nigel, may I suggest we take the reservations as read? Once again, I am your guest, admiring your well-appointed office and savouring your fine refreshments. Unless it is to be your innocent foil as you develop your thoughts, I assume I have a purpose here. May I know it?'

'Yes, enough of the bush to be beaten about. There are various complications.'

'I take it that Box Five is showing some resistance to the inquiry continuing, or at least to Fathers conducting it.'

'The Staff Counsellor has been brought in,' Sir Nigel said. 'I've ordered him off again, but he has at least served the purpose on this occasion of taking Five Hundred's pulse. And it beats somewhat uneasily and disquietingly. To the extent that Deakin, whom I've always regarded as sound, has entered his own report, criticising the use of Fathers whom he sees as irredeemably biased and finding Special Branch guilty of incompetence.'

'How convenient.'

'What bothers me is not simply that he has flouted explicit instructions and contravened all procedure, but that he has done it so blatantly.'

'The implication being?'

'That either he's extremely confident that he can get away with it – which means he's lined up the DG – which could lead to more difficulties – or that he's desperate.'

'Perhaps because he has something to hide?'

'And should therefore be a target in the follow-up,' said Sir Nigel. 'My thought also. Suspicious behaviour should be treated with suspicion. And Fathers is the obvious man to do it. Indeed, with so many potential suspects in Five, I feel I cannot give it to the ferrets in K7 who deal with leaks from within the Service. But it is placing a lot of trust in somebody I don't know. That's why you're here. I stand on the edge of a second step. Is Fathers the man I should take it with?'

'You are unseasonably blunt,' Hanson remarked. 'I'll reply in kind. I have had reason to doubt his judgement. Once, four years ago.'

'I've read that file,' Sir Nigel interjected.

'I understood it was withdrawn.'

'Even so.'

'And what was your own opinion?'

'His conclusions about this man's disappearance in New York were highly speculative. The evidence was patchy and second- or third-hand. His reasoning, however, I thought adequate.'

'You believed him?'

'I followed his reasoning.'

'I must confess it was impossible to break down.'

'Though you doubted it.'

'Your earlier candour,' Hanson said carefully, 'demands we be explicit at this point. The sensitivity of the issue is self-evident. His activities caused a lot of trouble. I doubted his judgement. His reasoning was not in question.'

'A not unknown predicament. Tell me more about him.'

'I have only rubbed so close to him that one time, till now. As a detective, he is an experienced investigating officer with an outstanding record. To be frank, that alone is reason enough to trust that the conclusions in his report are soundly based. I would add that the suggestion he is biased in favour of Special Branch, which I understand to be Deakin's view, is absurd. There is no detective more likely to mistrust his colleagues. As a man, he is arrogant, often grossly insulting, routinely insubordinate and habitually uncivil. He is strong-willed and more than a touch ruthless.'

'Combined with his obvious intelligence,' Sir Nigel said, 'I imagine that explains his success.'

'You would need to meet him,' Hanson continued, 'to understand how profoundly irritating he can be and the pleasure he clearly takes in it. His fine record is counterpointed by years of disputes with his superiors, cavalier disregard for orders, rudeness, short temper and sheer bloody-mindedness. People who admire him do so, in the majority, despite themselves.

'But there are those who admire him?'

'His immediate superior among them. He spends most of his time covering Fathers' back.'

'You make me wonder why he has not been transferred to some out-of-the-way place or to a dark corner of the bureaucracy.'

Hanson shook his head. 'It has been considered,' he said, 'but when those who do not have to tolerate his worst features contemplate him he is so obviously too great an asset to waste in that fashion.'

'And you, Jock, where do you stand?'

'For all his defects he is too valuable to be lost in the backwash of petty personal bickering. If it came to it, I would block any such transfer.'

'So you count yourself among those who admire him despite themselves. He sounds a likeable bugger in his own way.'

'Felicitously phrased, Nigel, even by Cabinet Office standards.'

Sir Nigel smiled briefly. 'You paint a vivid portrait, but is he the one to conduct the follow-up in the Crow inquiry?'

Chapter 28

The adrenal surge of success carried Fathers through the morning and into the afternoon. He handled the reporters, accepted the plaudits from on high, issued thanks and praise in his turn to the divisions who'd provided the extra personnel, got tired and exultant officers to write up their reports and instructed that the uniformed presence on the streets of the West End be reduced to only a few vans' worth more than normal. He dealt with all his paperwork for the night's operation and the bank robbery case. He called in Pardoner, Cathy Gordon and Yarrow, and outlined a further job of work for that night.

After that, he decided he'd had enough. His immediate tasks were completed and his energy drained. He was restless for a response to his report on Operation Crow. He had to get out and away from his desk. Announcing he was off for a late lunch, he put on his coat, told Cathy Gordon there was no need for her to back-tail him, and left. What he wanted was a walk. He crossed St James's Park, went through Admiralty Arch to Trafalgar Square and found himself on Charing Cross Road. He had gone there without a purpose, but now he found one – Christmas presents, naturally. He looked in various bookshops, working his way north.

He stopped buying when he suddenly felt painfully hungry. He'd bought four books, but only one was a present. As he left the last shop, he saw a face he recognised. The other man saw him, and his features registered in turn a puzzled frown, a spark of recognition and an amused grin. 'Dr Finlay, I presume,' Fathers said.

'Oh, it's all right,' said Paul Finlay, 'you can drop that old joke now and simply call me Professor. I've been elevated. Yourself? Are you still a Chief of Inspectors or have they made you a Super-duper-intendent?'

'Still a lowly DCI,' Fathers said humbly.

'I've been reading about you in the paper. Nice story – shame about the picture.'

They stood for a moment, in the awkwardness of acquaintances

175

who, having met by chance a long time after they last saw each other, don't know what to do next. 'Fancy a coffee?' Fathers suggested. 'Or something to eat? I'm just going to get a bite.'

Finlay checked his watch. 'Why not?' he said.

They fell into step, or almost, because Finlay was six inches taller than Fathers, as well as eighty to a hundred pounds heavier. He was wearing a heavy canvas coat with a fur collar that extended the full breadth of his massive shoulders. Quickening his pace to keep up with this colossus, Fathers felt like a child out for a walk with a grown-up.

When they entered the Italian bistro Fathers was aiming for, a waiter came up to them, and was brushed aside by the manager as he raced from behind the counter. 'Mr Fathers,' he said, 'how nice to see your face again, and not only on the front page of the paper. What is your pleasure?'

'To eat,' said Fathers. 'I think I'll have a lasagne and salad and a large black coffee.'

'Certainly, and your friend?'

'Just a coffee, please,' said Finlay.

'Try the cheesecake,' Fathers said. 'Best in town.'

'Why, thank you,' said the manager. 'Truly, we are rather proud of it.'

'No ta,' said Finlay, 'man of my build – got to watch me weight, you know.'

'As you like,' said the manager. 'Please, allow me to take your coats.'

Fathers handed him his Burberry. The manager held out his hand for Finlay's coat and his arm sagged under the weight. Finlay grinned and helped keep it off the floor. The manager departed, glancing suspiciously at the coat on his arm.

'What the hell's that?' Fathers asked as they sat down. 'Looks like it weighs a ton.'

'It does near enough,' Finlay said with satisfaction.

'Was that a fleece lining, or maybe the whole sheep?'

'Swedish army surplus, old-style Arctic issue. Twice as heavy as the thickest overcoat, so you work up a good sweat walking around, stay fit and never get cold.'

'I'm surprised at you, dressed in an army coat. Thought you were a man of peace.'

'Sweden's non-nuclear and non-aligned,' Finlay said. 'I wear it as a token of my support for a sensible defence policy.'

Fathers smiled and excused himself to go to the lavatory. As he

176

returned, he saw that Finlay was examining the books he'd bought. 'Finally decided to learn about the secret state, have you?' Finlay said. All three of the books Fathers had bought for himself were about spying. 'Find out just exactly what is the repressive system whose dedicated servant you are?'

'Christmas presents,' Fathers lied. He reached out to take the books, but Finlay gave them back one at a time, pronouncing professorially on each as he did so.

'This one's tripe,' he said. 'I'd go and get your money back if I were you. Jejune rubbish. Take twenty-one easily explicable incidents, exaggerate and distort them, weave a web of speculative fantasy and make a fortune. Crap. Now this one's more serious and intelligent, but more than a little starry-eyed. Read with care and discrimination. This is good, though. Probably the best in the field – best written by an Englishman, anyway. Interesting choice of presents for a copper to give.'

The food arrived and Fathers tucked in. 'Of course,' said Finlay, stealing a tomato from the salad, 'in some ways you can't do better than *Spycatcher*.'

'It's good, is it?'

'It's worth reading,' Finlay responded carefully. He munched thoughtfully on a purloined lettuce leaf. 'It's informative about attitudes, and the scandal's fun – the plot against Wilson when he was Prime Minister, that sort of thing. And in general terms it's got a lot of interesting stuff about MI5 as it grew up in the fifties and sixties, though apparently there's details which are wrong. But do you know what the most important sentence in the whole book is?'

'No. Haven't read it.'

'Well, I'll read it to you. I just got my copy back from a mate.' Finlay bent down to his briefcase, flicked the combination lock and opened it.

'I see you're a bit security-minded yourself,' Fathers commented, quickly eating some salad before Finlay swiped it all.

'Some rat nicked a set of exam questions from me once, which rather taught me to look after things,' Finlay replied. He straightened up with a copy in his hand of the best-selling book which Her Majesty's Government had spent a great deal of time, effort, money and prestige failing to suppress. 'Here it is. Second sentence of the prologue: "In January 1976 after two decades in the top echelons of the British Security Service, MI5, it was time to rejoin the real world." Makes you think, eh? It's also the most self-aware sentence in the whole thing.'

'But wouldn't you say that about your job?' Fathers objected. 'There's the academic world, and the real world.'

'Yeah, but for over twenty years he's supposed to have been telling his masters in government all about the real world. Yet only when he gets out of MI5 can he say he's part of it. What about you? You work in a tightly closed community. I understand most coppers find their friends among other coppers. You have a – what? – a collegial view of things. It's a highly consuming job, I should imagine. Not unlike many others in that sense. Would you say you're not part of the real world?'

'Well,' Fathers ruminated, chewing the last of the salad, 'no, I suppose not, though I'd say it's a part of reality that most people don't encounter.'

'Fair enough. And will you begin your autobiography with a statement that your professional life has been spent in an unreal world?'

'I won't write an autobiography.'

'No, you'll have someone ghost it for you. How about the second most important sentence? D'you want to know that? Where is it?' Finlay flicked through pages he had dog-eared. 'Here we are. There's an argument about whether MI5 should be allowed to circulate some highly damaging information about two people thought to be spies recruited in the thirties. In the course of the argument, our author says to somebody else, "If we filter out things we believe to be true just because we can't prove them, we're failing in our duty."'

'I believe a lot of unprovable things,' Fathers responded. 'I'll bet you do too.'

'But, if I voice them, I don't have an audience who takes everything I say on trust simply because I'm speaking for the state Security Service. And I at least try to be careful and distinguish between known facts and personal speculation.'

'I seem to remember us talking once about the difference between facts and truth.'

'That's right, and there's also a difference between facts and truth on the one hand and allegations on the other.'

'An allegation can be true.'

'And then again, it can be untrue. And if the prosecuting counsel who makes it also happens to be the judge and jury, which is how MI5's regarded, it's particularly dangerous. I just thought it was interesting they didn't think they had to prove things.'

Finlay sounded a bit downcast at the scepticism displayed by Fathers, who did not relent. 'It could be just one man's view,' he

178

said as he finished his lasagne and pushed his plate to one side. 'And one man who's long retired at that. It doesn't necessarily reflect MI5's view as a whole. I think I'm going to have some of that cheesecake.'

'I'll join you. You've made me hungry.'

'What about the diet?' Fathers said, turning to catch the waiter's eye.

'Sod the diet.' When the waiter had taken their order, Finlay said, 'OK, look, I'll give you a third chance.'

'A third chance at what?'

'At understanding.' Finlay flicked through the marked pages, found the right one, turned the book so Fathers could read it and tapped a large forefinger authoritatively on the page about three-quarters of the way down. 'Read from there to the bottom,' he instructed.

Fathers did as he was told. 'Dramatic moment,' he said.

'Right,' said Finlay. 'Philby's defected – disappeared from Beirut. But it's not just that. It's the realisation he must've been tipped off. Now they know there was another traitor – as well as Philby, Burgess and McLean. And, when they nailed Blunt the following year, they knew it wasn't him either. When Philby did a runner, the investigation started which finally convinced about half of MI5 that Hollis was the other traitor.'

'He was Director-General at the time, wasn't he?'

'That's right. And the other half thought it was Mitchell, who used to be his deputy. Dramatic moment, indeed, with a key question: who tipped off Philby? Gripping stuff.'

'So what's your point?'

'Now read this bit.' Finlay turned back to the page before and tapped the beginning of its last paragraph as the waiter returned with their cheesecake. 'From there, over the page, to the end of the next paragraph.'

When Fathers had finished his set reading he immediately went through it again. Finlay ate while he waited. Fathers looked up in puzzlement. 'But that's ridiculous,' he said. 'MI5 and MI6 tipped Philby off. This bloke Elliott they sent out to interview him, offer immunity and get a confession. He told Philby it was known he was a Russian spy. Then a few days later Philby defects.'

'Exactly,' said Finlay with satisfaction. 'And on that basis, seeking the answer to a question they already knew, these twerps in MI5 spend the next twenty years arguing that their boss was a Soviet mole. Staggering, isn't it? No self-respecting spy-novelist would dare offer such a flimsy plot.'

'Everything revolves around that question, does it?'

'Well, that's what began the mole-hunt. There's some writers who regard it as definitive proof there was a fifth man – that's why you gotta watch out with these so-called non-fiction spy books. The hunt produced a lot of circumstantial evidence against Hollis. Every bit of it has an innocent explanation, as far as I can see, but they stitched it all together and reckoned it proved he was the fifth man. The most important thing, which both the anti-Hollis and anti-Mitchell camps agree on, is that everybody inside MI5 who looked at the evidence believed there'd been a high-level traitor. How else to explain why so many operations fouled up?'

Fathers munched his cheesecake in silence. When he'd finished, he pulled out a cigar and lit up. 'How else, then?' he asked.

'Try incompetence. Seems to be the one hypothesis nobody ever tested.' Finlay got out his pipe, cleaned and filled it, and lit up in turn. 'Have you heard the expression a wilderness of mirrors?' he asked. Fathers shook his head. 'It's the title of a book about spies and suchlike, but it was coined by a bloke called Angleton to describe the world he moved in. James Jesus Angleton – he was head of counter-espionage for the CIA in the sixties and seventies. You heard of him?'

'No.'

'Died last year. He virtually tore the CIA apart with hunting for moles and traitors. There was this KGB defector, Golitsin, who said both the British and American intelligence services were penetrated by the Soviets at the very top level. Angleton believed him, cast doubts on the loyalty of anybody – including a couple of other defectors – who produced facts which contradicted Golitsin and did what the MI5 investigators did with Hollis, but on a much bigger scale. Constructed a series of circumstantial cases against various people.'

'Wilderness of mirrors,' Fathers reflected. 'Nothing is what it seems.'

'Exactly. Here's a defector. Is he fake or real? His information seems OK where it can be checked. Here's another. His information seems solid too, but, oops, now he's gone and contradicted the first one. How d'you choose between them if one says so-and-so's a spy and t'other says he ain't? Unless you find actual spying equipment – cameras, code-books, you know – all the evidence is circumstantial. Even if it's strong, you can't put the spy on trial 'cause you can't let the defector testify.'

'To protect him.'

'And because the defence counsel'd probably tear him to shreds. Apparently there's this thing called defector's syndrome. Once they've said everything they know, they're useless. To stay off the scrap-heap, they start to embroider and invent so they can still be the centre of attention.'

'We get witnesses like that. They give good QCs a field day.'

'Right, so you never know who or what to believe or trust. Guess what happened to Angleton.'

Fathers shrugged. 'At a guess, he was named as a mole himself.'

'Slightly more subtle than that, but essentially right,' said Finlay, approving his new student. 'Another CIA officer constructed a case against him on the basis that, if you wanted to disrupt the CIA, the best way to do it would be to go round hunting traitors, sowing dissension and demoralisation, having everybody look over their shoulders all the time. So he concluded Angleton was a KGB agent. It's not clear if this guy believed the case or not, but it was probably as convincing as most of what Angleton came up with. He got canned.'

'Angleton?'

'Yeah.'

'You seem to know a lot about this.'

'Well, it's a hot topic, isn't it? But it's also a case of know thine enemy. MI5 had me in for a little session a few months back.'

Fathers smiled inwardly. He knew for a fact that Finlay was on Special Branch's files, and F7 doubtless had one on him too. He wondered what the MI5 officers he'd interviewed might say or think if they knew he was in the company of a man one of their colleagues had interviewed – presumably as a security risk. 'What about?' he asked.

'Me and my loyalty. Honestly, what a prat the guy was who interviewed me. He asked me what I thought about this and that, and I referred him to my articles and books. He asked me what I'd been doing in Moscow earlier this year, and I told him it was none of his business.'

'What were you doing there?'

'Seminar on concepts for non-nuclear defence policies. They're very interested in that sort of thing.'

'So why didn't you tell him?'

'Why should I? What piss-worthy right does he have? Anyway, he probably knew perfectly well what I was there for, if he knew I was there at all. It was actually reported in the press in Moscow.'

'Was that it?'

'Oh no, we danced round the mulberry bush for ages. He turned all clever and super subtle and asked me if I didn't think all this *glasnost* and democratisation business is just marvellous. But I disappointed him by saying that *perestroika* still has a fragile social and political base and that, though it's very hopeful, I needed some convincing before I'd regard it as irreversible. Mentioned a few wicked things the KGB's done this year and generally refused to behave according to his stereotype. So then he said that I surely approved of Gorbachev's new diplomacy. I think that was meant to be the real clincher, the trap I couldn't avoid falling into. I gave him a long disquisition on Soviet arms control policy in the past three years, largely approving it, of course, but I think I used enough long words, acronyms and general jargon to baffle him. Threw in some learned comments about the problems Gorbachev faces and generally muddied his waters. Then I gave him the schedule for my graduate seminar series on Soviet foreign policy and suggested he come along if he was interested. Haven't seen him there though. Shame. I'd like to introduce him to my students. But I expect he's not quite so dumb he doesn't know that.'

Fathers smiled. He half sympathised with the man who'd interviewed Finlay. He'd done it once himself and got nowhere. Finlay had quite obviously regarded the session as an enjoyable sparring match and was a nimble and wholly unyielding opponent.

'They really do seem to be quite stupid,' Finlay said. 'Find it impossible to realise that just because I think our so-called defence policy is immoral, dangerous and intellectually shallow that I'm not therefore on the side of the Soviets. They don't seem to notice that I think and say similar things about Soviet policy.'

'No,' said Fathers, 'that's just good cover.'

'Yeah, I suppose so, in the wilderness of mirrors. But they are dumb, you know. It's like that incident when a woman wrote to Reagan after he'd had Libya bombed, calling him a senile fool, or something. Next thing, a couple of Special Branch officers turned up to check her out. Or that report a while back, about how Soviet special forces – the Spetsnatz – had infiltrated the Greenham Common peace camp. What a lot of bullshit. Stupidest place for Soviet spies to be would be freezing their toes off in a continually evicted peace camp right outside a military base where they're under the constant eyes of the police. Unless they're as stupid as MI5. Which is possible I suppose.'

Fathers was silent. He checked his watch and turned to summon the waiter. It was the manager who responded. 'Bill, please,' Fathers said.

'Compliments of the house,' the manager said. 'I insist. You have rendered more than usual service this last day.'

Fathers shrugged and Finlay mentioned something about police corruption.

'Don't see you grabbing your wallet,' Fathers responded.

As they left the bistro, Finlay said, 'I don't suppose you ever discovered the full truth about Michael?'

Michael Sampson, a former colleague of Finlay's, was the man whose disappearance Fathers had gone to New York to investigate four years ago.

'No, never heard another word about it.'

'Poor bastard. Serious side to these things. Makes the stupidity more worrying.' Finlay stood for a moment in silence. 'Well, it was nice seeing you again after all this time. If you ever want some more instruction about spying or whatever – including anything to do with the real world – don't hesitate.'

They shook hands and went their separate ways.

Chapter 29

Fathers walked through the cold, clear night, feeling the skin prickle on the back of his neck. He turned into a deserted street where there was a fruit and vegetable market during the day. The shop windows were dark, the occasional street-lamps cast mean pools of light to show the oceans of rubbish on the pavements – rotting produce, newspapers, cartons, wrapping paper, cigarette packets. He stepped out into the relatively litterless road and lengthened his stride.

The man who was following was good at his job. He moved carefully through the rubbish, quickening his pace as Fathers did so, staying on the pavement where the shadow was deeper. He saw Fathers turn down a small street to the right, ran quietly and cautiously till he got to the opening, paused to read the name on the street sign and pulled out his short-wave radio. 'He's going down Waldorf Street,' he said. 'You stay on him when he comes out. I'll take the motor.'

'Roger,' said the back-up man in the car. 'The girl's about fifty yards back on you and Pete about as far back again.'

The man acknowledged the information and shoved the radio back in his pocket. Following Fathers while the woman back-tailed him and was followed in her turn was the routine of the last couple of days, unbroken except very late at night and, oddly enough, that afternoon. He entered the narrow street, keeping to the edge. It was barely lit, but he could just see the tall figure, now eighty yards or more ahead of him. He decided to close the gap and speeded up a little. Although his partner would take up the job when the target emerged at the other end, he didn't want to risk losing the trail here, just in case there was another way out.

Suddenly he realised that Fathers' silhouette was getting bigger too quickly. The gap should not have been closing so fast. He stopped, but the figure kept getting bigger. In the poor light it took him a second to realise that Fathers had turned and was coming back his way. He pressed back into the shadow of the wall. He couldn't pretend just to be out for a late night stroll, keeping on his way and looking unconcerned, because Fathers knew he was being tailed. Twenty yards back was a break in the buildings which lined the street – a small derelict area, where a building had been burned or pulled down, probably used for parking. He could hide there, alerting his back-up once Fathers had passed. Flattening himself against the wall, keeping his eye on the target, he edged back into sanctuary.

'You joinin' me then?' said a voice. The man who was following Fathers jumped. Dammit, he thought, a tramp. But as he whirled round, he saw it was not. Facing him in an aggressive half-crouch was somebody wearing a leather jacket that was new enough to shine even in that dim light. He heard running footsteps and over his shoulder saw Fathers appear at the edge of the patch of rough ground. He looked from one to the other and his heart pounded. They were going to try to take him.

Fathers was a pretty good size. The other one looked around five inches shorter and about thirty pounds lighter. He pulled out the cosh from his pocket, tensed and made a dart at the smaller man.

Fathers let Yarrow get on with the job. It was his first opportunity to see his skipper in a fight, but afterwards he was unable to give a clear account of what happened. Yarrow appeared hardly to move out of the way of the attack and seemed to do little more than flick an arm out rather vaguely, yet he ended up with the cosh in his hand, while his assailant sprawled to the ground.

He tossed the weapon casually to Fathers and moved in closer to the man as he got to his knees. The man attempted to launch himself at Yarrow and butt him in the stomach. Yarrow swayed aside and appeared to use the edge of his fist as a hammer on the man's head, then sprang after him and got a hand to his throat. He held him out at arm's length. When Yarrow let him go, the man collapsed, his breath rasping. Yarrow knelt beside him for a moment and when he stood up the man was unconscious.

Fathers and Yarrow pulled the inert body fully on to the derelict patch. They could hear footsteps. Cathy Gordon walked past without giving them a glance. They waited in the shadows for the second man to appear. As he passed the rough ground, they moved out, Fathers in front of him, Yarrow behind. The man turned, saw Yarrow and made the same mistake as his colleague. He was stopped by a lunge-punch to his solar plexus, staggered gasping for air and fell as his legs were swept from under him. Fathers saw Yarrow feel for the pressure points with his thumbs.

Cathy Gordon reappeared behind Fathers. 'He's an impressive

little chap, isn't he?' she said, her voice high with tension.

'Not so much of the little, missus,' Yarrow said. 'Wherever these two come from, they didn't get a lot of training.'

Cathy smiled, pulled a radio from her bag and muttered into it. Pardoner's voice crackled back saying he'd be with them in a few minutes. They waited impatiently, stamping their feet in the cold. A van pulled up beside them and Pardoner got out. 'Number Three's in the back,' he said. 'No problems?'

'None,' Fathers affirmed as he helped the others drag their prey to the van. 'And you?'

'No. He was standing by his car, waiting for you in a nice quiet little street, so I clobbered him. What now?'

'I had a word with Herd. You and Yarrer can store them in his nick. He'll book 'em for something and handle the paperwork so they go in under his name. Cathy's going to park their car in a multi-storey and lose the keys somewhere. See you in the morning. And thanks.'

It's a long time since we've done that,' Sarah remarked as she switched the television off.

'Done what?' asked Fathers. He was sitting in his favourite armchair, leg hooked over the side, sipping a whisky and puffing on his cigar. Whoever had been tailing him, they were safely tucked away in three police cells. He'd see them tomorrow. No point in yet another late night when there was no need, and he was so behind on sleep and rest.

'Watched the evening news together,' Sarah replied. She was lounging on the sofa, shoes off and feet up, an empty wine glass on the table beside her. 'It's a long time since we've done anything together.'

'I've been very busy,' he said, skirting the real issue, yet also going to the heart of the matter. 'Worse than usual.'

'Will it ease now you've hit the headlines? You looked pretty good, considering how little sleep you're getting.' Among the items they'd watched on the news was one about Fathers's swoop the night before, complete with meaningless snatch of a short interview with him.

'It should do, but you know how it is. No sooner get one thing off your plate than another gets dumped on it.'

'I do know how it is,' Sarah agreed. She sighed. 'Tell me, how long do you reckon you can keep it up at this pace? I mean, you're pretty fit, even though you still smoke. You take the odd drink, but mostly not too much. You don't get enough exercise, but you're not entirely deskbound. You don't eat as well as you ought to, but not as badly as you might. But the weight of this job, Harry, how long can you go on taking it without something cracking? Heart, ulcer, something.'

'You make me sound like an old man.'

'No, but not as young as you were, yet still going as fast – no, even faster than you used to. And if you can take it at this pace indefinitely, how long do you think I can?'

'I've thought about that a lot,' he said. She looked sceptical. 'No, I really have, especially in the last couple of weeks. What's happening between us – or what's not happening more like – it's not what I want, Sarah, it's nothing like what I want.'

'What do you want?' she challenged. 'What's your vision of our life together – of what you'd like it to be? And how does it match with what we've got right now?' She stood up. 'Do you want another drink?' He shook his head. She got the wine bottle from the sideboard and poured herself another glass.

As she sat down, she said, 'It's something I ask myself too. And look, the way you are . . . I mean, you say you've thought about it, but if I were to judge by your actions I'd come to the conclusion that what you want is something I just can't survive. That you want to commit everything to your work and, if there's any leftovers on your plate, chuck me and the kids the scraps. And it's not enough.'

She took a sip of wine. 'I've always had my eyes open,' she said. 'You were, I think, as fair and as accurate as you possibly could be when we were getting set to get married. Do you remember? You told me all about how long your hours were, and unpredictable. You told me not to expect much of a social life, because our plans would keep on being disrupted at the last minute. You said that when we had children I'd have the major responsibility, that you couldn't be around enough, that I'd have to accept giving up my job.'

Sarah gestured vaguely with her glass. 'If my eyes hadn't been open already, they were by the time you got through. So I've never felt you conned me. Even when it's been hard, I've thought, you know, this is pretty much what he promised me. It's what I signed on for. But it's all gone over the top this last year or so. Not just the past few weeks, though they've been particularly bad. For Christ's sake, even the summer holiday, you arrived late and left early because of the bloody job. How d'you think it feels to be on the receiving end of that?'

Fathers shook his head.

'So anyway, after all that, I've got to ask myself, is this what he wants? Is this it?'

Fathers shook his head again. If only there weren't so many other things going through his mind right now, if only he weren't so tired, didn't have three people who'd been following him to think about, a response to his Crow report to wait for, a gangland investigation to run – and if only he didn't have his suspicions about Sarah.

'We've had good times,' he said at last, 'when I think you've been happy and we've been closer. And in among them we've had extraordinary moments of closeness. That's what I want. I've no big complicated vision to give you. I just want us to be close and happy.'

'Not that you give yourself a chance for it to be like that. Or me.'

Fathers held his temper. 'Look, a couple of weeks ago I got landed with something and told to get on with it as well as my usual stuff — '

'Which is already more than enough,' Sarah cut in.

'And it turned out to be more than I could've anticipated. Partly because it came at the same time as this whole gang thing boiled up. Now, I think – I hope – I'm getting to the end of it. And maybe I can take a breath and recover some energy and we can start again. Whatever happens, Sarah, I don't want to lose you.'

She looked at him for a time. 'I don't want to lose you either,' she said. To Fathers's ear she sounded dreadfully calm as she contemplated that prospect – but, then, that was how he sounded to her. 'I'm just hoping I haven't already.'

Fathers uncoiled himself, rose and sat on the sofa with her. She took his hand. Part of him wanted to confess his suspicions about her – to say, 'And I've been scared that I had lost you.' But he couldn't find the words before she spoke again.

'The thing is,' she said, 'it's not just about your time and energy and how you portion it out. It's about you, too, how you are.' She stroked his hand as she talked. 'We don't talk much in this sort of way, even when you have more time for me. We don't sort of characterise ourselves to each other. Maybe we don't need to. But – well, I don't know how you see yourself, but, thinking it through, I've realised one thing. In the past three or four years you've been getting harder. It's what you see in an ordinary day, what you come into contact with. Maybe it's only odd that it's taken so long to get to you. But you hardly ever talk about the job in the way you used to. There's no excitement in you nowadays. Just a sort of grim satisfaction when you break a case. And in the last few weeks I've never known you so – so held in about everything. You've had to develop a thick skin,

188

but it's started to grow inwards. It's working in and getting to your bones.'

The soft touch of her fingers eased the impact of her words, but didn't eliminate it. 'The man I married was a young, ambitious detective who cared about his job, thought it was important and, whatever filth he saw around him, including among his colleagues, thought that being a police officer was in fact a way of caring. He thought the job was important because he had a sense of justice. And he was ready to argue that case against anybody who confronted him with evidence of police corruption, bias against blacks, a whole series of imperfections. And against any policeman who came up with the usual cynical stuff and damned the public.'

She smiled at him sadly. 'The man I'm married to now never has such thoughts. He just gets on with it. He could still step back and say, yes, what I do is important to society. People need the police and need them to meet certain standards which I try to live up to. But he doesn't. I'm sure he still has those ethics somewhere, but they're getting pretty dusty now. He's almost indistinguishable from any other police officer. Except that he's cleverer than most and more successful. And that's what counts for him now. Not why he does the job, but how well, which he measures just like everybody else – cases cleared, where he's streets ahead. But back here at home, where his shirts still get ironed, his clothes laundered, his food bought and cooked – back here your clear-up rate is not enough.'

Fathers' thought was locked in icy paralysis. He sought a way to respond. None came easily. He took his hand out of hers. It was a long time before he said quietly, 'How well you know me. Without me telling you.'

'Oh, Harry,' Sarah said contritely, taking his hand back, 'you're exhausted. We should be toasting your triumph with champagne.'

He shrugged and shook his head. His successes of the last night and day had taken on a sour taste. Was too much bought by dubious means? he wondered, thinking about Queen and the fit-up, Yarrow manipulating his informants, letting Barker off the Hammersmith robbery charges.

'I should have picked a better time,' Sarah said, 'to let this all out. A more appropriate moment. But there are so few moments it's hard to find the right one.' She sat up to put her arms around his neck and pull his face to hers. 'The hardest thing is beginning again,' she said. 'But we can do it. Don't say anything now. Don't make promises. There's no — ' She might have said there was no point; instead she said, 'No need', and felt better, but uncertain. 'And

– oh, I don't know – all I want to say is, whatever you do, don't just hang your head, then shake yourself in that way you have and lose yourself in your work to get over it. Come to bed with me now. I don't want to make love. I want us to hold each other. Tell me with your body that you won't lose yourself. Won't lose your way.'

He put his arms round her. He still had no words to give her.

PART VII

Crow's Carrion

Chapter 30

Fathers started Friday slowly. He slept late, woke feeling rested for once, and went downstairs to have breakfast with Sarah and the children. When they'd gone to work and school – Sarah leaving him with a hug and murmured words of reassurance and affection – he took a long bath. As he lay there he wondered whether he ought to tell Sarah about his suspicions, to clear the air in the way she had cleared it last night. And he pondered his own passivity. It was she who initiated the catharsis of speaking it out, he who just sat and listened. But for him to respond to that by saying he thought – or had thought – she was having or had had an affair: it wasn't what she was looking for, it wasn't what last night was about. He rubbed the idea from his conscious mind.

When he arrived at the Yard just before ten, Pardoner followed him into his office. 'I've run the names through Crim Rec for you,' the DI said. 'Nothing there.'

'No surprise that,' Fathers replied. 'It tells me they're not from any of the mobs we've been dealing with – but I didn't think they were anyway.'

'It's to do with this MI5 thing then, is it?'

Fathers blew out a long breath and nodded. He hesitated over what to do next, then callously remembered Bastin's dictum that people who do you favours should be asked for more. Pardoner had been outraged when he'd learned somebody was daring to tail his boss all over London and, like the others, had brushed aside all warnings that they might be getting into something serious and didn't have to help – that this was a request, not an order. Fathers had finally stopped apologising for illicitly involving other officers in something he could not explain to them.

'Find out as much as you can about who they are, will you?' he asked.

'My pleasure.'

Fathers went to visit his three prisoners. Apart from insisting on their right to make a phone call, none of them would say anything.

He finished each interview with the remark that the charges were being changed to offences under the Prevention of Terrorism Act which meant he could hold them longer for questioning. He thought he saw a tremor of anxiety cross the face of the one who'd been following Cathy Gordon, but the threat didn't make any of them willing to talk.

Herd wanted to know what he was up to. Fathers lightly replied that he wasn't quite sure and would Herd mind holding the three until further notice? Herd replied he was happy to help. So many people are, Fathers thought as he returned to the Yard where he found a message asking him to call Hanson. He did so eagerly.

'I had three reasons for seeking a brief word with you,' Hanson said. 'Number one, congratulations on Wednesday night's show, which has not gone unnoticed, as I am sure you are already aware.'

'Thank you,' Fathers said.

'Number two, a more thoughtful and co-operative frame of mind is now to be found in Manchester.'

'Thank you again. Thank you very much.'

'An emolliative letter is on its way to Detective Inspector Pardoner.'

'That's very good. He'll be most grateful.'

'Number three, on another matter, the situation is indeterminate.'

'Oh.'

'Your efforts have been registered with appreciation, but no further decision has yet been made.'

'Ah.'

'So I must simply require you stand in readiness.'

'Oh well, thanks again for the first two anyway.'

'They also serve, Mr Fathers, they also serve.'

'Maybe, but standing and waiting is not my line.'

No, thought Hanson as he hung up, it's not. But he was struck that Fathers had effortlessly recognised the reference, which was not what he'd expect from most policemen, and was evidently keen to continue the investigation he'd been so brutally reluctant to begin. He called in his secretary and dictated a memo to the Assistant Commissioner, stressing Fathers' fine qualities, ignoring his others.

An hour later, Fathers rang the doorbell of a semi-detached house in the south London suburbs. 'Mrs Valerie Howell?' he said when his ring was answered.

'Yes.'

'I'm Detective Chief Inspector Fathers. Here's my warrant card. Could I have a word with you?'

The woman nodded and stood aside to let Fathers in. Her voice shook as she asked if the visit was about Pete. Fathers agreed that it was. Peter Howell was the second man Yarrow had rendered unconscious the night before. It had not taken Pardoner many minutes to discover that he had a wife called Valerie and a single phone call – 'Sorry, wrong number' – had confirmed that she was at home. What he had not learned was that she had reached that stage of pregnancy when her belly looked as if it was about to burst.

She led Fathers into a small sitting-room. She was pale and anxious, making a visible effort to remain calm. 'Tell me the worst,' she said.

'He's all right,' Fathers said. He didn't take the seat she offered him. Now he'd discovered she was pregnant it was such an obvious lever to use on her husband that he wanted to be on his way.

'He didn't come back last night. Are you sure he's all right? Oh God, I've been half expecting something like this, but it would be just now. Where is he?'

'He's fine.'

'Yes but where – oh!' Valerie Howell gasped and gripped the arms of her chair.

Oh Christ, Fathers thought, she really is going to burst. Almost literally. He watched as she took some deep breaths and then relaxed. 'Are you getting contractions regularly?' he asked.

She nodded. 'Every ten minutes or so.'

'You should have a friend with you.'

'Pete,' she replied. 'It's him I want with me. Where is he?'

Fathers did not intend to tell her, but it was hard, because there are not many things which can be refused to a woman in labour, even its early stages. 'He's with us,' he said, as gently as he could, 'helping us.'

'Well, I know that,' she exploded. 'But where is he right now?'

'Look, we shouldn't be talking about this. Do you have a friend I can call? Or should I get the ambulance? I mean, is this for real? Are you due?'

'Two weeks,' she replied.

'You're two weeks late? My God.'

'No, early. What's the problem with Pete? Is he hurt or something?'

'No, he's fine, really.'

'But what is it? There's a number to call in an emergency, but they don't know anything – or wouldn't say. But you – you can see – you can't not tell me.'

Fathers's reply was forestalled by another contraction. He watched with a welling of memories as she did her breathing exercise again. 'That was less than ten minutes,' he said when she came out of the contraction, 'and it lasted longer than the one before. This is the real thing.'

She brushed his concern aside. 'What's going on?' she demanded.

'Some sort of discrepancy has arisen. It's just a routine inquiry. I don't know the details.'

'Don't flannel,' she said sharply. 'Look, why can't you – oh God, what's happening? I think I've . . . ' She stood up in confusion, holding her legs apart, looking behind her at the damp patch on the chair.

'I think that's your waters bursting,' Fathers said, sounding calmer than he felt. Valerie Howell started to laugh with relief. 'If you tell me where the bathroom is, I'll get some towels.'

She told him and he ran upstairs, grabbed an armful of towels from the airing cupboard and came down again as quickly. She called out that she was in the kitchen, where he found her standing on tiptoe in a pool of liquid. 'There's gallons of it,' she said helplessly.

'Not literally,' he said, handing her the towels. 'Where's the phone?'

She pointed and he made the 999 call as she dried herself. She told him which hospital she was going to and the name of the consultant. He passed the information on. She went through another contraction as he hung up. Then she decided to change into dry clothes. When she came back down, she was carrying an overnight bag and, as they waited for the ambulance in the sitting-room, she complained that the baby shouldn't be coming two weeks early.

'It's only the doctor thinks it's early,' he said. 'The baby probably thinks it's just about the right time.'

'But first babies are supposed to be late.'

'It's your first?'

'Yes.'

Holy shit, thought Fathers, the situations this job leads me into. Today, it's your chance to tell lies and be generally horrid to a first-time mum who's just about to produce. What was that Sarah said about a thick skin growing inwards? 'Well,' he said, 'this one's different then.'

'Yes,' she said proudly. 'Oh-oh, here we go again.'

He waited as she breathed her way through the contraction.

'That was worse,' she said. 'I think I'd better transfer up a level.'

'Don't do it too quickly,' Fathers advised. 'You don't want to change your breathing pattern too soon, or you'll have nothing left in reserve if it turns out to be a long labour.'

'Are you a father? You sound like one. What you know, I mean, not just your name.' She chuckled.

'Yes,' he said, 'two, but they're quite big now.'

'Still, you'll know what to do if I have it here on the floor.'

'The hell I will,' Fathers said. He thought back in panic to a decade ago, trying to recall what he'd been told to do if Sarah gave birth before the ambulance arrived. All he could remember was the importance of the placenta being expelled from the womb. If it didn't come out immediately, it would do as soon as the milk started flowing, so the baby should be put to the breast. He also recalled the glee with which the class had been told that, if the baby wouldn't suck, the man should do the sucking himself.

'It's too long ago,' he told her, mentally crossing his fingers. 'You just keep your legs crossed.'

She chuckled again, then turned serious. 'I want Pete,' she said.

'Of course,' he replied. 'As soon as you're on your way in the ambulance, I'll arrange things.'

'But where is he? What's the problem?'

'Oh, nothing. It'll be smoothed over. Nothing, really, I promise you.'

As she left with the ambulance men, she turned to him. 'You will send him to me, won't you?' she said.

'Of course I will,' he replied. But as he got into his car he added: As soon as I get his story – if I like it.

Chapter 31

'The surprise, I would have thought,' Fathers said tightly, 'is that MI5 should follow me while I'm investigating it.'

He had watched Hanson's eyes and mouth carefully as he passed on what Howell – with no choice but to co-operate – had told him. He was certain the Home Office man's astonishment was genuine. 'A moment for thought and consultation is indicated,' Hanson said, regaining his composure. 'I shall get back to you shortly.'

'Don't think for too long or consult too widely. Whoever's behind this may be the one I'm looking for.'

'And it would be unwise to alert him,' Hanson agreed, noting that Fathers had said 'I'm', not 'I was'. The detective obviously regarded himself as back on the case. There was a certain justice in that, and possibly not much could be done to stop him, judging by his tone. It lacked the frivolous rudeness he so often adopted; it was probably the voice in which he habitually gave orders.

Twenty minutes after Fathers got back to his office Hanson phoned and summoned him. But on his way he was intercepted. The door of an illegally parked black Jaguar swung open as he came up to it. He skirted it warily, wondering if he'd been a bit hasty in telling Cathy there was no more need for her to back-tail for him. 'Good afternoon, Mr Fathers,' an urbane voice called out. 'I think we might have a talk.'

Fathers bent down and looked in. 'Good afternoon, Sir Nigel,' he said.

The Chief Intelligence Co-ordinator commented that he didn't think they had previously met and congratulated Fathers on his homework. They drove around London for half an hour. The discussion was intense, especially when Fathers explained his intentions and conditions. In everything he said Sir Nigel Laker read an implicit threat. If he did not authorise Fathers to find out why he had been followed, the detective could continue to hold the Watchers he had salted away in some undiscoverable place and might well take further action on his own account. There was a rage just beneath the surface which, though it was under control right now, was also both unmistakable and irresistible.

'There has been considerable dissent,' Sir Nigel said, 'about the external nature of the Crow inquiry. I shall tell you directly that I was on the verge of finding another means to pursue it. But you – or, to begin with, they – have forced my hand.'

If that was how Sir Nigel Laker felt because of the action of somebody in the Security Service and Fathers' consequent fury, he now proved equally adept at forcing other people's hands. Hanson's assistance was swiftly provided. The objections of the Home Office Deputy Secretary responsible for MI5 were overridden. The Director-General was bullied into submission.

'At this time,' Sir Nigel said, 'I hardly feel you are in a strong position to object to anything. You cannot control your ex-employees and the government has had to step in at considerable financial and political expense in a loyal attempt to bail you out. Now it appears you have some trouble controlling your current staff. One palliative effort has already been made with the Staff Counsellor's appointment, but much more and an exercise with further reaching effects may be set in train. It is not for me to take the Prime Minister's name in vain, but I wonder if you expect a sympathetic audience in Downing Street for any representations you might choose to make.'

At three o'clock a messenger arrived at Fathers' office in Scotland Yard and gave him a bundle of sealed envelopes. Two were addressed to him. The others he would deliver later. The Chief Intelligence Co-ordinator instructed him to find out who had authorised surveillance on him, and why, and to identify and explore any link with the failure of Operation Crow. Hanson described the terms of Fathers' access to St James's Barracks and confirmed authority for several telephone taps and mail interceptions. Separately two letters arrived from the Assistant Commissioner. Fathers left the one to Austin unopened. In the one to him, the AC announced his understanding that Fathers was engaged on a security matter, gave him permission to avail himself of all assistance he required from any police station anywhere within the Metropolitan area, released him from other tasks and ordered that queries or objections from any quarter should be referred to the Police Department at the Home Office.

The preparations took some time. Fathers visited the Barracks to ensure the arrangements which had been made were fully understood and would work smoothly, and added a few instructions of his own.

He phoned several police stations to line up the necessary assistance and then called in Yarrow and Cathy Gordon. He gave them a list of addresses. 'Organise some warrants,' he said. 'Be ready to roll these places over when I tell you. Really give them the works – top to bottom – rip them apart. Take your time. The one I've starred needs to be done tonight. The rest you can do over the weekend and early next week, but once you get going on them, do it all as fast as possible.'

'What offence?' Cathy asked.

'Secrets, Section One.'

'And what're we looking for?' Yarrow wanted to know.

'Anything hidden,' Fathers replied. 'And it may be well hidden. Don't just look *at* things, look *in* them. And anything odd. List everything. I'll tell you after if you found it.'

'Are these addresses occupied?' Cathy said. 'By somebody other than the suspect, I mean.'

'Except the starred one, yes. Be nice to them, but don't let them get in the way.'

'OK,' said Cathy, 'all clear. Anything else?'

'If you would. Something that is above and beyond the call of duty. But I'm sure you'll handle it.'

'What is it?'

'Take my kids out for a hamburger this evening.'

'Can I come too?' Yarrow asked.

So while Gary and Samantha were treated to junk food by two detective sergeants, Fathers collected Sarah from the library where she worked. They talked at their kitchen table. She was once again contrite about the night before – about her bad timing, and about saying it all more harshly than she meant.

He brushed that aside. 'You had to say it,' he said firmly, 'and you had to say it then. Getting the timing right is impossible when there's no time. Like now, for instance. I'm going to get a call in a few minutes and I won't be able to tell them to wait a bit. I'm in the middle of something I can't control and I have to see it through. What I said last night – that maybe I was coming to the end of it – has turned out to be about as wrong as it could be. So if you hadn't said it last night, God knows when you would've.'

Indeed, he told her, if she hadn't said it, he might not have thought to take the time to be sitting with her now, warning her that he would be away for days and nights on end. That he could not explain why without involving her – 'contaminating' was what he thought, 'involving' was what he said.

200

'I can't ask you to forgive me,' he said, 'because it's unforgivable. Any bloody time but this. I don't want to leave what we talked about yesterday where it stands. I suppose I want you to accept, and to' – he found the word hard to say – 'trust me, to take a deep emotional breath and wait for me to come back to you.'

'You will come back to me?' she said. And then she said it again without the questioning intonation. He put out his hands to her and she stood up, walked round the kitchen table, leaned over him as he sat in his chair and hugged him.

Two minutes later the phone rang. Fathers answered, listened and said, 'On my way.' He kissed Sarah goodbye and left her.

Chapter 32

It had been early on the Friday morning that Neil Deakin received a phone call from John Platt. Deakin could hear the alarm, but he did not feel the cold hand of his own anxiety until after he'd called Austin. Or, rather, until after Austin had called him back to say that an hour spent phoning round had elicited no information on the Watchers' whereabouts.

'Why the hell did you do it?' Austin demanded. 'No copper'd let himself be dogged around on his own patch for long. Asking for trouble.'

Afterwards, when Deakin had to explain his motives to Fathers, he reflected that it was simply standard operating procedure, almost an instinctive reflex. If you want to know about somebody, watch them. In addition, since Fathers was fundamentally unsound – as the withdrawn file on the 1984 New York investigation revealed – it was possible he'd do something which would add evidence to the case against him and his inquiry.

Deakin had had some difficulty persuading Platt to go along with it; the head of A4 eventually agreed only because of a history of favours traded and helpful short-cuts offered over the more than thirty years since they'd been together in the same intake. And his agreement was conditional on receiving written authorisation, though he didn't insist it go first to the Security Service Directorate for approval.

Platt's reluctance decided Deakin against even asking against Goreham, the head of A2, for phone intercepts. He didn't know Goreham as well as Platt and had often found the untidy little man an irritating, obstructive pest, forever complaining about inadequate resources and challenging the need for fuller surveillance. Had it not been for that, Deakin would have found a way round the restrictions that required authorisation from the Home Secretary so he could have had Fathers' various phones tapped as well.

All along, Deakin's strategy was damage limitation. From the beginning he'd smelled the danger of bias in the choice of Fathers to investigate what he insisted on calling the breakdown rather than failure of Operation Crow. His own interview, plus what McKellen and Thomas reported from theirs, convinced him the detective had already decided that the problem was a leak in MI5. Armed with that presumption, Fathers could do a lot of damage. When Deakin learned from Austin how quickly the interviews with Special Branch were being done, that fitted the pattern: Fathers was getting what he had decided were irrelevancies out of the way first, the better to concentrate on what he obviously regarded as the only real object of his investigation. When news came from Platt that every Watcher who'd ever followed Brown was being questioned and, when it became clear that Fathers was calling in the whole of K2, Deakin realised the net was being cast much wider than he had first feared.

So he felt fully justified in his initial wariness and the decision to put the shutters up round Lucy, to keep Kelvin Hay – Lucy's control – to one side. When Fathers went directly after Lucy, Deakin went to the Director-General, who backed his refusal to let Fathers in on the source, and prevailed on the Co-ordinator to see it the same way.

Heartened by that tactical victory, Deakin began to draft his counter-report. He also had Kelvin Hay insert an emergency request for information into Lucy's next set of instructions. He wanted to know about any aftermath to Scherchinskiy's abortive outing to Hampstead. Fathers himself put the idea into Deakin's mind by harping on about the need to ask Lucy exactly this question. He resisted it instinctively, then saw how it could be turned to his advantage, as long as Fathers didn't know about it. There was a possibility Lucy would turn up something to discredit or marginalise Fathers's work.

He kept all this to himself. Platt, of course, guessed what he was up to but said nothing. McKellen he no longer trusted. The head of K2 obviously preferred to keep his head down and hope the fire would clear sooner or later. It seemed he could not see or did not care that the Service was under direct attack and had to be defended. Thomas, on the other hand, was evidently eager to help, but that wasn't necessary and he couldn't be asked to take risks he did not wholly understand.

In the week after Crow's breakdown, Deakin set the different elements of his strategy going and waited. At first there were no results. Fathers was followed to and from his normal and temporary offices, his home, various pubs and other places. He was followed to Windsor Court in Hampstead. Do him credit, Deakin thought, he's putting up a good show of going through the motions. But his inquiry was to take only two weeks, and that was how much time there was for him to make some sort of useful mistake.

Deakin became a little impatient. He cast around for other possibilities and decided on a honey-trap, using a woman who found occasional employment in the dark side of recruitment efforts by K5. But she found it next to impossible to get close to Fathers. The one time she managed it, it was at the very end – he was with colleagues in a crowded pub and evinced a total lack of interest. By then, however, there'd been a small break. Fathers met Austin and exchanged a few words with him. Deakin decided not to ask Austin what was said, partly because the man complained every time he phoned, but mostly because Austin's team was the target of his counter-report. But even without the extra detail it was clear evidence that Fathers was unsound and had no regard for secure procedure; in itself, it justified putting the Watchers on him.

The fact that Fathers spotted his followers at some point and put a back-tail on them did not worry Deakin unduly, as long as their origin was not discovered. Indeed, since the woman who was doing the back-tailing was quickly identified as a detective sergeant in Fathers' squad, her activity simply confirmed that he was indiscreet and unreliable.

The best break, however, came the day after Fathers delivered his report and Deakin sent his in. Fathers not only met but had lunch with a left-wing academic whose file was heavily flagged by F7, a man who had actually been called in for questioning earlier that year, not in order to learn anything but to give him a scare. Deakin's report did not mention the surveillance he had placed on Fathers, nor the incidents it had unearthed. They would come in handy to defend himself when, as he expected, the Chief Intelligence Co-ordinator took issue with him, not on the grounds of what was in his report but on the grounds of insubordination. They were his justification for ignoring orders and taking things into his own hands.

So that Thursday, the first day of December, two weeks and two days after the black night in Hampstead, Deakin was congratulating himself on the whole business. True, though Lucy had acknowledged the emergency request, no information had yet come back. If it did, that would be a bonus. But even without it, he had enough to sink Fathers and his report with him, as well as ward off any attacks on himself.

And then it unravelled. Fathers took counter-action. Disaster loomed. Deakin could do nothing to avert it. He did not consider trying to evade it. Fathers could probably mobilise enough resources

204

to pick him up wherever he went. He could only wait for the blow to fall.

The brusque knock on the door of the flat where he had lived alone since his divorce twelve years ago came just after eight o'clock on the Friday evening. When he opened the door, Fathers swept in, accompanied by two men in plain clothes. One of them Deakin noticed, even as he braced himself, had untidy blond hair and eyes which were busy taking in every detail of the apartment as if it were a tasty meal he was about to consume. This was one of Fathers' ferrets. Two uniformed constables waited at the door as Fathers gave Deakin an envelope and curtly instructed him, 'Read that.'

It was a letter from the Director-General suspending him from duty until further notice, barring him from his office except in the company or with the permission of DCI Fathers whose every instruction was to be followed and question answered to the full, and threatening unnamed consequences if he failed to comply.

'It appears I'm in your hands,' Deakin said quietly.

'Indeed you are.'

He was taken to St James's Barracks where his shoes, jacket, tie, braces, watch and the contents of his trouser pockets were taken away from him. He was put in a small, white, windowless room, lit by a bright, bare bulb. There was a rudimentary bed in the corner. 'Get some sleep,' Fathers said. 'We start first thing in the morning.'

Deakin lay down but couldn't sleep. His mind raced and his eyes were attacked by the light which was left on all night. In the next cell, though he didn't know it, Gerald Thomas received the same treatment. By midnight Fathers had also called on McKellen and Naseby, and on Austin whose letter was signed by the Assistant Commissioner. But those three – still in the second rank of Fathers' modified hierarchy of suspicion – were, like Platt, allowed to stay the night in their own homes in the company of uniformed officers until he wanted them.

Fathers began with Deakin at seven the next morning. The K Branch Director looked tired and anxious, as he had every right to be. Two tape recorders with microphones sat on the table. Alongside Fathers was a man from Sir Nigel Laker's office, Waverley, on secondment from MI6. His presence was to drive home the message that there must be no deviation from total co-operation with Fathers. He looked with concern at the head of counter-espionage, but a glance at Fathers made him think better of suggesting the victim be allowed breakfast, a shave and change of clothes.

Fathers was used to questioning people for whom he had no sympathy. He had plenty of experience of dealing with individuals he found repulsive and evil. But he had only rarely questioned anybody for whom he felt a genuine dislike rather than distaste and, until Deakin, never anybody against whom he had a personal grievance. He shocked himself by his keen sense of anticipation as he approached the interrogation. He was relying on fatigue to combine with Deakin's sudden decline from eminence to powerlessness, to speed up the disorientation which would bring out a confession. He built on that with a calculated unpredictability. Some of his sessions with Deakin were long, covering the same ground time and again. Others were short – two questions and a curt dismissal. He alternated politeness with crude bluster. He jumped backwards and forwards in time as he questioned Deakin on the details of Operation Crow and its background.

As a further element of disorientation, Fathers played with time. There was a clock on the wall behind him in the interrogation room. He constantly had it altered. When Deakin had been back in his cell for an hour, the clock would tell him on his return that he had been away two hours, or thirty minutes. Like the cell, the interrogation room had no windows. Fathers would let Deakin sleep for an hour and make it seem like six, or for six and make it seem like one. The middle of the afternoon became the middle of the night or early morning.

Waverley protested at the technique one time when Deakin had been sent back to his cell. 'If you don't like it,' Fathers snapped, 'go and do something useful. Like make the tea.' But later he understood why Waverley had objected.

Fathers kept it going for nine days – two weekends and the week in between. But half way through he eased the pressure. On the fifth night – at a point when, having just eaten lunch, Deakin thought it was about two o'clock in the afternoon – he was allowed home. He walked into his flat to find it had been searched. No effort had been made to tidy the place up after it had been ripped apart. Two constables were waiting for him. They told him they would stay the night. They allowed him no privacy. When he went to the bathroom they insisted the door remain open. He discovered his medicine cabinet had been emptied. When he went to the kitchen he saw that all the sharp knives had been removed. Next morning at six they woke him, made a quick breakfast and took him back to the barracks.

He was shown into a new room. It had a window overlooking the park. There was a table, chair, pen and a pile of paper.

'Write,' Fathers said.

'Write what?'

'Everything.'

That afternoon, Fathers read what Deakin had written. 'You still don't understand, do you?' he said when he'd finished. 'I count six evasions, two downright lies and a handful of half-truths. Start again.'

Next morning, after a night Deakin had again spent in his own flat, Fathers told him he'd done better at his second attempt and instructed him to write a résumé of his entire career in MI5.

Between sessions with Deakin, Fathers questioned the others. Thomas got the roughest treatment but in the end he convinced Fathers, as he had Deakin, that he'd not talked to anybody about Crow at the critical time. The others went through a slightly gentler mill, though they all had to write out complete accounts of everything they knew about Crow, its conduct and aftermath. Austin and Platt also had to describe their careers and every contact they'd ever had with Deakin. Kelvin Hay was finally brought within the scope of the inquiry, questioned in detail like all the others, and wrung dry.

At the end of each day, a specially provided team of audio-typists transcribed the tapes. Between the different oral and written accounts, Fathers sought nuances of discrepancy which he hurled back at his victims, or slipped into interviews to trip them up, shatter their certainties, break them down. Meanwhile, across the weekend and in the first two days of the following week, Cathy Gordon and Yarrow orchestrated the ungentle and extremely thorough searching of everybody's homes. They all had families and had to explain as best they could to distraught wives and children what the hell was going on as clothes and possessions were dumped on the floor, electrical equipment was disconnected and its innards examined, carpets were rolled aside and floorboards ripped up, sniffer dogs roamed through gardens, correspondence, diaries and financial records were impounded.

None of the people into whose lives Fathers strewed this wreckage had any reality for him except as objects in his investigation. His determination was unqualified and his energy unremitting. He became the kind of policeman Sarah was anxious he was becoming – but to an extent beyond anything she could have feared.

In the course of it, as he learned more about Crow and the

sources, he found new needs for information and asked Sir Nigel Laker to ask some questions for him of people over whom his authority did not reach. He also changed his mind about how to deal with Joseph Perry, the magistrate.

At the end of it all, he was confident he knew everything there was to know about Operation Crow and why he had been followed. In fact, his conclusions were taking shape long before the end. But ever obedient to the rule of not allowing conclusions to leave logic to its own devices, he kept the process going, challenging himself to use the victims of his inquiry to prove himself wrong.

Chapter 33

Tuesday brought a distraction. That lunchtime, by a round-about route, a message arrived from Bastin. Between bouts with Deakin and Thomas, Fathers phoned. 'I really think that, if it's at all possible, you should get yourself round here this afternoon,' Bastin told him. 'Your new boss is somewhat eager to meet you.'

'Shit,' Fathers said. 'Myers. I'd forgotten all about him.'

'He takes over next week but he's a real eager beaver. Nosing around all over the place. Seems to be a bit impatient that half his complement of DCI's has disappeared.'

'Well, tough shit. I'm busy. Have you told him that?'

'Yes, of course I've bloody told him,' Bastin replied, sounding unusually angry. Normally he never displayed any temper. Myers must've got up his nose already, Fathers thought.

'Look, Harry,' Bastin continued more calmly, 'you don't need to tell me that what you're doing's important and urgent. I know that. If I don't know why. And I've told Frank. But. Well, I think you should consider the long term – for yourself – and get round here if there's any way you can. It needn't take very long. I really do advise you to.'

'Bad, is it?'

'New broom, wants to assert himself, usual sort of thing. I just think if you turn up – and if you're nice and polite and so on, hard though I know that is for you – well, maybe you can sweeten him for a bit, then pick things up properly whenever you get back to the squad. For once, Harry, be tactical.'

'Yeah, I see what you mean. OK, I'll try to be there about four.'

In fact, it was closer to five when Fathers walked to the Yard. He cast his mind back nearly a decade and a half. He and Frank Myers had been Detective Sergeants together in a north London CID. Myers was two years older and had three years' experience at DS level when Fathers arrived, newly promoted. Myers had offered to show the younger man the ropes, had even taken him under his wing to an extent. Or tried to – for Fathers was no chick to huddle round a mother hen and it was not long before he broke free. But he did it without friction and managed to maintain a reasonably friendly working relationship with Myers for a considerable period.

They were similar in many ways – middle class, university educated, rising fast through the ranks – and different in several others. Fathers took his career seriously, but Myers was nakedly ambitious. He would occasionally talk about making Chief Constable one day. Ambition made him a good detective, thorough and determined, yet it became responsible for a deep flaw. As a Detective Sergeant, Myers ran some inquiries independently, as well as working on others under the direct and detailed supervision of a DI. He had two distressing tendencies: one was to let his own cases languish while he sought to please the DI; the other was that on his own inquiries, he was apt to forget that he knew more about them than a senior officer, whose suggestions he was therefore too quick to take. Fathers' faults were the opposite: his own cases took priority and he was never slow to point out when he thought he knew more than somebody else – or understood more even if he knew less.

Fortunately for Fathers, the DCI to whom he was responsible recognised the Sergeant's instinct for the investigative jugular and let him get on with things by himself for the most part.

Myers had a bad reputation at the division. His arrival on duty each day began with what amounted to a tour of inspection. If he spotted anything which fell short of perfection, the Superintendent always got to know. At the time, the Metropolitan CID was under a lot of pressure. The Commissioner had made it a personal mission to root out years of ingrained corruption. As a sideline, he was also insisting the CID smarten itself up. War was declared on bomber jackets, jeans and trainers, long hair and tieless shirts. Heavy emphasis was placed on following approved procedure at all times, on being correct in appearance, manner and every detail of daily work.

Different detectives responded in different ways. The old school scowled and complained about the new restrictions and the harassment. The corrupt ones thought they'd carry on getting away with it – and a lot did. Fathers didn't mind the dress regulations – even then he preferred to wear a suit and had never been seen in a leather jacket – and, unlike most of his CID colleagues, approved of the anti-corruption drive, though he knew it would do little more than scratch the surface. And like numerous others, he found ways to appear procedurally correct even as he cut corners in the usual fashion, believing that to do all the paperwork properly would mean he'd never manage to get out and do anything about actual crime.

Myers revelled in it all. It met his preferences precisely. He projected himself as perfectly fitting the Commissioner's requirements for detectives, made sure his superior officers knew about it, and to hell with what his colleagues thought.

Which would not have bothered Fathers at all, except that, the more Myers strove to embody the new model CID officer, the less effective he became as a detective. At which point he developed a habit of horning in on investigations when most of the groundwork had been done, and claiming part or – if he could get away with it – all of the credit when the breakthrough came and arrests were made. While this caused resentment among the detective constables, it was no problem to Fathers until he got to work one Monday morning to find Myers had not only stolen one of his cases over the weekend but, because he didn't know the full background, had screwed it up.

To be fair to Myers, as Fathers was not at any point in the ensuing row, three car thieves had been arrested and charged and, since they'd been caught in the act, there was no doubt that convictions would follow. But Fathers' sights had been set on the dodgy dealer to whom they sold the cars and the even dodgier exporter who marketed English luxury cars to continental buyers at surprisingly low prices – neither of whom Myers knew about. Fathers had left precise instructions for what to do if the thieves were seen in action which, as a result of a carefully constructed surveillance operation, was possible at any time. Those instructions included calling him out. They did not include arrests. Myers simply happened to be on hand when the message came in that the thefts were in progress, and intervened.

That Monday morning, Fathers's withering contempt bellowed itself up and down the corridor and provided the hot topic of canteen gossip for several days. He refused to help Myers prepare the case against the trio who'd been arrested. Myers immediately reported him for falling short in his duties, which was a mistake because Fathers was happy to tell the whole world what Myers had done and certainly had no objections to telling the DCI and Superintendent who, in any case, could hardly have avoided hearing about it already.

Afterwards, the senior officers conferred. 'Harry just lost his temper,' the DCI said. 'Frank fucked up.' The Superintendent liked Myers and tended to see the episode as a minor error of judgement. But he had to concede that the episode should be noted in Myers's file. He did his best to qualify the harsher judgement of the DCI, who didn't like Myers one bit and was pleased at the opportunity afforded by what he thought was a grotesque miscalculation. But the result was that Myers' rise through the ranks was slowed for a bit as he put in the time needed to show – or to allow him to claim when he next went for promotion – that he'd learned from his mistake. And the consequence of that was that Fathers made the step up to Detective Inspector before Myers.

Well, Fathers thought as he rode up in the lift at the Yard, it didn't hold him up too much – he's long since overtaken me. I doubt he'll have forgotten – what're the odds he's forgiven me?

He went to Bastin's office, knocked and entered. Bastin was sitting behind his desk with Myers standing in a corner. 'Five o'clock, Harry,' Myers remarked as they shook hands, 'is not four, but let's not talk about that. What's keeping you away from the squad so much?'

Bastin cut in quickly before the unpredictable Fathers could do or say anything predictable. 'I did say — ' he began.

'I know, I know,' Myers said, 'hush-hush and all that. Who're you reporting to?'

This time Fathers got in first. 'Can't say,' he said.

'Can't or won't?' Myers challenged.

'I have been instructed,' Fathers said carefully, 'to say nothing. All queries are referred to the Police Department.'

'Well, let's not dwell on that,' Myers said, 'but in future, don't think you can go taking on all these other tasks all over the place.'

'From beginning to end,' Fathers said irritably, 'there's been no question of me wanting to do it. It's been forced upon me. Direct orders.'

'I can vouch for that,' Bastin added.

'I dare say,' Myers said dismissively, 'but I want my officers working in my squad and not for any Tom, Dick or Harry who phones up and wants to borrow one of them.'

Fathers wondered what Hanson and Sir Nigel Laker might think about that label, but he didn't say anything. Not because he was too polite but because it was secret.

'Since it seems I'm not going to get to see him properly for a while,' Myers said to Bastin, 'I'd like a word with Harry right now. This isn't my office yet, George, I know, but would you mind?'

Bastin's expression showed he did mind, but he got up and left. Myers took the chair behind the desk and gestured to Fathers to sit down opposite him. 'A lot of things need tightening up around here,' he began, 'your extra-curricula activities being only a small part of the story.'

'Honestly,' Fathers said, 'I did not go out and look for this. I have enough on my plate as it is.'

'Yes, yes,' Myers said testily, 'I'm not saying you did, but I think it's a bit reflective of how George has been running the show that his squad's at everybody else's beck and call.'

'That's hardly fair. He's been a very effective chief and the squad's got a good clear-up rate.'

'He's left you and your pal Cadwallader to get on with things by yourselves, is what you mean,' Myers said. Cadwallader was the other DCI in the squad. 'I can see the signs all over the shop. You've got your private empires and George has left you to it. Everybody knows it. Well, times change and so do the ways things are run. You'll find I'm demanding but fair. I pride myself on that. I'll be on your tail for results and, as long as you keep on producing, I'll back you up when there's a need. I want constant reporting on all your cases – regular review meetings – and I'm going to be along at the case conferences. I shan't tread on your turf, you needn't worry about that, but I've got a lot to do and I intend to ride hard to get it done. There's been a lot of slipshod behaviour round here and it's time— '

'Who told you that?' Fathers interrupted. 'There's nothing bloody slipshod about the squad. If everybody else did half as well as we do — '

'For a kick-off,' Myers said, 'you can sharpen your own attitude up. Lack of respect at senior levels inevitably percolates down the ranks. And I won't have it, not from anybody. And for all your reputation, Harry, I won't have it from you either. Don't think, just because we knew each other all those years back, that you can trade on it. I tell you this squad needs shaking up and I can see that includes you too, and I won't hesitate to do what's necessary. Do I make myself clear?'

Fathers stood up. 'Where d'you think you're going?' Myers snapped.

'Off.'

'I've not finished.'

'I've got work to do.'

'It can wait.'

'Not for this it can't.'

'I'm telling you to wait till I've finished and that's an order, dammit.'

'And I'm telling you I have to go,' Fathers responded opening the door. 'If you want to give me a pep talk or something, you can just as easily do it next week.'

'Is that when you'll grace us with your presence again?' Myers said.

'All queries are referred to the Police Department,' Fathers replied.

Chapter 34

When they forced their way in and Joseph Perry started to object vehemently, they silenced him with the search warrant. When they told him to accompany them, he demanded to know why. When they said he was suspected of offences under Section One of the Official Secrets Act, he replied that it was ridiculous and said he would call his solicitor. They told him he could do that at the police station. And when they took him instead to St James's Barracks, his anger knew no bounds.

'Mr Perry,' Fathers said, 'you have entered a world where none of that has any relevance. Sit down and shut up.'

The phone tap on Perry had revealed nothing of any obvious interest. There'd been several calls from Gavin Stone, who was out on bail, but Perry had always cut the conversation off in the first minute. There'd been other calls to numbers which, when traced, turned out to be family. There'd been a few incoming calls – an invitation or two to supper parties – a couple of friends or acquaintances asking favours, but nothing which made Fathers feel he was on the right track with the magistrate.

But he'd decided, while he was in the mood, to bring Perry in as well, even though his sights were mainly set on Deakin. It was worth using the almost unlimited resources he had at his disposal to establish whether Perry was a red herring or the real thing. It was not what he had recommended in his report, but doing it the quick way seemed at least as good as the careful, slow inquiry he had suggested then, and since it might bring a quick result – one way or the other – it was possibly better.

Perry continued to expound on his rights and Fathers' lack of them – at least for hauling him in – for quite some time. Finally Fathers got through to him that there was no question of being allowed to phone a solicitor, let alone leave, until they had had what he termed 'a conversation.'

'I want it to be recorded that this is under the strongest protest,' Perry said as he subsided.

Fathers gestured at the tape recorders. 'Now,' he said, 'I want to tell you a few things.' He gave Perry a truncated version of the story – attempted arrests, failure, inquiry, and conclusion that the problem was a leak. 'There's a very small number of people,' he said, 'who knew enough to sink the operation – who had the right information at the right time. And you, Mr Perry, are one of them.'

'This is preposterous.'

'If it is, it is made so by your own behaviour,' Fathers replied evenly. 'You knew the address for the raid because you saw it on the warrant. You knew it was a security operation because the justification was offences under the Secrets Act. And you knew both of those things early enough to make a key phone call.'

'But I didn't,' Perry said.

'Or tell the person who was with you on that Tuesday evening.'

'I didn't – I wasn't with — '

'Mr Perry,' Fathers interrupted, 'this is not a game. The fact that instead of answering my questions when I came round that time you chose to throw me out. The way you start to say one thing and then change to another. Two other sources of information. All these things tell me you are lying.'

'What other sources of information?' Perry demanded.

'Either you are lying because you are the person I'm after, in which case, believe me, I will get you sooner rather than later. Or you are lying because there's something else, entirely unconnected with my inquiry, which you're trying to hide.'

'What two sources?'

'If it's the latter,' Fathers continued, 'you should reflect on the following. Had you not thrown me out, it is most unlikely Gavin Stone would have been arrested for that car theft.'

'You will not cease hearing about this for a very long time, that I promise you.'

'It is also quite certain you would not now be here and my men would not be searching your house.'

'You – you cannot do this.'

'I can do it,' Fathers replied. 'I am doing it. And unless you show some sense, I shall have no choice but to carry on doing it. I can open up your life completely and I will do so.'

'I want to phone my solicitor.'

Fathers looked at Perry for a long time. All this bluster was either an extremely strong performance, or the magistrate was like

216

an amputee feeling his phantom limb. He didn't know his rights and authority had been cut off.

'My solicitor,' Perry repeated.

'You have that option,' Fathers said. 'If you exercise it I shall charge you under Section One of the Official Secrets Act.'

'For what offence?' Perry snapped, but Fathers' ear caught the quaver in the voice, the first sign that Perry's defences were beginning to weaken.

'Passing classified information to an agent of a foreign power on Tuesday the fifteenth of November. You will appear in court tomorrow morning and I shall ask that you be remanded in custody while I complete my investigations. Regrettably, due to your lack of co-operation, that process may take a considerable amount of time – conceivably several months – but I am confident the court will refuse bail. Now, do you want to make that phone call?'

'Yes, I – I, I don't know.'

'You can think it over for a while if you like,' Fathers offered, 'in a cell. I can have you brought back in an hour, tell me then what you've decided. By that time, the men back at your house should have finished the ground floor and started upstairs.'

Perry jerked as if he'd been slapped. 'Stop them,' he said. 'Please.' The words began to pour from him. When the torrent stopped, Fathers had him taken to the cell. The magistrate said nothing more about calling his solicitor.

Perry's original refusal to talk to Fathers had produced consequences which swept Gavin Stone away. Now that Perry did talk, the aftermath was almost equally unpleasant. It was on Friday afternoon that Fathers called on Jonathan Blair, QC, MP.

As soon as he mentioned the name Joseph Perry, Fathers could smell the fear. This is either it, he told himself, or it's another man of prestige and position fearing exposure.

'Joe's an old friend,' Blair said.

'I know that,' Fathers replied. Blair and Perry had been lovers at Oxford more than thirty years ago. Now that Blair was in politics it would not have mattered at all if it became known that he had slept with a woman before he was married – but to have slept with a man was still different.

'Mr Blair,' Fathers said, 'you can either make this difficult for yourself, as your friend Mr Perry has, or you can make it very easy and that way it will remain completely discreet. You understand what I'm saying. I must have answers to my questions. That is what Mr Perry

217

did not grasp. As a result of which he has had a very unpleasant time. Because if I don't get answers at first, I must keep going until I get them. And don't doubt that I will get them.'

'I understand you,' Blair said quietly. He was on the House of Commons Defence Committee, which meant he had access to classified information — its release to the Committee tightly controlled by the Ministry of Defence and rarely amounting to the whole story about anything but still sensitive and secret. Perry had not been his only male lover all those years ago, and he had often feared that something from those days might return to haunt him. It appeared that this was it.

'Did you spend the evening of Tuesday November the fifteenth with him?' Fathers asked.

'Spend?' said Blair. He blinked rapidly. This was not what he had expected. The policeman wanted to know about the present, not the distant past. Blair had not had a male lover since graduating. After Oxford, like Perry, he had married. They had each raised families, had successful careers and more or less suppressed their homosexuality which was not a qualification for success in their chosen professions, even after it was legalised. But they stayed in touch and could count themselves friends. Blair had gathered that, after his divorce, Joe found solace by returning to his earlier sexual preference. He understood that across the last six years there had been a few affairs with younger men.

Perhaps, then, the detective's interest was in Perry, Blair thought, not himself. He kept a tight grip on the treacherous relief he felt suddenly suffuse him. He did not want to drop Joe in any trouble; even less did he want to drop himself in it.

'Were you with him that evening at all?' Fathers asked when Blair didn't answer.

'With him?'

'With him,' Fathers agreed.

'Why?' Blair asked.

'Mr Blair, just answer.'

'How much do you know?'

'About what? I know a lot about many things. What specifically do you have in mind?'

'About me.'

'Or,' Fathers suggested, 'do you mean about you and Perry?'

'Yes.'

'I know you were lovers and I'm not very interested. What I don't know is whether you saw him on the evening of — '

218

'I think so, but let me check my diary,' Blair said, suddenly decisive, opening his desk drawer. He was astonished to see Fathers get quickly to his feet and move smartly round the desk so he could see in the drawer too. My God, Blair thought, did he think I was reaching for a gun? He took the diary out slowly and closed the drawer. Fathers returned to his chair and sat there as if nothing had happened.

'I apologise,' Blair said as he flicked the pages to the appropriate date, also pretending nothing odd had just passed between them. 'A man in my position with – well . . .'

'With elements of your past you'd rather remained secret,' Fathers said for him. 'The way to achieve that at this point is to keep talking.'

'I hope so. At least, I see I have little other choice but to hope so. I suppose you're not going to tell me what this is all about?'

'No.'

'No,' Blair said. 'Well, I was there. I remember now. There was a division that night, three-line whip. He lives close by the House, you see, so it's quite easy to drop in for a drink. Says here that I arranged to see him at seven thirty.'

'Do you remember what time you actually got there?'

'Not particularly. I had a meeting at five and another at six. I don't remember either of them dragging on especially. I should think I got there more or less on time. I usually do.'

'And when did you leave?'

'If I recall, the division came about nine.'

'You'd be paged, would you?'

'That's right.'

'Well now, Mr Blair, I'm very sorry, but I have to ask you to recall everything you and Mr Perry talked about for that hour and half.'

'Oh, come now. That's impossible.'

But Blair discovered that prompted by a smart detective who already knew what had been discussed – or at least had heard one account – it was not so difficult. Though it was slow.

'I suppose that was an indiscretion,' Blair said half an hour later, 'about the warrant.'

'It certainly was.'

'Is that what you're here about?'

'Not as such, but — '

'But you do, even so, want to know whether I talked about it to anybody later on. The answer is no, not that you could verify that. Or falsify it.'

But the fact was that since Blair readily mentioned Perry referring to the Special Branch warrant he'd just signed, the trail had probably run out. If Blair hadn't mentioned it, Fathers would have been suspicious, for Perry had said they'd talked about it for a good twenty minutes, speculating what a raid was like, how it felt when, whatever you were doing, it was violently interrupted by the police. It was not an experience either of them had had. Till now. No mention of the warrant by Blair, and Fathers would have swung into action against him.

As Fathers left, he asked himself whether homosexuality, past or present, made somebody any more likely to be a traitor than heterosexuality. And he wondered about secret lives. Had Blair or Perry ever told their wives they were gay – or had been gay? If they hadn't, didn't that ability to keep a secret suggest they would be good security risks? Or did guilty secrets make people more vulnerable – the conventional wisdom.

And he thought about the logic of security. Blair, Perry, Stone – all caught up in the swirl of events they had not initiated, could not control, nor stop. Stone: OK, a thief, but caught as a spin-off from the Crow investigation – caught doing something wrong, but not because he had done it. Perry: mildly indiscreet, true, but to a man after all who already had access to classified information – and otherwise put through the wringer, not because of something he'd done but because of where he was in relation to a different issue on which, stupidly but in some sense understandably, even creditably – protecting an old friend – he'd not wanted to answer questions. And Blair: if he'd not had a drink with an old friend one evening Fathers would not have been there scaring him with the prospect of exposure. And supposing Blair had told somebody? What if he'd said to Fathers, 'Yes, I just happened to mention it to a colleague in the division lobby. What time? Oh, about nine thirty.' Then Fathers would have been along to see that colleague, check him out first, find out about his background as he had with Blair. Or what if Blair had forgotten the warrant? Then Fathers would have been back at him, on him, turning him and his life inside out until the answers fell into place, tearing him to pieces, picking over his bones, chewing him up and spitting him out.

There was potentially an infinite progression through indiscretions and, contrariwise, misplaced secretiveness, all started by the demands and logic of a security investigation.

Fathers checked his watch as he arrived at the barracks. Time to see if McKellen has recovered from the way I ripped into him this morning and written a better account of Crow. And time enough to smell the strange odours in which I'm bathed when I finish this thing.

Chapter 35

On Monday, ten days after he'd found out who was following him, Fathers spent most of the day in the room with a window overlooking the park, at the desk where he'd set Deakin writing the previous week, and drafted his second Crow report. At five o'clock he took it to Sir Nigel Laker who offered him whisky and cigar, the sofa and a newspaper while he read.

'Not much there,' Sir Nigel said at the end. He topped up Fathers' whisky, poured one for himself, chose a cigar and joined the detective in the informal half of the room. 'I don't mean that critically,' he added. 'You have once again been extraordinarily quick and thorough.'

'There's one or two interesting things in there,' Fathers said equally. 'The little mole in your own office, for example.'

'Yes. Waverley. Christopher Waverley. He may yet turn out to take the biggest fall of all. What did you do when Deakin got to that part?'

'Ah,' said Fathers, 'I was hoping you wouldn't ask.'

'Why? A man of your resource, I'm sure you handled it perfectly, but it must have been a challenge with him sitting there beside you.'

'That's the point. He wasn't. I, er, I got into the habit of sending him off for tea and that sort of thing. One time when he was out of the room, Deakin stopped answering my question and started to dump on his pal.'

'Ah.'

'Bit of luck, really. I got the feeling he wouldn't do it when Waverley was there.'

'Fortuitous. So it seems I cannot reprove you for wilfully ignoring instructions.'

'No,' Fathers grinned. 'Ironic, isn't it? That's exactly what Deakin was counting on with all his shenanigans. That if he got the result you'd eventually turn a blind eye to how he'd done it.'

'Hmm, not so unlike yourself. Both of you laws unto yourselves.

Neither allowing much of anything to stand in your way.'

Sir Nigel lit his cigar. Such men, he reflected, were always useful – but sometimes only up to a point. Well, Deakin, it seemed, had gone beyond that point. Fathers so far had not, even if he had strange ways and, it seemed, stranger friends.

'Mr Fathers,' Sir Nigel said, 'I perceive you have been pushing yourself very hard throughout this inquiry. Your efforts are deeply appreciated. Yet perhaps I can prevail upon you for just a short moment more. Had you produced the Crow malefactor, the course ahead would be clear and simple. Since you have not, it is murky and complex. It might shed some light in my mind if you would now talk me through your report. It may help various elements assume their right proportions and places.'

Fathers expelled a thin stream of cigar-smoke. 'Happy to,' he said. 'There's two issues: the Crow leak and the Deakin sideshow.'

'Quite,' said Sir Nigel picking up the report.

'Hay is clean on both. Didn't know about the Tuesday night outing or about what Deakin was up to.'

'Naseby?' Sir Nigel said, turning a page.

'No role in the sideshow. No basis for suspecting him on the leak. Like others, he knew enough to do the damage. It could be him but I've found no evidence for it.'

'No.'

'Platt and Waverley. Both guilty as hell on the sideshow.'

'And both, I'm afraid, will suffer for it.' Sir Nigel penned a comment in the margin of the relevant page. 'But neither could have leaked on Crow.'

'No possibility,' Fathers said, picking up his whisky glass. 'No knowledge.' He took a sip. 'Austin had a small role in Deakin's production as a source of information and remains a possibility for the leak but – like Naseby – without evidence.'

'The same could equally be said of McKellen and Thomas.'

'Yes. They were obviously at fault for not answering my questions fully in the first round, but they didn't know what Deakin was up to and, as for the leak, they knew enough but there's no evidence.'

'So having cast a cloud on Thomas in round one you have cleared him now.'

'Cleared?' Fathers said. 'Found no evidence is as far as I'd be willing to go.'

'An appropriate precision,' Sir Nigel said approvingly, crossing out one marginal comment and replacing it with another. 'Which brings us to the head of UK counter-espionage.'

'Who did what he did for, he claims, the best and purest of motives. Saw himself as the defender of MI5's integrity and efficiency. I dunno about that. Suspect away if you like, but I've got nothing to suggest he's the leak. You may want to go over him again, but I put him under a lot of pressure and didn't get a sniff. And he was where I was looking hardest. He's been connected with failed operations before, of course.'

'Who hasn't?'

'But there's never before been a foul-up when he's been in charge where there was a hint of a leak. He doesn't even have a suspiciously perfect track record, if you're looking for things to suspect, which I suspect you are.'

'*Touché*, Mr Fathers. Point very much taken. We can drive ourselves silly – and in the past we have done so – casting doubt on everybody for every, any and no reason. His record's bad, that's suspicious. It's good, that's suspicious. He drinks a lot. He's on the wagon. He has a girlfriend. He doesn't. As you say, suspect away, but at the end of the day you have no evidence.'

'None. Not against any of them.'

Sir Nigel smoked and reflected for a while. 'Against the officers most closely involved, then,' he said through the smoke as he pulled out his pen to make another notation, 'there's no evidence. That, of course, does not mean that none of them was the leak. But let us consider the various other possibilities. First, what do you say to friend Deakin's own theory? Special Branch incompetence.'

'Possible – always possible – but he only made the case for it look strong in his report because he knows nothing of police work or how the Branch goes about this sort of thing.'

'You have faith in them?'

'Faith?' Fathers pouted. 'It's not the point. Austin's a competent officer leading a good team. I covered it all in my first report. The strong probability is that they didn't foul up. That the leak had already occurred and Brown and Scherchinskiy never got near Hampstead that night. I did also think of another possibility at one point, getting rather too subtle for my own good.'

'Which was?'

'That Austin might've messed up on purpose. But if he did, it was so brilliant it's invisible.'

'And you think that if you couldn't spot it, it didn't happen?'

'You make it sound like complacency,' Fathers said, 'but fundamentally that's right. I'm confident that after twenty years I know

224

all these procedures well enough I could spot a deliberate mistake as quickly as I could a genuine one.'

'And as for the rest of Austin's team, you didn't bring any of them back in, so the position is as it was in your first report.'

'Yup. Would've been hard for them to leak, because they found out so late. Just possible it could've happened, but no evidence.'

Sir Nigel sighed. 'You're not being very helpful, Mr Fathers,' he complained. 'All you seem able to manage is eliminating each possibility. Tell me about the magistrate.' He flipped through the report till he came to the part on Perry. 'You followed up in great detail on this, though it was a little outside your remit, hmm?'

'And got no result, so I'm for the high jump,' Fathers responded calmly.

'In fact, you do have a gap,' Sir Nigel said.

'Yes. About twenty minutes, maybe more, between Austin going and Blair arriving.'

'Blair – yes, an interesting entry for his file.'

'Peccadilloes in his distant past,' Fathers objected.

'It was illegal at the time,' Sir Nigel said, 'and is still not smiled on in many circles, especially including security-minded ones.'

Fathers tossed his head unhappily. Poor Blair. 'Anyway,' he said, 'Perry's gap. Frankly I don't know what to do with it. Long enough for him to make a phone call. But again, there's never been a hint of a problem with Perry before and Special Branch use him regularly for warrants so he's had plenty of chances. I suppose you could go back to my original recommendation – keep a close watch on him for a long period and see if anything breaks. But – well, I'm inclined to doubt it. His home's been searched. There were various things you'd regard as incriminating, but nothing in the spying line, no inexplicable phone numbers in his address book, nothing in his bank account which doesn't tally.'

'In other words, once again there's no evidence, and you have looked extremely hard for it.'

'Yes.'

'Hmm.' Sir Nigel turned a page. 'Ah,' he said, 'I was very struck by this section. You seem to have quizzed them about the possibility of disinformation.'

'It was Deakin raised that, when I had him write up a full account of Crow. He spent several pages defending Lucy against the charge – which I hadn't made – that this Pole's a dud source. He said the Director-General made that suggestion when Crow blew up. So I thought I'd better cover it. It's why I asked you about the other two sources.'

'And I did as you requested and have received from both Six Hundred and Langley affirmations that their respective assets – Six's Gerhardt and the CIA's defector – are sound.'

'Well, that simply confirms what I thought. You have to reckon the trade-off. As I understand it, to get a disinformer accepted you have to use him to pass over a lot of accurate and valuable material.'

'Quite so, and you're wondering if the secrets spilled over two years by Lucy and seven by Gerhardt are a sensible price to pay for the gain of making Crow fail.'

'Especially,' said Fathers, 'since if it weren't for Lucy there'd've been no Operation Crow to begin with.'

'Quite.'

'In fact, I did wonder – getting too subtle again, I'm afraid – if it might have been a complicated plot to give MI5 a false operation which, in failing, would bring on an inquiry and cause all sorts of internal trouble.'

'But Gerhardt and the CIA's man would have had to be part of the plot.'

'And there would've been no upheavals,' Fathers said, 'if Deakin had reacted differently to my appointment – or if you hadn't wanted an external investigator. So whoever set it up would've been gambling on some very long shots indeed.'

'No, it's just not credible, is it? We have to regard Lucy and Gerhardt as safe. So, another possibility eliminated. What else is there? While you're about it, perhaps you'd like to clear the DGSS.'

'Oh, I don't think it could be him,' Fathers responded gravely. 'He knew nothing about that Tuesday. He'd already given the necessary authorisation. Deakin didn't go back to him until afterwards. Of course, he knew Brown and Scherchinskiy would be lifted some time, but if he'd passed that on, they wouldn't't've planned to meet.'

The Co-ordinator was looking at him incredulously. 'You did consider it,' he said.

'Oh yes. I hope I've considered everything.'

'I'm glad. Did you consider me?'

'Didn't know a damn thing,' Fathers said.

The Co-ordinator blew out a long breath. 'Well now,' he said, 'in your first report, you had another offer – anybody, anywhere in the Joint Computer Bureau.'

'Yes, or anybody else with a high level of computer skills – anybody else in MI5, that is, not the whole country.'

'Thank heavens for that.'

'I've checked the transactions record, by the way, and there's nothing there which shows illicit access to any Crow material.'

'Which suggests?'

'A high level of skill, enough to break the JCB codes and evade or override the security barriers.'

'Well, we can always have a look,' said the Co-ordinator. He sighed dismally and drained his glass. 'I doubt it will take us much more than a decade. How many of them are there?'

'One hundred and forty-nine. I'm hoping to be let off that little chore.'

'Of course. K7 handles counter-espionage within the Service. Events prevented me from turning to them after your first report, but they are the appropriate tools for digging through the JCB. It'll take their minds off the nineteen sixties.' The Co-ordinator rose. 'So, Mr Fathers, my thanks. I think I can let you get back to your normal duties now. Needless to say, not a word.'

'If you are going after the JCB, you might start with the intake of ten years ago, the ones recruited through press advertisements.'

'Yes. Perhaps so. If you think of anything else, do let me know.'

'What'll happen to the people I've had in over the past week?'

'I shall have to take my time over that. Except for Naseby and possibly Hay, they'll all remain suspended and barred from their offices pending consideration. I imagine a transfer or two, even an early retirement. Austin, of course, is not my concern. His Commander will rule.'

Fathers nodded and stubbed out his cigar. 'Well,' he said, 'that's that. Can't say I'm sorry to be shot of it.'

227

PART VIII

The Christmas Penguin

Chapter 36

While Fathers was away, Detective Sergeant Elliot Yarrow had plenty to keep him busy. There was the Hammersmith bank robbery case to get straight so it could be brought to trial, and he took it on himself – since he knew Queen wouldn't – to make sure the cases against those arrested in the swoop on Connors and Garston all went smoothly. And he lent a hand to Queen preparing the case against Joey Wainwright for the Stubbs murder, harrying the laboratory to take less than the several months it usually needed to produce a report on the knife. On top of that, there were the searches he and Cathy Gordon conducted for Fathers and, just when they'd done all the ones on the list they'd been given, up came another one to do. Turning the places over was tiring, made worse in most cases by the objections and distress of the other occupants of the homes they raided. It was not easy to close his ears and mind to a six-year-old as his room was taken apart. And everything that was found had to be listed, in the knowledge that Fathers, scrutinising each report, was looking not only for what they'd found but for where they hadn't thought to search.

Through all of this, like the rest of the Serious Crime detectives, he had to put up with the arrival of the new Chief Superintendent who called in everybody of the rank of sergeant and above for get-acquainted sessions. Yarrow knew enough to restrict his side of the conversation to little more than 'Yes, sir' and 'No, sir'. He didn't like the way the new man went through his file picking out all the weak points, or the general sense Myers communicated of an impending revolution in just about every aspect of the squad's work. Cathy Gordon told him it would all blow over, but he wasn't so sure, though he didn't join the group of moaners who met in the bar each evening.

So it was not because he was idle that, all through Fathers' absence, Yarrow had a feeling of being at a loose end, of sculling around not quite sure what he ought to be doing. When Rita snapped at him a couple of times during the week, he sat down to try and

231

think through his sense of dissatisfaction. She told him outright it was ridiculous since he'd just had a role in breaking three big, connected inquiries – and that was when he found a focus for his unease. He explained it to her as much as he could – which was not very much since it amounted only to a series of questions – but she didn't think a lot of it. Putting it into words with her, however, made it possible for him to find a way of expressing it a bit more clearly when he dragged Queen away from the grumblers one evening.

The DI heard him out, lit a cigarette and said, 'Way I work, son, I told you before: if I don't like what I see, I try to find out more. You reckon there's a pong in the air, go sniff it out. You understand? Don't sit in the bath and think – go do something about it.'

So Yarrow went visiting. The man he wanted to see was out, but he knew enough about him to expect him back soon. He let himself in, helped himself to a beer, watched the news and even answered the phone. Half an hour later he heard the front door, switched the television off and said, 'Your nooky called and said she'd be here at half seven, which gives us nearly an hour together.'

'What d'you think you're up to, breaking into my place?' Davy Dawes asked truculently.

'Aw, don't take that tone with me, Davy boy, or I might talk about who's been saying what, where and how come so.'

'All right, what do you want?'

'There's just a little thing been troubling me,' Yarrow said. He got up and went into the kitchen. 'Want a beer?' he called. 'I saw you had three, so there's still a couple left.'

'Make yourself at fuckin' 'ome, why don't you?'

'I did, thank you. Do you or don't you?'

'What?'

'Want a beer.'

'Yeah.'

Yarrow came back, lobbed a can at Dawes and opened his own. 'Well now, this thing that's been troubling me. I was wondering, my man, why you waited so long before putting me on to the Hammersmith blag, and then so long again before you gave me Cy's name, seeing as it was you who put him on to the driver's job in the first place.'

Dawes said nothing.

'You see,' Yarrow continued after taking a swig, 'it's what we in the trade call a discrepancy. That means something which don't fit quite proper like. Do you follow me? Because you could've told me before the blag came down. Or you could've told me 'bout Cy Barker's part in it as soon as we started doing business. Or you could've stayed entirely shtum. 'Stead of which, you told me after it happened, and well after you knew about it, and then didn't tell me everything. As a result of which, if you recall, Davy boy, you lost more 'n four hundred nicker. Now, how come?'

'I didn't know it was a bank when I first told Cy about it.'

'No, Davy, that won't do. Please don't give me pork pies. Try again.'

'God's truth, Mr Yarrow.'

'Cy says different. Dunno 'bout God.'

'Well, no, all right, but I didn't know it was 'Ammersmith, not at first.'

'So what you could've done is bell me and say, "Now look here, Cy Barker's doing a wheelie for a bank blag that's coming down soon, though I don't know where." Why didn't you?'

'Well, 'e's a mate 'n' all.'

Yarrow darted at Dawes, knocked his beer aside and grabbed the knot of his tie. Dawes was a stone heavier but had nothing like the policeman's physical condition or fighting skills. He tried to resist, but it was no use. Yarrow pushed his forearm into Dawes's throat, forcing him back against the wall, held him there for a moment, then walked back to sit on the arm of his chair. He picked up his beer. 'Sorry, Davy,' he said, sounding not at all apologetic, 'it's just I don't appreciate bullshit. You're the most pathetic liar I've ever met. That was another discrepancy, you see. Since if you didn't tell me before it happened because he was a mate, why did you tell me after?'

'I needed the money.'

'Bollocks. If you did, you'd've taken my first offer and not let me drive you right down to fifty quid before you coughed up.'

'We had a fight.'

'Now that's more convincing, Davy, that's a better lie, but I know it's a pig in pastry, because if it was the truth you'd've said it straight away.'

'We did 'n' all.'

Yarrow shook his head. 'More balls,' he said, 'and in your case I've had just about enough of 'em.' He got to his feet again and looked pointedly at the other man's crutch. Dawes put his hands down to protect himself.

'Actually, Davy, that won't do you much good,' Yarrow explained to him. 'You see, I can kick so hard that, putting it in technical terms, the force of impact will transfer itself through your hands to your balls. All you'll get by covering up like that is some broken fingers to go with a pair of swollen goolies which'll quite worry your bird. Now, take your hands away and spread your legs. Come on, wider. No wider, that's right. Ah, your hands, keep 'em away. Good. Now, one more porky and I'm going to kick you. Understand?'

Dawes, pale, nodded. 'Right,' Yarrow said. 'Tell me all about it. From the beginning and don't miss anything out. Start with who told you to get a driver.'

'Guy White.'

'Guy White? He doesn't go in for blaggings. Pull the other one, it's got a steel toe-cap at the end of it.'

'No, honest, it was 'im. I mean, you know me, I wouldn't dare set 'im up, would I? I mean, you'd not be the only one to get back to me if I did.'

'Yeah, true enough,' Yarrow said thoughtfully. 'Go on.'

'He asked me one night – come round the club – said 'e needed a good wheelman for a bank job. Didn't say which one, honest. I mean, why would 'e? And I said I could get 'im Cy an' 'e said OK.'

'Go on.'

'Well, the gorilla told me not to tell Cy who it was for. Just to say there was a job an' if 'e wanted it, somebody'd get in touch. So I give Cy a bell an' 'e said OK. And I told Guy an' 'e gimme fifty quid and says to keep my mouth shut. Which I did. 'E tells you not to talk and you don't.'

'But you did, to me.'

'I'm coming to it. You said you wanted it from the beginning. Well, bit more 'n a week later, Sunday it was, 'e come to me again at the club — '

'Guy?'

'Yeah, and says there's another job for me with two 'n' a 'alf ton in it. Says I'm to pass you a message.'

'He said to pass it to me?'

'Yeah.'

'I mean, he mentioned me by name?'

'Yeah. An' e' told me to tell you the 'Ammersmith blag was down to Connors and Garston.'

'Is that exactly what he said, Davy?'

'Yeah, I mean, I asked if that was all, an' 'e said it again and made me repeat it. An' 'e said, whatever you do – I mean *you* –

I'm not to say anything more 'n that. An' 'e says to do it straight away. Well, when I called, you weren't in, so I left a message and you called me on Monday morning.'

'You told me exactly what he told you to?'

'Yeah. And then next day I got the two fifty.'

'You still got any of it?'

'No.'

'What happened next?'

Dawes took a deep breath. 'Well, next thing you started pestering me for a name.'

'Which you didn't give me.'

'That's right. But then Guy come by an' 'e said, you know, what's been going on, and I told 'im, an' 'e said to leave it a couple more days and then to give you Cy.'

'And you said, "Oh, I can't do that, Mr White, Cy's a mate."'

'I did actually, but, well, like I said, you don't argue with 'im, do you?'

'Rough you up, did he?'

'Oh, you know, nothing much, sorta picked me up and dropped me a coupla times.'

'Nailed me 'ead to the floor, guv,' Yarrow said, 'but I don't 'old nuffink against him. 'E was a prince.'

'What?'

'Never mind. How much'd he give you for your trouble?'

''Nother two fifty, and no, I ain't got any of it left.'

'You do go in for expensive crumpet. When'd he give it you?'

'Straight after I told you. When was it? Tuesday, two weeks ago tomorrow. 'E give it me next morning.'

'All right, Davy, you can stand up straight now.' Dawes blew out a long sigh of relief and leaned weakly against the wall. He rubbed the thigh muscles which had been stressed by the way Yarrow had had him stand.

'I've got a piece of advice for you, son,' Yarrow added. 'In future, you hear about a blag, you tell me. You hear some more, you tell me more. Somebody starts telling you what to say to me, you let me know about that too. If I get another whiff of something like this, anything, ever, I won't kick you more than a few times, but I'll let every gaff you've helped put in the nick know exactly what you did. D'you understand?'

'Yes.'

'You are mine. As long as you're clear about that, you'll get along fine. See you. Thanks for the beer.' Yarrow tossed the can to

Dawes, who dropped it so the remaining half of its contents spilled over the floor.

When Yarrow got back to the Yard Fathers, as usual, wasn't there. But there was a large piece of paper pinned to his office door on which was written in big black letters, 'Normal service will be resumed tomorrow at 9 a.m. precisely.'

Chapter 37

Fathers got home in time to help Samantha with a maths problem and comment on Gary's latest painting. Then he had a bath and when he went into the kitchen found Sarah opening a bottle of wine. 'I don't know to what we owe the pleasure of your company before midnight,' she said, 'but I thought it was worth celebrating. Unfortunately, we don't seem to have an awful lot of food in the house. I've dragged some pre-cooked garbage from the freezer. We can pretend it's lobster thermidor. That's what *it's* pretending to be anyway. There's some salad too, of course.'

'That's nice,' he said, hugged and kissed her and took over the task of opening the bottle. 'I'm back at a civilised time because I'm through.'

'Really?' Sarah said. 'And truly?'

'This time, yeah – really and truly.' He poured the wine, raised his glass and smiled tiredly. 'Cheers.'

'Your health, sir. You look like you need it. Must've been a rough old time. What was it all about? Can you tell me now?'

'Not really. Not a lot anyway. It's been a security inquiry.'

'Security? What – Special Branch?'

'Partly.'

'What? You mean the real thing – MI5?'

'Yeah. Please don't ask any more, love. Partly because I can't tell you and partly because I just want to leave it behind. That's the second time I've been summoned to the Home Office for a special task. And its the second time I've rooted around, turned everything upside down and come up with nothing.'

'And all the while you've been doing that you've been carrying on with your normal stuff? Christ, aren't there — '

'Any other policemen in London?' he finished off for her. 'Makes you wonder. But no, for the last while, since – when? – shit, since the day after we bust the Connors and Garston crowd, I've been doing this security thing and sod all else. Before that I was riding two horses . . .' He paused to curse the Assistant Commissioner

237

internally one more time. 'But there's nothing unusual in that. I'm always running more cases than I can count.'

'What happens while you're away? Does that sordid Queen take over? Or David – but surely he's a bit new, isn't he? As an inspector, I mean.'

'Nobody takes over. They just keep going with their own stuff, and anything they don't feel too interested in they let fade away till I get back and start bum-kicking tomorrow. And catching up on the cases they've been keeping on the go. And my paperwork.'

The oven-timer pinged and Sarah pulled their dinner out.

'Oh, my bloody paperwork,' Fathers moaned. 'That's the worst of it. I had a look at it this evening and it's appalling. All these sodding great files climbing the walls. And memos. Bloody memos. Myers has already written me about two dozen.'

'Oh yes, I was going to ask you about him. I think I've lost my touch. I didn't know it was possible to burn a frozen dinner.'

'Ha, you always used to, when that was all we ate.'

'That was never all we ate.'

'Yes it was,' Fathers insisted, feeling his energy pick up. 'Don't you remember?' he said as she put the food on plates. 'You always said that, since I got home at ridiculous hours, you were only going to cook things which didn't take any time, so you could start it when I got in and not let it spoil. Scrambled eggs, omelette if I was lucky and TV dinners were the order of the day.'

'Well, there you are,' Sarah said. 'Sit down, anyway, and don't look at it like that, it's all you're getting. You've already mentioned scrambled eggs and omelettes, so I didn't only heat things up.'

'Near enough. And you always used to burn them.'

'I remember. It was the fault of that awful cooker we had in the flat. Am I going to meet him on Wednesday?'

'Eh?'

'Wednesday.'

'Who? This isn't bad, actually. Burned to perfection.'

'Your new boss.'

'Do you want some more wine? Myers.'

'That's right. I remember him. Yes, please.'

'Didn't know you met him. Oh, of course you would've. Social do's and suchlike.'

'Mm. He patted my bum once.'

'He bloody what?' said Fathers, wondering if she was serious and if his indignation was genuine. 'I'll have his balls for breakfast.'

238

'Yuk,' Sarah said. 'Surely the lobster's not that bad. Didn't I tell you?'

'No. I'm sure I'd've remembered.'

'Oh well, happens so much it probably slipped my mind.'

Fathers looked at his wife. 'Is that a joke, Sarah?'

'Which? Saying he patted my bum, or him doing it, or it happening a lot?'

'All three. Oh, sorry, you said you did want some, didn't you?'

'Wine? Yes, thanks. Well, it wasn't a joke when he did it. More of an accident really. Meant to be a friendly hand on my back. It was before you fell out and he was giving me some advice. He sort of slipped.'

'Sort of slipped,' Fathers scoffed as he poured the wine.

'Oh well, maybe he fancied me. Nothing wrong with that.'

'And they all feel you up a bit, do they?'

'Who?'

'Colleagues of mine who fancy you.'

'Actually, I've noticed a decline in its frequency across the years. Either I'm getting old and shrivelled, or wives of DCIs are off limits.'

'That's true actually,' Fathers said. 'Section Two of the Metropolitan Regulations. Paragraph fifteen: fondling spouses. They draw the line at inspector.'

Sarah chuckled. 'Anyway, how is it seeing him again?'

'Well, I've only seen him the once, and that wasn't so good. Still seems to be a pompous, power-crazed, ambitious little git. What were you saying about seeing him on Wednesday?'

'It's George's leaving party.'

'Oh Christ, so it is. I'd clean forgot. So that's it, end of an era, tearful farewells and all that. I'll be really quite sad to see him go.'

'You're only saying that because he's on the point of departure. Imminent absence already making the heart grow fonder.'

'No, it's not that. It's because of his replacement. Anyway, are you coming to it? Isn't Wednesday your night for the history thing?'

'Normally, yes, but we've finished it.'

'Finished?'

'Yes, stopped for Christmas. No more until the New Year.'

'Christmas. Bloody hell. When is it?'

Sarah laughed at him and stretched a hand out across the table. He took it in his and laughed with her. 'Seriously, though,' he said, 'when is it?' He checked the date on his watch and worked it out.

'Fuck a duck,' he said, 'it's less than two weeks. Have we bought any presents?'

'Yes, dear, *we* have,' she said, letting go his hand.

'I mean, for the kids and so on.'

'Yes.'

'Oh, good. Well, I'd better get one for you, hadn't I? What do you want. History book? I'll give you one on the history of MI5, how's that sound?'

'Rotten.'

'I'd better take it back then. Couple of knitting patterns, maybe?'

Sarah made a face at him. 'If you throw in the needles,' she said. 'I think I could find a use for them.'

'What are we doing on the day?' he asked.

'You have been in another world, haven't you?'

'Something like that.'

Chapter 38

Fathers called for silence. The detectives in his section shut up and looked at him with interest. Was Daddy about to give them a pep talk?

'I'm back,' he said. 'I'll take you one at a time – in this order.' He indicated the list of names he'd stuck to his office door which he then opened and went through, closing it behind him. Some pep talk.

He spent the morning seeing his officers, going over their work. They got a few minutes each. A few cases were promoted in priority, a couple were dropped. None of the sessions was difficult, except for their complaints about Myers which he ruled out of order and suppressed. He may have joked to Sarah that he was going to kick some bums, but that was not his way. While he expected his commands to be followed immediately and without question, and his advice to be treated as a command, he very rarely bawled anybody out. Anybody junior to him, that is.

Of Cathy Gordon he asked an important question. 'Have we passed the hat round, you know, to get something for George's leaving present?'

'Yes,' she said, '*we* have. Your contribution was a tenner.'

'Oh, right,' he said, getting his wallet out, 'Ten, that's a bit stiff. What did we get him?'

'A bicycle.'

'What?'

'Didn't you know? It's his great pleasure. Cycling.'

'What? The way he looks. He's no bloody cyclist.'

'No, really. He was saying a few months back. Apparently it was his great joy for years, but then he stopped having the time. Said he was looking forward to retirement and getting fit again and pedalling round the place.'

'Really?'

'Really,' Cathy confirmed.

'Well I never. Of all people. You sure it's a tenner?'

'Privilege of rank. You get to give more. Everybody was very generous, actually.'

'Yeah, he's not such a bad old bugger really, is he?'

'Not by comparison.'

'Where've you got this bike?'

'It's at my place. I was going to bring it in tomorrow morning. Can I leave it here?'

'Sure. I'll be out, but just put it in the corner.'

'Out?' said Cathy Gordon. 'Oh no, not more of that lark.'

'No, just having my hair cut.'

The most serious business, and the most complex, was with Queen and Yarrow. Logan and Grey had disappeared – 'Done a wee runner, och aye,' as Yarrow put it – and the case against Hughes was not looking strong. Juries rarely liked it when the victims of assault cases were not there to tell their story, so the Crown Prosecutor had been reluctant to lay the more serious charges than mere possession which had been promised. In consequence the magistrate had responded to the urgings of defence counsel, and bail had been granted. Hughes was on the streets again, piecing things back together.

'I wonder where they've gone,' said Fathers.

'Not been seen back in Glasgow,' Queen answered.

'Maybe abroad. Why not put out a standard anything-known request? Can't hurt. What else is new? What've Connors and Garston been up to while I've been otherwise?'

'Regrouping,' said Queen. 'They've signed up some more muscle to replace what we put away and brought in a pair of expensive heavies – shotgun specialists, so I'm told.'

'Nasty. Names?'

'Nothing yet. Also, the Primrose sale is still on.'

'So Billy did know about that. Or he's accepted it now he's out. What about Gelchin? Any word from him?'

'I heard Billy went to see him.'

'What's that mean? Was Billy getting permission to launch himself at Connors and Garston or something?'

'Don't think he'd need it,' Queen said.

'Hasn't got the overcoats,' Yarrow put in. 'Anyhow, he'd not be selling the Primrose if he was planning on that.'

'And Boyars,' Fathers said. 'He's still the middle man?'

Queen nodded. 'But the actual sale's to be personal between Billy and the other two, so I'm told. And it's still in cash.'

Yarrow opened his mouth, then shut it and glanced over Fathers's shoulder at the window.

'What were you going to say?' Fathers asked.

Yarrow's gaze traversed the ceiling and the filing cabinet before he replied. 'I was just wondering where they got the cash from,' he said.

'Oh no,' said Fathers, 'that would be too sweet.'

'Hammersmith?' said Queen, catching on. 'Shall I have a word with my snout?'

'They must've been spending hand over fist,' Fathers mused. 'This is the second round of extra recruitment we've forced them into. And they may have big ambitions, but if you tot up what they've got at the moment it doesn't add up to all that much.'

'Connors brought a lot of the ready with him when they first hooked up,' Yarrow reminded him.

'Yes,' said Fathers, 'but they can't last for ever on that, can they? Unless somebody's backing them we don't know about.'

Queen sniffed loudly and sceptically, his normal response when anybody said something which implied that what he knew was less than comprehensive.

'Anything else?' Fathers asked.

Yarrow told what he'd learned from Davy Dawes.

'So Guy set Tom 'n' Jerry up, then he shopped 'em?' said Queen. 'Or had 'em shopped, anyway.'

'That's what Davy says.'

'And you believe him.'

'Well, I sort of think, the way we were talking to each other and everything, taking a leaf out of your book as I was, that, yes, it's the truth.'

Queen gave Yarrow a long look and nodded. 'Learning,' he said.

'That was a smart bit of thinking, Yarrer,' Fathers said, 'but where's it leave us?' He drummed his fingers on the desktop. 'With Guy White acting strange is where,' he said. 'Queenie, ask your snout about the money, and these shotgun merchants. Yarrer, I think it's time to fix up a permanent watch on Boyars, just to keep our options open. I'd put the eyes on Billy, but I reckon he'd spot them.'

'Let's hope we can do it better than the last surveillance op we came across,' Yarrow said indiscreetly.

And then, finally, there was Myers to see. It was still two days before he formally took over, but Bastin had stopped fighting for his rights in his soon-to-be-former office and the new man was well ensconced. He was already beginning to run things the way he wanted – regular review meetings, attending the case conferences –

243

and there were, he told Fathers, a great many more changes in the pipeline.

'I plan to have this squad shaped up by Christmas,' he said, 'so we start the New Year with a bang.'

'Having ended the old with a whimper,' Fathers suggested irritably and irritatingly, 'what with only busting most of Connors and Garston's crowd, nailing a killer and wrapping up the Hammersmith bank job – to speak only of my side of it.'

'Connors and Garston are still active — '

'And I'm still on them,' Fathers interrupted.

'And you shouldn't claim too much credit too quickly on that front,' Myers continued, 'or I might ask why you were so slow to move against them. Don't think I don't read the papers. And the memos. And the reports. All of which — '

'Unfortunately,' Fathers interrupted again, 'the extra strength we needed to stop them on the streets wasn't available until after it went so far it got to a killing. As you know, since you've read all the paperwork.'

'I know about memos,' Myers said. 'I know all about them.'

'Is that why you're drowning me in them?' Fathers muttered. He'd looked through the ones sent to him in his absence: six of them complained about him not being there, four set times for meetings he'd missed, five laid down various guidelines for daily work – reporting procedures, how to ask for an interview with Myers, when to call a case conference and so on – and one inveighed against the way informants were used, specifically the habit of letting them off charges. But the one Fathers prized above all informed him it was against regulations to keep alcohol in the office.

'And I know what it looks like,' Myers went on, 'when one's written purely to protect your back.'

'From experience, doubtless,' Fathers suggested sweetly.

'I mean I know how to spot them,' Myers snapped. 'And I also know how to spot trouble. You have just two days to decide whether you're going to be trouble, in which case I'll give you some. Be clear about that. You have a habit of throwing your weight around, but whatever you were used to with George as he got old and slow, with me you will have to change your ways. Do I make myself clear?'

'Being disrespectful to George,' Fathers said, 'won't endear you to anybody in the shop.'

'Number one, I don't give a toss about endearing myself. What I care about is getting this squad in shape. Number two, you are the last person in the world to talk about disrespect.'

'Number three,' said Fathers, 'I have some serious advice for you. I mean it. You're lucky that you've taken over a good squad – running well, reasonably happy, more efficient than most, with an OK clear-up rate. You'll want to make changes. That's all right. We all do it when we come into new postings. I did when I took over in my section. But don't make the changes too fast or everybody's energies will go into resisting you and instead of a squad you'll have a bunch of demoralised moaners watching the clock so they can get to the bar and share their grief. Do it slowly, get people on your side, give us a bit of praise instead of going on all the time about how we need whipping into shape, tell us how we're going to go from good to better. Use some psychology.'

'Fatherly advice, indeed,' Myers sneered.

'And seriously meant,' Fathers said. 'Take it in the spirit it's given.' He felt well pleased as he left. It was fun to tease Myers, and even better to turn serious and tell him how to run things. He enjoyed being wise, he decided – an unusual and satisfying role to play. Sadly, the odds against Myers treading softly would not have tempted a compulsive gambler. Fathers went to plot with Cadwallader, the other DCI in the squad.

But later that day, Bastin came into Fathers's office to deflate Fathers's self-satisfaction. He looked older, sadder, angrier, 'A word to the wise, Harry,' he said.

'Who? Me?'

'I hear on the grapevine – don't ask how – that Frank will try to shift you first thing.'

Father violated the instruction in Myers' memo and poured them both a whisky. 'I'd not be too unhappy to be out of his way,' he said.

'You would if you knew where he'll try to put you.'

'Where?'

'Well now, where's the sensible place to shift you to? Another squad, or heading up the CID in an inner-city division.'

'Rather a squad than a division.'

'Sure. But Frank's got something really tasty in mind for you. Like traffic. Or records.'

Fathers mouth flapped open. 'He can't do it,' he said when his jaw muscles were back under control.

'Do you mean he wouldn't try?' Bastin said. 'If so, you're wrong. Or do you mean he couldn't succeed? In which case, you may be right, but don't bank on it. Without me to cover your back you'll be in a pretty exposed position.'

He finished his whisky and held his plastic cup out for another. 'Unless,' he said, as Fathers poured.

'Unless?' Fathers said.

'You do one or both of two things.'

'Yes.'

'You have a friend in high places you could use.'

Fathers scowled.

'Remember the formula,' Bastin said. 'He's just done you a favour. No better time to ask again.'

'What's the other?'

'Put in for promotion.'

Fathers drained his whisky and poured himself another measure. 'Whenever I've thought about that,' he said, 'I've decided against it.'

'And maybe rightly,' Bastin replied. 'DCI's a good rank for a copper like you. But I don't like this bastard, Harry, and I worry about what he'll get up to. You can see the signs as well as I can and you know him from way back.'

'Basically, he's not changed.'

'So you know what he wants to do. This is just another step up for him. His plan – two years and he'll make Commander. Now then, how can he do that? By putting his prints on every successful case the squad handles.'

'There'll be precious few of those if he goes on the way he's started.'

'True, but he doesn't see that. You've got to follow his logic. Thing is, with you, with your rep, he'll not get a whole lot of credit for your cases. How you work, it's well known. You don't refer up more than you absolutely have to. You work it out for yourself, run your own show. So he's worried that any case you break, you'll get the credit. And he wants it. So the best thing is to get rid of you, put somebody else in post who doesn't have your record, and won't match your rate, but will do pretty well because it's a good team – and claim the lot for himself. Frank, I mean. Good whisky. Is there more?'

'Not if Frank has his way,' Fathers said, offering the bottle again. He'd never seen Bastin drink so much in the office. Presumably it was a sign of how unhappy he'd been made by Myers' talk about smartening up the squad.

'I saw that memo. What a pillock. Anyway, the long and the short of it is, he'd rather have you out of the way and, on top of that, he doesn't like you, so he's being petty and vicious about it.'

'If I do put in for promotion,' Fathers objected. 'he can put his black mark on my file and it won't go any further.'

'Not if you do it quickly enough. I've drafted a recommendation. Well, it's a general commendation actually. Should carry a bit of weight for a month or two. And the Commander would back you getting the up – the AC too, come to that. He tells me Hanson's just sent over a missive full of praise for you, which goes a long way.'

Fathers blinked. 'Well, well,' he said. 'So when do you think I need to decide?'

'Early in the New Year. And either way, see if you can't tell Hanson about it. He'd probably block transferring you somewhere silly.'

When Bastin had gone, Fathers sat for a while in thought but came to no conclusion. He decided to get home early again. It was good to be eager to see Sarah. Driving home, he reflected some more on what Bastin had said. A friend in a high place, he thought. So some good came out of Crow after all.

Chapter 39

During the two round of his Crow inquiry, Fathers had not managed to get to his hairdresser's, whom he normally visited once a fortnight. On the morning of Bastin's leaving party, however, he arrived as business started and began the day relaxing as Ron washed his hair and then chivvied it with his scissors back to style and respectability. The place was almost a traditional barber's. It claimed to be unisex, but its atmosphere and ninety per cent of its clientele were male. Fathers's attention slid to the conversation at the next chair. It was, typically enough, about the weather.

'Looks like it'll be colder this year 'n last,' said the customer.

'Yeah, well, let's hope it doesn't freeze the way it did the year before.'

'Ooh, that was something awful. You remember I went down the coast?'

'Yeah.'

'Terrible it was. My mate, like, he had a bet.'

'A bet?'

'Yeah, that none of us would go out on the water on Christmas Day.

'On the water. Oh, you mean skiing. You're a nut for that, aren't you?'

''S why we went down there. Anyway, I took him up on it. Near froze me privates off.'

'Brass monkeys, eh?'

'I tell you what, it was so cold that as I passed the pier, I swear I saw a penguin.'

Fathers joined in the laughter. 'Mind you,' Ron whispered into his ear, 'if you was out water-skiing on Christmas Day, you'd have every bleedin' right to see a penguin, Mr Fathers, wouldn't you now?'

Fathers laughed again and Ron had to explain the joke. 'Is that all right?' he asked when he'd finished, carefully holding the mirror so that Fathers couldn't see the back of his head.

'Just fine, Ron, thanks, and happy Christmas.'

He spent the rest of the day deskbound, grappling with piles of

248

paper, distracted by a nagging thought he couldn't put away, until at six o'clock Sarah arrived and they went off for a meal that was meant to absorb the vast quantities of alcohol which would flow that evening.

Bastin's leaving party was a great success. There were a lot of people, a lot of drink and a lot of noise. Everybody asked how everybody else was and shouted back that they were fine and either looking forward to Christmas or dreading it. Rita was there, braving the leers and occasional surreptitious fondles from Yarrow's colleagues, calmly tolerating the nervousness with which he introduced her to his superiors and their wives. Sarah said hello to Myers and exchanged edgy hypocrisies. Then she took Rita off into a corner and they began to swap confidences at top volume. Fathers caught Yarrow's shifty eyes long enough to exchange a look of mutual worry and they made their way towards their women before untold damage was done – or damage which should have been left untold. They were intercepted by Cathy Gordon, who shouted, 'Shall I tell Sarah about the woman in the bar?'

The Assistant Commissioner rang a bell which people began to hear after a few minutes and steadily they quietened down and gathered round. Then he made an eloquent little speech, singing Bastin's praises and telling of the pleasures of retirement, and presented him with a fine set of decanters and glasses. Sarah had sidled through the crowd to where Fathers was and whispered to him that Eileen Bastin's expression was like somebody getting a Christmas present and wondering if the receipt has been kept so it can be exchanged for something worthwhile. Frank Myers stood up and told everybody how difficult it would be to fill his predecessor's shoes. The murmur of 'You can say that again' was, fortunately, not quite audible at the front of the room where the speechifying was done.

Then it was the turn of those who'd worked under Bastin. DCI Cadwallader spoke about what a pleasure it was to work for somebody as sharp and as kindly as the Chief Super, and one of his team brought in a lawn buggy. Eileen Bastin's expression didn't seem to change. Sarah whispered that they obviously had one already. Or else didn't have a garden. Fathers took his turn, repeating that it was a great pleasure to work for somebody like George Bastin, except, he added, that there was nobody else like him. Cathy Gordon wheeled the bicycle in and Fathers told Bastin it was time to get on his bike and look for work. Bastin seized it with both hands and beamed. He tried the brakes, pressed on the saddle, lifted up the back wheel and gave the pedals a whirl. Then he beamed some more. His wife's eyes softened.

When he stoped beaming, he pulled out a handkerchief, dabbed at his eyes and stepped forward to make his speech. First, he asked the Assistant Commissioner if he could withdraw his resignation. This pleased everybody, including the AC who expansively said that of course he could, except Frank Myers who didn't seem very amused. Then he talked for a few minutes about the pleasures of working with such a fine body of men – 'And women, of course,' he added just in time to stifle Cathy Gordon's muttering – and how he wouldn't have changed a thing if he had his time all over again. He was genuinely moved and so was his audience. He spoke for about five minutes, and when he'd finished they cheered him, sang 'For He's a Jolly Good Fellow', cheered him again and raced to the bar.

'I think you're right,' Sarah said when Fathers gave her a drink.

'What?'

'I think you're right,' she repeated more loudly.

'About what?'

'That man really is an arsehole,' she shouted.

'What man?'

'The new bloke,' she yelled.

'Who? Myers?'

'Yes,' she shrieked, 'the one who's standing right behind you.'

He whirled round, but Myers was on the other side of the room. When he turned back, Sarah was laughing so much she was spilling her drink.

In the taxi home, Fathers asked her what she'd told Rita about him. 'Oh, nothing,' she said, resting her head on his shoulder, 'nothing much.'

So what had Rita told Sarah about Yarrow, Fathers wanted to know. 'Oh, can't tell you that,' she murmured, 'girl talk.'

'You haven't gone girl-talking since you were twelve.'

Sarah squeezed his arm. 'Actually,' she said, 'I gave her some advice.'

'What about?' he asked suspiciously.'

'Evening classes. She's thinking of taking some.'

'Oh. Good.'

'Yes.'

'Are you sure that's all you were talking about?'

'I didn't say that, did I?'

'Didn't say what?'

'That that was all we were talking about. I only said I gave her some advice about evening classes. The rest is classified. What was that Cathy said, by the way, about you getting raped in some pub?'

Apart from Yarrow, Myers was the only one who didn't seem hung over. He called the whole squad together and proceeded to tell them what was what. There was going to be a change of name, he said, to symbolise the change of regime and style and also to reflect the change of priorities he had been authorised to introduce. From now on it would be the Organised Crime Squad. He was also going to be handling cases himself, another change. To help him he would establish a central team consisting of a DI, two sergeants and a complement of DCs. He looked pointedly at Fathers when he said there would be no more swanning off round the place, and at several others, Queen included, when he declared there would be no more blind eyes turned to small crime simply to keep a bunch of informants happy.

'How's he expect us to do our work then?' Queen muttered. I don't have to listen to this,' he added and closed his bloodshot eyes.

Myers had a lot more to say and it took him an hour to get through it. The gist of it was that he wanted a lean, efficient, straight squad, working hard and with a good clear-up rate.

'Not without the snouts,' Queen mumbled, eyes closed.

At the end, Myers took a sip of water and asked if there were any questions. No hands went up but one voice asked, 'Yeah, do we puke up here or when we get out?'

As Fathers got a cup of something hot and wet from the machine in the corridor the bleary Queen bumped into him. 'I got something,' he said.

'So've I,' said Yarrow coming up excitedly waving a piece of paper he'd just picked up from his desk. 'The Primrose sale's being finalised tomorrow afternoon in Boyars' office.'

Queen looked at Yarrow. 'How'd you know that? 'S what I was going to say.'

'From the phone tap,' Yarrow said.

Queen shook his head, then grimaced because he'd shaken it too hard. 'Stone me,' he grumbled, 'and last night after all that partying and drinking I staggered out and about to get the same thing. Real work. Shit. Mind you, I bet I know something you don't.'

'I'll bet you do,' Yarrow said generously.

'What?' Fathers asked.

'Something what'll please young Sherlock here.'

'Yeah?' said Yarrow. 'Lemme guess. Your snout's seen the money they're using to pay.

'My my, i'n' 'e sharp? Sounds like a fair chunk of it's from Hammersmith. Mind you, we won't know till we get a dekko at it. Still, it's worth a go.'

'Sure as hell is,' said Fathers. 'Come and see me in five minutes.'

He took the would-be coffee back to his office, remembered what he'd decided about getting his own coffee machine, wondered if he'd have the nerve to go ahead with it and made two phone calls. The first was to Cadwallader. 'What do you think?' he asked.

'Don't like it. Anything we can do?'

'I may have a line on the snouts bit.'

'OK. I'll see about the other.'

On the second call it took a long time before he was put through to the man he wanted to talk to. 'I've had a thought,' Fathers said.

'Oh yes?'

'I'd like to follow it up.'

'What is your thought?'

'Er, I'd rather not say.'

'In case you're wrong?'

'It's more a feeling than a thought, not sure I could put it in words.'

'Do you need any resources to follow it up and transform it into verbal form?'

'No, though I'd need my stuff back and I'll have to get round and see a few people.'

'It's unorthodox, but please proceed. There's no identifiable progress at this end and little reason to expect any for some while. Any short-cuts you can offer would be most welcome. By your "stuff" I presume you mean the various files, reports and transcripts. You can come here to have access to them. As for the rest, you still have authority if you want to interview anybody. None of the letters endowing you with it has been withdrawn.'

'That's what I thought. Good.'

'And when may I expect your third report?' the Chief Intelligence Co-ordinator asked.

Chapter 40

'Jesus,' said Pardoner, 'it's one of the Piranha brothers.'

'Dinsdale,' Yarrow growled, 'Din-sdale.'

'I didn't know you were old enough for *Monty Python*, Elly,' Pardoner said.

'Seen the repeats. *I* didn't know anybody still dressed like that.'

'Early sixties nostalgia,' Pardoner explained. 'It's all the thing nowadays. Who's that with him?'

Their attention was focused on two men walking along the street beneath them. One of them was Garston. His camel-hair coat, patent leather shoes, greased black hair and pencil-line moustache were the objects of their comments.

Yarrow picked up the radio mike. 'Guv, Garston's here. Got somebody in tow – don't know him. Over.'

'OK,' Fathers's voice crackled. 'I see him. He's holding something under his coat. Can you see it? Over.'

Garston and the other man disappeared into a doorway. 'Hello,' said Pardoner, 'the bloke in the fur-lined leather number – that Connors?'

Yarrow picked up the mike again. 'Connors is about to check in, guv,' he said. 'He's got a pal too. Carrying his left arm sort of funny. Could these be the minders? That might be a sawn-off up his sleeve. Over.'

'Possible. Tell me when you see the van. Out.'

They waited in the bare room for another fifteen minutes, taking turns with the binoculars to avoid strain and maintain concentration. 'There's Billy,' said Yarrow finally. 'And there's a carload of his mates. I wonder where Guy is.' Pardoner passed the news to Fathers. Three minutes after Billy Hughes had gone through the same doorway as Connors and Garston, Yarrow saw the van and took the mike.

'Here it comes,' he said, 'parking right outside, oh, naughty, on a double yellow too. And there's Guy, up the other end of the street, pretending to look at the dirty books in the shop window. Looks like he's not going in with Billy. Keeping his eyes open on the outside, like the blokes in the car. They're not taking any chances. Over.'

'How it seems,' Fathers said. 'Stay there. Call up if anything happens. Out.'

Billy Hughes had signed the deed of sale, the money had been handed over to him and he'd turned down the chance to count it, saying he'd know where to go if it was short, when the door to the small office was opened and Fathers walked in, held up his warrant card and identified himself by name and rank. Garston's minder pulled his shotgun from under his coat and pointed it at the detective.

'Don't be stupid,' Fathers told him, clamping down on his nerves to keep his voice steady. 'As they say in the movies, the place is surrounded.' He pointed at the window. On the fire escape outside there were two detectives – Cathy Gordon with a camera she was busily using and Bunn talking into his radio.

As the gun was lowered, DS Graves squeezed his bulk past Fathers and relieved both minders of their weapons. 'Nasty,' he said. 'Very. This way, gents.' As he took them out, Queen appeared with DC Hands who produced a large notebook and closed the door behind her.

The sudden danger and its passing left Fathers feeling light-headed. 'Now,' he said, 'Mr Boyars, is this your office?'

'Yes, and I'd like to know by what right — '

'Shut up. It's your office. Mr Hughes, do I recognise this document as a deed of sale?'

'I'm here in good faith, Mr Fathers, to conduct an ordinary — '

'Cut the crap, Billy. Just answer the question.'

'Yeah. I'm selling the Primrose. And I want my lawyer.'

'Why? You're not under arrest. Now, are the contents of these bags the money which has been rendered in payment for the Primrose?'

'Yeah. I haven't touched it.'

'Mr Boyars, to whom does – or did – this money belong to? Yourself, perhaps?'

'No.'

'Then who?'

Boyars jerked his head at Connors and Garston and added that he wanted his lawyer too.

'I thought you were your own lawyer, Mr Boyars. Do I take it that the money belonged to Messrs Connors and Garston?'

'No,' said Connors.

'Oh,' said Fathers, 'well, whose is it then?' His innocent question

254

got no guilty answers, so he said cheerfully, 'It doesn't belong to any of you? Good heavens. Yet a few minutes ago I saw these bags being unloaded from a van which, when I checked its registration, turned out to be owned by a company of which Mr Garston is the proprietor. Would you care to explain that?'

'No,' said Garston.

'And here on the deed of sale I see that same company is the new owner of the Primrose. Are you telling me that, as payment, you used money which is not yours?'

Garston stayed silent and exchanged a look and a shrug with Connors.

Fathers dropped his playfulness. 'Right then,' he said, 'down the nick with the lot of you. You two are through. So are you, Boysie.'

It didn't take long. Fathers and Queen spent a while teasing Hughes and White, who seemed calm enough about the sale being aborted, that they might be charged with conspiracy to evade Corporation Tax – why else had they insisted the sale be transacted in cash? Then they let them go. Of the money in the bags, a small part – forty-seven thousand pounds – was identified by the serial numbers as stolen from the Hammersmith bank. Boyars, Connors and Garston were charged as accessories before and after the fact. The two shotgun carriers were charged with possessing illegal firearms, and one of them with threatening behaviour. With everything properly filed and everybody in their cells Fathers took his section out for a celebratory drink.

'So stuff that in your pipe, Mr effing Myers,' Queen said to Yarrow, 'and ask yourself where we'd've been on the whole thing if he had his way with our snouts.'

'Yeah, but what about the future? Yarrow asked.

'I reckon Dad's gonna use today's little show to kill the whole thing stone dead. He's got a pal or two somewhere now, he has – I'm not sure who, but someone with clout – and I reckon he can outgun Frank any bleeding time he wants. What you having?'

When Fathers got home, Sarah asked what his buoyant mood was about. He explained. She asked him more about it. He provided a detailed description and she exploded at him in fury. 'You bastard,' she said. 'You knew they had guns and you just bloody walked in there. Went in first for Christ's sake. And you, of course, had no bloody gun, did you? Nor any back-up with guns, I'll bet.'

'I haven't got the certificate,' he said.

'Don't do that,' she stormed at him, wiping at her tears, 'you know what I mean. You could've got yourself killed in there, or at least really seriously hurt. I thought you'd stopped the heroics. You're too old for it.'

'You think I should've sent somebody else in?' he asked. 'Or at least gone in second so they could draw the fire? Who should I have picked? Queen's too old, of course, if I am. Graves is pretty big, I could've hid behind him. Or let Yarrow take his chance, see if he's fast enough to dodge the shots.'

'You know that's not what I mean,' she sobbed.

'Yes,' he said, 'I know. I'm sorry.'

'I just think of you sometimes, covered in blood, cold and white, or stuck in a wheelchair for ever, or blinded, there's a thousand terrible pictures I can conjure up, and I know it doesn't happen very often these days, but you will just go and put yourself in places where all that can come true. And then when you've been away so much for the last while and it hasn't been good and I hardly know you any more, but we've begun the process of working our way back together, and you come in so pleased with yourself and so strong and I think what would it be like now – this minute, now – if the guy'd been some sort of maniac and pulled the trigger.'

The words were almost lost in her sobbing. Tentatively he moved towards her and put his arms around her. She rested her head on his lapel and leaned into him with her arms down by her side. They stood for a long time in silence punctuated only by her sobs and, when they subsided, the sharp intakes of her breath as she recovered herself.

'I'm sorry,' she sniffed, putting her arms round him and holding him tightly as if she feared that otherwise he might float away from her. 'Sorry, sorry. I know, you couldn't put somebody else in line to take a risk you'd not take yourself – it wouldn't – it wouldn't be you – wouldn't be honourable.'

'And there really wasn't a risk at all,' he said, 'not really.'

She relaxed her grip but kept her arms round him. 'Oh yes there bloody was. Don't you try to pacify me like that.'

'How should I try to pacify you?'

She looked up into his eyes and traced a line across his forehead and down his cheek. She slipped her fingers into his hair and grasped a clump of it. 'I love you, Harry, honour and all, sod it.'

'I love you too.'

Chapter 41

Much of the behaviour of Detective Chief Inspector Harry Fathers in the period between Bastin's party and Christmas struck the members of his section and his superiors as odd. To start with, having only just finished an extended period of lengthy, almost continuous absence from his office, he might have been expected to make himself conspicuously present, particularly since he'd so emphatically announced he was back, and even more especially with a new, rampaging and hostile boss around. In fact, he was out for most of the time and if his colleagues had known what he was doing, they would have been even more puzzled.

Myers himself was particularly unclear about it all. First, on the Friday morning, his second day formally in charge, he was visited by Fathers, telling him in advance about the operation planned against Connors and Garston for that afternoon. Not only was the DCI giving forewarning, he had used the proper procedure for arranging an interview, and arrived on time with a one-page typed report which he expanded orally in a manner that was precise, comprehensive and polite. He pointed out that there was a chance that this would finally bust the Hackney man and his American partner and simultaneously clear up the remaining loose ends of the Hammersmith bank robbery, and also a chance that it wouldn't. It seemed he was going as far as asking for Myers's opinion. Myers agreed there was nothing to be lost in going ahead, and was so put off his stride by this sudden display of respect and openness that he forgot to insist on being in for the kill before Fathers suddenly changed the subject.

'I wanted to ask about the issue of our sources,' he said.

'Oh yes?' said Myers, preparing to bridle.

'I've been thinking it might be a lot of help if you could put it down on paper as a formal directive, so we can really get to grips with it and talk about it properly in my section.'

Myers did a double take, then reached out his hand and picked up a two-page document. 'That was my thought too,' he said, pleased, 'and it's good we're working along the same lines. I've already done it. It's going to the Commander as well, of course, and the AC. It's not actually a directive, needless to say, till it has their formal endorsement, but they've already agreed it verbally. You'll call your lot together and have a session on it, will you?'

'Well, maybe not as such, sir,' Fathers said. 'It might give the grumblers too much rope. I thought I'd let them all have it, of course, but then talk it over with them one at a time.'

'Yes. Yes, maybe a better way. You know them. Good.'

Fathers stood up, Myers' memo in his hand. 'Was there anything else, sir?'

'No, Harry, no, except to say, well, I'm happy to be kicking off this way with you. Put the other stuff behind us and forget about it, eh?'

'I was in a difficult position, sir. I may have overreacted to the pressure.'

Fathers left a satisfied Chief Superintendent behind him. You poor bastard, he thought.

That afternoon Connors, Garston, Boyars and the two shotgun artists were arrested, and Myers came in on Monday morning to find a folder containing a full report about it on his desk. Intending to build on their surprising new rapport – and already reconsidering the idea of booting Fathers into a bureaucratic backwater – he phoned Fathers to ask him along to discuss how best to set up and man his new central section. Fathers wasn't there but had left a note: 'Regret that I have been called back on to case I can tell you nothing about.'

Myers left a message, but no response came from Fathers, so he phoned again in the afternoon. Fathers had come back, but gone again, leaving no further message. On Tuesday morning Myers tried twice more. Fathers had been seen briefly, with his coat on, either going out or coming in, but he wasn't there just then and, no, he hadn't left any word for the Chief Superintendent.

Myers banged his fist on the desk and called the Commander, who spoke to the Assistant Commissioner, who phoned Hanson at the Home Office and asked, 'Are you still using Fathers on this hush-hush thing of yours?'

Hanson said he would consult and phone back. Then he called the Cabinet Office and spoke to Sir Nigel Laker who said, 'Yes he is. In fact he's here now. Do you want a word with him?'

Fathers was unexpectedly cheerful and polite and commented that he'd been going to call the civil servant himself and could he come round and see him right now? Hanson checked his desk diary and suggested that two hours' time would be more convenient, but Fathers said that wasn't possible and he wouldn't take long, and Hanson found himself quickly postponing a meeting. The upshot of Fathers' visit was that Hanson called the Assistant Commissioner to explain that, yes, Fathers was sorting out a couple of loose ends, it wouldn't take long and he was once again combining it with his other work.

'But he is still on this semi-secondment to you?' the AC asked.

'Yes indeed.'

'Well, I wish you blokes'd keep us in the picture sometimes. He is supposed to be working for us, you know.'

'And has, I gather, just achieved another *coup*,' Hanson responded, 'on which, and to everybody involved, many congratulations. He's a real asset, is he not?'

The Assistant Commissioner agreed that he was, even if he was often a little difficult. Hanson talked to him for a few minutes about that, and finally the AC agreed that what he meant was that Fathers caused very little difficulty and was an enormous asset.

'There is another thing, by the way,' Hanson said, 'while you're on. I gather that the new chappie at the SCS – or OCS as I understand it is henceforth – is intending a crack-down on the use of informants.'

'Er, that's so, yes. How do you know?'

Hanson brushed the question aside. 'I understand the idea is that they will no longer have a blind eye turned to their misdemeanours.'

'That's the gist of it.'

'How would you assess the impact of such a policy on the rate at which reported crimes are cleared up?'

'Ah, well, I don't think I've gone into that yet.'

'Has anybody?' Hanson asked with a deceptive gentleness, practised and polished through a lifetime of such conversations.

'Er, no, I don't think so. I've certainly seen nothing.'

'You might find it useful to think that issue through before you implement the new approach.'

'Ah.'

'I would not, of course, stray into giving you operational directives, and I have to add it is no part of the policy of Her Majesty's Government to condone crime, even of a relatively low level.'

'Of course not, that's the point.'

'But I would suggest,' Hanson purred, 'simply as a matter of friendly advice, that were the new policy adversely to affect the clear-up rate, there might be considerable discontent in certain political quarters.'

'I see.'

'In the course of which the image of the police, which we all do our best to burnish at every opportunity, might suffer somewhat.'

'Ah.'

'There is the question of priorities to consider.'

'Of course.'

'Sometimes pragmatism motivated by proper concern for law and order may indicate that a small criminal is more likely to pass on information about a big criminal if he – the small fry – is allowed to escape the net once in a while.'

'That's how it's been done so far.'

'That was a purely personal contemplation, of course,' Hanson added. 'I am talking quite informally and, naturally, off the record.'

'Oh yes.'

'And on the basis of all those considerations, you may conclude it would be preferable to consider the impact of this or, indeed, speaking in very general terms, of any new policy direction on the delicate issue of the clear-up rate and to do so before you implement rather than afterwards, hmm?'

The Assistant Commissioner thanked Hanson for being so helpful, put the phone down, called in his secretary and dictated a memorandum to Myers ordering a pause for thought and assessment before introducing the new policy. For his part, Hanson doffed an imaginary hat to an absent Fathers and put in his filing tray the memo by Myers which Fathers had given him.

During that week Fathers followed people. He conducted a few very brief interviews. He went to one or two relevant places, made some phone calls, visited a library, sat in a room in the Cabinet Office for two or three hours refreshing his memory. And he made sure that most evenings he got home early enough to spend time with Sarah and build together on their new start. But mostly he followed people.

He even visited the Yard a couple of times, though only when he was sure Myers wouldn't be about. For the most part he kept in touch by phone. On Monday evening, Yarrow told him Guy White had been seen visiting Gelchin, and on Tuesday evening Queen said that Hughes and White were parting company, but amicably it seemed, since they'd been seen drinking together. He thought about those things on and off through the hours he spent dogging the footsteps of presumably innocent citizens.

In the crowded streets of the West End, he picked people at random and stayed on their heels as long as he could – in and out of shops, fighting his way through the avid consumers, along the streets, into cinemas, on to buses, into the tube, ending up anywhere from Oxford Circus to the wastelands where they actually lived. When he lost somebody, he picked another and started again.

Their behaviour, he decided, was eccentric. Getting from one place to another appeared, for the larger part of the humanity that thronged the streets, entirely a matter of chance. There seemed to be no such thing as a normal walking pace. They rushed – or tried to – or they dawdled. They retraced their steps to look at something in a shop window, stood there for a few minutes, went into the shop and were out again in thirty seconds. They got on buses and off again a few stops later, when it would have been quicker to walk, because the roads were as packed as the pavements. They took the wrong way through the maze of corridors in the Underground stations. They stood at the kerbside looking for a gap in the traffic, when there was a pedestrian crossing not twenty yards away, then dashed between oncoming vehicles as if their life so depended on getting to the other side they were prepared to risk it in the process. Once safely over, they meandered and dawdled again, taking the longest way round any obstacle.

On Thursday, two days before Christmas Eve, Fathers decided he'd completed his research, returned to the Yard and phoned the Chief Intelligence Co-ordinator to invite himself round the next morning.

PART IX
Song of the Crows

Chapter 42

That Thursday evening Fathers was in a sunny mood, despite having just seen Myers. Because of it, in fact. The new boss was furious at the postponement of his pet policy change on informants and had also learned that his plan for a central section was under review. He didn't know who to blame for either setback and that made him even angrier. What made it worse was that when he tried to take out his anger on Fathers, the response was an apologetic smile and expressions of regret that it was impossible to say anything about his other assignment which was, thankfully, now finished. Almost.

So Cadwallader did his stuff, too, Fathers thought. He called Queen and Yarrow into his office. It seemed the younger man was also feeling cheerful, for he was singing, 'They're in the money, they're in the money.'

'Who are?'

'Logan and Grey. Just got a call from Interpol to say they're in Spain. Date of arrival makes it look like they went there straight from hospital.'

'Nice place to convalesce,' Fathers said.

'Expensive place,' Yarrow suggested, 'at least the way they're living it up. Their hotel's in the guidebook. Very classy.'

'Hmmph,' said Fathers. He asked Queen what Guy White was planning now he'd left Billy Hughes.

'Setting up on his own. Seems he's picked up the franchise for the area west of Billy's. Nobody's in control there right now. He's picking up the pieces after Connors and Garston broke everything up.'

'Clever trick,' Fathers observed. 'Stand aside from the worst of the trouble, then swoop in when the war's over and end up sitting pretty.'

'Thing is,' Queen said, 'there's blokes down there who've lost all their credit on the streets. Nobody'd give 'em the time of day, let alone a percentage of the take. So it's an open door, beggin' to be walked through.'

'And we suppose that White's visit to Gelchin this week was to get the say-so,' Fathers said.

'Final say-so,' Queen corrected him. 'Billy'd already been to see Gelchin, remember?'

'Let's have a drink,' Fathers said. He took the bottle from his bottom desk-drawer and handed the plastic cups out. 'Now, I'm going to tell you a story. Yarrer, you like stories so you can help and, Queenie, you don't so you can pick it to pieces.'

'Go on,' said Queen, lighting a cigarette.

Fathers pulled out a cigar. 'Jesus Christ,' said Yarrow. He opened the window and stood by it.

'Wouldn't prefer carrot juice, wouldja?' Queen jeered.

'No ta, whisky'll do me nicely, but there are limits.'

'Well,' said Fathers, putting his feet on his desk and loosening his tie, 'once upon a time there was a pair of middle-sized operators called Billy and Guy, and a pair of slags who thought they'd put them and everybody else on the bonfire. So there were a lot of fights and Billy and Guy began to lose out. Only they weren't losing out as much as it seemed.'

'Here comes the story bit,' Queen said draining his whisky. 'Got any more of this?'

'Christ, you get through it. Help yourself. But they had a problem. They didn't actually have the ability to stand in the way of Connors and Garston, so they needed to out-manoeuvre them – to seem to give in, but in a way which wouldn't lose them any cred where it counted.'

'Why not?' said Queen.

'Because they planned to be around after Connors and Garston were through,' Yarrow said.

'So when they surrendered — ' Fathers said.

'Or seemed to,' added Yarrow.

'They had to do it in a particular way.'

'So Guy went north,' Yarrow said, 'and booked a couple of gits who hated Billy to have a go at him.'

'And they were well paid for their trouble,' Fathers continued, 'which perhaps turned out to be a bit worse than they had counted on, and then given some extra to get the hell out of it.'

'Would you let yourself be cut by an artist like Billy,' Queen asked, entering his first objection, 'however much money you was paid?'

'No I wouldn't,' Fathers said, 'but then I'm not them.'

'They didn't need to know,' Yarrow offered. 'Guy goes north, says, I'm sick of Billy, he's going soft, here's some money – I'll make sure he's not covered. So Logan and Grey manage to get to him, but Billy knows they're coming, smiles and they end up in hospital.'

'I knew you'd bring that effin' smile in,' Queen said.

'Whereupon,' Fathers took it up, 'Guy visits them in hospital and says, "Oh shit, you screwed up, we're all in trouble, you'd better get out of here, have some more money" – and off they go.'

'What's the point of all this?' Queen asked.

'It puts Billy inside, so his firm, with Guy now in charge, looks extremely weak and the new mob don't smell a rat when the normally indomitable White turns up and says, "OK, I'm selling out."'

'How'd they know Billy would be put inside?' Queen asked; his second objection. 'Only chance that there was a couple of witnesses and a pair of uniforms just round the corner.'

'You don't know it was coincidence,' Fathers said.

'Fair enough, but you don't know it wasn't.'

'Yes, but it's my story. If it hangs together so far, it's not beyond Guy and Billy to sort out details like that.'

'But Sherlock had a look at the eyeballs and they was clean.'

'They could've been there by chance,' Yarrow suggested, 'but Guy and Billy would know where the patrols were. Nothing easier than making sure the try comes just round the corner from a unit. Anyway, they wouldn't've worried if they had to do it again to another pair, nor again and again until Billy finally got copped.'

'No, that's true,' Queen conceded. 'But they didn't want Billy inside for ever, did they?'

'With Logan and Grey doing their disappearing act,' Fathers said, 'they knew we'd have a lot of trouble making the serious charges stick.'

'Bit of a risk.'

'Risk nothing, get nothing.'

'So when Guy went to see Connors 'n' Garston, did he say he was doing it with or without Billy's backing?'

'Doesn't matter,' Fathers said airily. 'Those two slugs would've believed him either way. Billy being inside looked like a serious piece of misfortune for him which they could exploit. To continue: as a result of White opening negotiations which basically mean he and Billy are pulling out, they get left out of it when the big wave of attacks start.'

'Here,' Queen said suddenly, 'what about Guy's missus in all this? Did he break her leg himself or something?'

'Genuine domestic accident,' Fathers replied. 'It does happen. And a lucky chance, from Guy's point of view, since it made it seem that he really was weakening. That was what we thought anyway.'

'Some of us,' Queen rumbled.

Yarrow shrugged. 'Made sense at the time,' he said.

'So, where've we got to?' Fathers mused. He poured himself more whisky. 'OK, Guy and Billy look weak, seem to be pulling out, but because Billy cut the Glasgow laddies up and because Guy's Guy, they've still got cred if they can bounce back. At the same time, they're out of the firing line while everybody else is in it, and how.'

'So what they need,' Yarrow said, holding out his hand, 'is a way of bouncing back so they can expand.'

'And here,' said Fathers, giving him the bottle, 'is where it begins to get complicated.'

'Begins,' scoffed Queen.

'Yes, the pattern of motives gets triangular.'

'Because Guy decides that there's openings for a man with his talents,' Yarrow said, 'and wants to carve out his own place, separate from Billy, when all the other small firms have gone down the drain.'

'Jumping the gun,' Fathers reproved him. 'First, we have to take the fact that, while Connors and Garston have a lot of money, their coffers are not bottomless.'

'They need capital,' Yarrow said.

'Thus Hammersmith, a job they give to their new recruits, Tom 'n' Jerry, so they can prove their worth.'

'Or just because they're handy,' Queen said. 'Don't overdo it.'

'So Tom – or Jerry – talks to Guy,' Fathers continued, 'who fixes up the necessary, because the defections of these two weren't real. They were simply doing what Billy'd told them to.'

'Why?' Queen demanded, getting up to relieve Yarrow of the bottle.

'To seem weak, so the offer to sell the Primrose would be credible, which'd mean they got left out of the war.'

'And to get an inside line on the opposition,' Yarrow said.

'Yes, a spy in the enemy's camp,' Fathers agreed. 'Now, here's the complex bit. Billy's idea is to make sure that when he sells the Primrose it's bought with stolen money. Before you open your mouth,' he added to Queen, 'he knew they'd use the Hammersmith money, because that's a good way for the septic and the Piranha lookalike to get rid of it, so they didn't have to lose a percentage by paying to have it laundered. Actually, in the end it turned out not to be so much because we'd stepped into the game and they'd had to spend a whole lot buying in more troops.'

'So that's why it had to be a cash sale,' Yarrow said, 'and why it had to be finalised in person.'

'But how did Billy know we'd pick it up and bust in?' Queen challenged.

'Because he made sure we knew,' Fathers said.

'Fuck,' Queen said with emphasis.

'Not just your talkative barman at the Primrose, but probably also your little lad in Hackney.'

'That's right. He knew Guy years back.'

'It's the same thing Guy did with Davy Dawes,' Yarrow said.

'They've been playing our snouts against us,' Fathers said, 'though since we've got from it the charges we were looking for, and a set of cast-iron cases, I doubt I'll go complaining about it.'

'Yeah, but wait a minute,' Queen said. 'All they needed was for us to turn up at the sale. OK, that does for Connors and Garston, fair enough, but why did Guy mess around with Dawes like that?'

'That's the third motive,' Yarrow said.

'Exactly,' Fathers agreed. 'Remember, Guy wanted to set up by himself. To do this, he decides to ditch Tom 'n' Jerry by running Dawes as a line to us. Then, when it's all over and Billy's still got the Primrose and the Piranha brothers are safely tucked away, Billy will be a bit weaker and he'll find it harder to take over bits and pieces nearby, and therefore Guy will find it easier.'

'So Billy set up Connors and Garston,' Yarrow said, 'but Guy, playing his own hand, set up Yates and Fenner.'

'And at the end of it all,' Fathers concluded, 'or maybe sometime before, it doesn't really matter, Billy gets Gelchin's approval for what he's doing and Guy gets it for what *he's* doing. At least to the extent that Gelchin says Guy can move into open territory and make it his. Maybe he didn't know all the details and maybe he did, but so what? Well, what d'you think. Few loose ends, but not bad, is it?'

'One thing,' Queen said, 'why did they try to put us off, acting so confident like that?'

'Did it put you off? By acting confident, they tempted us in, made sure we'd take the bait. And Guy made it even tastier by making sure we got contradictory versions of how his wife broke her leg. When you work it out, it's a treble bluff.'

'And what do we get out of all this?' Queen asked. 'Your story is they've run fucking rings around us.'

269

'What do we get out of it?' Fathers examined his cigar and the last of the whisky in his cup. 'Apart from putting away Connors and Garston, two bank experts, a bent brief everybody on the Met's been after for donkey's years, and a young killer – with Yates and Fenner as a bonus? And let's not forget a host of lesser rats when we hit the streets. We get a nice story, a chat, a pleasant way to pass the time, lung cancer and a hangover. As for the rest, leave it to another day. What Billy did by handing us Connors and Garston, it's the result we wanted. What Guy did by setting up himself and making sure Billy's stayed more or less the size he was – not a bad thing. People like Billy worry me when they get too big. Can't really complain about it. And when it comes to watching them run rings round us, well, so what? Take our revenge next year.'

'Yeah,' said Queen thoughtfully. He stubbed his cigarette out, tossed the empty whisky bottle into the rubbish bin and stood up. 'Well, guv, nice story. Wonder if it's true.'

'Why don't you ask them?' Yarrow said.

'Eh?'

'Not a bad idea,' Fathers said, 'just out of interest. After all, there's nothing we can touch them for. Billy's knife work on Logan and Grey won't wear in court. Guy's part in the Hammersmith job – that's something we can't touch without dropping Dawes and Barker in it, and it wouldn't stand up anyway. No other laws broken. Why don't you?'

'Maybe I will.'

He did. When he got in the next morning, he beckoned to Yarrow and they went into Fathers's office. 'You know that cock 'n' bull story you sold me,' he said.

'Well, it was fun, wasn't it?' Fathers said.

'It's all true, every bleedin' word of it. I saw both of 'em last night. Pleased as you like, they was.'

'Billy didn't mind about Guy sticking it to Tom 'n' Jerry then?'

'Ah, I saw 'em separately. Billy was pleased with his part of it, and Guy with his. Seemed a bit worried we knew what he'd done over the blagging. Which could come in handy some time when we want to set them at each other's throats.'

'Well, well,' said Yarrow, 'it seems that man, or at least criminal man, hasn't lost all enterprise and originality after all.' The other two looked at him. ' "The Adventure of the Copper Beeches",' he added, 'changed a bit, as is my wont, to fit the case.'

'You ever checked he's not makin' 'em up?' Queen asked Fathers.

Chapter 43

'No report, I see,' Sir Nigel Laker said. 'You perhaps found it hard to translate your unfocused feeling into written form?'

'I thought it might be better not to put it on paper,' Fathers replied.

'Oh? Why so?'

Fathers smiled slightly and tilted his head to right and left.

'Let us, in any case, wait for the coffee to arrive before you begin.'

'Sure. Anything breaking at your end of things?'

Sir Nigel pointedly mimicked Fathers's head movement. 'We've begun,' he said, 'but with that number of people it's a long road to travel.'

'How about Perry?'

'As a precautionary measure he is being watched, but having reflected, I hold out little hope there. It's the JCB we're concentrating on, together with a trawl for other staff who are – I believe the expression is computerate. Ah, coffee. Good, thank you. Yes, just set it there. No interruptions, please.' When his secretary had gone, Sir Nigel poured the coffee and leaned back in his chair behind the desk, opposite Fathers. 'The floor is yours, Mr Fathers.'

'Yesterday evening,' Fathers said, 'I sat with two of my detectives and made up a story. A hypothesis, you would say. One of them, who likes stories, helped me with it and the other, who doesn't like anything that sounds like a theory, had the role of picking it to pieces.'

'Indeed.'

'It involved an elaborate conspiracy, and a further counter-conspiracy within that, with criss-crossing motives, switched allegiances and fake defections, disinformation, the manipulation of our sources and so on. This morning I learned that the story was true in every respect.'

'I see. How satisfying for you. And I presume that you are now about to do the same with me – weave various facts into a narrative to explain what has hitherto been inexplicable, to develop a hypothesis which can be checked for veracity.'

'Well, not quite.'

'Oh?'

'I think you may find it something you would prefer not to check.'

'You fascinate me. Please proceed. Do I take it that my role is to pick your, er, story to pieces?'

'More or less,' Fathers said. 'There's another difference too. This is a sort of negative hypothesis. It doesn't construct a story but breaks one down.' He took a sip of coffee, pulled his cigar packet out and looked at Sir Nigel with eyebrows raised, wordlessly asking if he minded. He did mind.

'No, please, Mr Fathers, have one of these. I'm sure they're more to your taste.'

Fathers did as he was told, because he knew from the last time that Sir Nigel was right. 'Going through the Crow material,' he began, 'it's obvious that Brown is an extremely proficient agent of influence and a spy.'

'Yes.'

'Assume he's not.'

Sir Nigel sat up in his chair sharply enough to spill some coffee into his saucer. He poured it back into his cup, using the time to regain his composure. 'I beg your pardon,' he said.

'If you do, you will find there is no leak in K Branch, you will not need to worry about the reliability or competence of the Special Branch people, you won't have to investigate Perry and you don't have to distrust your entire computer staff.'

'I follow you thus far, and most welcome all that would be, but good heavens, man, you surely can't be serious.'

'If you make that assumption,' Fathers continued unperturbed, 'you then have various things – the contents of the Crow file – which need explaining. Shall we take them one by one? Starting at the beginning.'

'Yes, good,' Sir Nigel said. He reached for a pen and paper. 'To begin with, there's the evidence of the CIA's defector.'

The defector, Fathers thought. When first he began to see the truth about Crow, the defector had stood in his mind like a no-entry sign. It had needed a huge mental effort to surmount that barrier. If he began there now, the Chief Intelligence Co-ordinator would dismiss him out of hand. He had thought hard about how to organise his explanation for maximum effect and, though he had no notes, had formulated a plan to which he intended to stick to rigorously.

'I'd find it easier,' Fathers said, 'to take it more or less chrono-logically, the way the Crow file developed. We'll get to the defector in due course. If that's all right, the starting-point is Source Lucy.'

'Disinformation?' Sir Nigel said immediately.

'No, no. There's no reason to suspect Lucy. Unlike the other story I told you about, this one doesn't involve a conspiracy.'

'Ah. So, then, Lucy's evidence.'

'Which was that he'd overheard Scherchinskiy quietly commending Brown for the reliability of his information and the way he collates and analyses it, and commenting on the fact that he's influential and valuable. It was evident that Scherchinskiy and Brown were in contact.'

'Yes.'

'What's odd about that? Brown's a journalist and is indeed an influential one. Why wouldn't he talk to the Deputy Press Attaché at the Soviet Embassy? Scherchinskiy was simply praising his work which, if you've read any of Brown's articles, involves a great deal of collation and analysis of information from a wide variety of sources.'

'I haven't.'

'Pardon?'

'Read any of his articles.'

'You should do. I have. They're extremely interesting.'

'Perhaps. But look here, Scherchinskiy's KGB.'

'You know that, I know, MI5 knows. Where's the evidence Brown does?'

'Hmm.'

'He meets Scherchinskiy perfectly openly, and a lot of other Eastern bloc officials. So do plenty of people. Several of those diplomats may be intelligence officers. I think it was McKellen told me he wouldn't think somebody was a spy just because of that.'

'But it might be enough to want to keep an eye on him,' Sir Nigel said.

'Perhaps. Anyway, round one to me, I think. Lucy's initial information *didn't* mean Brown was an agent.'

'But there's all the supporting evidence.'

'We'll get to it. Let's stay with Lucy. In May, he was warned off asking questions about Brown.'

'Yes.'

'Maybe. It wasn't explicit. He assumed the dressing-down he received was because of that. He might have been wrong. Remember, by then he had been alerted to the fact that MI5 was very interested in Brown. A specific question about Brown was asked. That may be why Lucy arrived at the conclusion he did.'

'Perhaps. But assume he interpreted it correctly. What then?'

'I'm told the Russians have a rather disdainful attitude towards the Poles.'

'True.'

'Scherchinskiy simply didn't want Lucy treading on his territory and had a quick word which had the desired effect. End of story. Either it was professional jealousy – Scherchinskiy keeping his contacts to himself – or it was just an anti–Polish knee-jerk.'

Sir Nigel conceded the possibility that Fathers was right. They moved on to the next set of entries in the Crow file: Brown dropping his Watchers. 'What farcical admixture of fantasy are you going to use against that part of it?' Sir Nigel wanted to know.

Fathers waved an admonishing forefinger. 'It's no good,' he said, 'you can't throw me off my stride like that.'

Sir Nigel smiled a little ruefully. 'I do apologise,' he said. 'It's second nature. Continue.'

'Have you ever followed people?'

'No. I've been followed, but never done the following.'

'You should try it. I've been following people the last few days. Ordinary people, going about their ordinary business. They behave in the most extraordinary ways. You would think every one of them had a Watcher on their tail they were trying to drop.'

The response was an unimpressed grunt.

'Take the famous two-train tube trick,' Fathers said. 'If you assume Brown's a spy, then you see that action as a sophisticated and successful attempt to drop his tail.'

'Quite.'

'If you assume he's not, how then do you interpret it? Remember what happens. His train comes into a station. Just before the doors close, he jumps up, dashes off, on to the next platform and into a train which has just come in there. What's it mean?'

'No, Mr Fathers, by your own rules invention is *your* role.'

'He's been day-dreaming, missed his station, wakes up, realises with a start where he is, jumps up, just manages to get off, goes to the other platform to get the train which'll take him back to his station, there it is, on he gets, phew, what a stroke of luck.'

'Oh, come now.'

'I've seen it done.'

The Co-ordinator looked at him. 'Yes,' Fathers said, 'yesterday I saw exactly that happen. On Monday I saw it almost happen – all bar the arrival of the other train. In between I saw it not happen. The bloke who jumped up didn't get to the doors in time.'

'You've been spending a lot of time on the Underground.'

'Researching human nature.'

'Personally, I never use it.'

'All life is there, Sir Nigel.'

'Hmm. All right, given your premise – well, no. What about the arrival of the other train at that very moment?'

Fathers shrugged. 'Trains going in opposite directions have to cross somewhere,' he said. He drained his cup of coffee. 'I think that's another round to me. My assumption is still standing up. The next occasion was when he hopped off the train to York.'

'More day-dreaming perhaps? He got on the wrong train at King's Cross? How convenient.'

'No, not at all. His sister lives at Whittlesey.'

'Where?'

'Six or seven miles from Peterborough. He broke his journey to see her.'

'Did he? Is that known?'

'Not by me. It's one of the things you'd probably rather not check. But it's a reasonable explanation. It doesn't work if he's a spy, of course, but it does if he's not.'

'I don't think you can so confidently claim that round,' the Co-ordinator decided.

'Breaking your journey is not evidence that you are acting for a foreign power.'

'Not by itself, but combined with everything else.'

'None of which has stood up so far.'

The Co-ordinator sniffed. 'The third occasion was when he left home in the middle of the night,' he said. 'What are you going to make of that?'

'How do you know it was the middle of the night?'

'How do you know it wasn't?'

'I don't, but I don't have to either. The most likely explanation, if you assume he's not a spy, is that he was off to catch an early train somewhere.'

'And why was he not seen by the Watchers?'

Fathers smiled. He had been to see the Watchers who'd been in the hidey-hole at the end of Brown's street. They'd confessed that, with the street's poor lighting, Brown's taste for dark clothes and the lorry which blocked their view, they'd have missed Brown if they didn't see him come out of his front door. Fathers knew about long shifts spent doing that sort of duty, and he drew from one of them the grudging half-admission that at the end of the night he might

275

not have been wholly alert, might even have been making a cup of tea. He explained it to Sir Nigel Laker as gently as he could – every step he took in this inquiry seemed to land somebody new in the shit and he was getting fed up with it. Still, it had to be done.

'There were relying on the bugs to pick up any sound of movement in the house, you see,' he concluded.

'And why didn't they?'

'It's a phone-based system. Deakin and McKellen always resisted doing a proper search or sowing a whole lot of bugs all over the place. There's one phone in his study and one downstairs. It picks up voices and heavy movements but, unless his stairs creaked, it wouldn't catch him coming down them, or shutting the door if he did it quietly.'

Sir Nigel hummed and hahed for a minute before declaring that the least convincing of Fathers' demolition jobs.

'Perhaps, but all I'm concerned with is maintaining the validity of the initial assumption. I don't have to prove him innocent, just show you there's no evidence he's guilty.'

'Ah, rigging the rules.'

'British justice is the envy of the world,' Fathers expostulated with mock pomposity.

Sir Nigel chuckled. Despite his initial shock, he, too, was enjoying the discussion. 'And the Tuesday itself, when he jumped off the bus?' he said.

'Oh, that's absolutely normal behaviour. Everybody does it. Risky, stupid even, especially as dusk comes down, but normal. Can't possibly suspect a man of being a spy because of something like that.'

'Not in itself again, no, but — '

'But that's my point about all of these incidents. In itself none shows Brown to be a spy.'

'Granted, but aren't you rather too intent on missing the wood for the trees?'

Fathers turned the cliché round in his mind and came up with a rebuttal. 'If you see a pine forest,' he said, 'you think all the trees in it are pines. But some of them may not be. It's bad to miss the wood for the trees, but it's sometimes worse to misidentify the trees themselves.'

'Yet here we have a very definite wood, for on the day Brown innocently jumped off a bus in the Strand he was on his way to a clandestine meeting in Hampstead.'

'We'll get to Hampstead in a moment,' Fathers ordered. 'So far the evidence of Lucy and the Watchers is consistent with the

276

assumption that Brown's not a spy. But before Hampstead came along, there were a couple of other things.'

'Ah yes. Porton Down, Bath, the missile business and the defector.'

Fathers again deferred the defector. He dismissed Bath – it had been given no more than fifty per cent probability in the Crow file, the only connection was coincidence, a weak one at that, and there wasn't even enough evidence to call circumstantial. And Porton Down and the missile article were simply embarrassing pieces of investigative journalism. 'There's no reason to connect Porton with the incident on the tube,' he said, 'nor to suppose Brown held back some of the information and passed the rest to the KGB. You might get him or his sources – and he obviously must have them – on Section Two of the Official Secrets Act for handling classified information, but never in a million years on Section One – passing it to a foreign power.'

'The widely discredited catch-all Section Two, as the cant of the liberal press has it,' sneered Sir Nigel. 'If only it were catch-all – catch-anything, in fact. The new law will serve us far better.'

They moved on to Hampstead. 'First of all,' Fathers said, 'I want you to be clear that from what K Branch had seen of Brown for themselves, there was no evidence that he's a spy. All they'd really got the evidence for – though they could've done it simply by reading his articles – is that he's a very good journalist. But that's all.'

'For the sake of argument,' Sir Nigel said carefully, 'I'm prepared to grant you a certain cogency to your case.' He examined the pad on which he'd been writing notes. 'You've scored reasonably well so far.'

'Reasonably well? I'm way ahead. I've won most rounds, drawn a couple, lost none. At this point, without the defector, Brown's clean.'

'That,' Sir Nigel said, 'is a large qualification. But let us proceed.'

Fathers took it point by point again. He began with the information from MI6's Source Gerhardt. 'What did it amount to?' he asked. 'The USSR was planning a major propaganda effort, trying to set the agenda for the next round of arms talks in the wake of the US presidential election. Do you think that to anybody who reads the papers or has watched the TV coverage of Gorbachev's performances over the past few years do you think that's a secret? Or surprising? Or in any way unpredictable? Gerhardt's intelligence was accurate but worthless. And it didn't mention Brown, Scherchinskiy or Hampstead.'

'But it did mention London.'

'Along with the other major Western European capitals. Big deal.'

Sir Nigel argued about it for a while, but eventually agreed that Gerhardt did nothing to strengthen the case against Brown and they came to the fact that Scherchinskiy was going to Hampstead that Tuesday night. Once again, Fathers pointed out, Brown was not mentioned. Scherchinskiy could have been going to see any one of a large number of well-off, influential residents of Hampstead who had liberal, left-wing or pro-disarmament views.

'But Scherchinskiy dropped his tail,' Sir Nigel said. 'What happened there? More incompetence by the Watchers? Simply a chance event? Coincidentally with Brown chancing to lose his?'

'Possibly,' Fathers said, 'but I doubt it. I should think Scherchinskiy did it on purpose.'

'And why? If not to cover the fact that he was meeting Brown?'

'To cover the fact that he was meeting somebody else, thus saving them embarrassment or a further entry in their file, or whatever.'

'But Brown was also going to Hampstead.'

'*That's* the coincidence. Or part of it anyway. He could've been going for any one of a thousand reasons. Once you see that Scherchinskiy needn't have been going there to meet him, you realise Brown needn't have gone there to meet Scherchinskiy. It's like a house of cards. Everything needs to stand up or nothing does. If you collapse the Crow people's explanation about Scherchinskiy, the one about Brown falls automatically.'

'So what was Brown doing there?'

'Heaven knows. Late film show, drink with friends, assignation with a woman friend, supper party with the smart set. Who knows? There's loads of possibilities. Why don't you ask him?'

Sir Nigel cogitated silently. 'Like every good house of cards,' he said after a while, 'this one has a further support.'

'The flat in Windsor Court,' Fathers agreed.

'I rather think you may be on the verge of stretching coincidence too far.'

'No, not at all. I've looked into it.'

'And?'

'Deakin sent a bod up there who learned from a neighbour that a foreign gentleman had just been round to look at it.'

'Yes.'

'Deakin took that to be the visit by a KGB man to check the place was still clean. In addition, the rent was paid by a company listed in Liechtenstein whose ownership MI5 couldn't trace. It all added up.'

'Yes.'

'It doesn't any more.'

'Do pull the rabbit from the hat. It's obviously itching to get out.'

'The flat is now being prepared for occupancy by an employee of the Japanese financial group which owns the company in Liechtenstein.'

At that Sir Nigel's eyes opened wide, the second time his blandly calm expression had been disturbed. Fathers smiled with satisfaction as his interlocutor wrestled with the news. 'How did you discover that?' Sir Nigel said finally.

'I visited the flat, talked to the caretaker who gave me the number of the firm that delivered the new furniture and so on, talked to them, got another number and traced it up the line. It didn't take long. The company in Liechtenstein's just a convenience, one which many corporations use.'

'So why was the flat listed as a safe house?'

Fathers shrugged. 'I didn't have the authority or the inclination to find out. Perhaps the KGB did show interest in it at one time. Then K4 saw the rent was being paid by a shadow company, put two and two together and, like so many other people in this damned business, came up with four and a half. You could look into it if you wanted. All I know is that it isn't and never has been a KGB flat. And you see the meaning of that.'

'Brown and Scherchinskiy,' Sir Nigel said heavily, 'could never have planned to meet there. However, has it not occurred to you that the error may have been in assuming Brown and Scherchinskiy were meeting in that flat? They could have been meeting, and in Hampstead, but at some other place.'

'Yes, it did occur to me and there's no evidence either way. It's what you'd conclude if you began by assuming Brown's a spy. But if you don't assume that – and you've no grounds for it, despite a year's close surveillance, mark you – you don't get to that conclusion. Instead, you get a coincidence. The only one. And one tree, even if it has three trunks – Brown, Scherchinskiy and a flat wrongly listed as a KGB house, all in Hampstead – one tree does not a whole wood make.'

Sir Nigel lapsed into silence again, obstinacy written all over the lines on his forehead and around his mouth.

'There was the telephone tap as well,' Fathers said after a while. Sir Nigel looked at him. 'I must say I felt a bit stupid when I worked that one out. If Brown were a spy, you would assume that he would assume his phone was tapped. So does it seem likely he'd use it to

279

state the time and place of his meeting with his KGB control?'

'But that could have been — '

'Deliberately leading MI5 astray,' Fathers said for Sir Nigel. 'Yes, but only if — '

'You assume Brown is a spy,' Sir Nigel said for Fathers.

'Which you've no basis in fact for doing.'

'However, above all of this, there looms the CIA's defector, whom you have been so noticeably reluctant to address. What of him?'

Fathers thought back to his discussion with Finlay in the restaurant on the afternoon between sweeping up Connors and Garston's thugs and picking up the Watchers. The wilderness of mirrors, he thought.

'There's this thing,' he began, 'called defector's syndrome.' It took some time but finally Sir Nigel accepted that, if a defector were presented with the name of a man and told he was a journalist, he did not prove that man was a spy simply by saying it and claiming the journalism was mere cover.

'The fact is,' Fathers said, 'that if you watch someone like Brown that closely for almost a year, and produce no evidence that he's a spy or a knowing agent of influence, you should be a bit dubious if he's named as a KGB agent by a defector. But it's quite clear from the portion of the transcript they sent over that Brown was named by the CIA debriefers, not by the defector. He did little more than simply agree with them. So you have no reason at all to shake what should be a solid conviction: that Brown can be cleared.'

Sir Nigel nodded. 'What else is there?' he asked.

'Nothing,' Fathers said. 'There's nothing left of the whole damn case against Brown. And now you know why Operation Crow failed.'

Sir Nigel looked at his notes for a long time. 'What now?' he said. 'Would you care for a drink? It's almost lunchtime.'

'Please.'

'Scotch?'

'Thank you,' said Fathers, picking up the cigar from the ashtray where he'd left it to smoulder out.

'Please don't stoop to relighting it. Help yourself to another.'

'Heavens. Such extravagance. Thank you.'

When he'd poured the drinks and they both had cigars, Sir Nigel indicated that he'd prefer to continue in the corner and led the way – the wing-chair for him, as usual, Fathers lazing back in the sofa. He felt rather at home in the Chief Intelligence Co-ordinator's office.

'Well now, you've set me a pretty conundrum with this negative hypothesis of yours,' Sir Nigel said. 'What you are saying, really, is that there is no story, merely a prolonged misunderstanding, a set of repeatedly misinterpreted events that misled a group of senior and experienced counter-intelligence officials.'

'Oh, I don't think events misled them.'

'No? What then?'

'I simply mean you can't blame the events.'

'And I take it that you believe your negative hypothesis, that you are presenting it not as an alternative possibility but as *the* explanation.'

'Absolutely.'

'Why? I follow your reasoning to the point of accepting the hypothesis as possible, perhaps even probable, but why such certainty?'

Fathers enjoyed his cigar for a moment while he formulated his reply. 'I began by seeking the reason for the breakdown of Operation Crow. In the course of it, I decided the likelihood that it was caused by Special Branch incompetence on the night was extremely low. I was, in fact, prepared to rule it out. So that left me looking for a leak. And in Perry and Thomas I thought I had likely candidates. Then came round two, after which I was prepared to dismiss Thomas, thought Perry was most unlikely and had nobody else with any evidence against them. So when we talked, I went back to the JCB possibility. Not that I'd even had a first look at them. I was simply casting around to think who could be responsible for this leak.'

'I see.'

'But there wasn't a leak. There was nothing to leak. The flat wasn't the KGB's. Once I realised that, the whole operation became effectively non-existent. It was like being called in to examine a house full of murder suspects and wondering why I'm making no progress, only to discover that there hasn't been a murder. The operation didn't fail because it was blown; it failed because it wasn't real.'

'So then you simply asked yourself, what else wasn't real.'

'And discovered that none of it had any firm foundation in fact. Never was there anything I recognised as evidence, and always an alternative explanation was equally credible if not more so. There's another thing, too, though I don't set much store by it. Deakin asked Lucy to look out for any reverberations after the Crow failure. He hasn't reported any, though he has made his routine monthly information drop. More important was when I suddenly thought about what Brown said on the phone.'

'I follow all that,' the Co-ordinator said. 'The problem I have, however, is wondering why and how it happened.'

'Oh, I don't think that's complicated at all. It's all there in my second report, really, though I didn't see it at the time.'

'Explain.'

'Lucy was Deakin's, recruited on his decision, carefully nurtured, treated cautiously at first, then trusted, run almost personally. He wanted a big operation attributable to Lucy. Not consciously, but he was ready to snap at anything that floated past him. Thomas: well, Crow was his first file in K2. He, too, wanted a big one. He's ambitious; no fault there, and he can hardly be blamed, because he checked constantly with his superiors.'

'And McKellen?'

'Wanted to unite the two halves of his career – his past experience in F Branch and his current posting in K. Along comes a lefty who looks like an agent of influence and a spy, and he was ready to believe it. To a degree, with all of them, politics got in the way. None of them would have any sympathy or understanding for somebody like Brown, and it's difficult for them to regard his activities as legitimate. McKellen, for example, talked with virtual hate about him. Anyway, when they saw Brown linked in some not actually very substantial way to an identified KGB officer, and especially when the link was provided by a source with whom two of them had worked very closely for a year, between the three there were all the right ingredients for a strong reaction.'

'But as to conscious motivation, you would clear them all.'

'Oh yes. I'm convinced it was misjudgement. Look, these people are there to hunt spies. Hardly surprising that when they see a pattern of behaviour which they find distasteful they call it suspicious and identify it as spying. I've done as much myself, you know.'

'You have?'

'Certainly. It's terribly easy. A nasty crime has been committed. Such and such a bloke is a nasty piece of work and was in the vicinity at the time. So I look for the evidence to connect him and the crime. And very often find it. We work that way all the time. But it can go wrong. You want the whole jigsaw to fit together and so, lo and behold, it does. Then your superior destroys the whole thing in thirty seconds or, if you're less fortunate, the DPP or, if you're really unlucky, the defence counsel. Happens all the time. It's why we have judges and juries, you know.' Fathers thought of what Finlay had said. 'Except,' he added, 'that in this sort of work,

MI5 is the investigating officer, the judge and the jury. Until reality comes along and intervenes.'

Sir Nigel sighed and finished the whisky. 'Tell me, one last thing, what put you on to all this in the first place? A random thought in your bath one night?'

'As a matter of fact, it was my barber.'

'Your barber?'

'Yes. He explained to me why a man might think he saw a penguin while water-skiing on Christmas Day.'

'And why would that be?'

'Because he had a right to.'

Sir Nigel nodded. 'He sounds a man of great insight and wisdom. It all comes down to a question of perception.'

'Preconception and misperception. You see what you're looking for.'

'Look and thou shalt find,' the Co-ordinator intoned. He stood up. 'Well, Mr Fathers, I don't know whether I'm grateful to you for your time, your effort and your barber, but thank you anyway. Was there anything else?'

'No, Sir Nigel, and happy Christmas.'

'You too.'

When the detective had gone, Sir Nigel poured himself another whisky. He looked over his notes, thought about what Fathers had said and couldn't fault it. He pondered what it would take to check the hypothesis – asking Brown where he was on the Tuesday night in November, or when he left the house that time, or asking his sister if he had come to visit her, calling in on his way to York. Of course, as Fathers had said, such checking was impracticable.

He thought back, too, to a conversation with Hanson, when they had discussed the difference between reasoning and conclusions. The solidity of the former didn't make the latter less uncomfortable. And then further back to his first discussion with Hanson, to whether a rogue or a fool was the Crow culprit. And here was Fathers saying in so many words that the Service was a fool, or some of its senior officials at any rate. He had done little short of accuse three experienced counter-intelligence officers of constructing their own reality and making everything around them conform to it. And then gone further, to say that it was understandable; they mistook Brown for a spy because it was their job to hunt spies. Follow this reasoning and the destination was uncomfortable in the extreme.

There was, of course, a silver lining to the cloud, and a very sizeable one. There was no leak, no traitor. No need either to plough through the whole of the Joint Computer Bureau and, having still found no leak, suspect the lot of them, standing where they did at the heart of Five Hundred's information system. Nor would any other staff member who happened to be a computer enthusiast fall needlessly under suspicion. There was no reason to tear the Security Service apart with further distrust.

Yet – could he go to the Director-General and give him Fathers' explanation? Or to the Prime Minister? Would it look well in the next Red Book, circulating round the Cabinet? A single sentence perhaps: 'The breakdown in Operation Crow has been investigated and identified as due to the operation being based on a fiction and all its earlier findings mythical.'

On the other hand, to hunt through the JCB when there was no point . . .

As he put his coat on to go to lunch at his club, Sir Nigel Laker was beginning to decide that the best explanation to provide was based on the error with the flat, wrongly identified as the KGB's. Wherever Brown and Scherchinskiy had met, it was not there. Officially, he would not circulate Fathers's full explanation. He would, however, act on it. Deakin, like Platt, would take early retirement. McKellen and Thomas would move sideways into the administrative side. Crow would be closed down, quietly, permanently and without embarrassment. Brown's file would be weeded of its Crow elements and returned to F7 whence it came. It was fortunate indeed that Fathers had decided to commit nothing to paper.

Chapter 44

On Boxing Day morning they managed to drag themselves out of the house and away into the countryside for a walk. It was not a bad day – mild with a slight mist – and the parents' need for exercise had prevailed without too much trouble over the children's for television.

The day itself had been very good. Sarah's sister arrived about noon with her husband and their two children. There was drink – too much of it – and presents – too many of them – and dinner in mid-afternoon – equally excessive. Sarah's mother and father called round at six with more presents, there was more drink and the cake was cut. Later on, Sarah's brother and his latest girlfriend arrived, and there was more drink together with cheese, pâté, cold turkey and salad. While the adults stuffed themselves and rotted their livers, the kids had a marvellous time. Their ages were compatible and they knew and liked each other well. They not only avoided any serious squabbles but managed to pass the whole day without breaking or losing any of their presents, partly because they spent a lot of it in front of the television going from one film to another.

With her sister's family bedded down in various corners of the house and the other guests gone, Sarah got into bed beside her husband and ran her hand lovingly over his torso. He murmured with pleasure then gasped as she grabbed a handful of waistline. 'What say we go back on the raw food diet next week?' she said.

'Oh, not in the winter,' he grumbled. 'Can't it wait till spring? But let's go for a walk tomorrow.'

They drove to one of their favourite spots. They walked through a wood and out into the farmland, along a path between ploughed fields. The slight mist could not take the edge off the bleakness of the landscape, but that was what they most liked about it, the openness and the sense – ultimately illusory but enjoyable – of freedom. Sarah walked and chatted with her sister and brother-in-law, the children ran ahead, Fathers strolled along behind, alone with his thoughts and contentment.

He ran his mind over the presents he'd received and given. And thought about the biggest gift of them all – the one from Bastin. Bureaucratic politics had always been a weak and blind spot. Yet in one simple session Bastin had explained the trick and he had worked it. He still had no desire to become an office finagler, but it was a useful ability to have. Outflanking Myers over the snouts and sorting out Manchester CID for Pardoner had been Bastin's departing presents. And then there was the issue of promotion. He wasn't sure if his heart was in it. He'd been happy at his rank and didn't look forward to the extra administrative work which promotion would bring. If he could deal with Myers once, couldn't he do it again whenever need arose? Maybe – and then again, maybe not. Whatever – he had time to decide, to see how things went, before he committed himself. Leaving the Squad would be a wrench, but it was changing under his feet, and not only in name. It might be timely.

Up ahead he could hear the children calling, demanding to have the big black birds which had come swooping down on to the neighbouring field identified. Were they rooks or crows? Crows for sure, Fathers thought with amusement. There were three of them and he heard Samantha and Gary start up singing a song they'd learned at primary school:

'Three crows sat upon a wall,
Sat upon a wall, sat upon a wa-a-all,
Three crows sat upon a wall, so earl-y in the mor-*owning*.'

Fathers grinned and silently joined in. What with Operation Crow and Wainwright, the crow on the Hammersmith robbery and Guy White picking up the carrion left behind by Connors and Garston, the bird seemed to have dominated his life lately.

'The first crow couldna hardly sing,
Couldna hardly sing, couldna hardly si-i-ing,
The first crow couldna hardly sing, so earl-y in the mor-*orning*.'

No, that was back to front: there'd been an awful lot of singing – much of it to tunes composed by Billy Hughes and Guy White, until Yarrow had stepped in and wrung the truth from Davy Dawes.

'The second crow fell and broke his wing,
Fell and broke his wing, fell and broke his wi-i-ing,

286

The second crow fell and broke his wing, so earl-y in the mor-*orning*.'

That sort of fitted. Two horrid birds in particular had taken a nasty fall and broken a lot more than just a wing.

'The third crow was looking for his ma,
Looking for his ma, looking for his ma-a-a,
The third crow was looking for his ma, so earl-y in the mor-*orning*.'

That didn't fit at all, unless a Freudian motivation lay at the root of Deakin *et al*'s problems. Wait for it though:

'The fourth crow wasna there at a',
Wasna there at a', wasna there at a-a-a',
The fourth crow wasna there at a', so earl-y in the mor-*orning*.'

And wasn't that the truth of it? That was the solution to the Crow mystery: there was no mystery, no crow. Ironically it was the investigation into Connors and Garston which had taken him into the murkiness of plot and counter-plot, defection and disinformation. Somehow the two had flowed into each other, with him as the point of conjunction. The one which should have been complex turned out to be crushingly simple. And what should have been simplicity itself – a straightforward case of gang warfare – was the one with all the ins and outs.

And thinking of confluence, how the MI5 job had poisoned him. He'd taken the suspicion endemic to that world and applied it to his own at home, believing Sarah was having an affair, for no better reason than that she was finding things to fill her life while he was out till all hours. Believing she was falling out of love with him, when the truth was that he was committing nothing into his life with her and, effectively, giving her nothing to love.

Sarah left the others and came back towards him. Well, they had turned that corner now. She had been extraordinary: after that evening just before round two of Crow began, she'd put everything on hold till he came back to her, and since then they had reconnected, rediscovered each other. They were close again and warm, sharing their pleasure, their humour and their problems. Last night Sarah's sister had told them both what a wonderful, loving home they had.

287

Sarah fell into step with him. He smiled at her and put his arm round her shoulders. She put her arm round his waist and gave him an affectionate squeeze. They walked in silence for a little while. Then she looked up at him.

'Harry,' she said.

'Yes, love?'

'We need to have a talk. There's something I have to tell you. I don't want it to hurt and it doesn't mean anything now because it's all over, but I have to tell you.'

With eyes as bleak as the landscape he looked out across the field. A fourth crow flapped down to join the other three.